Praise for *The Orphanmaster*

"Jean Zimmerman's first novel, *The O[rphanmaster], ... mystery for readers who value the history as much as the mystery. Set in New Amsterdam in the mid-seventeenth century, Zimmerman's nicely flowing narrative is animated by robust characters who thrive on the edges of civilization." —*The New York Times Book Review*

"As Jean Zimmerman proves in her immersive first novel *The Orphanmaster*, careful and imaginative research can be exhilarating. The book's subject is colonial Manhattan in the tense period of the 1660s before the English annexed the port from the Dutch, and on nearly every page there is some unobtrusively offered word or description, of food, of architecture, of dress, that brings the period and its people into clearer focus." —*USA Today*

"Jean Zimmerman's seventeenth-century New Amsterdam teems with enough intrigue, lust, and madness to give our twenty-first-century Big Apple a run for its money. And money is what drives this book— liberating, corrupting, forming the only bulwark against a terrifying, chaotic New World. Zimmerman's wit and humanity shine light in a dark woods, creating an uncommonly rich debut." —Sheri Holman, author of *The Dress Lodger*

"A rip-roaring read, packed with action and dark suspense . . . features a strong and unusual female protagonist . . . I was captivated by Zimmerman's unforgettable evocation of New Amsterdam." —Mary Sharratt, National Public Radio, "The Year's Best Historical Fiction"

"This fast-paced novel keeps you enthralled in both the mystery and the romance while also immersing you in colonial life, with industry and opportunity on the one hand and violence and disease on the other." —*Woman's Day*

"Absorbing period fiction with the requisite colorful characters of the era."   —*The New York Daily News*

"A thriller, love story, and costume drama in one."
                                                                   —*Good Housekeeping*

"Here's American history turned inside out, animated by Jean Zimmerman's prodigious imagination. Monsters lurk in the shadows, chaos presses in, legends come alive, and one adventure leads with irresistible force to the next. *The Orphanmaster* is a breathtaking achievement."
                            —Joanna Scott, author of *Arrogance* and *Various Antidotes*

"Jean Zimmerman has written a fascinating saga of early Manhattan island—part mystery, part horror story, and part love story—in which every page is a pleasure to read. The characters are well defined and hard to forget. . . . Fast-paced, filled with period detail, and populated with multidimensional, conflicted characters, *The Orphanmaster* leaves you wanting more."   —*Historical Novels Review*

"This is an absolutely mesmerizing novel set in the New Amsterdam colony circa 1663. . . . Zimmerman spins a story as riveting and nightmare-inducing as any Grimm's fairy tale. . . . Beautifully written, sophisticated yet terrifying in its examination of human flaws, this stunning novel haunts long after the monster is named and innocence reclaimed."   —curledup.com

"[A] compulsively readable, heartbreaking, and grisly mystery set in a wild colonial America. . . . [Offers] a fascinating perspective on colonial politics and human behavior."   —*Booklist*

"A feisty young Dutch woman, an English spy, and a local demon all cross paths in 1663 New Amsterdam in this Ludlumesque historical thriller. . . . A successful mix of historical fiction, spy thriller, and horror."   —*Library Journal*

PENGUIN BOOKS

THE ORPHANMASTER

An honors graduate of Barnard College and the recipient of an MFA in writing from Columbia University, Jean Zimmerman is the author of several works of nonfiction, including *Love, Fiercely: A Gilded Age Romance* and *The Women of the House: How a Colonial She-Merchant Built a Mansion, a Fortune, and a Dynasty*. She lives with her family in Westchester County, New York.

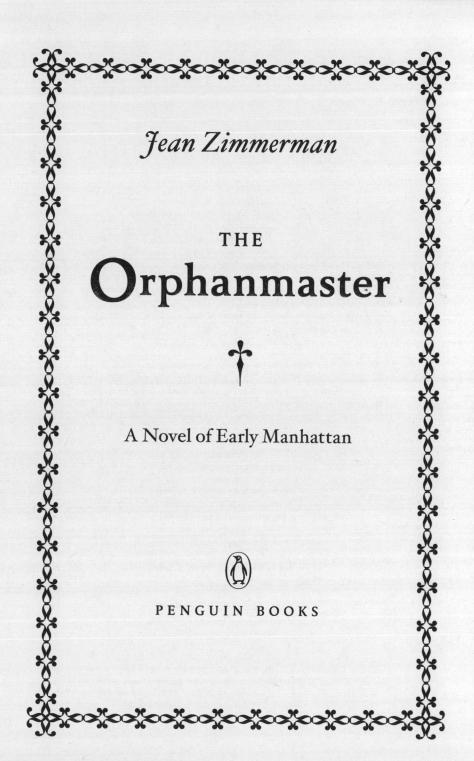

Jean Zimmerman

THE

Orphanmaster

A Novel of Early Manhattan

PENGUIN BOOKS

PENGUIN BOOKS
Published by the Penguin Group
Penguin Group (USA) Inc., 375 Hudson Street,
New York, New York 10014, U.S.A.

USA | Canada | UK | Ireland | Australia | New Zealand | India | South Africa | China
Penguin Books Ltd, Registered Offices: 80 Strand, London WC2R oRL, England
For more information about the Penguin Group visit penguin.com

First published in the United States of America by Viking Penguin,
a member of Penguin Group (USA) Inc., 2012
Published in Penguin Books 2013

THE LIBRARY OF CONGRESS HAS CATALOGED THE HARDCOVER EDITION AS FOLLOWS:
Zimmerman, Jean.
The orphanmaster / Jean Zimmerman.
p. cm.
ISBN 978-0-670-02364-6 (hc.)
ISBN 978-0-14-312353-8 (pbk.)
1. New York—Fiction. I. Title.
PS3626.I493O77 2012
813'.6—dc23   2011038593

Printed in the United States of America
1 3 5 7 9 10 8 6 4 2

Set in Carre Noir Std Medium
Designed by Francesca Belanger
Maps by Jeffrey L. Ward

Publisher's Note
This is a work of fiction. Names, characters, places, and incidents either
are the product of the author's imagination or are used fictitiously, and any
resemblance to actual persons, living or dead, business establishments,
events, or locales is entirely coincidental.

For the both of us

Our inheritance is turned to strangers, our houses to foreigners. We are orphans and fatherless, our mothers are as widows.

—*Lamentations* 5:2–3

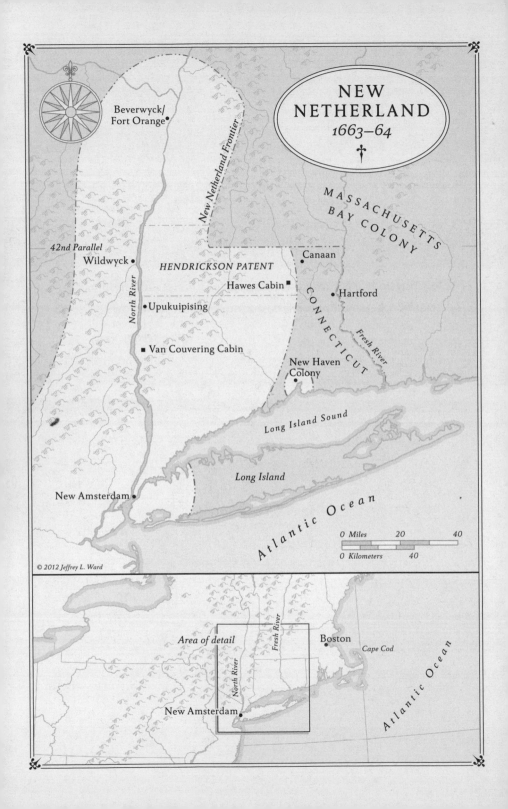

NEW
NETHERLAND
1663–64

Beverwyck/
Fort Orange

MASSACHUSETTS
BAY COLONY

New Netherland Frontier

42nd Parallel

Wildwyck

Canaan

HENDRICKSON PATENT

Hawes Cabin

North River

Hartford

CONNECTICUT

Upukuipising

Fresh River

Van Couvering Cabin

New Haven
Colony

Long Island Sound

Long Island

New Amsterdam

Atlantic Ocean

0 Miles   20   40

0 Kilometers   40

© 2012 Jeffrey L. Ward

Area of detail

Fresh River

Boston

Cape Cod

North River

New Amsterdam

Atlantic Ocean

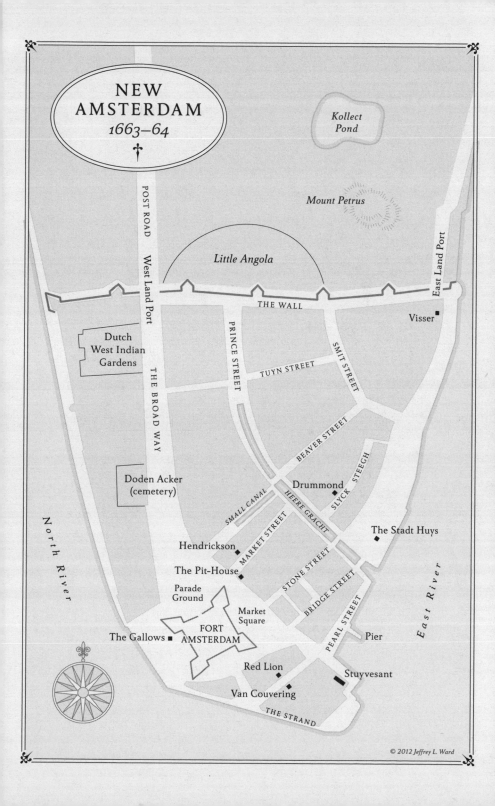

NEW
AMSTERDAM
1663–64

Kollect
Pond

Mount Petrus

POST ROAD   West Land Port

Little Angola

THE WALL

Visser

East Land Port

Dutch
West Indian
Gardens

PRINCE STREET

TUYN STREET

SMIT STREET

THE BROAD WAY

BEAVER STREET

Doden Acker
(cemetery)

SMALL CANAL

HEERE GRACHT

Drummond

SLYCK STEEGH

The Stadt Huys

North River

Hendrickson

MARKET STREET

The Pit-House

STONE STREET

Parade
Ground

Market
Square

BRIDGE STREET

PEARL STREET

East River

The Gallows

FORT
AMSTERDAM

Pier

Red Lion

Stuyvesant

Van Couvering

THE STRAND

© 2012 Jeffrey L. Ward

THE ORPHANMASTER

Prologue

On the same day, two murders.

In Delémont, in Switzerland's Jura, the regicide William Crawley lived with his sister, hiding in plain sight in a *pension* on Faubourg des Capucins, near the hospital.

As the bells of Saint-Marcel sounded vespers, Crawley's sister Barbara watched the dark descend upon the town from the second-floor terrace off the kitchen. Although ever vigilant, she failed to notice three figures slip from the Rue des Elfes, come through the black backyards across the street and approach the ground-floor entry of the *pension*.

A Saint Martin summer, unseasonably hot. Barbara went into the kitchen, stood at the sink, sopped her face with water from the basin. As she bent over, holding a cooling rag to her neck, they grabbed her from behind, muffling a shriek of alarm.

Crawley, working at his desk upstairs in the cramped and stifling third-floor garret, heard the disturbance. A crash of crockery.

"Barbara?" he called, rising to his feet. He went to the stairwell and saw them coming up toward him, taking the steps three or four at a time, a pair of blade-thin men in identical black waistcoats and small caps.

"No!" Crawley shouted, lunging backward into his attic study, groping for his dog-lock *pistolet*, kept at hand on a shelf near his desk.

They were too quick. They burst in on him, the first attacker wrenching the barrel of Crawley's gun upward. The hammer dry-fired, the powder pan fizzled, then finally exploded. But the lead ball embedded itself impotently in the garret's low ceiling, showering them all with plaster dust and bits of lath.

Thus he was caught, fourteen years, eight months and eight days after he affixed his seal (*"Ego, Hon Wm Crawley"*) to a document that doomed Charles I, a sitting king sentenced to have his head separated from his body. Puritan zealots, appalled by the Catholicism infecting the monarchy, demanded royal blood. The death warrant Crawley signed gave it to them.

On execution day, January 30, 1649, the condemned monarch wore two shirts, lest he shiver and seem to betray fear. The king of England, France and Ireland, the king of Scots, the Defender of the Faith, et cetera, asked the executioner, "Does my hair trouble you?" Charles I tucked the royal locks away from his neck beneath a cap, uttered a prayer, then splayed out his arms and received the blade.

And, inevitably, the revenge. It took a while. Charles Stuart, the murdered monarch's son, escaped (barely) the Puritan furies on his trail, slipped across the Channel to the Continent and entered into a decade of exile. Unimpressed by the young man's chances to regain his kingship, European royals turned their backs on him. Impoverished and ignored, he wandered, mostly in France and the Low Countries, anguished by his father's execution, feeling bruised by history.

But the dynastic destiny of the Stuarts took a turn. On September 3, 1658, Lord Protector Oliver Cromwell, rebel ringleader and "brave bad man" (Clarendon's phrase), died while attempting to pass a kidney stone. After two more years of succession chaos, the English Parliament invited Charles II to return home and assume the throne.

As a gesture of royal largesse and reconciliation, the newly restored young monarch issued the Indemnity and Oblivion Act, pardoning all former rebels against the crown.

All except the fifty-nine judge-commissioners who signed the death warrant of his father, Charles I.

Some of those fifty-nine had already died. These had their bodies exhumed, propped up in their cerements before the bar at the Old Bailey, judged, condemned and, in the singular phrase of the day, "executed posthumously." Cromwell's corpse hung in chains from Tyburn gallows while his head rotted on a spike at Westminster.

The living signatories, William Crawley among them, were hunted down like outlaws. Located by men of the king's chancellor, George Hyde, the Earl of Clarendon, who had them assiduously tracked to the provinces, Scotland, the Continent, America, to wherever in the world they attempted to hide themselves. Puritan protectors of the regicides made the task difficult as well as dangerous.

In this case, an agent of the crown named Edward Drummond beat the bushes of Europe to turn up the king-killer Crawley, following his spoor from Scotland to Paris, Münster and finally Switzerland. It was no simple task, finding a single needle in the haystack of the Continent, but Drummond made short work of it. The man, Clarendon believed, worked miracles. Without his efforts, the murderer Crawley would never feel the lash of the crown's revenge.

Clarendon could not ask a gentleman such as Drummond to perform the execution himself. He had other men for that, lean and hungry low-born men. After Drummond located the regicide, Clarendon sent out the assassins. Drummond was long gone by the time they arrived.

"Il se cache parmi les papists," one of the men come to kill Crawley hissed. He hides among the Catholics.

The other assassin closed his hands around the regicide's throat. The victim would have pled for a last moment of prayer, but found it impossible to speak. The attacker not busy strangling Crawley rifled quickly through the documents on his desk, stuffing them by hurried grabfuls into a greasy leather pouch.

Downstairs, Barbara squirmed in the grip of the third assassin. *"Chut,"* the man said, *"nous ne tuons pas les femmes."* We don't kill women. Meaning, unless they give us trouble.

In the garret, Crawley thrashed impotently, a minute, one minute more, the iron grip crushing his windpipe, a silent, terrible struggle. Then, blackness, blankness.

When the two killers were through, they dragged Crawley's body downstairs, his head banging hollowly on each stone step. Barbara, seeing her brother dead, gasped out a low moan and broke free. As she rushed forward, one of the men delivered a blow that knocked her to the floor.

The corpse of William Crawley, regicide, soared from the second-floor terrace of the *pension* on Les Capucins. The body landed not quite on the hospital grounds, but close enough that the infirmary nuns took charge of it, burying the Protestant king-killer in unconsecrated ground the next afternoon.

* * *

Altogether elsewhere, in the new world, morning. The Dutch settlement of New Amsterdam on the southern end of Manhattan Island. No indian summer there, but rather raw cold, with lowering clouds threatening an early first blizzard of the season.

A frail child, Piteous Charity Gullee, eight years old.

Piddy.

Alone in the forest near the Kollect Pond, north of the wall, yoked with two empty buckets, Piddy followed the beaten-earth path toward the water. Stood on end, the yoke she carried was taller than she was.

No one around. The dead of dawn.

Many times on her first trip to the Kollect in the morning—executed in total darkness during the winter—she kicked up whitetails, whistle pigs, squirrels, storms of screeching, warning birds.

This year the hunters had driven most of the animals farther up the island. The jays stayed around the swampy margins on the far side of the Kollect, mingling with herring gulls and common terns from the harbor.

Piddy humped the buckets over the last hillock. The pond's watery mirror turned pink-yellow with the morning, flecked with the black outlines of ducks and geese. Reed beds stretched around the shoreline, their purple floating tufts glowing in the early light.

The Briel household Piddy served was a thirsty, dirty, profligate bunch. But they didn't drink the water Piddy hauled, and they surely didn't wash in it. Where did it all go, Piddy wondered, the dozen buckets she carried each day?

She slipped down her secret path through the reeds and out onto a finger of crusted mud that crooked into the shallows. As she crouched to fill her buckets, she startled at a figure watching from the jackpines near the shore.

A devil of some sort, half-man, half-beast. To her small eyes, the apparition towered as tall as a tree. The figure wore European dress, a low beaver hat and a wilted lace collar around his neck.

Above the collar, fixed in the place of a human face, a deerskin mask. Flat, made of peeled skin, with blank, staring eyes.

Fear rose in Piddy's gorge. Still she thought that she could get away, that he would let her be.

The figure stepped into the water and splashed across the icy shallows between them. Just a few long-legged strides.

She turned her head so as not to see, but his breath came near and sour. From the mouth-hole of the mask, an odd sound, *"dik-duk, dik-duk"*—like the nursery rhyme the littlest Briel children recited.

"Oh, please God, no," Piddy managed, tripping backward over her yoke.

She made her body still smaller than it was, merging with the chilly mud and turning her face down into its grit, with the wish that if she could not see, then the monster would not see her.

Out of the corner of her eye, she glimpsed a pair of red hooves, sunk into the mud of the pond.

For a long moment all she heard was the rattling breeze that pushed the tops of the reeds. Then, *"Dik-duk, dik-duk."* He picked her up from the ground by the throat, shook her like a doll, and the air went out of her in little mewling cries, *uff, uff, uff.* Gripping her windpipe as though it were the handle to a satchel, the creature drew Piddy close.

Behind the scabby mask, red eyes. Her own gushed tears. He cracked her heavily across the mouth, loosening her teeth. Again. He drove his knee to force apart Piddy's spindly legs. She wanted to collapse, but he had her dangling by the throat.

It went on.

"Dik-duk." She found herself on her back. Piddy's blank brown eyes reflected the cloud-spotted sky above. Unconsciousness found her, but still her body wept and groaned as the creature worked on her.

When it was over, the killer dragged Piddy by her bare feet to the spongy edge of the pond. The corpus refused to sink. He leaned into the pond, weighting the small form with a stone folded into the thin linen of her dress.

Piddy did not hear the creature softly mouth two words, nor would she have understood them if she had.

"Deus dormit." God sleeps.

It began to snow.

Part One

Prince Maurice's
River

I

The counting rooms of the Dutch West India Company took the whole of the first floor of a redbrick warehouse, built along the East River on the southernmost flank of Manhattan Island.

The eighth day of October, 1663. Outside, a premature snowfall. In the crowded, noisy, tobacco-fogged counting-room quarters, merchants inspected the goods, the shipping barrels and one another. Beneath the din of voices, a musical ringing of coins and hollow clink of wampum, pleasing to all ears.

Everywhere were stacked colanders and kettles, pins and vinegar, blankets and Bibles and toys. The warehouse, like the colony itself, skewed heavily male, a realm of pipe-sucking traders, profane sail captains and percentage-minded excise officials.

But among the Dutch, profit was a promiscuous god, welcoming all supplicants, and in the counting rooms that fall day worked a scattering of she-merchants. One among them, a woman of twenty-two years, directed a young female assistant in the procedures of trade.

"When you fold, straightened edges go together," Blandine van Couvering said, watching her apprentice struggle with a length of duffel. The girl, fifteen years old, called Miep, was the youngest daughter of the Fredericz family.

Carsten Fredericz van Jeveren wanted Miep to learn commerce. To become a she-merchant like Blandine van Couvering. Blandine herself had no need of a protégée, but she did have use for Carsten Fredericz's patronage, so she took the slow learner on.

Miep displayed the refolded duffel to her mentor. "Good," Blandine said. "Now place it in the stack of others, and put the stack in—well, we have all sorts of cooperage, don't we? Which would you choose?"

The girl took the pile of duffel lengths and stuffed them roughly into a small cask. Fine. Not the barrel Blandine would have selected, and a bit messy, but let it go. She couldn't continue correcting Miep the whole day.

"You're next, madam," a phlegmy male voice said behind her.

Blandine turned to face the West India Company's ancient tax inspector, Chas Pembeck. The man wore a pair of the new Italian eye spectacles. He possessed himself of all the latest luxuries, a benefit of being the gatekeeper for the colony's imported goods.

"You are?" he said.

Blandine hid a pained smile. Pembeck's question stung. She thought of herself as a rising young trader of the colony. But the old fish pretended not to remember her. She stared at the ocular device affixed to the man's face.

Charming, the blush in her cheeks, the inspector thought. But was that insolence in her expression? He tried again. "Your name?"

"Blandine van Couvering, Mister Pembeck," Blandine said. As you well know. She thrust out her hand. A challenge to genteel tradition, which held that ladies never shook, but a business practice Blandine had lately adopted.

Pembeck took her hand unwillingly, limply releasing it. He ignored young Miep, who curtsied.

Blandine presented her bill of lading. Peering through his newfangled lenses, Pembeck soberly inspected the document, comparing its list of goods with the jumble spread around Blandine.

Company agents had marked off the counting-room floor in squares with quicklime. Blandine's bundles, firkins and barrels filled her square, spilling over the line. Pembeck nudged a stray cask back inside the border with his foot.

"This barrel?" he said. "Let's start there."

"Duffel cloth," she said. "From Antwerp."

"Better not to shut the tuns before inspection," Pembeck said.

Blandine pried open the top and displayed the contents, thick wool cloth, folded to better fit the container. "I have a smaller cask of duffel there," she said.

The inspector nodded and went on, ticking off the items one by one. "Two pony barrels of molasses. Brass thimbles, one score. A dozen long knives, a dozen jackknives."

"Sheffield Barlows, sire," Blandine said.

"Good," Pembeck said, popping open one of the English-made blades. "The river indians like these."

But there it had been again. That "sire" of the girl's had been pronounced with a faint air of condescension, of parody. Little Miss Snippy. He would level her an extra guilder in excise for that.

Pembeck clambered over the goods to reach the back of Blandine's marked-off square, tap, tap, tapping with his excise rod. "Six barrels Barbados rum. Five staves lead. Twenty pounds powder. A hundred ells cloth, red and plaid."

"I've got osnabrig, serge, diaper, Hamburg linen. Lawn and silk."

"And the duffel."

"Yes."

Pembeck made a note. "Hand tools, nails, saws and hammers." Rummaging, peering, checking against her bill of lading. She had a wide variety of goods, he saw, but no great quantity.

"Twelve iron pots, ten iron frying pans. The *wilden* prefer copper better, they like to shape it for arrowheads."

Wilden, what the Dutch called the natives. Savages.

"Forty white clay pipes—wherever did you get so many? Lace festoons. A wealth of those."

"For the women," Blandine said.

"Yes," said the inspector.

Every autumn fur traders—*handlaers*, they called themselves—paid hunters in advance with such trade goods, expecting in return fur pelts and animal skins. The river indians spent all winter trapping. *Handlaer* and native would then meet in the spring to complete their transactions.

The upcoming market weeks were crucial for Blandine's campaign to rise from her limited trade in minor peltry—soft-tanned deer skins, elk, mink, muskrat, otter and bobcat hides—to enter the elite world of the strange, mystical animal that had rendered life in the New Netherland colony viable.

Beaver.

Europe was avid for American fur, and valued beaver above all.

Blandine eyed Pembeck. "If I have the goods, I can make the trades, can I not?"

"Certainly," he said.

"There is no law or regulation stopping me?"

"You must pay the Company its tax is all."

Pembeck arrived at the black heart of Blandine's trading cache, her three long-barreled muskets. Providing weapons to the river indians had customarily been subject to Company regulation. She would brazen it out.

"Ah, these are fine," Pembeck said, his eyes lit with a familiar mercantile gleam.

Her father, Willem, had begun his life as a gunsmith, so Blandine could easily recite the characteristics of the weapons.

"Round, seven-five caliber, baluster-turned, pin-fastened, smooth-bore, iron barrels with wedding-band transitions, rounded banana contours and matching gooseneck hammers."

Pembeck blinked at her. "You're a sly one, ain't ye, lass? I had no idea."

No idea that the muskets were baluster-turned and pin-fastened? Or no idea that a green frill such as Blandine could know so much about gunsmithing?

Pembeck hefted one of the heavyweight muskets. He frowned. "Only . . ."

"Yes?" Blandine asked.

"We are not selling the indigenes flintlocks just now. The *wilden* are frisky enough as it is."

"These are simple pattern locks. You see?" She cocked the firing mechanism and displayed its brass powder pan to the inspector.

Pembeck performed a genial half-bow. "Permissible," he said.

He propped one of the muskets with its stock resting on the wide wooden floorboards of the counting room. "These will be pelt guns, and you will have the trappers bring back beaver skins to the same height as the length of the musket barrel."

The inspector held his hand, palm level, at the barrel's end. In exchange for the gun, an indian would be obliged to trade a fifty-nine-inch stack of "merchantable" beaver pelts.

Yes, yes, no need to tell me, Blandine said to herself. What does a man love more than to lecture a woman?

Inwardly, though, she reeled with contained excitement. After never having traded a single beaver skin, here were three five-foot stacks of them coming her way, each stack made up of, what? Thirty or thirty-five pelts?

Earlier in the day, she had quizzed Miep on the potential profit. "A thick winter beaver pelt is far more valuable than a skin having a thinner summer pelt," she said.

"Yessum," Miep said. At times she looked up at Blandine as the earthworm must look at the acrobat, in wonder that such things were done.

Blandine went on. "A hundred beavers, say, rounding out, at eight guilders, if the market holds."

"Eight hundred guilders," Miep said, adopting a pious tone whenever money was mentioned.

"Take away the cost of the pelt guns," Blandine said, "and the expenses of the trip, totaling perhaps two hundred seventy, being generous. Yielding what?"

She had watched the cogs of the young girl's mind turn. "Six hundred thirty," Miep said.

Ah, well, a gear must have slipped in there somewhere. "Five hundred thirty, isn't it?" Blandine said, gently.

Miep blushed, but Blandine could think only of the fatness of the number. In the spring of next year, she would be more than five hundred guilders clear.

On the musket guns alone.

A risk existed, to be sure. The hunter with whom she bartered might simply disappear into the fathomless wilderness with her weapon, giving no peltry in return the following spring. He could himself perish over the long winter with all its sundry dangers. He could fall to other *wilden*, be torn apart by beasts, lose his way to madness.

Without risk, no profit. Her father taught her that at his knee. More risk, more profit. From a young age Blandine saw buying and selling as a delightful game. Trade was all she ever wanted to do.

This year was her year. The portents others saw as grave she interpreted as omens of her coming success. A great burning comet flew nightly across the heavens. On the first of the last month of summer, a double rainbow aimed northward, pointing to the path of the North River. A woman at Corlaers Hook reported visions of pikemen in the sky. In Harlem, a cow gave birth to a two-headed calf.

Odd weather continued to descend upon the colony, like the early blizzard swirling outside the greased parchment windows of the counting rooms, snow mixing with flurries of multicolored autumn leaves.

"You embark on *Amsterdam Rose*?" Pembeck asked her.

"Tomorrow," Blandine said. "With the early tide."

"You bring the maiden with you?" Deigning to notice Miep, who curtsied again confusedly.

"No, she has not the experience."

"But with your giant?"

There it was at last. Pembeck's grudging acknowledgment that yes, indeed, he was well aware who Blandine van Couvering was.

"Always," she said. Blandine's most marked characteristic, to outside eyes, was that she went accompanied abroad by the tallest man in the colony, her familiar, her shadow, Antony Angola.

"Nasty weather," the inspector said. In quick order he affixed the Company seal to her bill of lading, calculated her excise at fourteen guilders and accepted payment.

Clink, clink, clink. The silver coins sounded their melody, falling from her hand to his.

Actual specie was rare in the settlement. Most of the trade went to barter or seawan, the wampum employed as currency. The carefully hoarded lion dollars Blandine had just given Pembeck represented the majority portion of her bank. She watched them disappear into the inspector's purse.

Nevertheless, exhilaration stole over her. It was done. She was on her way.

Naturally enough, because every good thing invites the bad, a cloud suddenly appeared in her blue sky. Her man Antony stood beckoning her, a hulking figure filling the doorway of the counting room.

Trouble. With the look on Antony's face, Blandine immediately took up her blue shawl. As soon as she did so, Antony turned and disappeared down the street, his outsized gait giving him a head start.

"Go home," she said quickly to Miep.

"Ma'am?"

"Your lesson's over."

Blandine van Couvering pushed through the counting-room traders to head into the snow, cinching the sash around her waist as though girding for battle.

2

The big-bellied flute ship *Margrave*, six weeks out of Rotterdam, three hundred twenty Holland tons burden, slid into the harbor waters of the Dutch colony of New Amsterdam. An ominous fall blizzard, a small wind, a swollen, inflowing tide.

Gerrit Remunde found the English gentleman at the portside rail, and they stood together staring into the snow and mist.

"Thick soup," Gerrit said.

"Aye," Edward Drummond said. "But we are close."

How could he tell?

"Because our soup has pigeon in it," Drummond said, as though reading Gerrit's thoughts. He gestured upward.

A pair of soft gray rock doves fluttered among the rigging, harassed by the gulls.

Clever Englishman. Gerrit had watched him covertly for the whole crossing, during which the man showed himself to be a calm, remote, unruffled presence. Much as he stood at the rail now. Dark, curly locks spilled past his shoulders, in the style of the English king.

He had boarded *Margrave* not in Texel, where her journey began, but at a stopover in Rotterdam, coming, he said when Gerrit questioned him, from the Jura.

Gerrit, a humble agent in cross-ocean trade, would be sad to see less of Edward Drummond. They both would disappear into the demands of their individual businesses. Though the compass of the Dutch colonial capital was small, they might never encounter each other again.

In the course of the passage the man proved devilishly difficult to pin down in conversation. But at random moments he surprised his listeners by offering titbits of adventure, intrigue, bloody engagements on horseback and at sea, diplomacy, feckless ministers, King Charles II, called the "Black Boy" for his olive skin and glossy hair, duels, smuggling, a lady's leg glimpsed behind the arras, an anecdote that demonstrated bitter familiarity with the pain of exile.

Vastly entertaining.

"You are a born raconteur, sir," Gerrit told him.

"*Raconteur*," Drummond said. "That is the French word for 'bore.'"
And everyone laughed.

His clothes were especially fine. Gerrit delighted in them. The man
portrayed himself as a grain merchant but did not, Gerrit noted with
secret glee, know the tare on a barrel of wheat.

A grain merchant! And him with velour on his back. But his incognito
lodged safe with Gerrit. Mum was the word.

In the sheltered bowl of the bay, the snow thickened, the wind died
entirely, the sails luffed, and *Margrave* was becalmed. One of the low
skiffs of the river indians loomed out of the weather, bobbed in the ship's
wake, became fog-swallowed.

For an interminable half hour they drifted with the tide, the only
sound being the muffled mutterings of the seamen.

No one else appeared concerned, but a familiar tension gripped Gerrit.
He felt it during every arrival, sure that they would wreck themselves upon
the rocks of the river. He would drown within view of his family on the shore.

Damned fog. Damned obscurity. An early October blizzard? They
were lost for sure.

Far off, a quiet lap of the surf and, yes, the yelping bark of harbor seals.
Suddenly it was there, a fat green band of coastline appearing out of the blizzard like a blessing. Gerrit recognized the lower tip of the isle of Manhattan.

Towering above a thin strip of rocky beach stood the town gallows,
poking proudly from the mist.

"Ah," Drummond said. "Civilization."

They hove aback off the island, heading toward the East River roadstead, the brick dwelling-houses and low taprooms of the Strand increasingly visible. Inhabitants poured into the streets, shouting and calling.
Behind the gibbet, the fort and the windmills.

Ten, twenty, then several whooping dozens ran along the shore, children and adults, pacing the new arrival's progress toward the wharf on
the island's eastern side.

A cannonade of welcome boomed, answered by the lone twelve-
pounder at *Margrave*'s stern.

Gerrit glanced over at Drummond and saw him tracking something with his eyes. As the crowd flowed east, following the ship, a single figure, trailed by another, pushed west, against the tide of townsfolk.

Gerrit recognized her. A young she-merchant of the town, wrapped in a shawl of Virgin Mary blue. It seemed the only color to enliven the whole scene. Behind her, the big brute, her giant.

Gerrit smiled. Well, the woman was appealing enough to attract a man's gaze, to be sure, her head boldly uncovered, her hair white-blond and arresting. Not to Gerrit's own taste, too thorny, too independent, but Drummond seemed momentarily taken by the vision of her.

"Civilization," he murmured again, watching the pretty miss with her trailing bodyguard.

Milady and milady's giant proceeded west along the Strand as *Margrave* continued east around the tip of the island.

Soon, home. In bed tonight Gerrit would tell Gerta all about his shipmates, and about the Englishman. "Very much a superior class of person," he would say.

Blandine threaded her way through the crowd of townsfolk rushing to the ship newly arrived from Patria. Normally, she would have been among them.

Speed, Blandine felt, was of the utmost urgency. Along Pearl Street to the market square, past the fort, past the vegetable gardens of the West India Company, leaving behind the hurrying crowds hallooing the ship heading toward the East River slip.

Off the shore, ghostly in the fog and falling snow, the Dutch vessel, catching small wind to lumber in the harbor swell. Blandine loved how the river indians called the sailing ships from Europe "cloud-houses." The flute ship—possibly *Sea Serpent*, since it hoisted a Frisian flag—indeed resembled a floating cottage with sail-clouds billowing above it.

She knew Antony would have liked to greet the ship. He enjoyed excitement. But he was her faithful shadow, even though she felt no need of one. Blandine had long ago stopped pleading for him not to follow her around. His devotion meant more to her than she cared to admit.

Three years ago, when Antony Angola had recently arrived in the colony as a West India Company slave, the town's *schout*, or sheriff, implicated him and a group of others in the killing of a fellow African.

Unable to determine individual guilt, Petrus Stuyvesant, the director general of the colony, had each member of the group draw straws.

Antony the tall drew the short straw, and the director general sentenced him to hang. The first time Blandine ever laid eyes on the giant, he stood on the gallows scaffold.

He made for a pathetic picture. Seven feet in height, twenty-three stone in weight, forty years old, he nevertheless cowered under the jeers of the crowd. The condemned man stared at the Bible they presented him to kiss as if he had never seen a book before.

The onlookers roared as the trap fell, but entered into a stunned silence when the double halters around Antony's neck (the hangman used two, in accord with the condemned man's size) both broke like puppet strings.

The giant fell heavily to the ground. He sat up, stunned and blinking, the tattered noose ropes hanging limp. He looked fearfully at the gape-mouthed colonists surrounding him, expecting to be set upon.

At that moment, the sun broke through the clouds, sending a bar of light over the Upper Bay. The crowd remained struck mute and frozen in place.

Except for Blandine van Couvering. She moved forward and knelt beside the dead man who had not died.

The crowd raised a huzzah then, proclaimed a miracle, cried out for mercy and insisted the giant be pardoned. The director general complied. At the crowd's urging, he granted Antony the "half-freedom" that was the colony's odd custom, manumitting him from Company enslavement. The double welts around his neck became emblems of his rebirth.

Blandine's compassion was flavored with pain. She had lost her own family to shipwreck four years before, so her heart went out to Antony, whom she saw as a solitary soul like herself. She drew the man out of the mob and took him under her own broken wing for protection and nurturing.

Antony had not left Blandine's side for any serious stretch of days since. He graduated from involuntary servitude with the Company to voluntary servitude with his "Blandina." She fed and clothed him and tried to shelter him, but he slept out of doors even in the foulest weather, using an open shed behind her dwelling-house.

He found ingenious ways to bring in money to the household. In the coves and shoals along the island's shore, he dove and swam as no giant could ever be expected to swim, scrabbling along the rocky bottom for lobsters. He would bring back a burlap sack full of the creatures and barter them in the market by the fort. Blandine knew he had gone lobster fishing only when a leg of pork or bundles of carrots suddenly materialized in her larder.

But somehow, no matter how far afield he went, Antony always knew if Blandine was ready to go out, materializing behind her, instantly and magically, whenever she stepped into Pearl Street.

The two of them, young Dutch-American woman and older African giant, bowed to the soldier at the land gate and passed beyond the wall. There Blandine found three other Africans, Lace, Mally and an elder, Handy, come to meet her.

"Piddy," Lace said. "A little eight-year-old orphan."

"Stolen," Mally said.

Aet Visser huffed aboard *Margrave* via the gangway, a round man with a florid face. The ship displayed the usual chaos of any newly docked vessel, but Visser was used to it, and threaded his way through the piles of cargo.

"Deck officer," he said to the first seaman he could grab. The sailor poked a finger aft. Visser found First Mate Barent Kouwenhoven at the whip staff, supervising the off-loading of a half dozen noisily complaining white-and-black Holstein dairy cows. Kouwenhoven wore hemp-canvas short pants notched off at the shin, a trim collared shirt and a twisted cap.

"I am the colony's orphanmaster," Visser said. "You have cargo for me."

"Aye," Kouwenhoven said. "You're here for your orphans. A sorry collection they are, too."

"How many dead during passage?" Visser asked.

"By the Lord's grace just one," the first mate said. "Disposed of at sea."

The mate could not recall the boy's name. In fact, all the circumstances surrounding the ocean burial were unfortunate. The captain stayed in his cabin nursing a vicious hangover from a rummy game the evening before, so there was no one to mumble the words. The purser objected to wasting precious sail canvas on an orphan's shroud, and the other boys needed clothing, so the child went over in his altogether.

"That gives me ten," Visser said, referring to *Margrave*'s manifest. "All boys this time, I believe?"

"Take 'em if you want 'em," Kouwenhoven said. "They've been no use to me." The Dutch orphans brought over by the *Margrave*, the first mate indicated, could be located in the ship's forward hold.

These were almshouse cases, burdens on the public purse in Patria. New Netherland felt the dire need of willing hands, lots of them, to make the colony work. The population of Europe was not yet convinced that decamping for a rocky, windswept island in America would improve their lot. Life in Holland proved all too comfortable. The new coffeehouses were just coming in, joining the tobacco houses already there. The cheese was as good as ever. No one wanted to leave.

Aet Visser recruited his orphan charges from three sources. Deaths of parents in the colony, deaths of parents on transocean voyages to the colony and these orphan shipments from Patria. Fortune proving to be a rascally mistress, the pool of orphans never dried up.

Visser descended between decks. The holds were reasonably well cleaned, kept shipshape in the way of the Dutch marine, yet foul-smelling after the long voyage. He found his charges, passage-stunned and cowering together in a collection of raglike hammocks.

"You have arrived," he announced, just to make sure the listless children, few over twelve years of age, realized they had successfully accomplished the transit from the old world to the new. Often he found on ships such as this that the orphans had little idea where they were, why they had been swept off the streets of Amsterdam, Rotterdam and the Hague or to what purpose they would serve in America.

"I am the orphanmaster. You will follow me." His ducklings.

Perhaps the orphans had visions of kindly couples, childless by circumstance or sterility, waiting to adopt their precious new wards, whisking them off to a thorough scrubbing in a hot bath, a steaming dinner of gussied fowl, fatty bacon and candied fruit, then a rosy sleep in a warm bed.

Visser could not recall that particular scenario ever coming to pass in the real world. No orphanages existed in New Amsterdam. The boys would be taken in by settlement families who needed laborers and servants.

In his frequent letters to the government of the home country, the colony's director general pleaded for "new blood." And here was what they sent him, ten gangly children. New blood? New to the colony, perhaps, but exhausted, thin and almost bloodless, as far as Visser could tell.

No kindly couples greeted the orphans. The wealthy burghers of the settlement would inspect the goods and make their choices, picking this or that orphan out from among the cowed assemblage. A servant from the great man's household, a downstairs maid, say, or a scullery cook, would drag the chosen one away by his filthy neck. Though not before, Visser would hasten to assure, the burgher paid the orphanmaster for the privilege with several strings of seawan, what would be referred to (with a wink) as "expenses."

He examined his charges now, climbing out of their hammocks and standing shivering in *Margrave*'s hold. They knew not what they were in for, Visser thought, but then, which one of us does?

"Single file," he barked at them. "Keep in line."

Puke-stained and filthy, pale almost to transparency, the orphans trooped after Visser through the ship's mazelike hold. Together they mounted a steep ladder and emerged on deck, to stand blinking in the fresh air and drifting snowflakes.

"Behold," Visser said, making a sweeping gesture at the rude collection of unpainted, snowcapped dwelling-houses clustered around the wharf. "New Amsterdam settlement, Manhattan Island, the capital of the New Netherland colony. Your new home."

Sponsored by a trading cartel, the Dutch West India Company, the colony of New Netherland existed to feed Europe's growing appetite for fur. Chartered in 1624, New Netherland's main settlement, New Amsterdam, clung to the wedge-shaped tip of Manhattan Island, posted alongside one of the greatest natural harbors on earth.

In 1663, almost four decades after its founding, New Amsterdam existed as a less than mile-square community of fifteen hundred souls.

A red cedar palisade running along its northern boundary lent a contained, almost besieged feel to the town. Digging waterways and erecting windmills, the Dutch colonists slowly made the place over in the familiar image of their homeland, which they called Patria, the fatherland. They lived at first in dug-out pits, then in cabins, and finally, as the colony grew more prosperous, in sturdy brick or clapboard dwelling-houses.

On the west side of the island's wedge, along Prince Maurice's River, stood Fort Amsterdam, a square redoubt with log ramparts and battlements at every corner. To the east side of the fort, protected by its walls from the winds off the bay, lay the town market, *het marckvelt*. Between the fort and river rose up three windmills, what the Dutch called *moolens*, and the town gallows.

Four streets ran north-south, up the island to the wall: Pearl, Smit, Prince and the Broad Way. Eight roads crossed the settlement east to west, including the Strand, on the island's southern tip, and Langs de Wal, Wall Street, the path that ran below the northern palisade.

Two gates, or *landtpoorts* ("land ports"), led through the wall to the fields and woodlands to the north, one on Pearl Street at the East River, and another on the west side of the island at the Broad Way. But settlers in the middle neighborhoods of the colony wearied of taking the long way around, and had kicked loose the logs in the palisade at several points, in order that they might pass through.

Carved from a stream bed, Heere Gracht, a canal navigable only at high tide, bent north almost to the wall from its starting point at the East River. The island's busy wharf district ran along its southeastern shore. The Strand, the waterfront street, offered tap houses to sailors and dockworkers. The wealthier colonists resided mainly on Stone or Market streets.

New Amsterdam's population comingled the dominant half who were Dutch with German, English, Swedish, Polish, French, Jewish and African elements in a fluid, uneasy mix. River indians walked freely down the settlement's streets, on shopping sprees for sweet pastries or bolts of cloth.

Beyond the wall lived small communities of Africans, strategically located to absorb attacks from maurading native Americans. The African settlements thus acted as shields for the benefit of the Dutch colonists in the town.

One man ruled over the colony, with an iron hand and wooden leg. Petrus Stuyvesant.

3

Piddy Gullee went for water and didn't come back in October 1663. Lace and Mally turned to the only person they could count on to help. Blandine van Couvering had forged a powerful link with the colony's African community, one that had been hammered home in July 1659, on a single afternoon almost four years before Piddy's disappearance.

Blandine turned eighteen that summer, and she knew no more of Africans than any well-born young New Amsterdam woman would. She often passed a collection of cabins outside the palisade wall. "Little Angola," the townspeople called it.

These were the homes of the "half-free" Africans, a full quarter of the black population of the colony, the ones who could own their land but had to pay a yearly tribute to the government.

Half-liberty. When Blandine thought about it as a young girl, she considered that granting such rights—the Africans also enjoyed a single holiday in spring, after May Day, when they were given free run of the colony—served only to highlight the condition of their servitude. Should anyone have asked, she might have said she opposed slavery. But it did not bear heavily on her young conscience.

Blandine's own family never possessed a slave. She occasionally witnessed enslaved members of the community as they labored to shore up the walls of the fort. The Company worked the majority, and the director general personally kept a score. Only the wealthiest members of the community could afford to claim ownership of human flesh.

For a long time, to Blandine, Africans represented only one more element in the growing horde that Manhattan drew to itself. All that changed one sparkling July afternoon.

The Dutch made war upon the Esopus tribe that summer of 1659. The violence of the Esopus wars, the retaliatory massacres, the burning of cornfields and villages, happened far to the north of New Amsterdam, near the town of Wildwyck. So far, nothing of it had directly touched the settlement.

Just to be safe, the *schout* ordained that no settler should venture out beyond the palisade wall without armed escort. But it was the high summer season, the raspberries on the hillsides only a short few leagues from town needed gathering and the colonists loved their summer fruit.

A band of a dozen settlers, primarily women and children but with two Company militiamen along, headed out from town through the land gate. The militiamen carried firearms.

Blandine joined them. She enjoyed raspberries as much as anyone, and liked the easy feeling of community among the pickers. It was a tradition. She had picked every year since as a child she went with her mother and father. Blandine always relished getting beyond the confines of the colony's northern wall to the wilder lands beyond.

The area where the tiny juicy drupelets grew seemed perfectly secure. *Bouweries*—the farms of the countryside—open meadows and dwelling-houses dotted the landscape, marked also by the major thoroughfare of the Post Road, the link between the southern tip of Manhattan and the territories to the north.

As the group passed Little Angola, one of the women there, Mally, hailed Blandine.

"You going berrying?" she asked, seeing the woven basket Blandine carried over her arm.

Blandine knew Mally casually, having employed her and her half-sister, Lace, to do hemming on linens she imported from Patria. The finished product—pillowcases, bedsheets, handkerchiefs—commanded a higher price than raw cloth.

Blandine saw Lace coming up behind Mally, carrying sacks for fruit. No one had any objections to the Africans joining the group, so Mally and Lace came with them.

If Africans had any status in the colony at all, they were usually called by the last name of the region from which they came. So Mally and Lace and others, too, all were given the same last name, Angola. There was no thought behind it, and it was by no choice of the ones so named. The Dutch authorities simply needed a distinguishing label to put down on paper if the Africans were ever hauled into court.

A hot July day. Insect noise swelled from the meadows, died and swelled again. Two sisters in the group, Tryntie and Aleida Bout, sang a hymn of thanks, "Nederlandtsche Gedenckclanck," a new anthem celebrating the Protestant victory over the Spanish Catholics in Holland.

> *We gather together*
> *To ask the Lord's blessing*
> *God our defender and guide*
> *Through the past year.*

A few of the others picked up the song. Blandine noticed that the harsh rasping of the locusts, katydids and crickets easily drowned out the quavering human voices singing God's praises.

She trailed behind the group. With the journey out of town, her abiding sorrow lifted a little, the sadness she had suffered since she lost her family. Yet these were haunted precincts for Blandine. It had been a different, more carefree girl who traipsed through the sweet berry bushes when she was young.

The road they followed up the island led them to a small rise with a view of the wide river to the west. The water's surface reflected back the gunmetal blue of the sky. Blandine noticed a flattened thatch of grass. Probably nothing more than a night bed for deer.

As they diverged from the road onto a path, Blandine saw that a collection of canoes had been pulled in amid a reed bed on the rocky Manhattan shore just below her. They stood empty, beached in a line.

From the water, she thought, no one would see the skiffs among the reeds.

The sky was patched with high white cumulus, the men had taken up the hymn along with the women and the group entered in among the scattered cane-fields of raspberries. The fruits dangled, crimson and abundant. Emperor and hairstreak butterflies sipped on the berry sugar. A cloud of them arose as the Dutch, crying out like children, plunged into the bushes.

In a first gluttonous spasm, the settlers didn't bother with their baskets, they simply stuffed whole handfuls into their mouths.

With Lace and Mally, Blandine wandered away from the others. The berry trail guided them in random directions. Each prickly, laden cane

led to the next, as though there would be a secret revealed at the end
of the path.

Blandine left off picking. She sat on the ground amid the canes, her
aproned skirts spread about her. She looked east toward the Post Road
and a massive stand of jackpines that lined the way. Mentally, she calculated the worth of the trees. Masts for the navies of the world.

Far off, on the roadway, a drover herded a pair of cattle, heading
toward town. Then, between one tree and the next, he abruptly disappeared. She waited for the man to show himself again. His cattle wandered down the road without him. She could hear their bells tinkling.

After a quarter hour, the clouds fully reefed the sky, hiding the sun,
and a breath of cooler air rose from the river. The colonists quieted, intent
on filling their baskets. Blandine struggled to maintain her lightness of
heart. The cows still roamed alone. What happened to the drover?

She quickly rose to her feet.

"Mally," she called. "Lace." They were nearby.

"We have to—" she said, but broke off. "We should join the others."
They threaded their way back through the berry canes to where the
dozen pickers worked.

Everything was all right. The clouds uncovered the sun, and the red-
stained faces of her fellow townspeople reassured her. She was a ninny
to be nervous. Odd how the wilderness struck her differently at different
times. Glorious one moment, threatening the next.

A hand fell on Blandine's shoulder. She jumped, surprised.

"Look within," Patricia Reydersen said, displaying a basket nearly
full with fruit. "What have ye been at? You've picked hardly nothing
for yourself."

"I've got more than anybody!" crowed the nine-year-old Reydersen
daughter, Ereen. Patricia Reydersen had been one of the matrons who
was kind when Blandine was newly orphaned, having been close to her
mother, Josette. Patricia's hearth offered the hungry girl cider and cookies.

Militiaman Jerominus Tyinck, his chin bloodred with berry juice,
stood nearby. Blandine approached him. "Did you mark the canoes?"

The man looked at her blankly.

"Along the shore," she said.

"No doubt they're over from Pavonia, lass," Tyinck said, naming the colony across the river from Manhattan. Indians there were known to be harmless. "No need to fear."

Tyinck dismissed her, a young goose of a girl pulling at her curls and trying to keep her hands free of berry juice. The militiaman strode away toward an area of heavy cane. He propped his gun against a stump and worked his pipe.

Silence. Out of that silence, a shout.

Vocalizing loudly, an indian warrior appeared, running pell-mell from the concealing forest. He swung his war club and dropped Jerominus Tyinck with a tremendous blow to the head.

Screams. As more natives showed around them, a wide-eyed panic gripped the colonists. They were outnumbered. The children clung to their mothers. The women moaned: *"Neen, neen, neen."* No, no, no.

Resoluet Waldron, the other militiaman, engaged his musket. The gunshot sounded enormous in the still glade. The bullet spun one of the attackers around in a bloody whirl. But that was all. Another raider grabbed the gun out of Waldron's hands and smashed him with it. He, too, fell to the ground.

The women and children were on their own.

Blandine stood with Mally and Lace. More and more *wilden* appeared out of the woods. Not river indians, she saw. By their markings, Mahicans, from the north.

The director general of the colony displayed a callous disregard for distinctions of tribe and clan among the natives. Armies of settlers during the Esopus wars attacked all indians indiscriminately, and in one recent engagement, decimated a Mahican village.

The action against the Mahicans, Blandine had heard, was particularly vicious. Soldiers set lodges afire with families still inside and shot the inhabitants as they fled. One army trio happened upon a young, pregnant Mahican, sewed her orifice shut with deer sinew, then induced labor by beating the girl with their musket butts. She died in her birth pangs.

Fury answered fury, and now here were the vengeful Mahicans on the settlement's doorstep.

Blandine huddled with Lace and Mally at the far edge of the group of colonists. Two of the raiders pulled Patricia Reydersen out of the group. She began to shriek. Blandine met the woman's agonized gaze and covered the eyes of Lace and Mally so that they should not see.

Within view of the other settlers, the two raiders tore off Patricia Reydersen's clothes. They alternately mounted her body to force her and, when she resisted, took up fist-sized stones to batter the woman's face.

For Blandine, it was as though she saw her own mother attacked. Why hadn't she moved to help her? Would she be next?

Several of the Mahicans gathered around the wounded Dutch soldier, Resoluet Waldron. Uttering short birdlike calls, they used the man roughly, pushing him back and forth, pummeling and kicking him. They stripped the soldier naked, too, laying him out prone, facedown. While two raiders extracted a souvenir fingernail from one of the bellowing man's hands, another worked the blade of a battle-ax in a straight line down the skin of his spine.

When the cut was sufficiently deep, the raider, a tall Mahican with a blue-painted face, dug into the wound with both hands, grabbing the bloody stretch of skin and peeling it off the flesh. The whole flap came up easily, with the sound of a raw beaver tail being split open. The flayed man thrashed, but the natives stood on his neck and arms to hold him tightly in place.

None of the raiders seemed to be in any hurry. Several threw themselves on the ground in attitudes of aggressive repose, chatting, laughing, slapping one another's chests. Those not directly involved in the attack on Waldron wandered easily in and out of the group of terrified colonists.

One of the warriors approached Blandine, fingering her yellow hair as she tried not to flinch. He yanked a trailing curl, hard, then strolled off, looking back once or twice, marking her. She had picked up a few words of the language while trading. She heard the man say "mine."

Mally and Lace clung together, their faces wet with tears. They prayed in a desperate whisper. Hysteria and paralysis gripped all the colonists, women and children both. Blandine knew that she had to act, discover some way out, or she would follow Patricia Reydersen into death.

Blandine said under her breath, "We have to get away. Now. The three of us."

Like everyone else in New Amsterdam, Blandine witnessed waves of blank-eyed Dutch refugees come south in flight from the Esopus war. Several told of being "freed" by their captors, experiencing an illusion of flight, only to be cruelly tracked down again. It was a common tactic of the native warriors.

Blandine sought to turn a false escape into a real one. She began to move, trying not to panic, leading Lace and Mally away.

Two raiders were close by, the one who had marked her before, painted with black-and-white zigzags, and another, a younger male whose whole body was stained yellow.

They bent over with laughter, as though women captives edging toward the forest made for a tremendously comical sight. They pointed and howled.

When Blandine, Mally and Lace were ten yards away from the mayhem, Zigzag and his yellow comrade broke off to follow.

"Where you go, huh?" the big indian called out in English, still laughing. "Where?"

"Keep on," Blandine said. "Whatever happens, we stay together."

Behind them, a raider in the larger group stood up from his task of wrestling down one of the colonial women and shouted in their direction.

"Bring them back," Blandine understood the raider to say.

Zigzag turned and called in reply, "We have them."

Suddenly Yellow Boy ran at Blandine in an abrupt, sudden charge, but fell to his knees and skidded to a stop a few feet away, laughing at her fright.

Zigzag dashed forward to slug Lace with a vicious punch, knocking her down. While Blandine pulled the woman back to her feet, the Mahican stood dancing in place, inches away, shouting threateningly into her face. But, abruptly, Zigzag turned his back on them and strode away.

The effect, Blandine knew, was designed for maximum fear.

In a staggering march, trailed by the two warriors, the three women left the scene of the berry-harvest attack behind. The shouts of the raiders and cries of settlers faded. Behind them, Zigzag and Yellow Boy continued their negligent pursuit. They would stop, plucking a leaf or berry, calling out to a hawk circling in the sky above them.

And then, suddenly, nothing. Blandine led Lace and Mally down a steep incline and turned them into a sheltered glade. They no longer could see their two pursuers. Silence. Even the faint whooping from the distant berry patch died out.

"Is it over?" Lace said, her voice half-strangled with fear.

"Keep going," Blandine said. Her heart raced. She did not dare to think they had escaped so easily. But it seemed true.

A keening scream. Zigzag and Yellow Boy stood on the crest of the slope above them. In a combative display, the Mahicans battered each other, slapping and pummeling their chests like two boys in a school yard.

As the raiders advanced downward, their nonchalance vanished. Zigzag freed his stiffened member from behind its cloth, waving it at them arrogantly.

"Lord Jesus save me," Lace whispered. Her hand gripped Blandine's, nails abrading the skin.

"Now we run," Blandine said.

The three women fled down the slope to the shore of the river. Blandine led them to the reed bed where the native dugouts were beached.

Mally leapt into the first canoe. Lace climbed into the unsteady craft with her.

"Come on!" Mally shouted to Blandine.

But, for a long breathless moment, Blandine stayed on shore, working to push the other canoes out of the shallows, casting them off into the river current. If their pursuers wanted them, they would have to swim.

Finally, she dove for the little boat.

Together the three women paddled the craft out into the current, working furiously. The raiders arrived at the shore and splashed into the water behind them. They lunged forward, swimming to within a few yards of the women in the dugout.

But they came up short. Blandine, Mally and Lace moved into deeper water, outdistancing the Mahicans.

When the three women arrived wet, bedraggled and still fear-stricken at the settlement, and once the Dutch director general sent a well-armed war party of his own to retaliate against the raiders, Blandine felt herself drawn into the lives of Mally and Lace and the community of Little Angola.

None of the others in the berrying party survived.

In the aftermath of the raid, Blandine noted with scorn some of her erstwhile suitors shying away from her as soiled goods. The men of the colony were never sure what exactly happened in the berry patch on the river.

Only the first love of her life, Kees Bayard, stayed true. "You are my brave girl," Kees said to her, solicitous in the wake of the tragedy. He defended her stoutly. He volunteered for the company that pursued the fleeing raiders.

Deep inside, though, Blandine felt that no one understood the terror she experienced that day. Only Lace and Mally. It was as though, when your house burns down, you want to talk only to other people who have had their houses burn down. Her later friendship with Antony only cemented her connection with the Africans.

So it was natural, when one of their own disappeared that fall four years later, when a child who went out to fetch water did not come back, that Lace and Mally should turn to Blandine.

4

As soon as she heard of Piddy Gullee's disappearance, Blandine sought out the orphanmaster.

Aet Visser was the man most important to her in all of New Amsterdam. Charged by the town government with looking after the interests of orphaned children, he had taken care of Blandine herself when she lost her parents at age fifteen.

Not that she wanted him to. Not at first anyway. Crushed by rage and grief at the news that her parents' ship, *Blue Hen*, had wrecked with the death of all aboard in the Channel off Kent, she walled herself away from human contact.

She was fine, Blandine told the orphanmaster when he came calling. I am old enough to take care of myself. A small stash of seawan made it possible to live as she pleased. When the disaster carried her parents to the bottom of the Channel, Blandine boldly marched into probate court, a girl of fifteen petitioning to sell her family's home, a two-story redbrick residence on the canal with five apple trees in back.

Such a transaction was the proper province of the orphanmaster, and Visser appeared next to her in court, but she rudely refused his help. She stumbled through her dealings with the magistrate. Visser interrupted to suggest that Blandine retain the fruit of the orchard trees for ten years hence. The magistrate ruled five.

That was nice. But she told Visser he should keep out of her affairs anyway. She smiled ruefully at the memory of telling him off, a squeaky-voiced girl trying to act grown up.

After that, Visser played patient. He had already reached middle age when they met, and had held the orphanmaster position forever, since the rough-and-tumble years of the 1650s, a time when colonists and natives seemed locked in irresolvable, deadly conflict. There were many new casualties of war.

He oversaw the means and property of parentless minors. He was an angel of death, appearing whenever parents perished. Among shipwrecks,

indian wars and rampaging contagions, the business of orphanmaster-
ing boomed.

Visser came to the new world from Friesland, in the Dutch Republic,
where the winds off the North Sea blew strong. He shared his back-
ground with many in the colony, including the director general, which
allowed Visser to cultivate the relationships that helped him secure the
position of orphanmaster.

Did Visser cut corners? Was he ever accused of dipping his hand into
the money pots of his wards? Inevitable, these accusations, when such
dealings were transacted. But Aet Visser bumped along as the colony's
orphanmaster, not totally honest, perhaps, but for the purpose of the colony, honest enough. Which is all that can be realistically asked of any man.

Rumor surrounded him. He had disobedient wards killed. He
fathered a whole family of bastards with a beautiful half-indian woman
north of the wall. He supplied young orphans to the Jews for their infernal blood rites.

Visser shrugged off the tales. He modeled openness.

"I myself am an orphan," he always said, neglecting to add that his
parents had both died at the comfortable old age of fifty-two.

The orphanmaster held forth in the Orphan Chamber, a special court
convened at the colony's town hall, the Stadt Huys, an imposing five-
story stone structure on the waterfront.

In the Orphan Chamber, Visser arranged for apprenticeships and
servitudes. He ensured that heirs inherited inheritances. He sent a few
of his wards back across the sea to Holland, to be cared for in the homes
of relatives.

Just in the last week, an issue came into the chamber when two
human heads were discovered while gathering in the cattle of settlers
who had disappeared "in the last disaster"—an indian incursion. Visser
officially declared the two heads were indeed those of the vanished men,
Cornelis Swits and Tobias Clausen, thereby rendering their children
wards of the orphanmaster.

"Pursuant to the intentions of this court," Visser ruled, "the cattle
shall be put to use for the benefit of the orphans."

The severed heads of the fathers, he suggested, should be remanded to the dominie of the Dutch Reformed Church, for possible reunification with their bodies, should such bodies ever be located.

Another case, Dorothea Janz, father drowned off Hell Gate in 1661, mother dead through ingestion of arsenic. Visser divvied up the family belongings. A blanket to the child's aunt, a string of seawan to the foster parents, a bedstead that materialized magically in the best chamber of the director general's sister. A cache of twenty silver rider coins, where did those end up? A mystery, thankfully unexamined by prying eyes.

Through it all, Visser maintained a rumpled, shambling, habitually hungover mien that concealed a shrewdness around the heart.

"Money is the root of all," he would proclaim.

When she first heard him say that, young Blandine archly suggested to the orphanmaster that he had left off the tag end of the biblical epigram. "Doesn't it say, Mister Visser, 'money is the root of all evil'?"

"Oh, right," Visser responded, chuckling. "I always forget that last part."

No matter what the monetary issue might be, he loved his orphans. He said it all the time, and people believed him.

A man of Visser's long experience could not be put off by the surliness of Blandine van Couvering. Surely, it was not customary for one of his wards to live independently at such an early age. But Visser hewed to the philosophy of letting well enough alone. The maiden, as far as he could see, was making her way in the world. To drag her kicking and screaming into a foster family's home would do neither of them any good.

He looked in on her often in her rented rooms, stopped her in the street to ask after her well-being, gave out small gifts of raisins and walnuts. Visser made the introductions to merchants who helped Blandine reach her current status as a trader-on-her-way-up. The orphan girl felt her heart melting, and iced it against the orphanmaster again and again. But eventually, he won her over.

Now, in the wake of Piddy's disappearance, Blandine sought Visser out. She knew where he would be after *Margrave* docked. He would have a flock of orphans from the ship, and would bring them to the yard behind one of the grand houses of the settlement. There, they would be parceled out for work.

She made her way through the snow to the dwelling-house of the

Hendrickson family. This is what wealth bought in Manhattan. The mansion was easily the largest private home in the colony. Two stories plus attics, a full seven bays wide, with grounds that could have sited several of the neighboring residences. The acreage stretched from Market Street to the family's own private waterway, which connected to the larger canal, the Heere Gracht.

The black prospect of the Hendrickson mansion, clapboarded in dark-stained wood, always struck Blandine. Built of milled lumber, the house didn't simply occupy its lot in the style of the other residences in Market Street, many of which were grand enough. The Hendrickson house didn't sit, it loomed. The prominent jetties on the second floor made the place appear as though it might topple down upon whoever might approach it.

The house had another odd quality, too. The windows were not the traditional casements, broken up into small individual lead-lights, but rather new-style sash affairs. The expanse of blank panes resembled nothing else in the glass-starved colony. The windows stared down at Blandine like blind eyes. She passed through the front gates, along the dwelling-house walk, beneath the overhanging second story to reach the stable yards in the grounds behind.

A solitary, pretty young female seldom approaches a group of adult men without at least a measure of trepidation. In the area to the rear of the house, many of New Amsterdam's worthies gathered to examine the orphans newly arrived on *Margrave*. Aet Visser was there, conducting business at the far side of the yard. Blandine's loyal suitor, Kees Bayard, stood with Martyn Hendrickson himself, the youngest of the three Hendrickson brothers, the wealthiest men of the colony.

And the orphans. A pathetic group of ten clustered together in the mud and snow of the yard, clothed in rags, still wobbly and filthy from their transocean voyage. Each face displayed the stunned, faraway "Where am I?" look of those new to the new world.

Ranged against the orphans, the gentlemen worthies, dressed impeccably in the style of the day, waistcoats, matched doublets and lace collars. They teetered on their scarlet heels, *les talons rouges*, a style imported from the French court of Louis XIV.

A chronic labor shortage afflicted the colony, and Visser's orphans-for-hire got snapped up soon after they stepped off the boat. The gentlemen checked the offerings, poking and prodding as though they were hell's ferrymen, examining lost souls.

Blandine recoiled at the scene. She knew what it reminded her of: the slave market at the foot of Wall Street on the East River.

"Blandina," Kees Bayard called, seeing her. The men all turned and straightened up, a pretty girl in their midst.

"We have another orphan up for grabs," Martyn Hendrickson called out. "What do we bid on her, gentlemen?"

Kees glared at him and took Blandine's hand. She withdrew it.

"If I had the means," she said, "I would gladly sponsor all of the boys here."

"Did you hear that, Visser?" Martyn called over to the orphanmaster. "We have a new proffer, you will have to top Miss Blandina's price."

Aet Visser, haggling with one of the gentleman worthies over a hollow-eyed scarecrow of barely ten years, looked over at Blandine and waved genially.

"I'll have half of these myself," Martyn said briskly. "Send them upriver to my brothers, work on the estate. Good healthy toil in the fields."

"Plus they don't eat much," Blandine said.

Martyn ignored the hint of bitterness in her tone and laughed. "Exactly," he said. "And if one of my brothers gets hungry, he can always cook himself up a couple of them."

"I beg of you, sir," Kees Bayard said, "not to be coarse in front of the lady."

"Miss Blandina knows well I am only jesting," Martyn said.

"Dear Martyn," Blandine said. "The way one knows one is joking? Is if the other person is laughing."

The two men stood on either side of Blandine as though vying for her favor. But Martyn Hendrickson could never be anyone's suitor. A notorious gambler, drinker, whoremonger, he preferred dissipation to romance. Tempting as he was, the young women of the settlement despaired of Martyn Hendrickson. Killingly handsome, green-eyed, rich as a god, he appeared too wild to tame.

Blandine always thought she detected a loneliness behind Martyn's unfocused eyes and brandy-slurred speech. Although the two of them could not possibly be more different in circumstance and outlook, they each had lost both parents. Martyn would never think of displaying vulnerability, but Blandine perceived it in him nonetheless. She recalled when she and Martyn were young, rattling about the settlement, lost and but shallowly rooted. Or perhaps she was just reading her hurt into his.

"I have just seen Lace and Mally," Blandine said.

"Ah, the Africans again," Kees said. He disapproved of Blandine's friendship with the two women. It brought up troubling memories of the Mahican raid.

"I come with bad news," Blandine said. "A little girl in the African community has gone missing."

"And what is your bad news?" Martyn asked.

"For pity's sake, Hendrickson," Kees said. But he laughed in spite of himself.

"You are unfunny, sir," Blandine said to Martyn, and crossed the yard to Aet Visser. She stopped beside him, waiting for him to finish his business.

With Visser was the orphanmaster's frequent shadow, Lightning, a half-caste Esopus indian who prided himself on his European father. Lightning dressed as a Dutchman, spoke as a Dutchman and wished desperately to be a Dutchman. Blandine found him repulsive. As if sensitive to her feelings, Lightning faded away when she approached, crossing over to join Martyn Hendrickson.

Visser stood resting a hand on the shoulder of one of his wretched orphans. These boys were healthy enough, he thought, feeling the bones beneath the boy's threadbare shirt. They'd serve anyone well as field hands.

The orphanmaster turned to his former ward.

"Miss Blandina," he said. "This is not a place for you."

"How much for that one over there?" Blandine cocked her chin at a young orphan boy.

"Please, it's not that way," Visser said. "I merely guide my wards toward gainful employment."

Blandine poked Visser in his belly, where the heavy clink of money bags sounded.

The orphanmaster nodded, acknowledging her point. "We must live in the real world," he said, sighing.

"The real world," Blandine repeated. The orphans looked like a collection of stick figures, leaning against one another for support. From the streets and workhouses of Patria to a hard-labor existence in New Netherland. She loved a part of Aet Visser. But not this part.

"The Africans report a child of theirs lost or disappeared," Blandine said. "Lace and Mally have gone frantic."

"I know," he said.

"You know? What do you mean? I just heard of this."

"The boy has been gone a good week now," Visser said.

"The boy? What boy?" Blandine said. "This is a little girl."

Visser took Blandine's arm and moved her to the far edge of the yard. "We must speak of this, but not now," he said. "We'll meet at our usual venue, after sundown, and have our sup."

There was nothing Blandine could do. She left, her heart rending. If her life had played out differently, she could have been among the orphans lined up for work, getting pawed over like cattle.

The Hendrickson house beetled above her as she stepped out into the snowy muck of Market Street.

5

Edward Drummond stayed with *Margrave* well into nightfall, supervising the unloading of his instrument case, his lenses and lens-grinding tools, purchased in the shops of London's Long Acre and Chancery Lane, crated and couched in beds of wood shavings and straw.

"That one, there," Drummond said of the coffin-sized wooden crate containing his prized brass perspective tubes. "Have a care."

The porter bumped the crate down the wharf.

Drummond said to the man, "Is there a glassworks?"

"A glassworks?" Drummond might as well have asked, *Is there an elephant?*

On his way from Switzerland to meet *Margrave* in Rotterdam, he had time for a detour to Rijnsburg, to the laboratory of Benedict Spinoza, the lens grinder. He picked out a set of plano-concaves, a pair of lovely biconvexes, a concavo-convex, extremely fine work, the man was a magician, plus a disassembled treadle apparatus, in order that Drummond might better learn to grind his own.

At the dockside warehouse, he questioned the factor. "You keep a watch?"

"Yes, sir."

"All night?"

"My man lives atop the stairs," the factor said.

Drummond stuck an English guinea into the man's hand. "I'll send word where to deliver my crates. Keep them safe."

Hat, doffed. Forelock, tugged. Plus a stiff-cocked bow. Perhaps the guinea had been too much.

He saw his impedimenta safely warehoused and then, at nine o'clock, left the docks and proceeded down Pearl Street into the heart of town.

One reason to tarry about *Margrave* was to divest himself of shipmate Remunde, who possessed an inquiring sensibility, and thus might well disrupt Drummond's purpose in New Amsterdam. Send Gerrit home to his Gerta, and leave the questions behind.

Drummond must appear a simple grain merchant, newly arrived, in search of his lodgings. He possessed letters of trade that would present him as such.

One thing he enjoyed about the Dutch, perhaps their best characteristic, was that they were always too busy with their single-minded scurrying after profit to pay anyone else much mind.

The contemporary wisdom: "The Dutchman is a lusty, fat, two-legged cheese worm, a creature so addicted to eating butter, drinking fat drink and skating on ice that all the world knows him for a slippery fellow."

Well, yes. But they were not all that way. Bento Spinoza, for example. A superior man in every aspect.

On his walk into the town Drummond saw himself clearly transported to the land of the cheese worms. A brawling, ruddy, crapulous bunch, snuffling along like pigs after truffles. The streets of the colony were alive even well after dark.

The new world, as far as Drummond could see upon first blush, was much like the old. Only dirtier.

If he squinted he could have been on any minor main street in a Kenmerland countryside village, in the muddy outer precincts of Assen, say, or Hunz.

Not the Flanders of the Van Eyck brothers, Peter Paul Rubens, Rembrandt van Rijn or even the Brueghels. New Amsterdam felt more like the pig-gravy-and-sausage hamlets in the backwaters of the Zuider Zee, where the peasant boys stared at you gape-jawed, never having seen a human being they didn't know from the cradle.

But no one stared at him here. Drummond, in his experiences in service to the crown, had attempted to perfect a posture of transparency. After periods of trial and error, in Amsterdam, the Hague, Paris and London itself, he found it a not difficult skill to possess.

Pull down your hat brim. Meet not the eyes of any passerby. Appear unlost, resolute in direction, with no hesitancy. Wear a dark cloak that swathes any identifying clothing. Keep to the marge.

Drummond once walked past a night watch in Bruges, passing within three feet of his lantern. Then a cohort, George Post, trailing behind Edward, waylaid the man and asked if he had seen anyone abroad in the street just now. The night watch had sworn not.

Invisible. Perhaps, only a shadow.

Ahead, spilling a rowdy clientele out into the bright pool of its window light, Drummond saw the Red Lion tap house.

His man Raeger would be there.

"And you, how are you keeping yourself?" Aet Visser asked Blandine.

"I leave soon for the Beverwyck market," Blandine said. "I need to go in order to pursue my trade, and I'll be gone for at least two weeks. But I'm worried, Aet. The Africans can get no one to care about the fate of this child."

Visser patted her hand. "I will look to it," he said.

"Will you?" Searching the man's lumpy face. The bulbous, comical nose had taken on the crimson hue that intensified whenever Visser downed more than one brandy.

Blandine sat with him in the chimney corner of the Red Lion, on Pearl Street a block from the Strand. A rough tavern, a sailor's haven frequented also by decadent gentlemen, but a place Blandine knew as a second home. Literally, since her dwelling-house lay just across the street.

Blandine's time at the Lion went far back. She accompanied her father there as an orange girl, hawking to the clientele fresh citrus fruits her parents shipped in from the West Indies. She once brought into the Lion a bright green parrot from Curaçao. A fistfight broke out as patrons vied with one another to buy the bird.

Her parents allowed her to keep her earnings from the tap house, and this was her first introduction to the thrill of trade. Blandine's French Catholic mother had met her Dutch Protestant father in Flanders. Both made their living buying and selling, along with her Amsterdam uncles, establishing the Van Couverings as a thoroughly mercantile family.

Blandine took many of her meals at the tap house. The Lion was renowned for the quality of the tobacco it sold, and the interior was as hazy as the fog-shrouded air outside. She could barely see across the room.

Blandine herself repudiated smoking. She had smoked at age twelve, but now at twenty-two she had given it up as a habit unfit for her moral universe. She still made room in her universe, moral or otherwise, for the Lion's beer and hard cider.

She sat with a mug of October bock squarely in front of her, tugging and releasing a stray blond curl that trailed at the back of her neck. Another habit, but one of which she was hardly aware.

Cats wandered the floor of the taproom, all of them scrawny and defiant. A litter of kittens rolled around in the sawdust under the bar. Blandine watched, marveling that the animals didn't get flattened by the red-heeled shoes of the drinking gentlemen.

Monday night, past nine o'clock, the weekday closing hour ordained by the director general, strictly enforced in the taverns along the Strand. But somehow the Lion had a magical dispensation to avoid the curfew.

Mostly sailors in tonight, dockworkers, factors. In an L-shaped casino annex hanging off the tavern's back end—"the Lion's Mane," wags named it—Martyn Hendrickson held forth with dice, drunk and losing. His companions of the bosom, Ludwig Smits, Pim Jensen, Rik Imbrock, the usual crowd, egged him on.

In the Mane, they drank Humpty Dumptys, an English import, brandy boiled with ale. The half-indian who went by the name of Lightning matched Hendrickson Humpty for Dumpty, hat tugged down low over his eyes.

The Lion's smoke-stained overhead beams were pockmarked with dozens of confiscated blades sunk deep into the wood, jackknives, hunters, kitchen cutlery, shivs, adzes, razors, hatchets, a silvered partizan minus its shaft.

The tradition began, legend had it, when a *wilden* struck one of the timbers with his battle-ax. The array of knives made for a pretty sight, but had a practical use as well, in the event of riot.

The gambler Pim had a blade out of his pocket and sharpened it on a whetstone. If he made a move to use it in the Lion, the knife would end up confiscated and embedded in the rafters. But he would, and did, employ it readily outside the tavern.

The Company imposed a jail term of six months for anyone drawing a knife in a fight. The measure failed to deter blade-men such as Pim and the other sailor-gambler-rowdies in his crew.

Martyn Hendrickson shrugged off the pretty whore hanging on him, the better to throw the bones. Hendrickson comported himself as a self-conscious libertine, returned a year past from a sojourn in Paris but still flaunting his debauched tastes. As he tossed the dice, he shouted for help from "accursed God" loud enough that those in the taproom could hear him.

Martyn and other members of his circle were among the many men Blandine had to fend off while spending her evenings in the Lion. Hendrickson was so wealthy he believed he could do what he wished. With her or anyone else. But Blandine always held her ground.

"Go upriver on your commerce," Visser told Blandine.

"And what of the African girl-child? You mentioned a missing boy?"

"I will let you in on a secret," Visser said. "An inquiry is already under way. Other children have disappeared. There may be a slavery ring at work. I consult closely with the *schout* and the director general."

Visser tapped his finger alongside his nose: *This is just between us.*

"And Piddy Gullee, she will be among those looked into?" Blandine could have added, "Even though she is poor and an African," but that went unsaid.

"All will be well, child," Visser said. He was a master at telling people what they wanted to hear. "Really, go about your trading. I know you have great anticipation of it."

She searched the orphanmaster's eyes. She did not quite trust him to be truthful with her. He turned away, looking thirstily across the room, gesturing for a refill.

An event of the last summer tugged at Blandine's mind, holding out a hint that somehow connected with Piddy's disappearance. The son of a settler had been killed upriver. She could not quite put her finger on it, but she felt a link there.

"I will look in on the Africans, you can rest easy," Visser said.

"I am friendly with Lace and Mally," Blandine said. "They'll be heartened by a visit from you."

The tall Englishman, the one Blandine had seen at the rail of the arriving ship that afternoon—she had discovered it was not *Sea Serpent*, but *Margrave*, out of Rotterdam—entered the tavern and stood as if posing, his face an insolent mask, eyes adjusting to the gloom and smoke.

A prinked peacock, Blandine thought, in his doublet of black brocade, with slashed sleeves, hair worn long and ringletted, in slavish imitation of King Charles. No doubt the man found the present public house and the whole Dutch outpost itself a shabby mirror for his vanity.

Blandine glanced at Visser and realized he was watching her watch the Englishman. In spite of herself, she blushed, and then tried to hide her blush behind her pewter tankard. Visser pretended not to notice, but Blandine caught the twinkle in his eye, the wretch.

The orphanmaster made an elaborate show of petting his dog. Visser kept a tiny white terrier tucked inside his coat, no more than a couple kilos of fluff, nestled against his belly bulge above his thick leather belt.

Maddie. The dog was so meek that when he set her down among the taproom's kittens she merely stood there and trembled. She needed Aet Visser's care as the orphans did.

Across the room, the peacock fanned his tail and spoke to the tapster, presenting him with a token. A coin? No, a short length of knotted rope.

The barman immediately turned, disappeared into the back and returned with Ross Raeger, the Lion's owner. Raeger and the Englishman went together into the upstairs gallery.

"I have to go," Blandine said to Visser. "The *schout* will come for curfew."

"Have a last beer," Visser said. He waved at the server.

Blandine stayed. And by this small decision, she considered later, her fate sealed itself as firmly as an iron-jawed trap.

6

"They are in Connecticut or Rhode Island," Raeger told Drummond. "Probably New Haven. Or, anyway, Goffe was seen there, public as you please, strolling the Green."

William Goffe and his father-in-law, Colonel Edward Whalley, had both placed their seals on the death warrant for Charles I. Now, evidently, they hid in the American colony to the north. Among his other tasks in the new world, Drummond had come to fetch Goffe and Whalley to justice. Rumor had it that a third king-killer, Colonel John Dixwell, was with them.

"I told Clarendon that I should better land in Boston," Drummond said.

"Massachusetts is a vast realm of ignorance," Raeger said. "They still believe that New England might be an island."

"But Boston is closer to the New Haven Colony, is it not?"

"No, no, Manhattan is much preferable," Raeger said. "If you ship into Boston Harbor, disembark, they make a mark next to your name, pretty soon the sheriff comes to interview you, he brings along a dominie."

By dominie, Raeger meant a cleric—probably, in Boston, a Puritan, the kind of man Christopher Marlowe, in one of his plays, called "a religious caterpillar." Drummond could never pass muster with such a soul. He'd be smoked out as a Catholic, even though he hadn't heard a *te deum* in years.

He sat with Ross Raeger in a four-by-four cubby at the landing of a flight of stairs. A second wood-paneled stairway wound upward to the few rooms the Red Lion let out to boarders. Tobacco smoke filtered from the noisy taproom down below. At Raeger's elbow was a Judas window he could slide back to surveil the scene in his ground-floor bar.

Drummond and Raeger were confreres, had been in London together on Oak Apple Day, the twenty-ninth of May, the birthday of the second Charles and Drummond's, too, the day the monarch took back the English throne.

A glorious time to be alive. A few months later, England's spymasters sent Raeger out as an agent-innkeeper to keep an eye on Dutch doings in New Netherland. Now, as host, the man laid out roast chicken, sliced venison, potatoes, fat chunks of smoked salmon. Drummond stared down at the spread, disbelieving the size of an oyster offered to him, nearly a foot long. New world bounty.

On the table also, two small lengths of rope, one from Raeger and one from Drummond, both tied in an elaborate wall-and-crown knot. Drummond had placed his down, and Raeger answered with his. Their code, the pass-sign, the emblem of the Sealed Knot.

The Society of the Sealed Knot devoted itself to the English monarchy. During the Civil War, to be caught with a wall-and-crown on your person meant immediate hanging. The knotted rope indicated Drummond was present to meet Raeger on the king's business.

Raeger brought out the good Canary sack, in order, he announced, "that we need not drink the vile Holland gin." Which, from the sound of drunken voices, the louts and bullyboys in the taproom downstairs were pouring down their throats as though the world might end.

"So, I'll have to go to Connecticut for the regicides," Drummond said, resignation in his voice, weary from tracking the king-killers all over creation. "But first I must head north to Fort Orange and Beaver Town, to establish this ridiculous incognito I am hauling around."

"Last few years, the wheat business is booming," Raeger said. "Maybe you could take a profit from it."

"To Fort Orange, then overland to, where, Hartford? Then finally New Haven and the regicides? What would that trip be like?"

"A horror. The Boston Post Road. Easier to come back here, and sail up the coast by boat," Raeger said. "Unless . . ."

Drummond eyed him. "Unless what?"

"Last July, the river indians made some kind of mess up north, and the Dutch are blaming the English. Anytime the Sopus act up, we catch the fault."

"And what could I do about it?"

"I was instructed that at the present time we are to avoid another indian war," Raeger said.

"Now I'm a preventer of wars? Whenever someone wants me to perform a miracle, I tell them, no, thank you, sainthood is much too dangerous an occupation, I'll stick to the safety of soldiering."

"Well, somebody should make a visit. I'd do it, but I have a public house to run."

"A visit. What are we talking about?"

"There's the Hendrickson plantation where the thing happened, on the east side of the river, opposite Wildwyck. Grisly sort of killing, we heard about it all the way down here, it's got everyone spooked. There've been pamphlets distributed around the colony with the bloody details."

He took a folded sheet of foolscap from his vest and slid it across the table to Drummond. *He came prepared*, Drummond thought.

"They're talking devils in the woods," Raeger said. "Ghosties and goblins."

Two texts, one English, one Dutch, written side by side. THE LATE MASSACRE AT PINE PLAINS, read the headline. "A faithful account of a bloody, treacherous and cruel plot by the English in America, purporting the total ruin and murder of all the Dutch colonists in New Netherland."

Drummond scanned the lurid prose. Blood spilled in the wilderness. Aboriginal demons, eaters of flesh. Esopus indians, English subterfuge to blame.

And this: "To God alone has the fearful tragedy been revealed."

He put the pamphlet back on the table and lifted his tankard. He felt the need to wash out his mouth.

"A ghost story," he said.

Raeger nodded. "The whole colony has an indian hobgoblin on the brain."

"I don't understand," Drummond said. "We English are said to enlist some sort of flesh-eater?"

"People are too scared to think clearly," Raeger said. "One of the Hendrickson brothers is downstairs right now. Do you want to talk to him?"

Drummond demurred. "I need sleep. You've secured rooms for me? Not here, I hope."

Raeger said, "On Slyck Steegh, next to the canal."

"I've heard about your canal. That it stinks like pig anus."

"The better part of town." Raeger laughed.

"And the workshop I asked for?"

"Abutting the back. Brick, with a glazed tile floor." Raeger drank up his wine. "You can stand one night in a room upstairs, can't you? Get settled tomorrow in the dwelling-house. Take your time. But you will go north to inquire about this awful business?" He flicked his finger at the pamphlet.

"I suppose." Drummond sighed.

"I just thought that if you were up there, you could damp down the flames of anti-English sentiment a little."

"But I can't go mucking about without drawing their suspicions," Drummond said.

Raeger nodded. "The Dutch," he said, "are a most suspicious people."

"Only in this case, their suspicions are entirely correct."

Raeger laughed and slid open the little window, giving Drummond a view of the downstairs.

The long-stemmed white clay pipes of the smokers bristled in the gloom. Voices rose from the taproom. Besides Dutch and English, Drummond counted snatches of French, Swedish and Polish, some Hochdeutsch, plus a few words of what he took to be Algonquin, the language of the river indians.

The multilingual chatter impressed Drummond. By the bowels of Christ (Cromwell's favorite oath), what a bestiary Raeger had himself here! As though someone had tilted up the globe and all the dregs flooded down into New Netherland.

"Who's that?" he asked Raeger.

The innkeeper peered around out the little window to see where Drummond was looking. "Aet Visser," he said.

Drummond shook his head and gave Ross Raeger a thin smile. Always joking.

"Visser's a minor Dutch official," Raeger said. "A sort of guardian they call the orphanmaster."

"Please," Drummond said.

"Oh, you mean the lady," Raeger said, putting on an innocent face.

"I saw her when *Margrave* came in," Drummond said.

"Blandine van Couvering. Styles herself a she-merchant. Grain, foodstuff, some small furs, working her way up to beaver. Striking, isn't she?"

"Very. She deals in grain? So do I."

"She's not for you, my man," Raeger said. He quoted Wyatt's poem about Anne Boleyn: "'*Noli me tangere*, for Caesar's I am, and wild for to hold, though I seem tame.'" Touch me not, the Latin meant.

"Caesar," Drummond said.

"Stuyvesant has Lady Blandina marked for his nephew," Raeger said.

"Stuyvesant," Drummond said.

"The director general."

"I know who Stuyvesant is," Drummond said. "Does he arrange marriages now?"

"The person our director general reminds me of the most is Cromwell himself," Raeger said. "Stuyvesant tells people to call him '*Mijn Heer* General.'"

"I heard he's not half the man that Cromwell was," Drummond said.

Raeger laughed. "Yes, yes, and *Mijn Heer* General has not a leg to stand on. We know the jokes. But it's serious. Like the wolf, the longer Stuyvesant lives, the worse he bites."

"And like Cromwell, he's a great builder of gallows."

"You saw that, did you, coming in? Stuyvesant had it erected down there on the point for a purpose, so it's the first thing newcomers see of the new world."

"I don't know," Drummond mused. "Perhaps it is a necessary measure, in the wild. I have only just arrived, and already I get a sense of lawlessness, beyond the wall, waiting to burst in."

"Extraterritoriality," Raeger said. "We have slipped the leash of civilization out here."

"And God, is he present and accounted for?"

"Oh, *Mijn Heer* General keeps God in his vest pocket," Raeger said. "You can ask him for a peep if you wish."

"And the nephew, the girl's beau? What's his story?"

"Cornelus Bayard, called Kees, 'like the call of the hawk,' he says, but 'Kees' actually means 'cheese.' The eldest son of the director's sister.

A shipbuilder-merchant. Something of a prig, and tied to the director general's purse strings, but he's on his way to becoming a very rich man."

Drummond gazed down through the window. "She can do better than that," he said.

The high-booted English peacock came down the stairs from the second floor, strode directly across the taproom and stood before Blandine and Visser.

He performed a courtly bow. "Edward Drummond," he said. "I'm told you deal in grain."

Blandine felt her face grow hot, and hated herself for it.

Visser saved her. "Why, yes," he said in his thickly accented English. "I trade in a little wheat, flax and barley. A Briton, are you not?"

"English," Drummond said, not taking his eyes from Blandine's downcast face.

"A grain merchant?"

"Yes."

"Aet Visser," the orphanmaster said, and held out his hand to Drummond.

Several loud bangs sounded against the street wall of the tavern.

"The *schout*," someone called.

"Time, gentlemen," a voice said from the outside.

Raeger emerged from upstairs and hurried across to the taproom entrance. "Yes, yes, yes," he said, disappearing into the street to consult with the sheriff.

The clientele drained down their last dregs and began filing out. From the backroom casino, the Mane, curses from the gamblers.

When Drummond turned back to the chimney-corner table, he saw that the woman Blandine had slipped around him and joined the crowd in leaving.

Drummond was about to follow, but Visser grabbed his arm.

"We should talk, sir," the orphanmaster said. "You and I should talk wheat and corn."

7

The next morning, Tuesday, a half foot of wet snow covered the ground. Kees Bayard visited Blandine before her departure for the trading market upriver at Beverwyck. He was preoccupied.

"Will you go around the island by Hell Gate or up the North River?"

"The North" is what Blandine should have said. But seeing Kees pace, glancing out the window of her rooms to the early morning foot traffic on Pearl Street, she felt an urge to tease him.

"We sail east across the wine-dark sea, the better to stop over at Holland."

"Yes, that's the proper way," he murmured, still distracted. Kees was anxious to get on with his business. He was always anxious to get on with his business.

They were in the ground-floor *groot kamer*, the great room of her dwelling-house, directly opposite the Red Lion. The taproom across the street presented a blank, shuttered face to the morning, the death-sleep of the drunkard.

"Your kit is stowed?" Kees asked, evidently not noticing her trunk, still half spilling out its contents.

Cornelus Bayard. "Kees." Ever since Blandine had been a little girl, Kees shone like a star in the tiny firmament of the colony. She loved him before she even knew what romantic love was, when she still wore her leading strings, under the close watch of her mother. All the maidens in the colony, and some married women, too, set their caps for Kees Bayard. And now here he was with her, in her rooms, wishing her a safe journey.

"Sea dragons will gobble up the *Rose* to the last timber," she said.

Kees stared out her window. "Devilish weather," he said. Then he turned to her. "I'm sorry, what?"

She laughed and patted him lightly on the cheek. It didn't bother her that his mind was often elsewhere. That "elsewhere" included his three flute ships plying the waters between the new world and the old, bringing timber and furs to the Netherlands, returning to the colony with lengths of linen, panes of window glass and kegs of gunpowder.

One thing she loved about Kees was that though others might question her passion for trading, he understood and encouraged her. They were going to be rich together. He had a fourth merchant ship already in negotiations for purchase. The day Blandine married Kees, guilders would shower down on her like raindrops.

He said he loved her, but she glimpsed him dallying with other girls, young things, at the market square on Saturdays. His idea of marrying Blandine always seemed hypothetical, held off to some golden, indeterminate future. "If we were to get engaged," Kees said, rather than "when." That was all right. She was too busy to marry now.

In Holland, the standard of a woman's honor hovered somewhere between the strict English version and the lax Parisian, and was perhaps a shade less rigid on the new world's frontier than in Patria. Blandine did not hold herself above getting amorous now and then. She would have gone further with Kees, if she could have broken through his gentlemanly reserve.

She held a terrible suspicion that she did not fully admit, even to herself, that their true love, each of them, was for profit. Kees liked to invoke one of his favorite sentences. "Out of every hundred guilders in Nieuw Amsterdam, I hold ten."

Blandine would complete the boast for him. "Soon to be fifteen," she'd say.

It was still early. Light came thinly through the orange shutters, falling on the clean-swept floor. Before dawn she awoke, and by the light of a candle had erupted in a frenzy of cleaning. The place was spotless, because Blandine kept it that way with soap and water every day. She cleaned that morning not to expunge dirt but because her Dutchwoman's soul required the ritual.

At first light, at her door, Antony, with the African elder Handy and Lace.

"Piddy is found?" she asked.

By their expressions, no.

"You still mean to leave," Lace said, unable to hide the disappointment in her tone.

Blandine stepped out into the street in front of her stoop.

"I leave, but I am with you."

Lace looked unconvinced. "You are with your trading," she said, moving to turn away.

Blandine said, "There is a thing I must look into in Beverwyck. Something that might bear upon Piddy's disappearance."

Did she lie? She felt low, as though she were skulking away from friends in need.

Antony had stayed with her, assuming his usual post outside the door. But Lace and Handy departed, still unsettled and, Blandine thought, angry with her.

Now day had broken and the river sloop *Amsterdam Rose* would soon launch. She rummaged in her *kas* for an extra chemise, looking to take it along but also perhaps hoping to embarrass Kees Bayard a bit with the sight of it.

"You are very pretty this morning," he said, eyeing the frill of the undergarment.

"The hunt suits me, Kees. Profit excites me. Advantage gives me pleasure."

She fluffed the chemise and stowed it in her overflowing trunk.

"The tide turns," she said. "I must go."

She shut the trunk and tied a gray cloak over her olive linen gown. "You know what is the softest fur?"

"Beaver," Kees said automatically.

Blandine shook her head. "Mink. I'll bring you back a pelt for a fur collar," she said. "Or would you rather a bearskin muff?"

They stepped outside. Antony waited on her, hefting her trunk effortlessly onto his shoulders. The snow in the middle of Pearl had already been tracked to mud, but lay bright white along the margins of the street.

Kees displayed an attitude toward the giant that he had toward all servants, an oblivious disregard—until he required attendance. Then, finger-snapping hauteur.

He held out his hand to Blandine, a gesture that was meant to be friendly but came across as somehow patronizing. She was leaving. He was staying. She felt an odd, heart-flutter rush of anticipation, the sense of slipping out from under the gaze of Kees, beyond the town, away from all constraint and expectation.

Kees bowed, touched her cheek and set off down High Street toward the fort. He had apologized for not being able to see her off at the ship. "Business with Uncle," he told her. Stuyvesant, the director general of the colony.

Blandine didn't care. As she watched Kees's rigid, squared-off form disappearing down the street, she felt lighthearted and free. She locked her front door and turned the other way, toward the docks.

"You know the indian? Lightning?" Antony said, walking along beside her. "He's one of Aet Visser's men."

"Yes?" Blandine said, diverted by her eagerness to board ship.

"He watches you," Antony said. "He's been around. Last night. And he was here this morning."

Lightning. The skeletal half-indian habitually wore a stove-in black felt hat, covering a scar that people gossiped came from a Mahican scalping with a sharpened clamshell. He had tattoos of stars along his jawline.

"If he's watching me," Blandine said, "he won't have much to see for the next few weeks."

They turned along the wharf and found the sloop that would carry her and Antony north into the wilderness. She could see her goods being loaded onto the *Rose*. Joy coursed through her.

It was all she could do not to break into a run as she reached the pier.

8

Drummond lodged the night in the Lion, sleeping alongside a loutish sail captain. Emperor Nasty-Pants erupted with vile-smelling vapors the whole time, waking bright-eyed, jubilant with the triumph of a new day, just as Drummond fell back into an uneasy doze.

He dreamed of the colony's lone pet peacock, seeking for advantage among the seagulls and pigeons of the town. He killed the bird and fed its heart to a street mongrel.

When Drummond woke, a smear of blood showed on the snow as he went to empty his bladder behind the Lion. But it was only the telltale aftermath of the tavern's cook slaughtering a chicken. It turned out the colony owned no peacock.

He took breakfast with Raeger, who afterward sent a boy with Drummond to find his rented rooms in Slyck Steegh. His landlord was a Swede with an unpronounceable name. Trount, or something like that.

The rooms were acceptable. Drummond asked to see the outbuilding. A rectangular space, well windowed, the tile floor finely grouted, the whole place as licked-clean as the king's boots.

"I informed Mister Raeger the shed would be three guilders a month extra," the Swede said. "I'll take it in seawan if you don't have coin."

The business of wampum mystified Drummond. Raeger possessed barrels of the stuff stored in a keep at the back of the Lion. The Dutch, Drummond knew, established seawan factories on Long Island, protected by armed guards. Inside, they churned out whole wreaths by drilling holes in clamshells and stringing the bits together. The purple being more valuable than the white.

Which seawan the river indians and everyone else in the colony cheerfully accepted as legal tender for all debts public or private. So the Dutch literally were able to mint money. Incredible. Drummond couldn't fathom how it worked. Designs for shell-drilling instruments and more efficient seawan-stringing machines naturally occurred to his mind.

"It is cold in here," he said to the Swede as he inspected the shed. "Might you install a stove?"

Trount said he would be pleased to, and Drummond charged him with having his equipage fetched from the wharf warehouse. "Breakable furnishings," he said. "Have your boys be extremely careful with it."

"Certainly, sire," the Swede said. He appeared continually offended by something, and Drummond wondered if the cause was not him. No matter. Landlords, in his experience, lived to fuss.

Later in the day, he uncrated his treasures. The snow of the early blizzard melted from the roof of the shed, but there would be another freeze that night. Drummond worked as dusk fell, not bothering with assistants, loving to do the tender labor himself.

He opened Spinoza's lenses, carried in slots of red velvet within an oaken case. He remembered Bento, his kindness, his diamond intelligence, his monk's existence.

The lens grinder tended toward the philosophical, too, and along with his optics Drummond had taken away a hand-copied manuscript of Spinoza's work, *Korte Verhandeling van God,* which full title in English would be *A Short Treatise on God, Man and His Well-Being.* Drummond had gained fluency in Dutch during his ten years of exile with Charles II.

The writing had impressed Drummond on his tedious voyage across the sea to America. It had, in fact, become his nightly companion, his candle burner. But Drummond did not wonder that the author of such a work had been driven out of his community. The thought behind the book was incendiary, a challenge to Christian and Jewish orthodoxy both.

In his workshed now, Drummond moved on to his prize, the perspective tube he had recently purchased in London. Safe in its nest of wood shavings and hay, the two-yard-long instrument made Drummond shiver with anticipation.

Becalmed on the ocean one moonless night, Drummond had set up the tube and aimed it at the caudal light that streaked across the southwestern quadrant of the sky. He allowed Captain John Grudge, the other officers and a few of his shipmates to peer at the comet through the glass.

"It resembles a grain of rice," was Gerrit Remunde's comment.

A ship at sea offered no suitable base upon which to steady a perspective tube such as Drummond's. He would take it to the highest hill in the colony, he would ask Raeger where was best, he would erect it on the darkest night, and wrapped in a warm blanket with a flask of brandy he would look into the heavens to his heart's content, all night if he could manage it.

The comet, the planet Venus, the stars of Orion, the oceans of the moon.

And he would pour molten glass in his little shed and grind lenses. Spinoza had demonstrated that lens-grinding could be a suitable enterprise for a gentleman. The great Galileo occupied himself with grinding and optics. Drummond meant to do the same.

If all the king's urgencies would let him.

"Halloo!" a voice called. The Dutchman from the Red Lion, the one who wanted to talk wheat and corn, showed himself in the yard. "Edward Drummond?"

No peace. Get rid of the man, remove himself to his rooms, some mulled claret, an early night.

"Mister Drummond."

"Yes?"

"Aet Visser. We met last night at the Lion."

"Yes, I'm sorry, Visser, I am just in the midst of getting settled."

"A man of the new learning, I see," Visser said, poking his head into the doorway of the workshop.

"May we speak in the future?" Drummond shut the shed door in the man's face and moved off toward his dwelling-house. A little rudeness often did the trick of discouraging unwanted acquaintance.

"I don't mean to disturb you," Visser said. "I know you must still be getting your land legs under you. Have you help? I can send you over one of my orphans, very good, very reliable."

"No, thank you," Drummond said, sidling across the yard.

"No bother at all."

"I bid you good evening," Drummond said.

"One moment, if I might trouble you, I have a small request to make upon your time."

"I'm sorry, Mister Visser."

"Please, it won't take a moment. It has to do with my work as the orphanmaster here, about the welfare of children, sir, always a worthy occupation of any gentleman."

Drummond had his hand on the knob that opened the door into his rented chambers. Inside were unpacked boxes and bags. An unsuitable environment for guests.

But something made him hold his hand from turning the knob. An expression on the man's face, an invitation to openness and congeniality.

Drummond at bottom always liked the Dutch. He joked about them and often found them risible, but every people (apart from the Italians) had their saving graces. An essential goodness underpinned what some saw as the Dutchman's natural greed. Goodness and sturdiness were, for Drummond, an unbeatable combination.

He'd fought alongside Russians, Frenchmen, Poles. After his own countrymen, he would choose the Dutch to have beside him if he were ever caught in dire straits, in a castle, say, long besieged. They would eat well to the end, starve together gaily, and he could count on them to stick when the situation turned ugly.

"I have mulled wine in the kettle, but no crockery out yet," he said to Visser. "We'll have to drink directly from the ladle."

Visser bowed. "An option to which I have often resorted in the past, I am unashamed to say." He passed from the yard into the dwelling-house in front of Drummond.

Boots propped on the andirons, slouched side by side in a pair of heavy chairs, Drummond and Visser drank in the light of a single candle as the dark welled up outside.

Drummond appreciated his guest's initial silence, his respect for the ancient, sacred act of imbibing. Drink first, talk later. Even if the wine did dribble down one's chin because you were using a bent kitchen spoon to drink it. Never mind, the act was still sacred.

Visser displayed the scarlet heels favored by the colony grandees, a style that no doubt would soon be outmoded. Fashion was a thing so ridiculous, Drummond thought, that it had usually to be abandoned immediately upon being adopted.

"I am here in connection with my role as the colony's orphanmaster," Visser began, after a pause to let the glow of the wine take hold. "Are you familiar with the office? Have you orphanmasters in England?"

"Not as such, no," Drummond said. "But I have spent a great deal of time in Flanders, and in Holland, so I believe I've encountered the practice before."

"The parents perish, and the surviving children are vulnerable to exploitation," the orphanmaster said. "I prevent that. It is merely a recognition by the state of the obligations of Christian charity."

"You are very good," Drummond said.

"You were afraid I came here to talk wheat and corn," Visser said.

Drummond laughed. "Well, last evening . . ."

"I attempted to deflect your attentions from the lady. She is the trader between the two of us. She does a good deal of grain bartering. I merely dabble."

"You sought to place yourself between us as a shield for her virtue," Drummond said. "I am not so predatory as that."

"She is a former ward of mine. Grown up now, and I really have no standing to direct her actions one way or another. But she is very dear to me."

"I am an honorable man."

"I've spoken to some of your shipmates on *Margrave*, and this looks to be the case. But I had no way of knowing that when you presented yourself to us in the Red Lion. Acquaintances begun in taprooms often come to smash."

Drummond began to feel impatient, and wondered what the meddler might be getting at. Checking with Drummond's fellow passengers on his bona fides! It wasn't as though he had asked for the young maiden's hand, for pity's sake.

"No doubt you question my motives, sir," Visser said. "You speculate that I am here to talk about Blandine van Couvering. My motives are pure, and I propose to close that subject and move on to the real matter of our interview."

"Of course," Drummond said.

"May I?" Visser asked. He gestured toward the kettle of blood-dark wine, helping himself, then refilling the ladle for Drummond. He blew his red nose with a well-used bit of lace, then leaned toward Drummond in his hard-backed chair as though the two had long been confidants.

Drummond thought Visser appeared plump that evening, but surmised it was the dog he kept with him, stuffed into his waistcoat. He was not wrong. The animal's small head popped from its place in Visser's vestments. The orphanmaster extracted a piece of cheese rind from behind his left ear and fed bits of it to the pup.

He picked up his story. One of his charges, he said, was a six-year-old orphan, William Turner, a child of some little inheritance, whom he had placed in the care of an English family, George and Rebecca Godbolt. William saw his mother and father die within a week of each other from the small pox.

"I placed William with the Godbolts in the spring. A loving household, with a number of other children. When I asked how many, the father, George, joked that they ran around so much he had been unable to make a count. But I think there are five, all unfledged."

"Mister Visser—"

"Call me Aet, sir. I have the intention that you and I shall become friends. And the best way to make a man a friend, I believe, is to bind him to you with the asking of a favor."

Drummond was not so sure of the truth of that proposition, quite the contrary, from his experience. But he let it pass.

"My quandary is this," Visser said. "I visit my charges often, at least monthly, to see how they are getting on, to perform my role as guardian. For reasons I lay entirely at my own feet, I let a few months pass in between visits to William."

"He was securely placed, was he not?" Drummond asked. "No blame accrues if he was well taken care of."

"When I came again, I had a strange experience. They brought the boy William in to me, and an odd whim gripped me that it was not the same child."

"He looked not the same? I mean, children change rapidly as they grow, that is axiomatic."

"The same color of hair," Visser said. "The same age and general stature, similar features, but an uncanny sense of difference."

"But the Godbolts—is that the name?"

"The Godbolts put him forth as William Turner, the one I had placed in their care those fifteen weeks before."

"What did you say to them?" Drummond asked.

"What could I say? I thought perhaps it was my own mind that was playing tricks, a possibility I considered much more likely than some mischief originating with the Godbolts."

"You said nothing?"

"I blurted out, quite stupidly, 'This is the same Billy?' George and Rebecca chuckled as though I were an aged relative wondering at the growth of a grandchild."

Drummond felt certain some deeper story lay behind Visser's actions. Why had the orphanmaster sought him out? A newcomer to the colony? It didn't make sense. He had the vague feeling of being a mark, dealt a hand of cards by a sharper.

"You're wondering how this concerns you," Visser said. "On that first visit, I left the house with my thoughts unsettled, doubting my impression. But after passing a night of disquiet, I returned immediately the next day. And now, for the first time, I attempted to communicate my doubts to the Godbolts."

"A delicate task," Drummond said.

"Indeed, sir. I had no wish to alienate a family of competent guardians by making wild accusations. Well, they denied the idea."

"They disavowed the possibility," Drummond said.

"With more bafflement than vehemence," Visser said. "Their reaction appeared very natural. I was a crazy man, proposing an insane charge against them. They asked me what I thought. Did I contend that they had spirited the other child away? Murdered him? That they were some sort of witches?"

"Let me ask you this," Drummond said, his curiosity aroused in spite of himself. "Did the child you placed have birthmarks or identifying characteristics? A prominent tooth, for example, or some deformity?"

"You are quite right, quite perspicacious. And I have in the past noted the birthmarks of my orphans. But I did not do so in the case of William Turner. I wracked my memory trying to recall a mole, a wine spot, something, anything."

"Well, Mister Visser—" Drummond began, but the orphanmaster held up his hand.

"We are almost there. As I left, purporting to be satisfied with their denials, I said I would come again. When I did, the next day, a strange thing happened. The Godbolts, man and wife, professed to have difficulty understanding me."

"Why you could make such a charge against them."

"No, not that. They played themselves confused, again and again, over the accents of my speech. They asked me to repeat my sentences. They would look bewildered, one to the other. They even asked me to 'Please, sir, speak the king's English,' which of course I was already doing. I don't know if it was the king's, but it was certainly the common tongue."

"What was the difficulty?"

"The Godbolts both claimed to find my speech more or less unintelligible."

"And this was not the case when you had met with them before."

"Never," Visser said.

"Your English is as fine as any native speaker," Drummond said. "Finer than mine, in fact. You used the word *perspicacious* before. That's not the sign of an uncertain man."

"Thank you," Visser said. "I have spoken it from childhood. I am aware my accent is rough, but I have never had a problem with making myself understood."

Impatience stirred in Drummond. Whatever could the man want?

Visser drank again. "There is something about an orphan, sir," he said. "They attain an almost mystical status within a community. They live beyond the pale. No parents, and thus, no stops against a child's natural urges."

"You have more experience with orphans, of course," Drummond said.

"Mister Drummond," Visser said, again tipping himself conspiratorially toward Drummond, "I would like to enlist you, as an Englishman, and as a native speaker of the English tongue, to visit the Godbolt household, and try to make some progress in this affair."

Good Lord, Drummond thought. The orphanmaster wants me for a nursemaid.

9

I n London, the queen consort, Catherine of Braganza, had a cold. Samuel Pepys, the diarist, was also ailing ("I see I must take besides keeping myself warm to make myself break wind and go freely to stool before I can be well"). Strange weather for England in 1663: an extremely cold summer, with frost in August, followed by a summery fall.

A decade before, the first Anglo-Dutch war concluded, but the trade rivalry between the Dutch Republic and England was left to fester, so the two countries, though many of their citizens did not yet realize it, were preparing to fight a second round.

At Fontainebleau, Louis XIV displayed his new affection for collars made from the sheared fur of mink, and his mistress Louise de La Vallière debuted the style of pendant necklace that would later bear her name.

The Royal Theatre opened in London's Drury Lane. Jan Vermeer completed *Young Woman with a Water Pitcher*. Through microscopic examination, Robert Hooke discovered the cellular structure of cork. "Little rooms," he called the cells. In Japan, an emperor abdicated. The Turks again invaded Austria.

The new world saw its native population decimated by unintentional but extremely effective biological warfare. Newcomers from Europe beheld the land as a great emptiness, confronting their fragile souls equally, it seemed to them, with a bitterness and an invitation. The great sea yawned. The forest primeval towered.

This was Edward Drummond's reality. He was both like and unlike other men, those puppets who stared mesmerized at shadows on the wall of the world's cave. He welcomed the mysteries of the new world, as he embraced the sophistication and hot baths of the old. Science saved him. He pursued the new knowledge as though it were a woman.

The travails of life at the court of Charles II had begun to wear on Drummond. He preferred solitary travel. He had lost one wife, Alice, to childbirth, in which the baby died. He was determined never to marry again, until he did, Simone, and lost her to illness, too. He had loved both well enough, but to his torment found that he could not remember with which of them he shared, one Christmas, a midnight supper of pears and chocolate.

His dispirited years in exile, living in penury with the throneless king, had marked him deeply. Never again could he see the world as a trustworthy place. Alliances shattered, promises faded, love failed. He continued to serve his king and faction not out of any special zeal, but simply because it was what one did. After spending his life as a soldier, if he had any politics left at all, it was the politics of weariness.

Drummond's status with Charles II depended entirely on his youthful friendship with the king's younger brother, Henry, who died in 1660, four months after the restoration. Grief over Henry sent Drummond staggering from London on the crown's business, a second exile.

The king handed him off to his chancellor, the Earl of Clarendon, a cowardly good man to match what he once labeled Cromwell, a brave bad one. Clarendon gave Drummond to Lord Mordaunt, and afterward to the spymaster Sir George Downing.

They all agreed this Drummond was a useful man. Intelligent. Got the job done, whatever the job might be.

Edward Acton Drummond. A cavalier in England, a *chevalier* in France, a *ritter* in Germany, a freebooter on the high seas, *persona non grata* in Spain and Rome. Of the royalist faction labeled the Swordsmen, member of the secret society called the Sealed Knot. With Prince Rupert on his naval adventures privateering in Guinea and the West Indies. Lately operating in Switzerland and the Low Countries.

Now, America. His merchant mask in place, ill-fitting and awkward.

"Beneath the stones of the palace," a Paris courtesan told Drummond once, "there is common garden dirt."

He was thirty-three, the same age to the day as the restored monarch. He had seen war, massacre, insult, pride, lovers, fanaticism, riches, loss, pleasure, faithlessness. His task, he realized, the only one left to him until his death, was one of discovery.

How does the superior man live in a godless world?

Late at night, when the street lanterns on the parade ground burned down and the moon had begun to set, Martyn Hendrickson slid through the side door to his mansion's hearth-room. He removed his big leather belt and set it on the sideboard, where the heavy buckle clanked as it fell. He picked up a small brass bell and rang it.

Though Martyn kept entirely random hours and oftentimes did not return to the big dwelling-house on Market Street for whole stretches of days, he required that a servant always be at the ready when he did. Tonight Myrthe Mueller stood on call, a gawky girl who at the age of fifteen was well nigh Martyn's own height. His brothers, Adias and Abraham, chose the house servants for Martyn. They liked them ugly and at least in their mid-teens. Fewer problems that way.

All the girls had crushes on handsome Martyn. When she heard his bell, Myrthe rose from a pallet in front of the smoldering fire.

"Good evening, sire," the sleepy-eyed girl said, with a heavy German accent. She gave a halfhearted curtsy. "May I get you something?"

"Tea," said Martyn. Tea had barely arrived on Manhattan. Most residents could not afford it. But the Hendrickson family's merchant ships sailed regularly to East Asia. Martyn could have had a tea party every day if he so chose.

As Hendrickson waited for the kettle to sing, he leaned back in a silk-embroidered chair by the bay window in the spacious new *groot kamer*, an addition to the dwelling-house that looked out on the grounds. A shadow moved in the settlement's four a.m. stillness. A black cat, crossing the yard toward the fort.

Martyn never asked that the tapers be lit, as he favored the dark. With a grunt, he offered Myrthe his high-topped boots. Kneeling before him, she yanked them off. He stretched out his legs and waggled his toes.

It had been a long, cold night. A long, pleasurable night. Suzy, the drunkest, most slatternly, cackling witch of a whore on the Strand, offered up her services for the measuring of men's members. Taking on all comers, so to speak. Kees Bayard failed to measure up. The laughter was loud enough to drown out the howl of the wind off the harbor.

The house lay chilly and empty. Martyn's brothers had not come to town for many months. He did not miss them, as they tended not to amuse him.

Myrthe set the tray in front of Martyn with a steaming cup of tea and a cone of white sugar. The tea china came from England, a pattern only a gentleman could afford. The sugar, a rich man's treat as well. Martyn brought back so many of his tastes from Paris. Chocolate, an aphrodisiac that children loved.

"Anything else, sir?"

"Cake?"

Myrthe disappeared through the doorway, but looked back as she went. There sat the master, his dark eyes glittering like his many-jeweled rings. He leaned his head forward on one hand as though he were weary. Myrthe wondered after him, as always. Whether he might be lonely. Whether he might fancy her.

Myrthe readied the master's cake on a plate. She had cared for two families before the Hendricksons, one in Germany and then, when she lost her parents, one here in New Amsterdam. She found Martyn breathlessly good-looking, with features that were almost delicate, womanly. Those marvelous green eyes of his.

Yet Martyn gave off a disturbing body odor. When he sat at the close-stool in the cubby off the hearth, his *scheisse* could stench up the whole house. Myrthe had the job of emptying his chamber pot, and the man's excrement showed black as blood sausage.

In Germany, they liked to interpret such things.

"Master, might I inquire about your diet?" she made bold to ask Martyn once, after a particularly loathsome bowel movement appeared in the best chamber pot.

Her master did not take the question well. He appeared not to be accustomed to the German openness about bodily functions. In fact, he directed Myrthe that if she did not like the way his turds looked, she should take them into her mouth and swallow them down herself.

Then he laughed and tugged on her braid, the way he often did. But after that, Myrthe shut up about the motions of her master's bowels.

Not all dogs take the collar. Not all men accept the strictures of civilized society. And not all New Amsterdam orphans recognized the authority of Aet Visser as their master.

Settlers glimpsed these renegades only occasionally, flitting down alleyways, prowling the Strand. They filched day-old bread from the bakeries and slit the purses of drunkards exiting the taprooms. Any normal person contemplating a street urchin's existence would conclude that such ones had two possible paths forward. They would be dead before twenty, or they would grow up to be rogues. The former was much preferable to the latter.

Twelve-year-old Tibb Dunbar was an orphan renegade who lived outside the colony's authority. At least, Tibb Dunbar was one of his names. He had many. Werner van der Boorsum, when he wished to pass for Dutch. Brian Wilkins, when he wanted to be English. Frederick, Jules, Sven. He was not above dressing as a girl to get away with a crime spree.

"Heya," he'd say to his street urchin gang, batting his eyelashes and swishing his petticoat. "My name is Prunella." The gang laughed heartily.

Even dressed in female attire, Tibb always had a red kerchief about his person, tied around his neck or stuffed into an inner pocket, his marker, his signifier, his nose-wiper and meat-sopper.

The townsfolk knew the red-kerchiefed orphan boy as Gypsy Davey, and the *schout* had him registered on the colony rolls (the veracity of which the boy strenuously denied) as Davey Burrows. Preachers stalked him as a heathen, ripe for baptism.

"The Devil will steal your soul, Gypsy Davey," the churchy ones warned him.

"The Devil best be watching out," Tibb responded, "that I don't steal his."

Most householders hated Tibb and shooed him away whenever they saw him. But a few matrons doted on him. He had regulars—Blandine among them—who left meat pies out on their stoops for him. Ah, Gypsy Davey. Dashing, debonair, even with dirt on his face.

His exact age, his whereabouts whenever he was sought, all particulars of his parentage and how long he had been in the colony remained a mystery. Aet Visser attempted to make arrangements for Gypsy Davey to "go up the river," to work at the great estate of the Hendrickson family. But the boy slipped the leash.

Tibb didn't need a goose-feather pillow. Gypsy Davey liked rooftops. Werner van der Boorsum haunted the wharves. Prunella vanished whenever the *schout* turned the corner.

In fine weather—and to Tibb, any weather that didn't involve a howling blizzard was fine—he slept under a great oak on the east side of the island, beyond the wall. He welcomed all urchins into his gang, which he called the High Streets, after the address of the work yard behind Missy Flamsteed's taproom, where a boy could always cadge a beer.

Tibb had his partners in crime, their numbers ranging from a handful in winter to a good two dozen in summer. The High Streets lived high. They loved to prank the burghers, slipping straight-pins into the hanging laundry. They ate, swam, slept, stole, laughed, ran, drank, smoked entirely at their leisure. One June day they picked every bloom out of Sacha Imbrock's flower garden and sold the roses before anyone could catch them at it. Tibb himself had a great taste for pickles, so pickles were always a target.

"Fetch the pickles" became a code-phrase for "let's get it started."

The early October blizzard bothered Tibb not at all. But a worry nagged him as he lay on a tattered beaver pelt under his oak, the last remnant of snow melting beneath his body. He chewed a sassafras stick.

Something bad was happening. Well, something bad was always happening, but this was special bad. A beast went abroad in the colony. That didn't mean anything either, but this beast had a special liking.

Children.

Nobody in the settlement realized it yet, but Tibb Dunbar did.

10

That their ankles became moistened as they passed through the thick drifts of autumn leaves made no difference to Johanna de Laet and Hans Bontemantel. They felt eager, randy. The freak snow had kept them away from their private glade for a week.

Now they ran off into the forest near the Maiden's Brook, holding hands. Hannie toted the basket. She had told her mother she would collect morels for supper.

Yet even a growth of *Phallus impudicus*, the common stinkhorn, could not distract their attention from the matter at hand, which was (Hannie reached brazenly into Hans's trousers) the matter at hand.

"What does that look like?" Hannie teased about the mushroom. "It looks like yours."

"Except mine's bigger," said Hans, laughing.

She laughed, too, and ran away deeper into the woods, toward their private place.

Hannie and Hans slowed and walked solemnly together through groves of oak and birch. He told her he loved her, she said she loved him. There were many private places on the island of Manhattan, out of sight of God and parents.

Hans grabbed Hannie around the waist as they reached the clearing they had visited nearly every day over the summer. He pulled her to him and clutched a handful of her glossy chestnut curls.

"Wait until we get to our place," she said.

The spot lay beneath a black elm, where the grasses grew long and full. Just like a feather mattress, they always said.

The weather was a little cool. Hannie had a sense of sadness. They would not be able to come here much longer, once the snows began in earnest.

Even as it was, a pretty fall day, she was glad she had brought a woolen blanket in her basket. They would go underneath it, hiding like children. With the difference of having shucked off their clothes.

Hannie lay down, throwing back her arms in an exaggerated posture of repose. Hans did not take his eyes off her, but removed his jacket as he kneeled.

They were really going to marry. No one believed it, but everyone would see.

With her eyes closed, she lifted her skirts, the bunches of white petticoat, to reveal black stockings that reached to her thighs. She saw no reason to kick off her clogs.

When he had lain atop her for a while, she smilingly pushed his face back in a gesture he understood. He complied, turning over onto his back. Hannie rose on her knees, readying to position herself for utmost pleasure. A horsefly buzzed near her face. She brushed it away.

She suddenly realized that the branches of the black elm above her were studded with silent crows.

Then she saw it.

In the center of the clearing appeared the remains of a cook-fire. She knew it had not been there the week previous, before the storm. Wooden stakes had been driven into the ground in a circle around the blackened ash-pit. A cord of some kind hung from the stakes.

"Hannie?" Hans said, as the girl rose unsteadily from the patch of grass that was her prenuptial bed.

"Wait," she said. "Wait a moment."

She stepped toward the center of the clearing, brushing down her petticoat as she walked. The bombinating flies swarmed, targeting her eyes.

"Hannie!"

She needed to get to the cook-fire. To see. She felt she could not turn back.

Bones. Bones piled in a neat tower on the scorched earth. Big bones, too, nothing like those of a chicken or the remains of a pig roast.

Bones bladelike and white as frost.

The cord swung a yard from her eyes. Soft and viscous, it resembled the intestines of the lambs her family butchered every spring.

She turned around to see Hans lying inert, on his back, his hand thrown over his eyes.

"Hans, come see." He ignored her. "Hans!"

A rustle from the woods at the far end of the clearing. A deer?

She looked back to the ash-pit, not wanting to, unable to resist.

Next to the bones, a fan of . . . What was it?

Fingers. Tiny fingers, such as those of her little sister Trude. Splayed out carefully in sequence, as though they were still part of a hand.

Next to the severed fingers, a corn-husk doll directed its mocking gaze toward Hannie.

And a symbol, drawn in blood everywhere, on the trees, the stones of the fire ring, the half-burnt logs. A circle cut by a cross:

The last thing Hannie saw was a piece of cutout deerskin stuck with an indian hatchet to a pinewood tree, fashioned into a kind of mask, with gaping holes for eyes and an eerie, twisted shape for a mouth.

Hans looked up when Hannie started shrieking. She didn't wait for her beloved to come and see. She started moving her feet in the direction of home.

The tiny golden bat folded its wings, clung upside down to the ceiling of the lodge and whispered to Kitane of his coming death.

"Brother, why are you alone?"

"You, too, are alone," Kitane responded soundlessly. "Where is your colony?"

"Where is your family?" the bat echoed. It spun slowly around into the shadows, then again caught a golden light. Hunching its leathery wings, it made the reddish hairs on its neck ruffle up like the collars of the Dutch.

Outside, the locusts raised a dry-husk chorus. "Why are you alone?" they said.

An old lodge, long abandoned, its mother and children no doubt dead from the plague. The lice inside were lonely for their people. They welcomed Kitane.

Mid-moon in the harvest month. Kitane played his mind over what should be happening now, the sunlit life he should be leading, seeing it from the shadows of now.

Bringing in maize from his clan's plantings. Hunting deer. Dressing deer. Cutting the venison into strips, hanging it above a fire. Looking toward winter.

Kitane and Showma and Munn, together with the clan.

That life gone. Swallowed by shadow. Instead, he was alone in an empty lodge on the edge of a pond-fed marsh. On his back in bed, watching a yellow bat hunch across the rough bark roof.

"It's morning," the bat observed. "I'll be going to sleep now."

"Go ahead," Kitane said.

"You'll be all right? I'm worried about you."

"Sleep well."

"Why don't you sleep, too? This is, what, the third day of your waking?"

Kitane rolled away to face the wall, the willow sticks of his bed snapping in their dryness. If the lodge were alive, the women would have watered the beds once in a while, keeping their woven branches supple and comfortable.

The swannekins came, the swannekins bore sickness, the swannekins wrecked everything. The Dutchmen. The English. The French.

Kitane heard the *scritch, scritch, scritch* of the bat crawling down from the ceiling. The creature appeared before his face, glowing like a little moon.

"Jesus," Kitane said, taking the name of the swannekin's lord-god in vain. "Get away from me."

He closed his eyes and turned his mind to the girl Makitotosimew. Her name meant "she has large breasts." And she did. They grew larger and larger in Kitane's mind until they became gross and hideous.

He opened his eyes again. Brother bat spoke.

"Why are you alone?"

"I am Chansomps, a man of the locusts," Kitane said. "Hear my friends outside the lodge. I am not alone. I don't need to listen to you."

"You are Kitane. The brave, the chronicler, the survivor, the slave, the godless, the revenger, the smasher of faces. You walk without sound."

Last night, Kitane heard the witika calling him from the darkness at the edge of camp. He had never been more afraid.

And he envisioned not his past but a future life, one he had been seeing in his mind for the recent few days. He was walking down the street in Dutchtown. He had been there often, and he remembered well what it looked like, the swannekin lodges that it would make a stone sick to live inside.

As he walked a round-headed war club came magically into his hand. He touched his face and it was painted. He had burned the hair from his head with hot stones, leaving only a single roach, a rat-tail woven with turkey feathers that hung down his back and beckoned his enemies, "catch me if you can."

And in this future life of his, Kitane would break into a run and lift the war club. He would pass quickly down the street killing men, women and children. Counting how many swannekin heads could he possibly crush before they got to him. Five? Fifteen? A score?

His father told him that before Kitane went into battle, he should know what he would do when he saw his own blood. Would the sight of his own blood mean that his fight was over? Or would it mean his fight had finally begun?

Perhaps he could kill thirty. He was Kitane, smasher of faces.

The vision of this future life was horrible and pleasurable at the same time. He returned to it again and again, like an itch.

Dying with Dutch blood on his hands. His blood and his enemy's blood, comingled. Horror and pleasure. Afterward, they would place his body in a canoe and set it adrift from the shore.

Why are you alone?

"Because the world is on fire," Kitane answered, out loud this time.

"Have you seen Kitane?" Blandine asked the question of every river indian she encountered in Beverwyck, getting only negatives in reply.

Well, perhaps not *every* Lenape. There were too many, hundreds, stalking through the town, mixing with the Five Nation natives from the Mohawk River and interior lake valleys, all of them eager for trade.

"Swannekins," the river indians called the Dutch. No one knew what the word meant, none of the Lenape would tell them. One theory had it translated as "fake men," another as "a sharp stick upon which I mistakenly sit," and another as "the saltwater people." Likewise, Manhattan either meant "place of hills," or "the place where we all got drunk." And the Mahican tribal name, some said, actually meant "flesh-eaters."

During the trading season, Beverwyck burst at its deerskin seams. From the steep promontory that marked the end of the town, it was possible to see straight down Yonkheer Street to the narrowing, placid river, now full of small-boats and anchored ships. A palisade encircled the community, surrounding dwelling-houses and shops, offering protection against the creatures, human or otherwise, that inhabited the wilderness.

A paradox, since those same inhabitants were welcomed, carrying heavy loads of furs, especially in the spring and summer months. In these two mid-fall weeks, after the first turn of leaves but before the harvest fair, *wilden* and *handlaers* haggled over the next winter's furs, with trade goods exchanged for a promise of pelts. A hundred thousand beaver skins passed through Beverwyck in a single season.

Purple seawan streamed like gold. The village population swelled tenfold. When they slept at all, which was seldom, traders stacked themselves four to a bed. They could not often find one to rent. Landlords let every corn-husk mattress 'round the clock, in four six-hour shifts. Tents and lodges encircled the rude streets of Beverwyck proper.

It wasn't a circus atmosphere, really. There were no jugglers or players. Trade, trade, trade, that's what everyone was here for. A single-minded passion seized the whole town. Forget the hunt, forget the harvest, forget eating and sleep.

Profit was afoot, and the Devil take the hindmost.

"Yay, dearie, want a job of work?" a prostitute hailed Blandine in passing. "On your back, your beaver'd fetch a beaver easy."

Antony made a fake lunge at the offending woman, who cackled and made a dash for her hovel.

This was Antony's second year at Fort Orange's Beverwyck market.

When he had accompanied Blandine the year previous, the milling crowds disoriented him, a crush of people so different from the land of his birth. He was repeatedly baited to fight. Blandine managed to extricate him each time, but she hadn't planned on taking him along again.

He surprised her by begging to go. "Are you sure?" she asked. "You didn't enjoy it last time."

"I did," Antony said.

"You fought, you remember?"

"So what? Look at me. What's fighting to me?"

So the giant came along, and seemed to feel more in his element than before.

"You're a big one, now, ain't you?" the laughing whore taunted Antony. "Come, let us measure it, see if you're big all over."

Antony lifted his blouse, and the prostitute screamed in mock horror.

Blandine laughed and passed on.

She was feeling good. What merchandise Blandine still had left, she held back for the climactic market Saturday, the culmination of the annual autumn trading fury (second only to the spring trading fury) that gripped the whole district.

She had already placed her pelt guns, her hand tools and metal implements, most of her cloth. Her only mistake, she noted for the future, was to ignore the fundamental draw of iron traps. She had none, and could have traded a score.

She saw indians of both sexes parading through the streets, flaunting the ropes of wampum around their necks that represented so many hundreds of guilders to the visiting Europeans. The dense odor of rum hung in the air along Handlaer Street, the drink being sucked down and traded with equal avidity.

Houses and shops of red moppen and yellow Gouda brick anchored the town. Blandine could see the tips of merchant masts riding in the Fort Orange harbor. Everyone was here. One last final push. Let it begin. She was more than ready.

And yet she couldn't shake off the idea that someone was watching her. It was partly what Antony said about Lightning. But it was also Blandine's own notion, a physical, prickly sensation that dogged her.

She stopped to confer with a trio of Mohawk women, translators she knew from her earlier seasons at Beverwyck. Two of them had ax heads suspended over their breasts on necklaces of deer sinew, while the third wore a gigantic spoon from an English silversmith.

She asked if any of the three had seen Kitane at the Beverwyck market this year.

"He's gone mad," a crooked-toothed woman named Oota said.

"You know this?" Blandine said seriously.

"I refused him my body," Oota said, "and he lost his mind."

The other two women hooted with laughter.

Blandine persisted. "I want to ask him about the killing across the river, the tenant farm boy in Pine Plains."

The group fell instantly silent, looking sullenly away from her.

"Perhaps one of you might know about it," Blandine said.

"Nobody talks about that," Oota said. She pronounced the Iroquois word that meant "taboo." "You won't find anyone around to say anything on that subject."

Blandine hoped that Kitane would. Throughout those market days, she sought him out. They had been cohorts, she and the Lenape trapper, in a small company of merchants who had journeyed up the Mohawk River to trade during the market weeks of the previous fall.

Kitane proved himself the most competent scout, the best hunter, the most artful trader. He out-*handlaer*-ed the *handlaer*s and out-natived the other natives.

Blandine believed she had formed a friendship with Kitane in the weeks along the Mohawk River. When their paths came to part, though, and they said their farewells, the native had displayed a dead core that frightened her. She realized that any real connection with him could exist only on some faraway plane to which she herself had no access.

It didn't matter that she was a European-American female and he was an Algonquin male. That wasn't it. It was more the reality he inhabited, where the trees spoke and the animals were full-on individual beings, with names and voices. That world was simply beyond Blandine.

Out of that strange realm, she knew, came the demon-beast apparition called "the witika."

II

Drummond traveled upriver by the sloop *The Faith*, marveling, along the way, at the vastly timbered shore. Here amid bights, hills and reaches (the Dutch called them "racks") were masts for the king's navy. Arrowroot and pinweed lower down gave way to black spruce and bog moss as they proceeded up the Northman—a fond name the traders had for the river.

Mother Mary, what a rich land! Sassafras, chestnut, red oak and white, cedar, elm, water beech, tulip trees, sumac, poplar, hundred-foot jackpines, tangles of grape, sword grass, nutwood.

At Tappan reach, at nightfall, great fires lit the sky. The river indians had set the woods aflame to clear meadows for planting. The embers spangled the darkness overhead like orange-colored constellations. The scene was magnificent. The underbellies of the night clouds still glowed behind them at midnight, after *The Faith* left the fires far in its wake.

As dawn rose, the forests revealed themselves to be painted with autumn in ways Drummond had never seen in England or on the Continent. Glorious colors, a spectacle. The fall leaves were themselves political: Dutch orange contended with English red for supremacy over the woods.

Why did the great river flow so straight? It hewed to a north-south line, remarkably strict, so unlike the rivers of Europe that Drummond knew, the meandering Rhine, the Seine, the Thames.

A highway. An arrow-straight river highway to the fur-rich wilderness of the north.

From the start the Dutch colony followed "Prince Maurice's River." Named after Maurice of Nassau, Prince of Orange, the immense waterway that the early Dutch settlers also called Mauritius River offered a route north from Manhattan for traders looking to penetrate the interior. Later it would be renamed the North River, and then the Hudson, after the dead Englishman who discovered the region for the Dutch.

In America, New Netherland remained a thorn in the paw of the

English lion, a sliver, a rude finger, thrust in between and separating the two crown colonies, New England to the north and Virginia to the south. If New Amsterdam and the great harbor represented the stem end of the thorn, then Fort Orange and its trading-post town of Beverwyck were the sharp, pricking point.

"What does one do with a thorn?" Clarendon had asked Drummond, who well knew that the English chancellor preferred to answer his own questions. "You pluck it out."

By the 1660s, nearly all the beaver had been harvested from the valley of the North River. The Dutch traders and native trappers had to go farther afield for their prey.

Into the impossible depths of the forest, where God did not bother.

Along the North River's shore, Drummond saw many deer, a family of red foxes, a catamount. The waters swarmed with eels, sturgeon, tomcod. Mostly, though, he noticed the birds: ducks, geese, widgeons, herons, bluebirds, fish eagles in amazing abundance. The sky ran black with a species of dove in great swooping flocks, numberless. Darkness fell at noon as the birds blocked out the sun.

Drummond slept little on the voyage north. He didn't feel like it. He stood at the stern, near the wheel, and brooded. The unbroken wilderness that lined the shore appeared able to absorb any perception Drummond might have of it and survive unchanged, intact, immune. If it spoke to him at all, it said only, *oh, little man.*

How far did the woods stretch away? The Dutch heard strange place-names from the river indians. *Cain-tuck-kee. Ohi-yo.*

And if the wilderness ran on forever, empty of God and man? Where was a place in it for Drummond? The idea both attracted and repelled him. He didn't want to admit that it made him afraid. Perhaps *challenged,* he thought, would be a better word.

Aet Visser and his Godbolt quandary occupied Drummond's thoughts occasionally, a mildly interesting puzzle he must solve. A boy who all of a sudden wasn't the same boy. He felt silly even considering it. What did he care about some minor colonial official and his problems? Drummond was a soldier. He didn't often have doings with children.

The whole question would be a waste of his time, were it not for the fact that Drummond needed English allies, English contacts, English friends in the colony, and George and Rebecca Godbolt, Raeger told him, headed up the New Amsterdam community of English settlers. Where they led, the rest followed. That was part of Drummond's mandate from London, to rally his countrymen to the crown's cause in the new world.

He had, the day before embarking for the north, visited the Godbolts. He portrayed the visit as a courtesy call. Drummond's aristocratic presence inflated George Godbolt like a pig-bladder balloon.

"We are simple people, sir, and we very much appreciate your condescension," Godbolt said. His wife, Rebecca, bobbed alongside him.

"I have heard of your exploits, Mister Drummond, with Prince Rupert during the late wars, and your attendance on poor Prince Henry," Godbolt continued. "As you see, my wife and I profess the personal faith, but never, in all our years, have we supported the rebellion or the Commonwealth."

"Long live King Charles," Rebecca murmured.

Drummond let the couple gas on for a bit. The Godbolts appeared visibly distressed when he brought up the name of Aet Visser. George Godbolt, who had been sitting nicely in a spindle-backed chair, sprang to his feet.

"Aet Visser!" George Godbolt said, "The man is completely addled. He's not to be trusted."

"Husband," Rebecca Godbolt said, "Mister Visser means well. He does good work. He brought us William."

The Godbolt residence showed the unruliness of a household with many children. Dolly, the youngest, had been displayed for Drummond's gratification when he first came in. Rebecca presented the swaddled, pink-faced infant to be cooed at and chucked, then whisked her away.

Strolling about the great room, speaking with the Godbolts, Drummond felt uneasy. He pondered what kind of game the orphanmaster might be running. Did Visser have some unscrupulosity afoot with the orphans? It would not be the first time in the history of this misguided world that a guardian mistook his task.

Drummond felt sure he was being used as Visser's cat's paw, enlisted to a task that for some reason the orphanmaster did not want to do himself. The man's motivations were as yet beyond the reach of Drummond's understanding.

His strategy had always been to propel himself into a given situation and then employ his native intelligence to get him out. His intelligence, and perhaps a Scottish flintlock carbine.

Glancing upward to the unplastered ceiling, Drummond could see the adze marks on the joist rafters that supported the rough planking of the attic floor above. He was brought up short.

Through a gap in the planking, the eye of a child stared down at him. He turned to the Goldbolts. "May I see the boy?" he asked.

"Our children are at Roeletsen's school," George Godbolt said. "Are they not, Rebecca?"

"All of them?" Drummond asked.

"Except the baby," Rebecca said. "And Georgie, our youngest son—he's six—he's at home with a catarrh."

"Might Georgie be up and about?"

"Sleeping," Rebecca said.

Drummond pointed upward, directing their gazes to the ceiling.

The Goldbolts stared. "Why, the little imp," George said.

"William!" Rebecca shouted.

The furtive eyeball between the planks vanished.

A minute later the young gentleman himself stood before him, William Turner, aged six, parents deceased, orphan ward of the Godbolts. He looked up mutely at Drummond from under the mop of his black hair.

"This is our William," Rebecca said.

"It seems he stayed home from school," George Godbolt explained. "He wanted to keep his brother company."

Rebecca had her hand on the child's head, not as though she were petting him, Drummond noticed, so much as gripping his scalp.

"A great pleasure to make your acquaintance," Drummond said, bowing slightly and holding out his hand to the boy. William looked up to both the Goldbolts' faces before placing his small, soft hand in Drummond's.

"How are you, son?" Drummond asked as gently as he could. The boy managed a stiff nod.

"He don't speak," Rebecca said. Mute, yes, but to Drummond's eyes, William Turner looked perfectly healthy.

"We find the boy a great help in our business," Godbolt said.

"Visser mentioned that you are in preserved meats," Drummond said.

"Hams and wurst," Godbolt said, with obvious satisfaction.

A family of sausage-makers, for Lord's sake. Drummond concluded that the suspicions of the orphanmaster were ridiculous. The Godbolts should be praised, not accused.

He looked into William Turner's dark eyes. Drummond considered himself a fairly good judge of character. Something in the boy's gaze spoke to him. He picked up his beaver and prepared to take his leave.

"I am sometimes in need of a responsible boy to help safeguard my optic equipment, my glass lenses and other scientific instruments. Would you consider making William available to me once in a while for that purpose? I can provide a small stipend."

"He has many responsibilities with us at home," George said.

"Of course," Drummond said. "Well, think on it."

"You will tell the orphanmaster . . . ?" Rebecca said.

"That his fears are unfounded," Drummond said.

"Yes, thank you," Rebecca said.

They shook hands, George Godbolt opened the door for Drummond, and that had been that. A fool's errand. From nothing came nothing.

Caught up in preparation for his journey, he had not thought much about William Turner. But the boy's silent, open-eyed gaze must have stuck in his mind, because now, at the rail of *The Faith*, he decided the whole incident had been a little strange.

He tried to dismiss it from his thoughts. What was the boy to him, or he to the boy?

But he might yet speak to Aet Visser about it. If he remembered. If Visser was still riding this particular hobbyhorse when Drummond returned to Manhattan. If Drummond survived his arduous trip upriver, to Beverwyck, overland to New Haven and back to New Amsterdam.

First, he had to inquire as to a murder.

12

"It's very much spoken about," Drummond said. "We heard of the killing down in the capital. The story has gained great currency."

His host, Adias Hendrickson, looked uneasy. "I wish it had not," he said.

"Yes?" said Drummond. "And why's that?"

They sat before the hearth in the Hendrickson dwelling-house on the east side of the river, near the northern frontier of New Netherland, but still south of the Dutch trading outpost at Beverwyck.

The great room was the largest Drummond had seen in the new world, at least twice the size of those on Manhattan. It was filled with an array of chairs and tables draped with Turkey rugs to rival the furnishings of any English gentleman.

The floorboards beneath Drummond's boots had been cut of yellow virgin pine, from a tree that had to have been the width of a wagon.

The place had an undeniably male atmosphere. No wallpaper or curtains graced the room, only whitewash and plain wooden shutters. A wolfhound curled up near the hearth and lifted its snout lazily whenever Drummond moved. There were no women anywhere around.

The patroon Adias Hendrickson owned a massive swath of wilderness that extended east from the North River all the way to Connecticut. The heart of the territory of the Esopus tribe, recently the site of much war and bloodshed.

In Europe, such holdings would have established Hendrickson as a lord. Here, they only seemed to make the man nervous. He appeared worried over indian trouble and angry at encroaching settlers from New England.

Drummond kept to himself the private knowledge that Hendrickson's days as a local aristocrat might be numbered, as the New Netherland colony's days were. Soon enough the entire new world would be English.

We will relieve him of all his landed worries, Drummond thought.

"I am interested in the tale," he said out loud. "I came across a pamphlet in New Amsterdam."

"Lies," Hendrickson said.

"Then I wonder if you might regale me with the true story."

"The less said about that business the better," Hendrickson said. "A bloody awful crime."

The room lay in fallow darkness. The candles guttered, and the only real light came from the flaring embers of the fire.

Drummond persisted. "I ask your pardon, but I have reason to ask," he said. "You see, I am an Englishman, and upon arriving on this coast, I found the tale much bruited about, and my countrymen blamed for a horrible murther."

"It was a crime of the *wilden*, sir," Hendrickson said.

"The indians of the Esopus are perceived as allies of the English, are they not? Thus their sins are attributed to my countrymen. I feel bound to defend my nation's honor."

Something was holding Hendrickson back. Fear? Something else, a furtiveness, as if the patroon knew much more than he would speak.

Drummond prompted him again. "It is a tale on everyone's lips in the town, but I fear it has lost truth in the retelling. I'm confident that I can hear the real story only from you."

Pursuing Raeger's errand "to damp down the flames of anti-English sentiment," Drummond had disembarked *The Faith* at Rhinecliff Landing. He made his way inland to Hendrickson. He required a mount for an overland journey to New Haven, he explained. He plucked at the harp of Ad's vanity, saying that everyone had directed him to the Hendrickson place when he said he was in need of good horseflesh.

Hendrickson received him coldly. Hendrickson's patent, what he liked to call "the estate," seemed an empire in and of itself. In the dreary afternoon light Drummond saw peonage-style work gangs, many of the workers not much more than children, bringing in the harvest. He watched one boy, gaunt and sullen, attempt and fail to lift a full sheaf of wheat. The child simply could not summon the strength. The boy stared around with despairing eyes, looking for help that didn't come.

Across the landscape, clots of laborers, dressed in tatters and wearing clogs, appeared as a forlorn army. No happy harvesters here, no milk or honey. Only recently, on a trip to Russia, Drummond had witnessed serfdom in practice, and he was reminded of it now. Not much of a life for children.

Their lord and master, Adias Hendrickson, became animated only when he approached his stables. The patroon paddocked his complete herd, a dozen horses imported from Curaçao, he said.

Drummond liked a well-muscled roan, and he and Hendrickson concluded a deal. The man treated his horses with more respect than he did his farmworkers.

Drummond held off getting to the covert reason for his visit until after dinner, when his host offered buttered hard cider and tobacco. Only then did he ask about the strange Jopes Hawes killing, which Raeger told him about.

"Can you tell me, sir?"

Hendrickson worked his clay pipe with great sucking drafts. But still he stayed silent and frowning.

Drummond waited. Ham—Abraham, Adias's brother—sat slouched in a chair at the back of the room. Ad looked over at Ham, both silent as monks.

Hiding something, thought Drummond again. He was about to entreat once more when Ad drank in a choking gulp of smoke, spewed it out (along with copious amounts of spittle) and spoke.

"Have you heard, sir, the name *witika*?"

Across the room, the heretofore motionless Ham Hendrickson stirred and coughed.

"The goblin of the river indians," Drummond said.

"Very good, sir," Ad Hendrickson said. "You've been schooled. You impress me."

He sucked noisily on his pipe. "A demon, it is," he said, "and a damnable one, too."

"Superstition can have its uses," Drummond said.

"What do you mean by that?" Ham demanded.

Ad said, "The witika stands three yards tall in its bare feet, and its feet are always bare, since it never wears shoes or clothes. This better shows the rotting flesh of its body, green and gray and speckled over with grave wax."

"You paint a pretty picture," Drummond said.

"In its chest lodges a beating heart made of ice," Ad said. "Long, stringy hair, fouled with the dried blood of its victims. Great, red-rimmed eyes, but their centers are blank and black as a Bible."

"Brother, for the Lord's sake," Ham said. "The man shouldn't hear all this."

Ad shook his head and continued. "For all its decrepitude, the witika is strong as a bear and fast as a lion. No man can outrun it. It can dash across the surface of water and leap in great bounds."

"And who has seen this beast?" Drummond asked. "Have you?"

"Most who lay eyes upon the witika perish of fright," Ad said. "Those who don't, the beast murders. Those who survive go mad."

"Then the question naturally occurs," Drummond said, "as to how we know details of the creature's appearance?"

"You are European, sir, an Englisher, you hail from the safe and sane precincts of the world. Here in this terrible new land, we are bereft of God. His glory has not yet penetrated the wilderness. The brutish old gods remain, the false idols and wild deities of the savages."

"And the victim?" Drummond asked.

"The son of one of my tenants. Joseph Hawes, called Jope, twelve years of age. A smallish boy; we knew him. The family worked a farm plot on the eastern edge of our patent, past Pine Plains."

Ham spoke up. "We told the Hawes people it was dangerous, living there. We thought the Sopus would rape the women to rags, skin the men alive, roast them all up and eat them."

The obvious satisfaction with which Ham relayed his words made Drummond look over at him. But the man's broad face remained inscrutable, either by expression or because it was lost in the gloom.

"But the indians didn't get young Jope Hawes," Drummond said. "Their demon did."

"You are skeptical," Ad said. "I understand that. I expect it. It was why I hesitated at first to traffic in such tales. You are a man of modern faith, sir?"

Modern faith. He meant nonconformist views. Drummond sidestepped. "And the circumstances of the killing," he said. "What were they?"

"Jope has a living mother and two young sisters. They tell he left the homestead last July ides at dawn, with the view of a hunt in the mountains to the east. Even at his young age, he was well-armed and experienced."

"He served as ensign for a scout at Fort Orange," Ham said.

"His parents found him dead?" Drummond asked.

"Here is where it gets interesting," Ad said. "The mother, Christina, Kitty, avers she had a terrible dream that night, one of blood and fire, wherein her son stepped out of a hole in the ground and ascended skyward trailing flames."

"A portent," Drummond said.

"Exactly so. The goblin appeared to her also, a long-armed wracky creature with fangs."

The Hendrickson brothers spoke Dutch with each other. Drummond's fluency had been honed in his years in the Low Countries with the exiled second Charles. The brothers, he noted, used a northern dialect. Ham told Ad to be careful with his words and Ad told Ham to shut his mouth.

To Drummond, Ad continued. "The son Jope did not return when the family expected. A day later, now some ten weeks ago, poor young Jope's body turned up in the woods, ravaged beyond belief. He lay beside a well-known spring, as if the killer wanted the body to be found."

Ham spoke from the darkness. "Do you wish to hear the details, Mister Drummond? Listeners always want to hear the bloody details, don't they, brother?"

"Who discovered the body?" Drummond asked.

"A freeholder from Canaan," Ad said.

"From Connecticut?" Drummond asked. Now they were getting to it. "An Englishman?"

"You may well ask what he was doing abroad in our woods," Ham said. "But your countrymen here make themselves very free with other men's property."

"Brother, you are rude to our guest," Ad said mildly.

"That's quite all right," Drummond said. "I understand the borders remain unsurveyed."

"They are clear, sir!" Ad said shrilly. "The borders are very clear!"

The next words out of his mouth, Drummond thought, would be "damned English." But Ad settled back on his chair, and sucked his pipe.

"His rump was eaten," Ham said. "That's what you want to hear, don't you?"

It's evidently what you wish to tell me.

"The witika is a great consumer of human flesh," Ad said. "He himself is born of starvation. The more the witika eats, the more he hungers."

"It gorges, yet still finds itself ravenous," Ham said.

"I know how it feels," Drummond said. "I've had such meals myself."

The elder brother gaped at him, and then burst out laughing. "My word, sir, you are a pippin." Turning to Ham, he said, "He's had meals like that!"

"Could not the depredation of the body be from animals?" Drummond asked. "On my journey up here, I saw many beasts, including some sort of wolf-dog and the one you call a bobcat."

"Humanlike teeth marks," Ham said, practically crowing now. "Witika teeth marks on dear dead Jope's rump, his shoulder, his cheeks. The monster ate out the young boy's eyes. And it proved a great relisher of the male genitals."

"Do the natives here customarily indulge in cannibalism?" Drummond said.

"There were other indications of the river indians," Ad said. "Certain totems left around the body in the ritualistic way."

"Sopus totems?" Drummond asked.

"Yah," Ad said. "They make a sign, a circle with a cross, like this."

He drew in the ashes spilled from the hearth.

The sign seemed to agitate Ham. "What does it matter!" he shouted. He raised himself out of his chair and stormed over to the fire, stamping his foot on the hearth bricks to erase the sign his brother had drawn. Ham stood over Drummond and brandished his flagon like a war club.

"Zelf kalm, broer," Ad said in Dutch. Calm thyself, brother.

"If one would seek to sow dissension between the peoples of New

England and those here in New Netherland," Drummond said, "he need only spark another Esopus war such as the one near past. Is that not so?"

"It is the damned English who stir up the Sopus against us," Ham said, vehement.

Finally, thought Drummond, the English had been damned, as he knew they would be.

"I don't mean to upset you," he said. "And I sorrow over any trespass committed by my countrymen. I only mean to get at the truth of the matter."

"Are you a representative of the crown?" Ad said.

"As I told you, I am only a grain merchant, en route to Fort Orange on a mission of trade in wheat. One of my confederates asked me to shake out the details of this matter. I do so in a purely unofficial way."

"We don't believe you," Ham said.

"We'll say no more, say no more," Ad said quickly. "Lest we wind up poisoning our acquaintance with barbs and accusations."

That was all right. Drummond judged himself ready to quit anyway. The Hendricksons' excellent, butter-heavy cider foxed his brain, and he didn't want his probing to further alert the patroons about English interest in the area. They were clearly touchy about the subject.

He managed a cordial good-night to Ad. Taper in hand, Brother Ham conducted him to a bed in a rickety lean-to, where a servant man already snored loudly.

As Ham was leaving, Drummond said, "There is a third Hendrickson brother? Martyn?"

Ham turned to stare at him.

"I saw him briefly in New Amsterdam at the Red Lion," Drummond said. "He's an important man in the capital, is he not?"

Ham snorted derisively. "You don't know nothing," he said.

Drummond caught a look at his face, lit from below by the candle. An expression crossed Ham's features, violently seizing the man, then just as abruptly vanished. Drummond couldn't call it by any other name than fury.

"Don't go on about Martyn," Ham said, "or I'll whip ye good." He blew out his candle, plunging Drummond into blackness.

13

Blandine came to the big Saturday market with a jug of good Barbados molasses, planning on letting the Lenape and Mohawk children get a taste, and draw in their elders that way.

But she was glad she had it along, since a Beverwyck landowner named Embers de With immediately sought it in trade for a small wooden keg of saltpeter.

"I don't need the stone salt myself," he explained. "But the molasses I can use."

The natives flooded Beverwyck's central square, coming in from the lodges the local merchants made available to them for sleeping during market time. The taverns, at ten o'clock in the morning, already had eager customers.

Beverwyck. In English, "Beaver Town."

The open square at the intersection of Handlaer and Yonkheer streets, the site of heaviest trading, went by the name of "the Fuyck," a Dutch transliteration of a native word. Understandably, the usage gave rise to much bawdy punning on the part of the English traders allowed to do business there.

The snows of the past days had vanished. The sun beat down on the scene, offering one of the few hot days left to the season, before cold and winter dark descended on this part of the world.

Blandine luxuriated in the warmth of sunshine on her neck, and loosened the lace scarf that propriety demanded she wear, a demand she honored more in the breach than in the observance.

She could not afford a huge wardrobe, but the clothes she did possess tended to the bright and feminine, and today she wore a cornflower blue dress with a tight bodice, blousy sleeves and a yellow petticoat underneath. She considered caps foolish.

Sunning herself in the Fuyck, seated atop her barrel of saltpeter, knocking her heels against its staves, Blandine saw Edward Drummond before the man saw her.

Drummond, the grain merchant from the Red Lion.

The Englishman, dressed simply in a flowing white blouse, leather breeches and knee-high jackboots, strode up the hill from the fort, toward the sprawling market where all the day's trading would take place.

She watched Drummond talk volubly in the middle of a small clutch of grain merchants and fur *handlaers*. This was a man, it struck Blandine, who was acting a role, and who certainly thought it a great lark to be Mister Edward Drummond.

Well, Mister Drummond, she lied to herself, *I had forgotten all about you.* She was surprised to see him in the north. Could it have been Drummond who these past few days she felt watching her?

The men and women surrounding the Englishman attended to him slavishly, hanging on his every word. Blandine felt disgusted by the fawning sycophancy that colonists directed toward aristocratic Europeans.

As one born and bred in America, Blandine van Couvering had the opposite feeling. She knew that people in New Netherland were somehow stronger, more resilient and braver than their transatlantic cousins. At least she felt herself to be.

Drummond saw Blandine across the crowded market. Smiling broadly, he gave her a full Court of St. James bow.

Ugh. The pompous English fop.

She jumped down from her perch, turned away from him, kicked the cask of stone salt in front of her and attempted to disappear among the numberless traders that had flocked to the big market day.

All morning, though, she felt as though she had a shadow. Another one, apart from Antony, whom she could plainly see.

She would glimpse Drummond occasionally, passing through the crowd or standing with his fellow grain merchants. He never looked toward her, but Blandine got the sense that he was somehow posing for her benefit.

She decided to ignore him and go about her business.

The molasses-for-saltpeter trade proved lucky. Daniel Voorhees, one of the main munitions dealers in the settlement, came to market looking for all the sulfur and saltpeter he could buy. Much of his supply had been ruined in the recent storms.

Embers de With returned to Blandine, eager to trade back for his original keg of stone salt, but she had already heard of the need, and approached Voorhees herself.

"A pony keg," Voorhees said, when Blandine rolled the little wooden barrel toward him. "I have six bolts of bleached Haarlem linen for it."

"I'll take twelve," Blandine said. When the man refused, with curses, she kicked the keg backward, away from him, and followed after it. He called her to return, offered the twelve bolts and was dismayed when she demanded fifteen. He yielded them to her, sourly, but they were hers just the same.

She found a good home for the cloth, too, trading up for six barrels of seed corn. Then the corn went for wheat, a trade to a plantation owner whose maize had gone to rust that year. He had wheat, he needed corn, so Blandine bartered his ten barrels for her six.

She had the good luck to be the first trader to greet Blue Shirt, the Seneca sachem, when he came in with sundry pelts he had held back from spring market, hoping to get a better price in the fall. He had otter, muskrat, cat, deer, but was particularly well stocked with good, merchantable mink.

Blandine immediately saw what he had, knew that mink was at a premium just now with the new fashion set by the French king for soft, turned-fur collars.

"I have no use for wheat," Blue Shirt told her when she made her offer. "You know that."

Blandine eyed the other traders at the fair. They hadn't noticed Blue Shirt yet, but they would soon enough. She didn't have much time.

"Wait for me here," she told the Seneca chief, using the trading patois. "Please, I'll come right back."

She stuck a pipe filled with tobacco into Blue Shirt's hand, hoping to occupy him.

Blandine hurried across the Fuyck, thinking, *Wheat, wheat, wheat—who needs wheat?* Not wanting to say it out loud. Thinking for an instant of Drummond, the erstwhile wheat trader.

She was going to lose the trade, she knew. She couldn't let that happen.

A bearded, stench-ridden savior appeared to her in the person of

Skag Smith, a toothy English frontiersman who sat amid a scattered pile of rum casks. Trying to control her urgency so as not to spook the man into upping his price, she bartered her wheat laterally, ten barrels for ten of rum (what the indians called "English milk").

Seconds later, she returned to Blue Shirt and suddenly found herself in possession of twelve dozen finely cured mink pelts.

The other traders also knew the whim of *le Roi Soleil*, knew what mink would fetch the next season in London and Antwerp, but they didn't get to Blue Shirt in time. Blandine had virtually cornered the Beverwyck market.

A small crowd of *handlaers* gathered around her. She fended off furious offers and counteroffers. Antony glared at the traders whenever they got too close to her bale of pelts.

Blandine felt splendid. She was at the top of her game. She had a brief, glancing wish that the English popinjay could see her now, but immediately banished the thought as unworthy of her.

Embers de With emerged from the clutch of traders around Blandine and approached.

"Fashion will change, that's what it does," he pronounced. His opening gambit. "Who knows how long mink will hold its present inflated value?"

"And yet, the whole world tags along after Louis," Blandine said. "Are we not sheep? What he wears, the courts of London, Portugal, the Empire, even Spain are sure to adopt."

"Not Spain, surely not Spain," De With said.

"They dye the fur black," Blandine explained.

De With countered, "And of course there is an ample supply of mink from Russia."

Suddenly Edward Drummond was there by her side. "You've not heard of the tsar's edict of embargo?" he said to De With.

De With flinched. "An embargo?"

Drummond nodded. "Total and complete. To protect the Siberian mink population, which has much diminished in the wild."

Blandine almost laughed, but she also had the concomitant urge to smash Drummond in his supercilious, hair-draped face.

"Please, sir," she said, sotto. "I can well attend to my own affairs."

"An offer of pertinent intelligence, merely," Drummond said loudly. "I have just recently come from the Grand Duchy of Muscovy."

Have you really? Have you just come from there, you precious English ass?

Blandine focused on De With, who paced, hyperventilating, practically popping the buttons on his vest. He was less cool than in the morning, when he and Blandine had conducted their molasses-for-saltpeter barter.

The pressures of trade affected different men in different ways. Some could not see their way clear to consider it as she did, as merely a great game.

"You know, I've heard of a scheme to farm-raise the creatures," Blandine mused. "Perhaps that would be a way to assure oneself of a steady supply of mink. But getting the husbandry of it might take a few seasons."

"By which time," Drummond interjected, "the French king could have returned to ermine."

"Or sable," Blandine said, smiling sweetly.

Shadows lengthened around the Fuyck. Men had begun to stumble for the taverns, exhausted by the frenzy of bartering. The day of trade was nearly over.

"All right!" De With said. "What will you take for the bale?"

"My whole supply? Wouldn't that be foolish of me?"

"Just tell me," the maddened trader said.

"I really wouldn't know. What can you offer?"

"For the Lord's sake, woman!"

Blandine fingered the silky pelts in her suddenly golden cache. "You have a holding in Beverwyck town, on the heights off the river," she said. "Almost an English acre, I think, from the looks of the plat map."

De With stared at her. Land, solid ground, earth-and-soil property, in exchange for the skins of dead animals. "That piece is just off the Post Road," he said, a faint tone of accusation in his voice.

"Just so," Blandine said. She waited.

"It is a full acre," De With said.

"Oh? I didn't mark it exactly."

He paced, bulging in gut and eyeball, furious at the thought of being beaten by a girl.

"I would need a signed and witnessed deed of transfer," Blandine said.

At this, De With erupted. "My word is good!" he shouted at her. "Ask anyone."

Blandine looked around. A crowd of traders attended the deal in amused anticipation. Drummond looked on attentively.

She waited for De With some more. Come on, man, come to it.

Finally, the exasperated merchant said, "The acre plot is yours," and a laughing cheer went up from the assembled traders.

Blandine looked over at Drummond. In spite of herself, she exchanged a small smile with the Englishman.

"One thing," Blandine said, turning back to De With. "Or two things, really."

"What are they?" De With said.

Blandine yanked one of the mink pelts from the tightly wrapped bundle. "I keep one out," she said. "A gift for a friend."

"For her lover," the *handlaer* Warner Wessels shouted, and again the whole crowd laughed.

"Yes?" De With said. "And the other thing?"

She knew what she wanted. Her original trade, the one with which she had started out the day. "I am in need of a jug of good Barbados molasses," Blandine said.

Across the faces of the stones were written the name of the sun, the name of the wind, the name of the heart and the kidney and the liver. But what was written most and written largest was his name.

Lightning.

The sun blazed copper-bright. Behind the warrior swayed the deer he had netted and killed, still draining its fluids onto the gnarled roots below.

The tree from which the carcass dangled stood at the mouth of the cave. His cave, Lightning's own secret. The Place of Stones.

The clearing at the top of Manhattan Island sang with the rushing river of stones, clacking together in the stream the Dutch called Spuyten Duyvil. The song made this the Place of Stones. The stones made this a castle for witika.

As a child Lightning had visited, on the Manhattan shoreline below, the great Lenape village of Shorakapock. A place of summer feasting. Chepi lived there, Alawa, Nuttah and old mother Hausis. Now they were all dead.

He could wade into the ancient shell middens of Shorakapock, dive so deeply into the pile of cast-off oyster shells that he was buried to his chest. He could thus swim through the past banquets of the village. The middens stretched around the end of the island. Endless shells, as many as there were stars in the sky.

And he was well aware that there were shells in the pile that he himself had tossed away during the feasts of summer, sweet salty water pouring down his chin as he gobbled the succulent flesh of Brother Oyster.

The blood of the deer still drained.

Before dawn that morning, he had cut away a slice of its hide, ragged with reddish cold-weather fur. He laid out the skin as he prepared himself to do the work for his master. Lightning's blade had shone scarlet with blood, like a sunrise sun.

But he scraped the hide in the old way, not with a knife but with a sharpened clamshell. He flipped over the skin and touched the remnants of flesh. He crouched above the stone and punctured his palm, dripping his life blood to merge in a swirl with the deer's innards. Rubbing a finger across the welts of blubber, he brought the blood to his lips. A milk of life, even in death.

The hide called out to him from the hot stone on which he had laid it out. *Where will be my eyes?* the skin asked. *What shape for my mouth?*

He had to lie down awhile to think. He flopped on the open grass, the skinned shank of a swannekin child a foot from his face.

Brother Deer had his own memory, he thought. Brother Deer held within himself the crown of antlers and the troubles his people had suffered at the hands of the swannekins.

I will help you in your fight for vengeance, said the deer.

Lightning thought of how he might slice the raw leather, with a sure hand and a woman's finesse. Over these last months, he had developed skills he never knew he had.

The eyes, the mouth, he would carve them beautifully. As witika requested.

All the while his languorous mind coursed slowly over the laying-outs that had taken place in the past and would occur in the future. Inside the cave opening behind him, trophies stacked themselves haphazardly.

Heart, kidney, liver. Fingers, many fingers, and toes, collected from the laying-out places around the island. Each of them so small, as precious as the seashells from which seawan beads were carved. His master preferred to keep orphan garments, stained or clean, as mementos, but Lightning treasured the parts of the body.

All that was missing was that which was given up to the feast.

The dead called to him, too. *Where are my eyes, where is my penis, where is my uterus?*

Ho, ho, he answered, they are here.

He loved to witness rot.

He had lain for hours, motionless as a stone, flat on his belly in the grass. A few feet away, his totems. Silently, patiently, he watched the progress of putrefaction, the leg shank crusting yellow, the blackened ooze from the organs, the way things transmogrified into other things.

The process of decay held for him a majesty greater than any he had ever felt in the song circles of his people, the vision quests, the ceremonies that made him a man.

The dangers were constant. All of nature seemed determined to raid his bounty. *Heart, kidney, liver, I will be your protector.*

Buzzards flapped down, eager for a meal. Brothers, this is not your time. He crooked his arm and chucked at them lazily with rocks. Go! They rose away, lazily also, apologizing.

Sister Coyote whined, snuffling under the rock ledge, pleading for some meat. *Brother, please, please,* she said, *I beg of you.*

His heart was as of stone.

He held himself warily against them. He must guard even against the resolute armies of ants.

But some he favored.

Come, Brother Fly, friend moth, beetle chieftain with your legion of followers. He watched them carry their morsels away. One after another, numberless. Still he lay quietly, until the maggots burst out of their eggs and began to eat. He could hear the tiny tusks munching.

I am ready, brother, a soft voice whispered.

It was the mask, calling him. Its outline revealed itself, perfect in shape and dimensions.

He got to his feet and crossed the Place of Stones to approach the sacred skin. He petted the scabby, mottled surface, uneven with fat globules and veins.

Witika's next mask.

He lifted the blade and began to cut.

Part Two

The Stadt
Huys

14

Drummond left Beverwyck and took Peterson's ferry across the river, finding himself once again traveling across the sprawling patent of the Hendrickson brothers. But he felt eager now to initiate his New Haven mission against the regicides, and had no time to waste on Ad Hendrickson's natterings about goblins.

Picking up the roan at the inn on the eastern shore where he had stabled it, he set out upon the Post Road toward New England. The land was wild. The road, really no more than a track carved out by indians, led through a succession of small but difficult fordings.

It did not help to ease Drummond's mind that every other farmhouse had been burned out in the recent Esopus wars, leaving charred timber skeletons exposed to the elements.

He stayed over at an informal farmhouse hostelry, for once not having to share a bed.

That night a woman cried in the forest. Moaning, sobbing, inconsolable. Drummond rose, the night still pitch dark. He padded out to the porch of the farmhouse, peering into the inky black.

"What the devil?" he murmured to himself. The weeping crescendoed and fell, then mounted again. It sounded as though a woman were being murdered, or her child had been taken from her. Great, gasping yowls that went beyond pain to get at the horror of existence. Drummond felt lost and alone.

"Catamountain," his host said, suddenly appearing, disheveled but wakeful, by his side. "They cry at night."

The next day, the terrain turned mountainous, and the track climbed through hilly rumps of dense deciduous woods, alternating with deep gullies and swales, the Taconic Range. The forest floor lay thick with the golden litter of autumn leaves.

Taking up the Mohawk Trail, he drove himself onward even as a pelting rain began. The roan had difficulty keeping its footing, slipping often on the wet, slushy leaves.

The miles proved monotonous. To help himself along Drummond repeated, in a sort of singsong, the names of the three New Haven regicides. "Whalley and Dixwell and Goffe." Over and over.

He switched to the names of the saints. "Francis and Stephen and Paul." Then back to the regicides.

The crown had been trying for years to get at the regicides who had taken refuge in New England, living incognito in Cambridge. In 1661, the second Charles issued an order of arrest for the three. The document arrived in Boston on the heels of the fleeing outlaws.

They were old men now. Whalley, father-in-law to Goffe and son of the sheriff of Nottingham, signed his name next after Cromwell's on the king's death warrant.

As a young lieutenant, Drummond served with General Keith on the field at Worcester. He had met Whalley in battle, in front of Powick Bridge. Now he had the honor of helping to crucify him. He left unasked the question of whether the man was a traitor or a zealot. Whalley existed on the other side of the line of battle, and that was that.

Drummond had never actually sunk the blade into any of the regicides he tracked, leaving that to more sanguinary hands. His spymasters did not deign to ask someone of Drummond's rank to get his soul dirty, any more than they would do the job themselves. His assignment was only to seek out the renegades and convey information about their whereabouts to the crown. Someone else killed them.

The French, if they knew about Drummond, would have labeled him "*le doigt-homme.*" The finger-man. But the French did not know about him.

After they fled Boston, Whalley, Dixwell and Goffe easily found allies to hide them. There were plenty in New England who hated the king, feared the papistry and adhered to the deceased Cromwell and the republican cause. Somewhere among them, in the Massachusetts Bay colony, or perhaps in Connecticut, the regicides had discovered what they considered a safe nest.

Drummond would flush them out.

The downpour turned vicious, the rain coming at him not from above but on a howling slant, a northeaster storm. He tightened the shaggy bearskin around him. It provided some comfort, even soaked as it was.

The massive pelt had been a gift from Blandine van Couvering when they parted after the trading days in Beverwyck. A begrudging gift, a strained mercy, granted, she said, in acknowledgment of Drummond's intercession in the Embers de With trade.

After her mink-for-land triumph, Drummond had lost Blandine in the crowd of *handlaers*. They loved her, and loved most that she had managed to trade back for her original jug of molasses. She started with the jug, and ended with the jug plus an acre of prime Beverwyck land. Now that was a trader.

Drummond found Blandine again off the Fuyck, just as she was about to enter an inn. The crude, single-story log hostelry faced a burbling stream the Dutch called Tweedle Kill.

The darkness had come on completely, but there was a little light escaping from the windows of the inn. Drummond caught sight of a head of white-blond hair and called out Blandine's name.

She turned to him solemnly, unsurprised. As Drummond approached, the woman's giant loomed out of the darkness, hefting the bearskin, folded into a mattress-sized bundle and tied with deer-sinew cords.

"I want to give you this," she informed Drummond, "but not to encourage you to enter into my affairs again. I simply don't wish to feel myself beholden to you."

Antony laid the gift at Drummond's feet.

"So we are even," Blandine said. "You helped me with the trade, even though I did not ask it. This is a good skin of a nice-sized western bruin. We are quits."

"We may be even," he said. "But perhaps we are not quits."

Blandine turned away. "Good night, Mister Drummond," she said, and disappeared through the lantern-lit doorway.

Blandine was miles behind him now. Drummond had no idea where the woman was. Still in Beverwyck? On her way back to New Amsterdam? But if her mind ever played over him—would it? did it?—it made him curiously happy to think she might think that he was thinking of her. Out in the wilderness dark.

The bearskin was immense, wide as a tent, taken off some sort of gargantuan she-bear. Inside it had been provided with arm slings and tanned to the softness of deer leather.

Getting her hands on such an impressive specimen no doubt represented a coup for Miss van Couvering. The young she-merchant had her contacts, though, among them the well-adorned Mohawk women with whom he'd seen Blandine in the Fuyck. And of course this man Kitane, the legendary Lenape trapper Drummond had heard so much about but never seen.

The roan's head, streaming with icy water, hung in a most dispirited manner. The wind lashed, the blackness of night settled, the storm howled. Again and again, Drummond lost any sense of the trail, having to double back to locate it.

Footing turned from merely treacherous to downright lethal, with jumbled rocks and crisscrossing roots hidden under the layer of wet leaves. He considered that only Blandine's bearskin, draped over him and falling across the withers of his mount, kept him from freezing to death.

He dismounted and led the roan, both of them exhausted, stumbling forward through the forest. If he didn't find a haven soon, he would have to make a very ugly, very uncomfortable camp. He kept an eye for rock shelves beneath which to crawl.

Another thought brought him up short, one that indicated the gift of the bearskin might not be so straightforward as it seemed. Yes, the robe was big. Massive, in truth. Just the thing in nasty weather. But he had ignored one salient fact about it. The pelt's bulk meant there were bears the size of horses abroad in the American woods.

To Drummond, lost and alone in the unfathomable wild, the mind played tricks. Rampaging she-bears hid behind every boulder. If one approached, he decided, he'd give it the roan.

He envisioned what would happen to him. The she-bear would insist on taking back her skin. His blue corpse would be found months later, the frozen flesh gnawed upon by the hungry witika. The soul-wrenching night-crying of the catamount still infected his mind.

Drummond knew his thoughts were rambling, but he couldn't help himself. He hunched down into the pelt and wished the journey would end. He considered the person of Blandine van Couvering.

During his years of exile in the Netherlands, Drummond had encountered many other independent Dutch women, so different from the docile handmaidens he had left behind in England. Beguiled and bedeviled, attracted and affronted in equal measure, Drummond had never been able to grasp what it was these women wanted.

To be taken for a male? To destroy the space between man and woman? To possess the world on their own?

And now, this one. Pretty as a painting, but thorny as a rose.

Put her out of your mind, man.

But he couldn't, or wouldn't, and his fussing over the memory of Blandine almost made him lose the way.

When a low stone tavern revealed itself, he slogged right past it. No lights marked the place. Only his horse's tug at the reins alerted him to halt.

To Blandine's surprise, Antony had evidently developed Beverwyck connections of his own, since by the end of market, he was able to inform her where the Lenape trapper Kitane had last been seen.

They took the *Rose* again, sailing downriver, but stepped off the sloop when she put in at Wildwyck, the Dutch community at the head of Ronduit Kill. Blandine hired a skiff to ferry them across to the eastern shore of the river. From then forward, they proceeded on foot, penetrating the forest along an unnamed creek. This was where Antony had heard Kitane might be.

She had a sense of urgency, wondering what was happening in New Amsterdam, spurred by the idea that the Lenape might help her understand the abduction of an orphan child. The disappearance of Piddy Gullee connected in her mind with the ritualized killing of Jope Hawes, and Blandine felt certain that Kitane could give her insight into the mystery of the witika.

The storm winds of the previous night had stripped most of the remaining autumn leaves from the trees. What few remained were a golden shade of copper, on the oaks, which were always the last trees to lose their foliage. The night's rains freshened the forest air, the walking proved cool but not uncomfortable and Blandine followed Antony easily along the barely there track through the woods.

The stream they followed pooled into a swamp, which in turn led to a lake. At dusk Blandine and Antony entered the ghostly precincts of an abandoned native village on the shore of the lake. Lodges—the river indians called the larger ones their "castles," adopting the word readily from Europeans—dotted the forest floor beneath an expansive stand of sugar maples.

Lenapes loved the "sweet water" sap from maples, and considered the tree itself inhabited by beneficial spirits. Maples, Kitane informed Blandine once, were great tellers of jokes.

But there were no jokes to be told here. The lodges were empty, decrepit, their tree-bark wall panels curled up and admitting rain to the interiors. Maple boughs had fallen to collapse the roofs of a few of the castles. In the flats around the lake, fields once cultivated with corn lay overgrown with quick-growing sumac and bracken.

This was once the great village of Upukuipising, haunt of the Wappinger federation, tribal brothers of the Lenape.

"Here?" Blandine asked Antony, looking around at the devastated village.

"She told me, look in Upukuipising," Antony said, mangling the Algonquin word.

"She, who?"

"I said already. The Mohawk woman."

"What would she know of the Wappinger?"

Antony shrugged. "This is that village?"

"Yes, but there is no one here," Blandine said.

"We can at least camp the night," Antony said. "I'll build a fire."

The place gave Blandine a disconsolate feeling. She would have rather not stayed. Sickness and death marked every lodge. Even the breeze, passing through the plague-decimated village, shushed itself forlornly. But the evening came on, and there was nothing for it. They had to halt for the night.

As Antony gathered wood, she laid out their dinner, dried pippins, salted venison ham, chunks of sweetened bread buttered with beef tallow. When she went to fetch water, she discovered the stream had a pleasant taste. Upukuipising, she knew, meant something like "lodge among the reeds by the little stream." She had visited here as a girl years ago, in the village's heyday, with her father.

"All dead," she murmured to Antony, as they ate together by the fire.

"Or gone across the river," Antony said. "To get away from us."

She would go back to New Amsterdam, she thought, marry Kees Bayard, have a family, construct a trading empire, leave the past behind. Edward Drummond would no more figure in her life except as a fleeting memory.

Full dark, no moon. Bats rose into the night sky, darting black dots against the blue stars.

Later, Blandine felt compelled to visit each of the old lodges in turn, not the ones far afield, scattered in the woods, but at least the dozen or so that were bunched together on the slope above the lake. Taking an oil lantern, she wandered through the deserted village.

At times such as these, evenings in the forest, loneliness seized her like a black dog. She kept telling herself it was pure weakness, that she had to be strong to stay alive in this world. Her orphanhood hung about her like a cloak. You shall not feel sorry for yourself, she commanded, and then disobeyed.

Wilderness was where she lost God. She had not known her sister, Sarah, for that long, only a few years. But some children charm you, bewitch you, warm you with their glow. Sarah had a way with her . . . but what was the use? How to describe to anyone what Blandine had lost?

She realized what she was looking for as she traipsed from one empty lodge to another. Her family. She imagined herself going about the whole world, street after street, knocking on doors. Finally, behind one of them, she would discover her mother, Josette, at the hearth.

Blandine's secret: beneath the surface veneer of stubborn independence, she needed desperately to belong to somebody.

She could see the fire that Antony had built, beneath the trees down the slope toward the lake. She felt as though she were orbiting the thin, wavering light in vain, circling, never to come home.

In one of the last lodge houses, a small one along the far edge of the maple grove, she found strange totems strewn about the floor. A willow branch bent into a circle and lashed to a pair of cross-sticks. A mask.

In the dead embers of the lodge fire, some kind of half-crusted entrails, human or animal, she could not tell. Had someone been cooking there? The whole interior was cold and odorless.

One of the corn-husk fetish dolls the river indians kept in every lodge, this one stained black, sat upright beside the cold ashes. Fascinated, she picked it up. Discolored with what? Blood?

She lifted her lantern.

At the far back of the lodge, she saw Kitane.

Dead.

The Lenape trapper lay naked and motionless on a half-collapsed bed of willow sticks. By the dim light of her lantern, she recognized him by his bird tattoos. A fine gray ash covered the man's skin from head to foot.

For a long moment Blandine halted, unwilling to venture farther into the darkened interior. Silence. Could he be alive? But no movement, no breath.

She moved forward and knelt next to the body of her friend. She touched his hand, which felt as cold as stone. Kitane had been the one who opened the wilderness to her. On their trip up the Mohawk River, he had shown Blandine not only how to survive in what the European might consider trackless wasteland, but how to embrace it, glory in it.

He was also a man. Kitane had the most striking physical presence of anyone Blandine ever encountered. Now here he was, wholly unclothed. She had never seen a grown man naked. Enthralled and horrified at once, she studied his ash-dusted body. The flesh showed no signs of decomposition.

Some of Kitane's charisma had vanished with death. The bird tattoos across his chest, animated before, appeared lifeless. The ropes of muscle in his arms and shoulders, his flat belly, his strong thighs had subsided, the flesh sunk back like clay. His member rested inert alongside his leg, flaccid.

She bent her head down to his chest and listened. Nothing.

"Kitane Chansomps, prince of the locust clan," she murmured. "What happened to you?"

She rose, turned her back on the corpse and crossed to the door of the lodge.

"Antony," Blandine called out.

Behind her, Kitane reared up out of death.

The Lenape shouted a few unintelligible words of Algonquin, lunged forward and attacked Blandine, seizing her arm. He wore a deranged look and, strangest of all, snapped his jaws open and shut as if he would bite her.

Which he did.

Kitane sank his teeth into Blandine's shoulder, tearing through the cambric of her dress. She cried out. The pain was intense.

The Lenape ripped his mouth away with a piece of her flesh. He looked ghastly. His muscles were slack and his skin had a green tinge. But in the small lodge Kitane appeared immense, filling the interior with his crazed, naked presence. Blandine knew her friend was out to kill her.

Jabbering loudly, Kitane tilted his head back and swallowed his bite of Blandine's flesh, looking like a baby bird choking down some regurgitated morsel from its mother.

The lantern dropped from Blandine's grasp. Pain shot through her arm and ran up her neck. She felt fear, but most of all astonishment. This was not Kitane. This was a rabid animal that had shape-shifted into the form of Kitane.

Bleeding all over herself, Blandine backed out of the lodge. Kitane came at her again. It would have gone beyond strange, had it not been so horrible, how he gnashed his teeth. She could hear them clack and snap as the Lenape bore down.

Antony appeared, slugged Kitane with a single roundhouse from one of his ham-sized fists, and the crazed indian slumped to the floor.

They stared at the collapsed figure. Blandine's blood glistened on his lips. She clutched at her wounded shoulder, thoroughly shaken.

Antony bound Kitane by the legs, brought him away from the lodge and laid him lengthwise on the other side of their campfire. Later, the Lenape regained some measure of consciousness. But though his eyes opened, he remained catatonic.

Antony tended Blandine's injury. "I'm sorry," he said.

"What are you sorry for? You didn't attack me."

"I should have been there."

"I'm not sure what happened," Blandine said. "He lay on his willow cot. I thought he was dead. Then he leapt up like an ambush. He would not have done it if he had known it was me."

"It was chicken-hearted."

"No, Antony, no," Blandine said. "Look at him. The man is ill."

Antony gazed across the fire at the comatose Lenape. Once more, Kitane seemed still to the point of death.

"A madness comes upon them, a witika madness," Antony said. "He thinks he has become possessed by witika. He needs to eat human flesh."

A sick feeling stole over Blandine. She admired Kitane greatly. But she knew him to be near the settlement when Piddy disappeared. He had also been up north when the Jope Hawes murder occurred. Here in his lodge were the totems, a fetish doll such as Hannie de Laet found in the forest.

Blandine felt she didn't know enough about witika madness to judge whether this was a case or not. Was it even real? Could it be contagious?

She lay down close to the fire. Her shoulder throbbed. Antony stayed with his back propped against the trunk of a maple. Sleep didn't come to either of them.

Midnight winds rose in the night sky, blowing loose the stars into darkness. Antony laid more wood on the fire. Blandine reached a tentative decision. She would nurse Kitane back to health. But she would do it warily.

After a long time, Antony said, "You saw that he didn't attack me."

"Yes," Blandine said.

"You know why?"

"No," she said.

"Too big to eat."

15

Two weeks later, moonlight made the night into day. Blandine decided to return directly to New Amsterdam that evening, instead of staying over at the director general's *bouwerie* as she planned. She had been gone from home for almost a month now. First the Beverwyck market, then the aftermath of Kitane's attack. She needed to get back. Aet Visser's claim of a pattern of child disappearances weighed heavily on her mind. She and Antony made their way along the shoreline of Manhattan, following a trail she could see clearly, though a scattering of clouds at times obscured the radiance of the sky.

They had left the convalescing Kitane in the care of a village of Canarsies near Hell Gate. Over the past two weeks Blandine had nursed the trapper. After his attack on her, the Lenape fell into a fever, but she stayed at his bedside. She sweated him with steam infused with herbs. Antony brought in a native healer.

Kitane slowly recovered his wits, but remained in a weakened state. The prospect of him relapsing into witika madness receded somewhat. He became aware of what he had done to Blandine, and writhed in shame.

Blandine's shoulder healed. It was good to be going home, back to New Amsterdam. Her trading days at Beverwyck had been a fantastic success, so much so that she almost felt guilty. She knew she would soon see Lace and Mally. It was early November. As Blandine and Antony walked south toward the settlement, an unease rose in her, a sense of coming back to responsibilities too long left untended.

Still, what could be more beautiful than the white light of a full moon on the breast of the new world? The birch groves they passed shone incandescent. Night birds hooted as though they were calling to Blandine directly. The smell of autumn, delicious and bitter, hung over the forest.

The trail led them along the western flank of Mount Petrus, a low knob whose promontory indicated that they were only a half-league from the palisades wall.

"Up there," Antony said.

"What?" Blandine asked, searching where he pointed. She could see nothing.

"A man," Antony said.

A voice hailed them, a voice she could not believe, one that she had last heard in Beverwyck three weeks before. He came hurtling down the side of the hill, his boots sending up clouds of crackling leaves.

"Come," Edward Drummond said, taking Blandine's hand. "You must see this."

She thought of extracting her hand from his but found she could not make herself do so. His sudden appearance was so surprising, his tone seemed so urgent—not panicked, but excited, happy.

"You, too," Drummond called back to Antony, as he led Blandine up the slope.

"Mister Drummond," she said. But it was as if she were caught up in a whirlwind.

He brought her, breathless, to the bald crown of Mount Petrus. A child stood there, mute and motionless. A cloud suddenly dropped away from the moon and light flooded over them, making the child appear unearthly, like a ghost or a fairy.

William, the Godbolts' ward.

"Here, take a look," Drummond said.

Beside the boy stood some sort of a weapon, a brass cannon the likes of which Blandine had never seen. Stood on end, it was taller than she was. The device rested on a metal tripod, aimed at the sky.

Drummond, Blandine noticed, was wrapped in the bearskin robe she had given him.

Antony reached the top of the slope after her.

"Please, you must," Drummond said.

The boy stepped forward, like a little page at a royal court, and indicated a small cylinder fixed to the lower end of the cannon. He bent down and placed his eye to the cylinder. The pantomime was perfect. "Like this," William seemed to say, entirely without speaking.

"Go ahead," Drummond said. "You won't be sorry, I promise."

Blandine looked over at Antony. He stared, not at her but at the cannon, lost in admiration for the apparatus, its long brass lines gleaming in the light of the moon.

"What is it?" Blandine asked, hesitating. Drummond merely gestured her forward.

Blandine bent as the boy had done and placed her eye at the end of the brass tube. Nothing. A blank. This must be the Englishman's idea of a prank.

"Close your other eye," Drummond said, leaning uncomfortably close to her.

She did so, and suddenly gave a startled cry. "Oh!"

Through the brass tube shone the moon, the moon as Blandine had never seen it, close enough to touch. Its mountains and oceans could be read clearly. An immense beauty filled her eye and gripped her heart. She dared not breathe. Here was another new world, not America but a celestial one, presented to her as a gift, full of mystery, drenched in light.

Wholly involuntarily, she trilled out a laugh. She could not help herself. It was that wonderful.

Blandine had trouble keeping the moon in view. She did not understand how she was seeing it. It danced and moved, she lost it, found it again, laughed again.

That is a sound, Drummond thought, that the world needs to hear more of.

They were all aware of it, boy and giant and English spy, how lovely was the delight of this woman, bending slightly at her waist, her white-yellow hair the color of moonlight.

Blandine straightened up. "Oh, Mister Drummond," she said. As if compelled, she immediately returned her eye to the tube.

"I can't get it," she said. "Yes, I can."

"Antony," Drummond said, and Blandine straightened again.

"Oh, yes," she said. She guided her man's eye to the tube. His size made it more convenient for him not to bend down but to go to his knees. He at first also had difficulty registering the view.

"Lord God," he said after a moment. "My dear Lord God."

He, too, laughed, throwing his head back with a bursting guffaw, then immediately returning for another look. He stopped, gazed up at

Drummond with an immense smile, as though he had received a Christmas present.

"What is it?" Blandine asked Drummond.

"It is called a perspective tube," Drummond said. "It works by bending rays of light."

"That is the moon? That is the real moon?"

The expression on Blandine van Couvering's face would have been impossible for Drummond to describe or render. Her lips, parted in excitement, the blush of her cheeks, the radiant pale blue of her eyes, framed by dark, ash-colored lashes. He himself was the moon, poor and lifeless, with no light of his own, merely reflecting her sun.

The four of them returned again and again to the tube, boy and giant and man and woman, a small colony of the entranced. Drummond taught Blandine to adjust the device so that it tracked the moon's transit of the sky.

The night passed. It was cold, but none of them felt it. Drummond had shucked off his bearskin, offering it to Blandine, but she declined. The boy William crawled under it instead, comically moving about, a midget caught beneath a bed-mattress.

Down the slope, placed well away from the perspective tube in order that its light would not dilute the radiance of the moon, a small fire burned. Every so often, William moved down to tend it.

It had been difficult to persuade the Godbolts to let the boy out for a whole night, but again, some small flatteries convinced them. Rebecca, at least, became more comfortable with hiring out her ward. William proved extremely helpful to Drummond, silence being an attractive virtue in a servant.

From time to time Drummond would pose a question to him, trying to unlock the orphan boy's secrets. William stared at him but never spoke, mute as a millstone.

Allowing Antony to take over the tube, Blandine and Drummond followed William down to the fire. The boy stirred it into flame and squatted nearby. Drummond threw the bearskin down, and they sat.

"You have been ill," Drummond said. Her face, drawn and pale.

"Yes," Blandine said.

"And your arm. Is it stiff?"

"A wound," she said. "It's all right now."

"But since Beverwyck, you have been tending to your commerce?"

"I have been nursing a friend," Blandine said.

"An angel of mercy," Drummond said.

She shook her head, as if the comment had broken the mood. "I am no angel," she said.

"You look it, though."

Again, she drew back, refusing the trend of the conversation. "We are not at the king's court, Mister Drummond."

"Oh, they would love to see you at Whitehall," he said, laughing.

She tossed her head, unsmiling. "And you? How have you engaged yourself? You made your way to New England, I believe."

"New Amsterdam really is a small town, isn't it?" Drummond said. "Everyone knows everyone else's business."

"A grain merchant?" Blandine shook her head dismissively. "Farro, durum or spelt, which is the best for fermentation of beer? What is the purpose of an apple placed within a tun of flaxseed? Soft wheat or hard wheat for bread making, which has the high gluten? Here in New Netherland, would you counsel planting to sprout in late fall or spring?"

Drummond was silent.

"I never believed you were a grain merchant. Nor any merchant at all. You have not the commercial gleam to your eye."

"Whatever gleam I have, you have placed there."

Blandine snorted derisively at the compliment. "Said the courtier to the king's mistress."

"I find myself checked at every move," Drummond said. He flopped back on the bearskin, as if flattened by her logic. "If I'm not in trade, what would you suggest is my purpose for being here?"

"Me? I'm a provincial cousin. What could I know about such a glorious world as yours?"

"Nevertheless, the whole court would be amused to hear you guess."

"Let us leave off the artificiality, please. This night has been so special to me, and now you wreck it. What did you do in New England?"

Drummond was not about to tell her his business. In New Haven, he had not discovered the regicides. But he had discovered how to discover them. He would return to set the trap, and let others spring it.

What he had found in New Haven Colony were a great many hard-nosed people. He knew the type well. He had fought against them in the late wars of the Commonwealth. Religious caterpillars who disdained ever to become butterflies. He had not been able to find a decent draft of hard cider in the whole town.

Antony came and crouched beside them, extending his immense hands, palms out, to the warmth of the fire.

"This friend of yours that you nursed, did she survive?" Drummond asked Blandine.

"He. And yes, he did."

"The pox, or the hot sickness?"

"He was afflicted with a malady of the mind," Blandine said.

"Ah," said Drummond. "As are we all."

"No, we are not all. Really, your frivolity grates upon me at times. The man was entirely beside himself. He suffered from horrible delusions. He attacked me. He bit me."

"Your friend bit you?"

"Yes, he did. He is a river indian, a famous Lenape trapper. A man with great personal dignity. And this madness gripped him. It is common among his people. They call it witika, and a fancy convinces them they are eaters of human flesh."

Drummond sat up. "What did you say?"

"My friend—"

"Kitane," Drummond said.

Blandine looked surprised that he knew the name.

"His fame is widespread," Drummond said.

"Kitane thought he had been turned into a cannibal," she said. "By a demon that his people believe haunts the woods."

"He babbled about all the men he had eaten," Antony said. "He said he had cooked and consumed Petrus Stuyvesant."

"Our director general," Blandine explained.

"I know who Stuyvesant is," Drummond said, exasperated.

"I told him that the director general lived, and that I had seen him on Pearl Street not a month past."

Antony said, "Kitane told us he had eaten the director general and then crapped him out."

"What I saw walking down Pearl Street was Stuyvesant transformed into Kitane's excrement," Blandine said.

Antony laughed, and Blandine laughed, too, slightly embarrassed.

"What was it you said?" Drummond asked. "The word for the demon?"

"Witika," Blandine said.

"Witika," Antony said.

"I have heard that name only recently."

"In New England?"

"No," Drummond said. "Well, yes. They are inflamed by rumors of it there, too."

He had in fact seen a pamphlet in New Haven, the exact mirror opposite of the one shown to him by Raeger that first night in the Red Lion. In place of the English plot against the Dutch, this one had the parties switched. But it used identical language. "A faithful account of a bloody, treacherous and cruel plot by the Dutch in America, purporting the total ruin and murder of all the English colonists in New England."

"Kitane, he attacked her," Antony said. "But he didn't attack me."

"No?" Drummond said.

"No. Do you want to know why?"

Drummond looked over at him. "Because you are too big to eat."

Antony laughed heartily. He was beginning to fall in love with the Englisher.

They took the warmth of the fire and then walked back up the slope to gaze at the moon through the perspective tube some more.

"Can this see other things?" Blandine asked. "Make things on land far away appear close?"

Drummond trained his tube on the waters of the East River, the waves frosted by moonlight. They all took turns looking.

He said, "Look there," swinging the tube around so that it was pointed at the dark patch of forest to the north of them. "Someone has a fire in the woods."

A tiny orange flame, a league or so up the island, just in from the shore at Corlaers Hook.

He adjusted the tube, stared, adjusted some more. "I had it, and then I lost it."

"Let me," Antony said.

He put his eye to the lens. Forms moved through the darkness, backlit by firelight. One of them towered hugely, taller than Antony himself. But then he bumped the apparatus, and lost the vision altogether.

"I got only a brief look," Drummond said. "It appeared to be indians. Were you troubled by *wilden* on your way here?"

16

Earlier that afternoon, a gentleman approached an orphan as the boy walked among the bustle of the docks.

"Ansel Imbrock," the gentleman said. It wasn't a question.

"I am Anse," the orphan said.

"Do you know me?" the gentleman said. "I'm the orphanmaster."

Anse stared up at the man, who towered over him. He could not quite see his face, which was wrapped in a scarf against the cold. Mister Visser, Ansel's champion, had once given the boy a dried apricot. Perhaps, this day, he would have another.

"Come along, Ansel." The orphanmaster turned on his heel and set off. Anse had to hurry to keep up.

Ansel Imbrock often strayed to the wharf on his way home to Auntie's house. One day, he swore to himself, a seven-year-old's boast, I'll sail away in a tall ship. I will be a captain, and my sloop shall be very fast and be called *God's Truth*. Last month he had seen a ship named that at the New Amsterdam pier, and he liked the ring of it.

The gentleman did not stop. At least, Anse believed he was a gentleman. He wore the shoes with scarlet heels, and only gentlemen wore those. Besides, he knew the orphanmaster's business.

Up Lang Straet, away from the busy wharf to the more boring area of warehouses and idle small-boats.

"Mister Visser, sir?" Anse said. "I should tell my auntie."

"Your auntie knows already," the gentleman said. "Hurry."

He directed Anse to a rowboat moored to a finger pier. The man's hat brim shielded his face. "Get in," he said. "There shall be chocolate where we're going."

Anse did as he was told. He had never tasted chocolate, but he had heard of it. "Mister Visser?" he said.

The gentleman did not reply. He shoved the skiff into the shallows. Anse clambered into the sheltered nest of the high-gunwaled bow. By the time he turned around, the man already heaved at the oars. Anse saw only the blank expanse of his back.

"Sir?" No answer.

A sailor must be stalwart. If he ever were to become a captain, Anse had to learn to weather the harshest conditions at sea. The wind blew up the East River from the bay, and the waves showed whitecaps farther out on the water. The golden light of sunset faded upon the hills of Breukelen.

The gentleman pulled north, keeping to the Manhattan shore, far past the palisades wall. The farms and dwelling-houses became less regular, and patches of forest showed between the plantations. Soon, nothing, no sign of human habitation. Anse had never been this far from town before.

Whatever could Mister Visser want with him up here? Ansel knew that somewhere, he owned property passed down from his father. The orphanmaster had solemnly told him so. That must be it. He was being taken to see his land.

He wanted to inquire of the gentleman if it were necessary to make the journey at dusk, when the cold came on with the autumn dark. Anse decided to stay stalwart and silent.

Putting up the oars, the gentleman hooked a lantern onto the trammel, lit it with a twist of punk and then used the same wavering flame to ignite his pipe. Rich, molasses-tinged smoke wafted up from the stern. Anse loved the smell of a pipe. It recalled to his mind the smell of his dead father.

"Mister Visser?" he said timidly. No reply.

A gigantic moon rose, but its light offered him no comfort. Instead, the world became ghostly, unreal.

They drifted with the tide. The shoreline poked out here, and there was a house, but they passed it. The gentleman worked the oars again and they put in at a tiny cove. Before Anse could look at him the man splashed past and climbed up the ragged tideline on the beach, where the soil had been eaten away by the waves to expose a jumble of stones.

"Sir," he called out, as soon as he clambered from the skiff onto the beach. "I don't want to go."

The gentleman, about to enter the forest, turned to him. Anse found it difficult to see his face in the gloom.

"Could whoever we are to meet come here? I don't want to go."

"Then you'll be left," the gentleman said, and abruptly he disappeared into the darkness of the woods.

Sailor that he was, captain that he would be, Anse did not believe he could handle the skiff alone. Quickly, he scrambled through the fringe of rotted seaweed on the shore, climbed up the overhanging tideline and entered the forest.

The gentleman was already far ahead. "Please, sir," Anse said. "Wait."

Onward they plunged, on no path that Anse could discern. He fought off the slap of branches from the gentleman's passage in front of him.

Fear, real fear, not just the uneasiness that had gripped him since stepping into the skiff, but outright terror, closed about Anse's throat like a strangling hand. He could no longer summon the temerity to call out. He felt short of breath, either from being scared or from the exertion of making it through the undergrowth, he couldn't tell.

A shred of hope. A light shimmered in the woods in front of them. The black outline of the gentleman's form blocked it out, it reappeared, was gone again, then resolved itself into a familiar sight that warmed Anse's heart.

Firelight.

It would all be fine.

The undergrowth was thicker than ever. It took an agonizingly long time to reach the fire ring. When they did, the gentleman simply strode through the circle of light.

"Wait here," he said, gesturing to a log set on the ground amid a circle of pounded wooden stakes. He wore his hat brim pulled down over his eyes.

"Sir?" Anse said. "Mister Visser?"

But the gentleman had already stalked out of sight.

A small voice echoed Anse's. "Sir!" it cried. "Sir?"

Anse peered into the darkness. "Sir?" the piping voice said again. "Mister Visser?"

An echo? With a jolt, Anse realized he was not alone. Two children, two African children, vaguely familiar from the streets of the town, sat piled together at the other side of the fire ring.

They shivered in the November cold. Somebody had pulled all their clothes off, leaving them stark naked. Anse felt embarrassed for them.

One of the children, the bigger one, a boy of about Anse's age, had a rope loosely tied around his neck. A much younger girl sprawled across his lap. At her feet lay a small dolly.

"Will Mister Visser come?" the boy said in his curious piping sing-song. He grinned. There was something wrong with his face. It was swollen and bruised and caked with blood, which turned his smile into a gaping, twisted hole. His little sister slept soundlessly, as though she would never wake up.

"Sir? Sir? Sir?" the boy repeated, still with the same mocking voice.

Another sound, from the darkness. "*Dik-duk, dik-duk.*"

The beast strode out from the forest and walked directly into the fire! Standing upright amid the embers, a hundred feet tall!

The demon wore an immense mask, and sparks of fire shot from its mouth. It kicked through the flaming logs and lunged at Anse.

That was enough. Anse yelled and fled into the woods, floundering and thrashing in the undergrowth.

Late the next afternoon, Ansel Imbrock stumbled babbling into the guardhouse at the director general's *bouwerie*, far up the island from the settlement. The boy had gotten turned around in the darkness, and wound up going north instead of south, away from town instead of toward it.

When the *schout* questioned the child, Ansel churned up details of the scene that hadn't fully registered at the time.

The doll by the fire. The strange indian symbols, including a circle-and-cross sign painted in blood on the forehead of the African boy. The absolute stillness of the little girl.

Fear rendered Anse Imbrock imbecilic. He constantly muttered to himself about God's truth. They had trouble getting a straight story out of him.

The *schout* decided part of the boy's tale was an obvious lie. Aet Visser had not led him away from town. He took no skiff ride up the East River. No one witnessed Ansel Imbrock that afternoon in the company of any Dutch gentleman. The orphanmaster was ascertained to be elsewhere.

The boy was simply an orphan, known as a runaway, spinning tales to cover his feckless wanderings.

But the fire ring in the woods rang true. The resemblance to the bizarre scene that Hannie de Laet described was uncanny. No one had been able to discover the *wilden* ritual site she stumbled upon while mushroom picking. But here was the same tale told over again, recounted in confused snatches by poor little Anse Imbrock.

The *schout* knew well what it all meant. He must raise the hue and cry.

From the wilderness north, the witika had now slouched south to haunt New Amsterdam.

In London, Charles II chartered a new American colony, naming it Carolina after his murdered father. Spain found itself newly afflicted with its own monarch, also called Charles II, the product of a hundred years of Hapsburg inbreeding, a deformed and weak-witted descendant of Joanna the Mad. At Whitehall, Pepys overheard James, Duke of York, say that he would wear a wig, afterward gleaning from court gossip that the king avowed he would also wear one. A style was born.

Milton completed his epic *Paradise Lost* and sold the copyright to his publisher for ten pounds. The mathematician, philosopher and inventor of roulette, Blaise Pascal ("All of man's misfortune comes from one thing, which is not knowing how to sit quietly in a room"), died in a room in Paris.

Buxtehude took his seat at the great confectionary pipe organ of St. Mary's, in Helsingor, Prince Hamlet's home city. On the boards: *Theatrum Mundi*, "the world as stage." Molière's *Tartuffe* was produced for the first time.

The American missionary John Eliot, who oversaw the excommunication of Anne Hutchinson (he declared the number of deformities on the body of Hutchinson's stillborn baby corresponded with the exact number of her heresies), translated the Bible into the Algonquin language of native Americans. The Harvard Puritan Michael Wigglesworth published his apocalyptic catechism, *The Day of Doom*. Eventually, one out of every twenty people in New England owned a copy.

The Maryland, Carolina and Virginia colonies promulgated laws making it illegal to free enslaved Africans, contravening English law, which held they could be freed if they converted to Christianity.

In autumn 1663, the English emissary James Christe penetrated the western, Dutch-controlled end of Long Island, informing the settlers there that the territory was no longer under the jurisdiction of New Netherland, but that they should instead heretofore think of it as part of Connecticut.

For the first time, all over Europe but most especially in Italy, Holland and England, human beings placed their eyes to lozenges of shaped glass and peered into secrets of the universe. The Dutch scientist Christiaan Huygens debuted the magic lantern, an optical device that projected images upon surfaces. It was initially referred to as "the lantern of fright," since in early applications it was used most often to display fear-inspiring images of the Devil.

Nowhere on earth were women more legally unencumbered than in the Netherlands and its colony of New Netherland. For their elementary education, girls received identical instruction to that of boys. Under a unique Dutch legal tradition, a woman could choose a form of marriage granting her legal standing equal to her husband's, allowing her to represent herself in court, sign contracts and inherit property. Single women also enjoyed these rights, which would not be fully extended under British law for centuries.

Blandine van Couvering, aged twenty-two in 1663, took for granted her independent status before the law, though she herself could not feel free, oppressed as she was by her status as an orphan girl. In particular, she suffered nightmares of her sister's death by drowning, and often waked with the agony of reaching out to six-year-old sister Sarah, only to have the seas sweep the child roughly away.

An able student, she lacked fluency in Latin but could converse readily in Dutch, English and French, plus the trade language that combined pidgin English, peddler's French and Algonquin. As a child, working as a hawker of citrus, she lent her profits out to farmers at seven percent. She kept pigeons and refused to allow them to be sold for meat. A year later she had graduated to rabbits and was carrying on a brisk trade with New

Amsterdam meat-mongers. She explained the contradiction by saying, "Rabbits are much more stupid than pigeons."

As she attained her majority she became avowedly parochial, preferring everything of the new world to anything of the old. For a time, her favorite reading was Anne Bradstreet's *The Tenth Muse,* but she left this behind as her religious views shifted. She had seen war, massacre, pestilence, indigenes, lust, terror, loyalty, tobacco, hard cider, bobcats, intolerance, frugality, faithlessness.

She never wore a cap.

17

The director general hated the day. Every year, when the annual *kermis* rolled around, he felt his bowels tighten. During the harvest carnival, the populace threw themselves into drinking and brawling and fornication with unseemly abandon. An air of lawlessness descended upon the colony—his colony. Settlers poured into New Amsterdam from the outlying districts, so many that he could hardly recognize the faces on the streets. Because of knife fights, surgeons did their best business of the year.

Stuyvesant would have outlawed the whole festival if he could. Herded them all into church, given them a good tongue-thrashing sermon to mull over. The fair's promiscuity troubled him deeply. Africans and river indians and good Company men, thrown in together without thought of proper social forms.

The whole task of the new world, the director general considered, was to bring its morals in line with the old. Already the stays had been loosened. Between men and women, intimacies occurred openly on a daily basis that would be unheard of in Patria. Kisses, fondlings, passionate exchanges between unmarrieds, random adulteries on the part of those who were linked to others before God.

He recalled interrogating his nephew Kees about his dealings with the Van Couvering girl.

"Hast thou kissed?"

Yes.

"Touched?"

Yes.

"Does she remain intact?"

"Uncle!"

Among all the peoples of Europe, behind only the French, the Dutch were notoriously randy. The women, if not promiscuous, were open to suggestion. In fact, they were the ones who sometimes offered up the suggestion first. It did not necessarily matter that a woman possessed her virginity on her wedding day.

"It is a legitimate concern. Answer my question. Is she intact?"

Yes.

Or so the young suitor averred. From what Stuyvesant knew of his nephew, Kees would be no threat to any girl's honor. What he did with the prostitutes down along the Strand was his own business. With a proper lady, Kees would pull up short before things went too far. But not every man in the settlement would be so circumspect.

He, Petrus Stuyvesant, acted as the dykemaster, holding back the flood. The carnival challenged all that he tried to do. These things went on in his jurisdiction, he knew. But at *kermis*, they burst out into the open. They were goading him, his colonists, challenging his authority.

"Do you know," the director general said, "that this market carnival business was originally a religious affair? *Ker-mis*—it means 'church mass.' Now look at them!"

George Godbolt nodded in agreement, attempting to put the correct expression of distaste on his face. Godbolt was the sole petitioner in the director general's audience chamber at the Stadt Huys that day. Stuyvesant granted him a private audience as a show of favor to one of his loyal English residents. He had an idea that he might need Godbolt's support in the future.

Crowds flocked past the Stadt Huys along the wharf, gabbing and laughing and calling to one another, streaming toward the market square next to the fort. They reminded the director general of a gaggle of geese.

"*Labor omnia vincit,*" murmured the director general.

"I'm afraid M'lord General's learning is superior to mine," Godbolt said.

"Virgil," the director general said. He was Latin-proud in the extreme. "Work conquers all."

"A great truth, M'lord General."

"But no work gets done during *kermis*," Stuyvesant said.

Godbolt startled as the director general turned abruptly from the window, pivoting on his wooden peg so fast that he instantly came around.

The apparatus, Godbolt noticed with fascination, boasted strengthening seams of inlaid silver running along its length of oak.

"You know we have these indian murders to deal with," the director general said.

He did not divulge to Godbolt that there had been a new incident, with the orphan Ansel Imbrock's fantastic testimony.

"I understand, of course," Godbolt said. "I appreciate your seeing me during a time of trouble. This petition of mine is a very small matter."

"Aet Visser believes he can dodge authority," Stuyvesant growled.

"It's not Aet Visser," Godbolt said quickly. "Not him so much as this other one, the grain merchant, Drummond. I would be thankful if you could back him off."

"I've had some report of him," the director general lied. In truth, the man Drummond's name had not entered the lists, as far as he knew. An unlicensed presence in the colony always caused Stuyvesant anxiety. He wondered at Godbolt, an Englishman, complaining about this newcomer, his countryman.

Someone shouted drunkenly amid the circus outside his window. "A profane time," the director general said.

"Amen," said Godbolt. He felt relieved that the director general seemed to look with favor on his petition.

"These murders, too, must be signs of the Lord's displeasure. The De Laet child was quite hysterical about what she saw out there in the woods. Her father wouldn't let me alone."

Godbolt had served this function before, as soundboard for the director general's musings. Truth was, he wished to present his petition and—he felt himself a hypocrite—slip off to *kermis* to join his family in the revels.

"We thoroughly searched the area where Hannie de Laet said she saw the monstrosity," Godbolt told the director. "We could find nothing."

Godbolt was part of a crew platooned by the Company to investigate the fire ring in the forest. The merchant Jean de Laet had been so hounded by his fear-maddened daughter that his wife, Clara, had forced the man to ask the director general for redress. Something must be done, De Laet had said, to set my darling daughter's fright to rest.

The party, a dozen colonists strong, was organized by Kees Bayard, who, as far as the others could see, did none of the searching himself, but stood around smoking and directing others.

What were they looking for? A charred patch in the wilderness. A scrap of leather hung from a tree. The fingers of a child.

They found nothing. A young girl's flight of fancy, grumbled members of the search party. But Godbolt had a secret worry. Any inquiry into the loss of settlement children hove dangerously close to home.

Which is why he appeared before the director general on the first morning of *kermis*, asking that scrutiny of his mute adopted child cease immediately. On the part of Visser or the new English busybody aristocrat, Edward Drummond.

"The colony is inflamed with visions of the indian devil," the director general said.

Rumors were already abroad. This morning, the director general had reports of a witika effigy paraded in the marketplace during the fair. The Africans were making noises about disappearances of their own.

The director general would not be able to keep a lid upon Ansel Imbrock's new report of witika mischief for very long. He would have to organize another search party to get lost in the woods again, searching for a shadow of a mirage of a chimera.

He considered telling all to Godbolt, and thought the better of it. The man was a booby. He appeared eager to depart from the director general's presence. Probably to get himself off to the festival drinking booths.

But Petrus Stuyvesant knew a thing or two about ruling a colony of men. He understood the manifold uses of fear. He thought of a way to spring Ansel Imbrock's terrible story upon the populace, and curtail the excesses of *kermis* at the same time.

"I shall declare a day of prayer and repentance," the director general said. "To bring our jurisdiction more in line with the Lord's wishes."

"Very wise, very necessary, M'lord General," Godbolt said. "Shall you also look into this man Edward Drummond's activities in the colony?"

"I have the sense," Drummond said to Raeger, "that a single frigate with a brace of twenty-four-pounders could blow this whole business down."

They had strolled through every precinct of New Amsterdam that morning, pretending to be friends out for a constitutional, but in truth performing a careful inspection of the settlement's defenses, its palisade walls, its sea roads, its anchorage in the East River. You could walk the whole colony in two or three hours.

And now, the stronghold. Fort Amsterdam. A four-square citadel on the southwest edge of the island. At one time, it might have furnished a suitable defense against attack. And it still would serve as a refuge from marauding river indians. But for any real bulwark against a modern cannonade, the place was useless.

Crumbling curtain walls, rotted battlements, collapsed roofs. Inside—the gates were left open to all comers—one corner of the bailey played host to a great pile of manure, which seeped out into the enclosure and fouled the unused, leaf-covered cistern. Neglect spoke from every corner of the fortress. The roof of the keep, such as it was, served merely as a perch for doves.

"I don't think we'll have any trouble," Raeger said. He meant that England would have no difficulty with the planned move by the crown to take New Netherland.

"By 'we' you might as well say you and I," Drummond said. "I think the two of us could take it on our own."

Raeger laughed. "Deliver it up to King Charles with our compliments."

He sucked on his clay pipe. Raeger had picked up some of the local habits during his time in the colony. Pipe-smoking, he informed Drummond, was useful. The wreath of smoke could be employed as camouflage, he said, to hide one's expression during a conversation, say, or a negotiation.

"This settlement is waiting to be plucked," Drummond said. "The Dutch are like sleepwalkers. They pile up the gold, but forget to lock the door of the counting house."

Some sort of carnival or market day held sway on the lee side of the fort. Raeger had assured Drummond that no more favorable time could be had for a guided reconnaissance of the town. "The beast fair," Raeger called *kermis*, an autumn festival and trading opportunity. A time when colonists bartered cattle, and became beasts themselves.

"The folk go a little unbuckled during the fair," Raeger told him. "They indulge themselves in holiday play after the labor of the harvest and commit all kinds of drunken silliness. If you would ever want to steal a kiss from a pretty miss—say, for example, Blandine van Couvering over there—the beast fair would be the time to do it."

They had rounded the corner of the fort and were thrust into the noise and raucous anarchy of the harvest market.

Blandine was indeed there, in the midst of the crowd, but Drummond could hardly recognize her.

They had not seen each other since two mornings past, when the four moongazers had wandered into the deserted town at dawn, tired but merry after their rapturous night.

Drummond and Blandine and Antony and William felt as though they had just emerged from under a spell cast by the heavens. The full moon, setting in the west, still hung before them, a mystery realm, a few of whose secrets they had unlocked that night.

The woman who Drummond saw at the fair seemed a different creature altogether. Blandine looked a wonder, dressed to be seen in layers of scarlet, purple and green, with a black steepled hat that made Drummond think of the piled-high hairstyles of the French court.

But it wasn't just her costume. She struck a formal pose, mincing forward step by step, her hand outstretched and placed archly in the grasp of her companion, an equally up-rigged colonial gentleman.

The two of them were characters in a dumb show. Goggle-eyed crowds of wrights, rude boys and rustics surged around them. A few other high-caste couples, similarly accoutred and stylized, passed through the fair, swans gliding over a lake crowded with wood ducks and widgeons.

Blandine and her partner stepped delicately aside to allow for passage of a yoke of oxen, hawked for sale by its drover.

Drummond almost laughed out loud. It was as though Blandine were playing at an appearance for the royal court at Whitehall. But she should be careful not to step with her pretty little beribboned shoes into the pile of ox dung just dumped in her path.

Drums beat to announce the opening of *kermis*. Already boys in yellow stockings and monkey jackets roamed the market, eager to spend the few stuivers given to them by their parents at just the right food stall or the most enticing of the spectacle booths.

Touts, mongers and hawkers lured customers to the booths with flatu-
lent blasts of brass trumpets. Ribbons, bunting and flowers garlanded
every surface. The fair lacked a maypole, but that was another festival,
another season. The atmosphere of frolic was the same.

Drinking and food counters lined the fairway, offering wine stiffened
with sugar, ham pasties and sweet pies, cakes with chips of candied
citrus peel.

"Here it is, here it is," the waffle man called. He had no need of a brass
trumpet. The wafting aroma of his hot fried cakes drizzled with honey
ensured that he and his missus had all the customers they could handle.

Most of the smells of the fair were not nearly so fragrant, and the
stench of the assembled pigs, sheep, goats, oxen, cattle and milk cows
mingled with the yeasty odor of spilled beer.

Spectator booths lodged against the fort wall, away from the public
promenade. A fire-eater, a dwarf. One booth displayed the invitation
"See the Jew!" charging a stuiver for country gawkers to stick their heads
through a curtain and gaze upon a member of the tribe, complete with a
fur hat and trailing side curls. The money, it must be said, went toward
the establishment of a temple.

Blandine and Kees Bayard conducted their promenade north through
the market to the parade ground, turned and made another promenade
south, stilt-stepping all the while.

Blandine encountered the rare exhibition of a miniature human, not
more than a foot tall. Dressed in a tunic and cap, the homunculus danced
and hissed atop a cabinet, a thin collar and metal chain around his neck.

"Hello, little one," cooed Blandine. The creature had tufts of cream-
colored fur around its grimacing, disapproving visage, and tore apart an
apple with childlike fingers.

"Just a monkey," said Kees. Since he had traveled to Suriname on
one of his ships, Blandine noticed that he affected not to find anything
wondrous anymore.

"He's a little man, isn't he?" Blandine said. She reached out to touch
the paw of the beast, but Kees pulled her back.

"It's dirty," he said.

* * *

In the Doden Acker, the town cemetery off the Broad Way north of the parade ground, a dozen children went unsupervised that afternoon, their nearby parents letting them run free. The kids played Deadman's Bluff among the graves.

"Deadman, Deadman, come alive," their singsong child voices called. "Come alive when we count to five. One, two, three, four, five."

The blindfolded "Deadman," Bo Dorset, stretched his six-year-old arms in front of him, grabbing at the air as the other girls and boys weaved and dodged away from him.

Suddenly young Bo blundered into a pair of tree trunks. There were the solid adult legs of Mister Martyn Hendrickson, planted right in the middle of the game. He towered above the boy, charming, smiling and totally smashed. His drinking pals Ludwig Smits and Pim Jensen stood next to him, holding him up and being held up in turn.

"You know what this means, Luddy," Martyn said.

"Whut?" Ludwig Smits said.

Hendrickson tugged the blindfold from Bo's head. "It means I'm the Deadman." He slipped the rag over his eyes. Ludwig and Pim howled with laughter.

As soon as the blind dark descended, an old childhood rhyme came back to Martyn, one his mother used to sing to him as a baby. When he was a child, Martyn lost his eyesight to fever for a week. During that time, his mother perished of the same fever.

> *Kiss-kiss, kiss-kiss*
> *Don't my fishy-fish go like this?*
> *Tick-tock, tick-tock*
> *Time it is for the crowing cock*

For the next few minutes, as the yelling children scattered, a sightless Martyn did the Deadman. He tripped and tumbled funnily against gravestones, chasing his prey. He had to leave off once to vomit, but manfully returned to the game. The drunken man lunged, knocking over laughing children like bowling pins, grabbing at them, missing.

Finally the blindfolded Martyn managed to tackle nine-year-old Greetje Breit. The girl giggled uncontrollably, thinking it was fun.

"Moeder, moeder, moeder," Martyn babbled. Mother, mother, mother. Beneath the dirty rag tied around his eyes, Martyn shed tears. He collapsed upon Greetje, suffocating her until she screamed. Pim and Ludwig peeled him off her.

The contagious shrieks of the children passed to the adults, who joined in the merriment.

18

Kees Bayard had myriad things on his mind. For one, he wished to slip away from the fair and nuzzle with Blandine. The rules were relaxed for *kermis* time, and Kees meant to take advantage. But at the same time, he needed to stay right where he was, at the carnival. Criers had just announced the commencement of Kees's primary reason for being there, his main event, the goose-pulling challenge. His uncle had in fact outlawed goose-pulling several years ago. But the edict had not stopped the practice, merely thinned out the ranks of Kees's competition.

To the north of the market square, in the parade concourse across from the large, fine dwelling-houses of Stone Street, the games were about to begin. The test: to gallop a mount full-speed from one end of the course to the other end, where a live goose hung upside down, dangling ten feet in the air. Grab at the angry, squawking bird's head.

The colony declared whoever pulled the bird down to be king of *kermis* fair. There were other contests at the festival—"kitten in a casket" was a favorite—but goose-pulling reigned supreme. At times the bird's legs snapped off at the halter tied around its feet, other times a contestant would pull its head off its body in a great spray of blood and feathers.

Festival organizers made the snatch more difficult—devilishly hard, in fact—by liberally greasing the animal with bear fat. Onlookers and contestants alike had to be drunk enough to appreciate the spectacle.

"I drink the bottle of fire," repeated a beered-up farmer, staggering in circles beneath the suspended goose. "Bring me the bottle of fire!"

Kees found it delightfully easy to meet the game's challenge. Without bragging about it, he was made to pull the goose. Kittens! Pah. He had left off killing cats as a young boy.

"Wish me luck," he said, grinning at Blandine as he prepared to organize his mount. He would ride Fantome, a coal-black charger of which he was inordinately proud, a horse he swore had Spanish (other times, Moorish) blood. For the fair, he dressed Fantome in colors and braided its mane with ribbons.

"Your good luck is very bad luck for the goose," Blandine said. She had watched Kees at this ritual many times before.

Edward Drummond appeared at her side. "Mister Drummond," she said, surprised. The Red Lion innkeeper stood with him.

"Raeger," Kees said, shaking hands.

"My friend and compatriot, Edward Drummond," Ross Raeger said. Drummond bowed to the director general's nephew. *Of course*, he thought, *the girl would have some bright boy by her side.* They probably thought of marriage.

Kees looked curiously at Blandine. "I met Mister Drummond at the Lion," she said, stammering.

"We share an interest in astronomy," Drummond said.

"Are you a horseman, Drummond?" Kees asked. "You should take a run at the goose." The Englisher stared most insolently at Blandine, Kees thought, and he had an urge to best the man at mounted combat.

"Goose-pulling," Raeger explained.

"Oh, I know goose-pulling well," Drummond said. "I spent a long while in the Low Countries, where there are quite a lot of geese."

"So, then, you wish to ride? I will lend you a mount," Kees said.

"I prefer other prey," the Englishman said, still gazing at Blandine.

She raised her eyes to him. In truth, Drummond had so wearied of killing and death on the battlefield that he no longer enjoyed even butchering small game. Geese—and kittens—were safe with him. Blandine van Couvering, on the other hand, might not be.

On closer inspection, the woman's costume looked much less outlandish, even charming. A crimson petticoat peeked out beneath a looped-up violet apron, raised to display the tease of red silk. Above a vivid green and blue waistcoat, her fine, full breasts showed amid a burst of white lace. Fat curls fell around her face.

Drummond noticed that although she still grasped Kees's arm, Blandine's eyes strayed again and again to his.

"I'll lay a wager on your win," Raeger said to Blandine's fidgety suitor, who was evidently anxious to leave her side and climb onto his waiting steed.

"I'll bet the goose," Drummond said.

Kees judged the Englisher an insolent rounder. "I've been king of the fair three years in a row," he said, hating to have to spell it out, then realizing the claim meant nothing to the man.

"Good-bye, Mister Drummond," Blandine said, extending her hand. They shook. Seen side by side with Kees, the Englisher did not measure up. He appeared old. What had she been thinking?

Kees disliked his girl's recently adopted habit of public handshaking. He performed a curt bow and stalked off with Blandine trailing behind him.

"Very pretty, as we said," Raeger remarked to Drummond, watching them go. "And if one had the bad luck to fall in love with her, she'd be downright beautiful."

"Fall in love with any woman, and suddenly she's irresistible," Drummond said. "Your luck doesn't even have to be bad."

"Oh-ho, Mister Drummond is already far gone," Raeger said, shaking his head in mock sadness.

Kees located Fantome, the stallion trembling with eagerness, knowing what was about to happen. "What I should have done," Kees said to Blandine, "was to take the man's stinking wager."

Blandine buttoned his waistcoat, preparing him for battle. "Don't think on it now," she said soothingly. "In a moment you will be king of the fair again, and nothing will matter."

"I do adore you, Blandina," Kees said. "In spite of all."

He left her without a word of farewell, and rode to goose.

Blandine assumed her place in the gallery of spectators, on the parade ground in front of Pieter Laurensen's majestic stone dwelling-house.

"Boom," came a voice from behind her, and Blandine felt a swat to her backside.

"Just me," said Pim as she turned around.

Pim Jensen attended school with Blandine before leaving at the age of fourteen for work at his father's tannery. He had by then proved himself a great fighter, but no scholar. He stood smirking at her, a long-stemmed pipe tucked through his jaunty yellow hatband.

"You're looking fine today," he said. Blandine had dressed with an eye not for the leering likes of Pim, but for Kees (and Drummond, too?). She remembered all the times Pim had tried to force a kiss in the schoolroom. The boy was a menace.

"Blandine," Pim said, "let me sing a little song into your ear."

She didn't want to answer him.

"A lot of people," Pim said, his words sounding rehearsed, "a whole lot of people have a problem with you having a problem."

Blandine had no patience for this. There were times when the settlement was just too small. "For heaven's sake, what are you talking about?" she said.

She saw Mally and Lace across the square. They watched over cages made of bent willow branches, selling robins they had captured. Robins were always in demand, they brightened one's *groot kamer* so with their *cheerlup-cheerlup* song and orange-red breasts.

Kees had given Blandine a bird once, years ago, when he noticed her again after their childhood together, seeing his former playmate as a woman for the first time. His gift was not a live bird but a preserved specimen. He had smothered a hummingbird and carefully pressed it between sheets of clean white parchment, as though preserving a flower.

She recalled extracting the paper-thin pressing from its wrapping, a luminescent, almost transparent figure of a trapped animal, arrested in mid-flight. Its wings shone green like those of a dragonfly. Kees professed himself unable to decide if the thing was insect or bird.

Pim noticed Blandine looking toward Lace and Mally. "You know, you know," he chattered. "Too much time. You spend too much with them."

"Why could it be any of your business?" Blandine said.

"Let the blackamoors take care of their own."

"Stick it," Blandine said, a school-yard taunt.

"You ask too many questions about them African children," Pim said. "Leave off or you'll be hurt."

He slapped her butt once more. She retaliated by giving him a sharp crack across the cheek. "Don't touch me again," she said.

He laughed a harsh laugh and disappeared into the crowd.

Angry at the assault, Blandine turned from the concourse back toward the market square.

She did not see Drummond, but at the waffle booth was the orphan-master, crouched on the ground holding a thick, steaming waffle and breaking off chunks to hand to a group of boys and girls crowded around him. By Visser's side, mingling with the children, was Lightning.

"May I get a piece of waffle?" Blandine said, smiling at Visser.

"You can take over for me," said Visser, half-rising, staggering, being saved from a fall by Lightning. He was drunk.

"Aet, I see your dinner coming by," Lightning said.

Theo Michaelis, the town's most popular butcher, led a fattened beeve along by a leather strop. He had painted lines on the beast's hide, marking off the cuts he would make at slaughtering time. His *kermis* customers need merely point out which part of the animal that they wished to buy. Visser made haste over to Michaelis so as to reserve the rump cut he favored.

Blandine found herself left alone in a crowd of children with Lightning. They had nothing to say to each other. The man wore his customary felt hat, greened with age, covering his scar. He stared languidly at Blandine.

"I think you might be frightening the little ones," she said. The children had, in fact, sidled away from the half-indian to cluster around her.

Lightning smirked and stepped back into the flow of fairgoers, again taking his place at Visser's side.

Blandine approached Mally and Lace. She leaned down and made kissy sounds at their caged robins. Mally stared at her. She was taller and thinner than Lace, and had a stern streak running through her right alongside her good parts.

"Two others now," Mally said.

Blandine straightened up. "Oh, Mally, no," she said.

"The slave Steven, up at Stuyvesant's farm, he tell a tale about a Dutch boy coming in from the wilderness. Say the boy saw two of our kids being flayed alive by an indian demon. Didn't say who they were, but Small Bill Gessie and his sister, Jenny, they gone."

"Why were they alone?" Blandine asked. "We said no child should be north of the wall without an adult."

"They don't have parents to watch out for them," Mally said.

"Orphans," Blandine said.

"Uh-huh," Mally said. "Who knows what happened? We put out the word, yes, nobody go out alone. God may mark the fall of every sparrow, but we ain't him."

"Our people are crying," Lace said.

"Did you send for the *schout*?"

Mally and Lace stared blankly at Blandine. "I'm sorry," she said.

She knew as well as they did that the officials of New Amsterdam, from the *schout* up to the director general, would not trouble themselves about the disappearance of an African child. They had never done so in the past, so why would they do so now?

It was impossible to overstate how death-inflected New Amsterdam was, all of the new world, all of the globe, really. There were celebrants present at this *kermis* festival, and not just one or two, either, who would be dead within the month.

Children died. Especially children. Love failed to save them. Prayer failed. Influence failed. They were born dead, of course, or died in infancy. But other times the parents were allowed to get to know them, to love them for a few years before they were taken. Children died from contagion, from marasmus, from a cut finger that became infected.

The enemies of the young were legion. The triple-threat killers, typhoid, dysentery and cholera. Yellow fever, a.k.a. dock fever, a.k.a. "King Death in his yellow robe." An onslaught of other fevers: winter, spotted, camp, puking, putrid, congestive, diary, ship, remitting, black, blackwater, brain. The small pox, a great victimizer of native Americans.

Nothing to be done against any of it. Get them abed, cram them with ineffectual potions, bleed them. Pray. Sit at bedside through the night.

Nothing helped.

What did it mean to love a human child, a creature with such a tentative hold on life? Who might at any moment vanish into the long deep dark? Does a parent's love become more guarded, more careful, perhaps a little withholding? Or does it become more fierce in the face of constant, imminent threat?

Piteous Gullee. With all this death, did it matter that one child more had disappeared? And a child who was from "outside the wall" at that? Her death had taken place almost a month before. Old news.

Now two more. It was happening again.

Inside Blandine's head, a small chirping robin's song repeated, "There's nothing I can do! There's nothing I can do!" Over and over, rising to a panicked shriek. She beat the voice back.

"I'll go to the *schout*," she said.

"You do that, Miss Blandina," Mally said. She turned away.

They were disgusted over her lack of action on Piddy, as Blandine was disgusted with herself.

A roar rose from the parade ground. Blandine guessed that she had missed Kees's triumph at the goose-pulling.

The carnival turned nasty on her. She reeled through the market toward her home on Pearl Street, confused and ashamed. The red faces of the fairgoers appeared crass and wolfish. The crowd seemed to teeter on the edge of violence.

A bare-chested bald man passed Blandine hoisting a green-skinned, long-fanged effigy strung up on a pole: the witika. Children and a few adults coursed after him, pelting the goblin figure with clods of dirt.

Blandine saw Tommy van Elsant, the son of the funeral caller, hunkered down with some of his friends at the edge of the market-place, behind a stall that was not in use. He held a glass jar in his hands, and the youngsters around him leaned in, openmouthed, to gaze at its contents.

They each had paid a small token—a jaw harp, a knuckle-buckle, a string of seawan the length of a finger—for the opportunity to peer at a tiny fetus, adrift in its small bath of saltwater, cast off the last time Cara Reynoutsen miscarried.

As drink took the populace, the Dutch country dances on the parade ground became more and more frantic. Cross-dressing ran rampant. In the aisles of the drinking booths, brandy-boiled fairgoers lay where they fell. The recently harvested fields of the Company near the Doden Acker turned into crowded rutting grounds.

Blandine fled. Away from *kermis*, away from her countrymen, away from sickly sweet waffles and fat-smeared geese and her guilt over missing children. Lost in her thoughts, she made her solitary way down Pearl Street toward her dwelling-house.

"How-do, Miss Blandina," the street urchin Gypsy Davey said to her, appearing suddenly at her side.

"Hello, Davey, you little imp," Blandine said. The sight of the renegade orphan always cheered her. "Come with me, I'll treat you to a pickle."

"You best watch yourself," the red-kerchiefed boy said. "Walk the straight and narrow line."

Blandine laughed. Gypsy Davey wouldn't recognize the straight and narrow if it came up and bit him. She was going to tell him so, but when she looked again, Davey had vanished.

19

"**R**emember that the Devil is chained up, and wholly at the will and beck of God," preached Johannes Megapolensis from the pulpit at the Dutch Reformed Church.

As soon as the fair was over, to counter its sinful excesses, the director general had declared a settlement-wide day of prayer, fasting and contrition.

Visser sat in his pew, his brain bursting with the headache that had been waiting for him at the end of *kermis*. There was nothing like a good sermon after a spree. It settled the gut and righted the soul.

"Remember that Christ hath conquered the Devil in his temptations, on the cross, by his resurrection and ascension. The prince of this world is conquered and cast out by Our Lord, the prince of the next. Wilt thou fear a conquered foe?"

Through the fog on his senses Visser perceived the thrust of the sermon. It really concerned the witika, the only subject anyone in the whole settlement seemed to be talking about.

Witika fever swept through town quicker than the plague. The *schout* enforced a curfew for children. Parents locked their sons and daughters inside, day and night. Sponsors of Adolph Roeletsen's school had a debate whether to close temporarily, for safety's sake.

"Remember how you honor the Devil by fearing him, and pleasure him by thus honoring him. As tyrants rejoice to see men fear them, so the Devil triumpheth in your fears as his honor."

Ah, Visser thought, now the dominie was getting to it. Johannes Megapolensis and the director general were famous enemies. Even though the minister had acceded readily to this day given to the service of the Lord, he could not resist inserting a swipe at Stuyvesant in his sermon on the witika.

"As tyrants rejoice to see men fear . . ." Yes, yes, that was the dominie all the way.

An odd political declension had developed in New Amsterdam over the last year. The Dutch colonists, chafing under the harsh rule of the director general, had begun to rebel against him. The director general, in turn, increasingly sought his partisans among the colony's English populace.

Visser was sure it would all come to a bad end. The Dutch governor fought his own people and favored the foreign-born. Up was down. Sixes were at sevens.

The orphanmaster picked his nose, inspected the product and flicked it away. He himself avoided Stuyvesant as much as he could.

No worse a powerful man can there be than an impulsive one, and odd whims seized the director general with regularity. He shuttered taverns, ordered work details, issued proclamations on trade, all purely on impulse. Once the man attempted to place a ban on the Humpty Dumpty, the brandy concoction, which came to the colony direct from London.

Visser was afraid that if the director general's gaze should ever happen to fall upon him, he would end up much the sorrier for it.

Already, George Godbolt had high-hatted Visser at this very service. He and Rebecca passed him by with not even a bow of their heads. Resentful, no doubt, the two of them were, for Visser having sicced Edward Drummond on them.

Drummond himself sat two rows behind Visser. He listened first to the director general scare the living daylights out of the assembled by telling what Ansel Imbrock saw in the forest, implying this new attack was judgment for the colony's sins. Then Drummond attended as the dominie talked about the Devil. Also known as, just at that moment in the colony, the witika.

Day of prayer. More like the day of pride, Drummond thought. He had long ago turned his back on this personal God the preachers preached about. No god heard your prayers, no god watched over you, no god could be summoned for a throw of the dice. That was all just human vanity.

Especially vain were men who claimed God spoke to them, Drummond thought, such as the two who had mounted the pulpit at this church today.

Vanity, saith the preacher. Pride goeth before the fall, and also before the winter, spring and summer.

The new world, Drummond found, was an excellent place for doubting such a personal God. Inside the soaring cathedral at Reims, say, it was easy to believe. But in wilderness America, how could you venture to think that the Supreme Being pays humankind any mind? Take a short walk out your back door, brother, head into the desolate forest and tell me your old graybeard God is around. And if God wasn't present there, then he wasn't infinite, and if he wasn't infinite, he wasn't God.

No, Drummond was much more interested in this new God of Spinoza's. Not a father in heaven at all, but rather a . . . Drummond found it hard to describe. An entity, an endlessness, a totality. There were moments, on the voyage to New Netherland, at night in his hammock on *Margrave*, reading Spinoza's *A Short Treatise* by candlelight, when faith in this sort of God seized him and wrung his soul completely out.

Call Spinoza's God nature, the nature Drummond met wrapped in a bearskin robe in a pelting rain on the trail to New Haven. Call it infinity, which he glimpsed through his perspective tube when he stared at the night sky.

An inhuman God? A god that didn't care whether you capitalized his name or not? A god for which the terms *caring* and *loving* made no sense, since these were human terms, and thus too limited to apply to the God of Spinoza.

A god of space. A god of infinity. Of wilderness.

An inhuman God. Could Drummond live with that? Thus was his constant struggle, whether he was in church sitting two rows behind Aet Visser and smelling the alcohol on the man's breath from that distance, or if he was at an afternoon's fair, gazing at the face of Blandine van Couvering.

He would not, he decided, return to Europe.

Rumor, the real and true witika, a hobgoblin more powerful than any other, tore through the *groot kamers* and taprooms of New Amsterdam. It struck first during *kermis*, running like a virus among the reeling fairgoers. A new witika killing had been discovered, it whispered, this one close to home, right outside the wall. The name Ansel Imbrock became known to the populace. The boy had actually witnessed the demon doing its dark work.

Stuyvesant's fearmongering address to the congregation at the Dutch Reformed Church helped fan the flames. As November bled into December, reports of murder jumped from house to house like a crown fire. The Jope Hawes killing up in Pine Plains four months before resurrected itself in people's minds.

Rumor stalked the colony, seeking a victim.

The name of Blandine van Couvering kept cropping up. Wasn't she inordinately interested in the witika business? The fever that infected the colony needed a target upon which to focus. An independent woman, unmarried, an orphan, probably wanton (and pretty, that was always a plus), one who consorted with Africans and indians, who spoke her mind, who had some sort of relationship with the drunkenly corrupt Aet Visser, the orphanmaster himself, not to speak of the suspect Englisher she went around with—Blandine fit the role of sacrificial lamb perfectly.

Kitane knew none of this as he entered the settlement by the East River land port and passed down Pearl to the heart of town. He stayed with a small community of Long Island indians, the Canarsie, who lived in a collection of lodges on the shores of northern Manhattan, near the swirling waters that the Dutch called *Hellegat*, Hell Gate. Blandine and her giant had situated Kitane there, wanting him to be closer to them, so they could monitor his return to health.

At first, his town visit went along fine. He entered a clothing shop. He purchased stockings as a gift for a Canarsie girl he liked.

He left the store and walked through the settlement. He was hungry for sweets. Though he did not readily admit it to himself, Kitane wanted to see Blandine. Her presence was like a cool cloth on his forehead during an illness. She had not come up the island to see him for many days now, sending Antony instead.

Sickness had humbled Kitane. As he passed among the colonists working on the wharf, he dreamed not of a war club materializing in his hands, nor of stoving in swannekin skulls. All that had been burned away during the time he imagined himself a witika.

He dreamed instead of a Dutch bakery he had visited once in the past, and of the pastries they offered for sale there. He headed toward the shop. And suddenly a darkness rolled through the streets of New Amsterdam like a mist.

Did he imagine the colonists on the street staring at him, pointing their fingers? Kitane had been in New Amsterdam many times before. He could not remember ever being the object of any special attention. Yet there they were, that woman there, the man in the doorway, glaring strangely.

He did not know the townspeople had been infected by rumor.

Dissipating wisps of his former illness sometimes still blew through Kitane. During his witika sickness, fear of losing his mind caused him to lose his mind. Now a shadow of that fear crept back upon him. He felt unsure. Had he already killed? In his nightmares, surely he had. He saw children, too many to count, stretched out all around him. Were they really only dreams?

The swannekins all turned to look at him as he passed. Perhaps he had a smear of blood on his lips. He resisted the impulse to put his hand up to wipe it off. He knew it could not really be there.

The harbor gulls hung in the wind over his head, asking him what the master of the forest might be doing among the stone dwelling-houses of town. "Are you lost?" they shrieked.

Kitane told them to mind their own business, which was, as far as he could tell, rotted fish.

The bakery he remembered was no longer there. A tavern had taken its place. Kitane had noticed that was the main characteristic about New Amsterdam, that nothing was allowed to grow old there. Things changed with a baffling quickness. Shops, houses, people—they all shuffled and rearranged constantly.

A slight blade of panic worked its way behind Kitane's eyes. He should go back to his Canarsie lodge, return at a run. He was not ready. His mind remained unhealed.

Disoriented, he turned a corner onto another street. Where was he? A spasm of waking dream gripped his mind. Not a war club in the dream this time, no, and no bashing of heads. Just him, Kitane, running down the street, tearing and ripping with his teeth at every settler he passed. Eating and eating and never finding his fill. A witika nightmare.

Like a miracle, another bakery shop appeared on the street into which he had stumbled. When he walked inside, the she-merchant owner uttered a little yelp of alarm, like the bark of a dog, and disappeared into the back of the store. Her man came out soon after.

"What do you want?" the baker said.

Kitane pointed to a frosted cake with raisins, not trusting himself to speak.

"Can you pay?"

He took a short string of seawan from his bag, held up three fingers and traded the shells for three of the cakes.

Wolfing down the sugary treats in the street, Kitane felt better. Sugar, he knew, came from far away, brought by the Dutch in their cloud-houses. *The Bar-bay-dos.* The Dutch owned many slaves there, Africans.

Kitane had never been so weak. He had always been the strongest among any group he found himself in, the quickest, the surest with a hatchet or trap. Now just the whisper of the witika had killed him. He was not himself. He should never have come to town.

A troop of urchins ran past him, coursing down the street like a flock of chirping birds. Were they repeating "witika, witika," or was it only the voice of his mind?

He knew the settlement well. It was small. It was impossible to get lost. But Kitane wandered that noonday up and down streets he didn't recognize. When he approached the palisade wall, a lanky boy threw stones at him, driving him away.

"Kitane!" a voice called to him. A familiar voice, but one he had a hard time placing. It sounded like the voice of Brother Bear. But what would a bear be doing in the streets of town?

The Dutch, Kitane thought, were capable of anything. He recalled a dancing bear he had seen once in the marketplace. "I am ashamed," the bear told Kitane, when at the beck of its trainer it reared up on its back legs and shuffled slowly in a circle.

But the call came again. "Kitane!" Far off, like the wind.

Down the street, he saw Antony, big, lumbering, smiling Antony, gesturing to him. A friend among all the strangers. Relief poured into Kitane.

He was saved. He would not have to eat the swannekins after all.

20

The weather came in damp that day, but the caudle was warm and spicy, so all eight women drank copiously of the hot wine mixture from Margaret Tomiessen's set of dainty silver cups. Despite the head colds that some of the participants brought with them to the gathering, they felt determined to finish Elsje Kip's trousseau this Saturday morning. In a circle they sat, their lace lappets covering their ears, huddled over their work.

Elsje herself was absent. She lounged, the women who gathered imagined, in her father's house, fancying her future life as a bride, in the new home her family planned to convey to her. It had already been purchased: a wooden house on the upper part of the Broad Way, with a bright red door and several windows glazed with real glass, imported from Amsterdam.

"I haven't seen the inside," said Gertrude Pont, taking a sip of caudle.

"Nor have I," said Barb Stryker. Nor had any woman at the gathering. But they imagined it was the perfect spot for newlyweds, just so, with a scrubbed plank floor and smooth white plaster walls, the whole arrangement clean and fresh and decent.

Margaret Tomiessen's house was also just so, and she easily fit eight chairs in her *groot kamer* to seat her guests that afternoon. The location of the dwelling couldn't be more proper. The Tomiessens resided on Stone Street, steps away from the fort. A person could actually walk out her door without dragging one's skirts in the mud, as Stone was the first street in all of New Amsterdam to be set with paving blocks.

Margaret maintained the home spotlessly, raking out yellow sand on the floor every morning, dusting the cabinet and the candlesticks atop it, gathering the cold ashes from the hearth and dropping them into the gutter outside.

The hostess sniffled as she refilled the caudle cups of her guests. Each hausfrau balanced a length of fabric upon her lap and sewed minute stitches to hem them all around. The fabric was white, as was the thread. The linens had been bleached in Haarlem, and they were smooth and especially fine, an excellent gift for a newlywed, if you asked the women at this gathering.

When she stood on the new cobblestones outside her dwelling-house, Margaret could see all the way down to Pearl Street, where Blandine van Couvering kept her rooms.

"You know who's in there now?" said Margaret, tasting her caudle without blowing upon it first, burning her mouth a bit.

"The big fellow, probably," said Jacintha Jacobsen. "Angola."

"Not this time," said Margaret. "The big Lenape buck, Kitane. You've seen him?"

"He was at the bake shop this morning," Elsbeth Trompetter said. "Scared me half to death."

"They love their sweets," Jacintha said. A moment of silence, as everyone's thoughts went to the sweets tray on the cabinet, as yet untouched by the guests.

"And, *and*, do you want to know what else?" Margaret said. The others at the gathering leaned slightly forward, chickens cocking their beaks at a worm. "Sunday at dawn, Miss Blandina was seen coming in from the woods with her English fellow."

A silence fell over the group. One of the guests present actually was English. Lucy Hubbard's husband managed a taproom, and she had become acquainted with some of the finest ladies in town.

"That day," Lucy said, eager to demonstrate where her allegiances lay, "was the day the Imbrock orphan turned up at the director general's farm, scared imbecilic."

"That day," contributed Veltje van Borsum, her small wet tongue licking her thread to put it through the needle, "there was no church for Blandine van Couvering."

"Not unusual," Margaret said, hovering over her guests with the caudle ladle.

"Not at all," Jacintha said. "She avoids church like the pox."

Margaret said brightly, to keep up the conversation, "Ever since she was ravished by the indians."

Lucy Hubbard was a skeptic. "We don't know about that," she offered. "She said she was not. She escaped."

The other ladies blanched at a word spoken, however mildly, in Blandine's defense.

Margaret was quick to tamp down the incipient rebellion. "Escaped along with her African friends," she sneered.

Everyone else was confident. Blandine had been raped. Years ago. When her parents were still alive.

Margaret finally picked up the tray of izer cookies and offered them around. The women fell upon them with gusto.

"Is that why she has never married? She is the same age as Elsje, and look at us here, now, finishing up a beautiful trousseau for a proper young woman's *kas*." Jacintha munched on a cookie, spilling buttery crumbs all over a pillowcase in the process.

"Who would she marry?" said Maaje de Lang.

"Martyn Hendrickson," pronounced Veltje van Borsum, and all the women laughed.

"It would take a plumper hen than Miss Blandina to bring that rooster down," Jacintha said.

"No," Margaret said emphatically. "It's Kees Bayard."

Said Femmie Gravenraet, "He won't marry her." Margaret wondered if her cookies were not just too crisp, as all her guests seemed to wind up with crumbs in their laps.

"Not now. Would you?" said Jacintha. The topic excited her. "A little pretty thing she is, but headstrong. Like a man, almost. Then what would that make Kees? Her bride?"

The women laughed easily.

"A fine young gentleman," said Femmie. "I'd take him."

"Hoo-hoo!" said Maaje.

Jacintha was more stern, as was her way. "He is the nephew," she reminded them.

"So Miss Blandina, she brushes away Kees Bayard," said Femmie. "Pretty as you please."

"With those fine, fine shoulders of his," erupted Maaje. She was the greenest of them, and had known Kees in her school classes. Had a sweetness for him, in fact.

The chickens cackled. They well knew young Maaje's infatuation.

Femmie said, "She takes up with an African, an English monarchist, probably a Catholic—"

"He is!" Margaret interjected.

"—And now an indian," finished Femmie, pulling a nose-cloth out of her bosom and sneezing into it. "She's an orphan, with no parents to keep her straight."

"That African is always around," Jacintha said.

"You needn't worry about him," Femmie said. She lowered her voice to a whisper, gesturing toward her lap. "Castrated in the Barbados before they shipped him here."

Another long silence fell, as the women contemplated the possibility.

Margaret struck up the assault again. "She rejects her church," she reiterated.

"She has gotten herself caught up in this witika mess," said Jacintha. "What good woman does that?"

Margaret shook her head. "You have to wonder. What is her story anyway? Does anyone really know her?"

Every guest took a bite of her crumbling cookie and a draft of her caudle. Margaret crushed the drink and made her pronouncement.

It was the first time that the word *witch* was spoken in connection with Blandine van Couvering.

Drummond had not been able to get a peep out of William. Not speech, anyway. They were together in the workshed in the yard behind Drummond's rented rooms. He heard the boy humming to himself as he cleaned the slick tile floor. William came to his rooms every day but Sunday, cleaning the workshop top to bottom, polishing Drummond's brass scientific instruments.

Drummond made inquiries about the Godbolts. Through Raeger, he found a probate judge, Eberhard Luybeck, who knew something about the family's finances. Luybeck wore an ornate, steel-gray wig that framed a doglike countenance.

"I am considering a business arrangement with George Godbolt," Drummond told the man. "I am wondering how solid his credit might be."

"He don't do much in grain," Luybeck said. "Meat's his custom."

Prying information out of Luybeck did not prove easy. The man, like a lot of financial men, held his cards close. Drummond worked on him and discovered nothing more than that the Godbolts seemed to be well-off, as far as anyone could tell. Sausage wasn't their sole line. They were landlords. Parsimonious in the extreme, as the wealthy sometimes were. But comfortable, nonetheless.

The threadbare chairs he noticed in the Godbolt great room, Drummond concluded, merely indicated thrift, not poverty.

"Have you been long in the colony?" Drummond asked Luybeck.

"May I tell you an amusing story?" Luybeck said, not waiting for Drummond's response before launching in. "In the early days of New Amsterdam, this was thirty years ago now, the *burgomeesters* and *schepens* of this place decided that in order to be a real city we must needs have a lawyer in residence. So they sent to Patria for one. He came, his name was Asmar Schwarthole, he declared himself open for business. None came. He had no paying customers at all."

Drummond could see where this was going.

Luybeck continued, "Counselor Schwarthole became disheartened. He resolved to return to the Netherlands. The grandees of old New Amsterdam could not understand it. Why was there no lawyering business? Then some clever soul proposed that instead of sending the first lawyer home, the colony should send to Patria for another one. The second lawyer came, and do you know what happened?"

"Plenty of business for both," Drummond said.

"Exactly!" Luybeck laughed heartily.

"Dutch or English, it would be the same," Drummond said.

"Your countrymen seem to be in favor with the director general just now," Luybeck said. "If you have business with the Company, you should strike. I myself have capital, which I let out at nine percent."

Drummond politely put the man off. He left Luybeck's believing that his initial theory did not hold up, the idea that the Godbolts kept William from greed, wanting the orphan's payments from his inheritance.

He would have to find another reason, apart from monetary interest, that the Godbolts might go to the trouble of switching one of their wards. And if it were true, what happened to the other child?

Then again . . . the rich could be as greedy as anyone else. His great friend Prince Henry Stuart's avidity at collecting gambling debts taught Drummond that.

Today would be Drummond's first attempt at pouring glass into molds. He had the smelter fired and a mix of clean-washed river sand, nitrum and lime heating inside it. An even temperature rise, Bento Spinoza instructed him, was as important as the cooling and annealing. But at last, gazing into the molten admixture, he decided he was ready.

His orphan helper mopped on the other side of the workshop. Drummond beckoned him over to see the pouring of the molten glass.

"Do you know how the greatest hero of the Dutch Republic was called?" he asked the boy. "William the Silent. That's what we shall name you."

William Turner always saw his time at Drummond's as a refuge from the Godbolt household. He loved the cheery atmosphere of the workshop, especially now that the winter snows had come and the stove warmed the air inside so cozily.

William knew that Dame Rebecca had a worried mind about letting him out of the house. She both mistrusted Drummond and was in awe of him.

This morning, his mother-not-mother had entered the *kamer* as William sat at his toast-and-buttermilk breakfast. She looked at him in a way she no doubt considered loving, a frozen smile on her face.

"William, dear," she said, hauling him awkwardly up onto her lap. "We love you so much."

The warm body smell of Rebecca assaulted William's nostrils. She hugged him, jiggling his face into her chest.

"Honey, honey, honey," she cooed. "You would never say anything, would you? To Mister Drummond or anyone else?"

Crammed into her pillowy bosom, William nodded.

"It might be better," Rebecca Godbolt said, "if you would never talk again. Could you do that, honey? That wouldn't be too hard on you, would it?"

Encompassed in the warmth of his not-mother's body, William had an early memory of his real mother. Her bathing him, kissing the top of his soapy head.

Then came the pinch. Rebecca twisted the flesh of William's arm. The good mother had turned bad.

"Because it would be very, very naughty of you, you'd be an awful little boy, if ever you said a word."

Rebecca pushed him roughly away.

"You're thinking on it, ain't ye?" Suddenly snarling now, her face in a grimace. He backed away from her. He had seen storm winds blow in suddenly before, and knew what was coming next.

"What's your name?" Rebecca shrieked, pummeling him about the head with a Bible. "William!"

Bam! "What's your name?" Bam! "William!" Bam!

Until she was breathing hard and sank down again in her straight-backed chair.

"Go to the attic and catch flies," she said. "Stay up there. Don't say a word."

No, I won't say a word, William-not-William said silently.

An orphan's prayer soars to heaven like a lark, say the French. But in this wicked world, perhaps the steeple of heaven stands empty, its landlord closing up shop, so that there is no one to hear prayers, be they sent from orphans or anyone else.

William would not speak. Until that time—he was planning it, carefully, cunningly, during the midnight hours—when he would open his mouth and the words would spill out. Then there would be ears to hear.

"Aet Visser is a fool at cards," Martyn Hendrickson said to Drummond. Though he knew well who Hendrickson was, Drummond was a little surprised to be addressed casually by the man.

They watched the hapless orphanmaster losing at Bone-Ace in the Mane. In twenty minutes since Drummond arrived, Visser took the bone only a single time and never once hit thirty-one.

Clearly, part of the reason for his poor play was the man's drunkenness. Everyone in the Lion felt extremely comfortable and content that evening, since English-style roast beef was on the menu. The tapers flared high with the vapor of brandy in the air, only to be snuffed back down by the thick tobacco smoke. Visser drank gin.

"How do you read him?" Drummond asked Martyn.

"Visser? He's as honest as men come, but then again, when you get right down to it, how honest do men come?"

"He has information on every orphan in the colony at his fingertips?"

"Ah, yes," Martyn said. "They are his bread and butter. And perhaps a little of his marmalade jam, too."

At the table, Visser lost to Pim Jensen again. He wore a dirty and rumpled doublet, and looked as though he had been at it for a long time. After his day of glass-pouring, Drummond had dropped off William Turner at the Godbolts and come to the Lion to see Raeger. But he was distracted by the gaming in the Mane.

Drummond had witnessed the world's best gamblers at play, including Prince Henry, a demon at cards. Bassett was Henry Stuart's game, and he could win a hundred pounds on the turn of a queen, only to lose it in the next hand. Drummond knew the action well enough to understand the play was not really about winning and losing.

It was about faith and belief.

The field of battle and the gaming table. Drummond once stood beside an officer, a good man judged by all to be lucky and deserving, only to see a dressed-stone cannonball take off his head. Every soldier learned the harshest lesson of battle in ways that reordered his very soul: Luck had nothing to do with it. Randomness ruled.

The gambler wanted to believe differently, that the world held some secret order to it, one that would accord him a special measure of good fortune. Every play tested the gambler's faith in that belief.

At the table in the Mane, Visser rose up and sat down again, as if forgetting what he was doing. "Shall we move on to La Bête?" he suggested, slurring his speech. "Let's move on to the Beast."

Martyn laughed, commenting to Drummond, "A different game, but the same player. He is in no shape to keep track of the play."

"It is difficult to believe that Visser can keep track of anything, let alone dozens of orphans in the colony."

Martyn focused his intense green eyes on Drummond, who found himself wondering if Hendrickson ever bathed. He had encountered the man several times as a colony grandee, with whispers of great wealth surrounding him. Martyn always moved within a cloud of overpowering French *eau*. Drummond knew nobles at Whitehall like that, who thought their *scheisse* was perfumed, and no one dared to tell them otherwise.

"Two hundred and twelve," Martyn said.

"What?"

"There are two hundred and twelve parentless children on the Orphan Chamber rolls in New Netherland." He pulled a solemn face. "Of late, a line has been drawn through the name of one or two."

"I am interested in one that is alive," Drummond said. "William Turner."

He again felt Martyn's penetrating gaze.

"Are you a gambling man, Drummond?"

"Not with a deck of cards," Drummond said. "I don't trust anything that a Frenchman designed."

"Dice? We don't use knucklebones here, do you know? We have 'em out of the antler bones of the whitetail."

He picked up four dice from a cup on an otherwise empty green baize side table. The cubes, carved from the rosette of the deer antler, shone with a high-polished gleam, the pips painted on the die with coal-tar ink. At an inch square, they were larger than the four-sided sheep-bone dice Drummond had seen in Europe.

"Venus, Vultures and Dogs?" Martyn asked. "Or perhaps Hazard?"

He clacked the cubes together in his cupped palm, lending the movement a practiced air. Theirs was a private game in a corner of the Mane. No spectators. Most of the boys—Pim, Ludwig, Rik and the rest—were too busy watching another spectacular plunge by Aet Visser to pay Drummond and Martyn much mind.

"I make it a rule never to play when I don't know the stakes," Drummond said.

"An English guinea against what I know about Aet Visser and William Turner," Martyn said.

Drummond looked across the room at Visser. Any information from that quarter would likely be a confusing meld of half-truths and self-serving pronouncements. The well-connected Martyn Hendrickson could conceivably turn out to be a better bet.

"Your toss or mine?" he said, slipping out from the pocket of his waistcoat one of the coveted new golden English coins, much favored in the colony.

Twenty minutes later, Drummond had triumphed, four games to two. Martyn had a pair of shiny guineas in his pocket, and his opponent possessed a much clearer idea of Aet Visser's operations.

One, according to Martyn: Visser knew the names and particulars of almost every orphan in the colony, not only New Amsterdam—born children, half-indians and the foreign-born, but also Africans—enslaved, half-free and free. That included the three orphans missing from Little Angola.

Martyn pronounced their names: Piteous Gullee, William Gessie and his little sister, Jenny. When Drummond looked strangely at him, Martyn explained: "I've been charged by the director general to look into this affair."

Two: Visser had only a weak alibi for the stretch of time when Ansel Imbrock was taken. The dominie vouched for him, but the times did not exactly correspond. It was conceivable that Visser had been in the woods, as the boy himself alleged.

Three: William Turner was heir to a considerable inheritance from relatives in England, which was the reason Visser moved against the Godbolts: he wanted to take charge of the boy himself.

Four: colony gossipmongers had Visser keeping a whole sheepfold of his own bastards, north of the wall.

The new English guineas were machine-milled of the purest African gold (from mines along the Gulf of Guinea, hence the name), worth twenty shillings, with a profile of the second Charles stamped into the obverse ("*Carolvs II Dei Gratia*," read the inscription, "Charles II by the grace of God").

"Your English monarch," Martyn said, admiring the fresh yellow metal. "Is he really as meaty as all that?"

In the land of seawan, the gold piece was king. Martyn Hendrickson, from the wealthiest family in New Netherland, had no need for more pretty coin. Still, even a rich man stoops to pick up a penny now and then.

Information for gold. Both Drummond and Martyn counted it a fair exchange.

21

Kees Bayard trotted Fantome toward Pearl Street. He withheld his riding crop, since the stallion did not really need any encouragement to keep a brisk pace.

Kees liked to make an impression atop a horse, but on this chill December afternoon, few onlookers were out and about to admire him, and the ones that were kept their heads down to avoid the biting wind off the bay. He did tip his beaver to two old biddies and one young one, the red-nosed Maaje de Lang, who smiled worshipfully up at him.

"Ladies," Kees said.

"We come from trousseau-making for Elsje Kip," Maaje said, apropos, as far as Kees could tell, of absolutely nothing.

"Women and their weddings," he said grandly, and put Fantome into a canter.

"Will we see you at the wassail?" Maaje called after him, but he was too far away to answer.

He passed across the stone bridge over the canal and proceeded down Pearl Street. Blandine stood on her stoop as Kees approached and dismounted, tossing his reins over the iron fencepost.

"Come inside," Blandine said. "I've just been putting out the chicken bones from supper." She clutched her blue shawl around her.

Her great room sparkled, as usual. It was an attribute Kees loved about Blandine, her good Dutch homemaking skills. Odd in an orphan, when you thought about it, but praiseworthy nonetheless.

"Hot cider?"

"Please," Kees said. A look of annoyance crossed his face as he glanced out the window to the backyard. Gathered around a brazier near the lean-to in the garden were Antony (naturally) and the two African women, Lace and Mally, pulled up on stools of turned wood.

Farther down the yard, another of Kees's least favorite individuals slouched against the garden wall, the big, strapping indian trapper,

Kitane. Blandine had met him in the north and insisted on further association with the man whenever he came to town.

Kees had no use for him. Antony, at least, protected Blandine when
she walked abroad. But Kitane did nothing for anyone but himself. The
first mark against him was his insolence. Even now, the buck appeared
to be staring directly at Kees.

As much as Kees admired the way Blandine cleaned a hardwood
floor, he despised the promiscuity of her friendships.

"What kind of a circus do you run here?" Kees said, taking the mug
she offered him, a pained expression on his face. She had spiced the cider
with cinnamon, exactly the way he liked it.

"They are nothing for you to worry about," Blandine said.

"*Kermis* is over," Kees said. "They can all go home."

"What's the matter, Kees? You are peevish."

"Nothing is the matter. Not with me."

She took his meaning. "I see. You do not like the way I am talked
about in town."

"I am surprised you know anything about it. You usually keep your
own counsel. To a fault, I might say."

Blandine crossed to the back door and opened it. "Antony," she said,
"perhaps Lace and Mally need some help with their burdens home."

Antony saw Kees in the room behind Blandine and immediately
understood. He and the two women gathered up bundles of linen and
passed out of the garden by the gate. A grim-faced Lace and Mally waved
to her as they left.

The indian stayed, still staring impudently into the interior of the
house.

"Him," Kees said.

"Kitane has been ill," Blandine said.

"For heaven's sake, you can't be nurse to the world."

Kees edged past Blandine in the doorway and called out. "You there!
Move on!"

"Kees, please," Blandine said. "He is my friend."

"That is exactly the point. Why must you have such friends?"

"This is my house, my rooms, my garden. What is the matter? Tell me what concerns you."

Kees closed the door, slamming it a little too sharply for Blandine's taste. She turned her back on him and stood gazing into the hearth. He went to her.

"Please, my darling," he began, but she shrugged his hand from her shoulder. "I come not to harm you, but to help you."

"So much is on my mind right now," Blandine said.

Kees understood. She meant her expectations of their marriage.

"I don't think you do know what they say about you in town," he said. "The gossip is vicious. They use dangerous words against you."

"People will always talk about a single woman."

"This is serious. There is this insistent friendship of yours with the Africans—"

"The Africans have three children missing!"

"What concern is that of yours? Let the blacks take care of their own."

Blandine snorted. "Pim Jensen just told me that, too, and he's not a good man."

Kees took her by the shoulders and turned her to him. "You have to look to your behavior, especially at this time. This business of the hobgoblin has the whole town in a panic. Think of us. Think of me."

"I do," Blandine said.

"I still want you." He took a deep breath. "I see us marrying, Blandine."

Blandine stood still. It was what she wanted. She said softly, "Is that a proposal?"

"Yes. I want to—" Kees groped for words. "I want to take you away from all this. I want to protect you from gossip and false report."

"You are asking me to marry you."

"Yes, yes, yes—don't keep asking me that!" He paced the room, exasperated. This was not the way he expected it to proceed. He wanted it to be more, he didn't know, more noble than this. He wanted the grateful and loving Blandine he had borne in his mind.

"It must be—I have conditions."

"Ah," Blandine said. She fell silent.

"You must give up Antony," Kees said. "You'll need no bodyguard when I am your husband. We'll have plenty of servants. You must cut your absurd ties to these African women."

Blandine held her hands out to the hearth fire, as if the room had suddenly turned cold. She abruptly seized the iron and stirred the embers until tongues of flame crawled up the wide-throated chimney.

Kees knew Blandine wouldn't like his ideas about her comportment. He had thought the benison of a real proposal of marriage after all these months of courtship—years, really, if you counted their inconsequential childhood fumblings—would render his demands less harsh.

But now he realized he had misjudged. He had learned as a very young boy what Blandine van Couvering looked like angry. In the schoolyard, she had knocked his ears plenty. And here she was with a poker in her hand.

"Anything else?"

"Well, Kitane . . ."

"How about Mister Drummond?"

Kees was taken aback. "Drummond? What has he to do with it? Are you—?" He broke off, dumbstruck at the mere suggestion he could be betrayed.

For Blandine, everything flipped. The circumstances of her life became roiled and mixed up. This was what she wanted, wasn't it?

But she decided no. And she realized the refusal of Kees Bayard had been gradually forming within her heart for quite some time.

What was she going to do, walk down the aisle with him and *then* decide it was wrong? Leave Kees standing at the altar?

"I have known you a long while, Cornelus," Blandine said. "I have always balanced your faults with your goodnesses."

My faults? Kees thought, nonplussed. *Mine?*

"But I think overall I have been wrong to encourage you, and for my part to indulge in fantasies of our life together."

"Drummond, the Englishman?" Kees said. Good goddamn, he thought. I will strike him down! Then, his mind stirred, he considered the falseness of Blandine. If only she weren't so infernally pretty, he thought. Blond hair and dark eyebrows, a bewitching combination. She was the strongest person he had ever known, and the most infuriating.

"I cannot marry you, Kees," Blandine said.

Kees erupted. "The word *witch* has been spoken! Did you know that? Do you know what they do to witches? They burn them!"

Blandine's voice went from quiet to quieter still. "Then it is all the more important for a man of your stature not to associate with me."

"I defend you and defend you, over and over, to my uncle, to everyone—" Kees began, but Blandine simply walked to her front door and opened it.

He thought of her as a yellow-haired school lass, their first innocent kiss. She had done so many amazing things since then. He admired her because she made her own way in the world. Not like him, under the thumb of his uncle. A dark thought occurred to him and then passed. How would he survive her rejection?

Kees retrieved his black felt hat. The door seemed a mile away.

"If you go down this road, you will be alone," he said. "Not even God will be with you."

"Then what kind of God would he be?"

In the street, Fantome nickered at his post. Kees passed Blandine in the doorway. He stopped and made as if to kiss her cheek. But she pulled her face away. He felt as though he might cry. A thing he had not done, he told himself, since his best dog died.

Along the street, moonlike faces at the windows, witnessing the humiliation of Kees Bayard. The girl, he swore to himself, would yet feel regret for her rejection. And the Englisher would be made to pay, too.

He knew just how to begin his campaign.

Once again, before anyone else, Tibb Dunbar knew. Prowling the alleys along the Strand, he encountered a sight that beggared his mind. The square-chinned nephew of the director general, a prominent figure in the colony and therefore someone whom Tibb instinctively avoided, stood beside his glossy black stallion, rummaging in his saddlebags and getting himself up in a costume.

A strange one, that, but one which the urchin recognized.

Witika.

The man masked himself in the little walkway behind the dwelling-house of his sweetheart sugarplum, Tibb's own meat-pie patroness, blond Blandina.

Yawks, the man had it all wrong. The mask was a stupid flour sack with a pair of black-rimmed eyeholes cut into it. Nobody was going to be fooled by that.

Tibb guessed the game. M'lord Nephew would play scare-the-lady. No better way to send a woman into your arms.

Suddenly Kees Bayard turned and caught Tibb staring at him from the shadows.

Vanish, Tibb thought. But he stayed. Maybe he should warn Miss Blandina. Flour sack or no flour sack, the beast actually looked pretty frightening.

Tibb's philosophy: lots of scary things in the world, but not many that were really dangerous.

"I'm going to a masquerade," Kees announced, his voice sounding muffled and uncertain behind the mask.

"I didn't say nothing," Tibb said.

"A masked ball," Kees said.

"All right," said the boy. When an adult was nervous, Tibb knew, it usually meant he was lying.

Kees jerked the flour sack off his head, displaying his handsome mug.

"Yawks," cried Tibb, putting on a look of terror. "Now you're scaring me."

Kees performed a quick lunge toward the boy, who by that time was no longer there, had never been there and would not be there again.

Blandine knew New Amsterdam intimately. Since she was a small girl, she'd had the run of it. She knew its nooks and crannies, its alleys and yards, which houses had hidey-holes in case of indian attack, which root-cellar doors were left open to trespass. The plan of the entire colony, river to river, wall to Strand, floated in her mind in perfect microcosm.

When Antony returned from guiding Lace and Mally home, she asked that he escort Kitane back to the Canarsie village. A childish restlessness possessed her, and she suddenly felt elated that she had the whole town to wander in.

She loved Kees Bayard. Or rather, the girl in her loved the idea of Kees that the girl in her had created. A sense of loss propelled her out into the cold afternoon.

Blandine knew exactly where she wanted to go. She headed west to the fort, turned north through the market grounds and found Bevers Gracht, the cross street that led to the canal.

It struck her as interesting that she had remonstrated with Kees for childishness and here she was, spooking around town like a school-girl. Blandine skirted along the side of the waterless ditch, fetid now at low tide. Then she left the street through a secret gap in a hedgerow and slipped through an orchard to Edward Drummond's backyard. The whole circuitous route was as natural to her as breathing.

She didn't recall how or why she knew where Drummond lodged. Had Visser told her? That morning after the moon-viewing, so exhausted with happiness, had the inhabitant himself pointed it out?

At any rate, she knew the place. Tamra Smith lived there when Blandine was young. Back then it had been a family dwelling-house, but it had long been chopped up into let rooms. She thought of going up to the front door and asking if Tamra were home.

The brick shed in back was a handsome addition. There appeared something tidy and well-used about the low one-story building. Blandine lifted the latch and stepped inside.

The interior of the workshop was still warm, although the fire had gone out in the stove. In the afternoon light the brass instruments gleamed like gold in a king's counting house. There it was, resting upon a velvet stand, the long perspective tube through which she and Drummond had peered at the moon. Other, smaller tubes, a whole collection.

She ran her fingers over the brass filigree of an astrolabe. Someday she might ask Drummond about the strange triangular device. She had seen them often in the hands of sailors on ships but never understood how one worked.

Glass. Plates of it, ornate globes made from it, rough-formed opaque lozenges. Shards of broken glass filled a whole wheelbarrow parked in one corner of the shed. Drummond had more glass than an ordinary person could dream of in a lifetime.

The man was rich, perhaps wealthier even than Kees Bayard. Blandine caught herself. She did not want her thoughts to trend that way.

She looked out the glazed windows of the shed to the rooms of the main dwelling-house across the yard. With immediate certainty, she realized that Drummond was not at home.

She was a spy. She left the shed, crossed the yard and tried the back door to the ground-floor rooms. Open. She had not been inside the place since her childhood friendship with Tamra Smith, who seemed so exotic because she was English.

Another Englisher lived here now. In the silent, deserted great room, the bricks of the fireplace were still warm, and embers glowed behind the fender. On a table in the corner, two cameos, by different artists, of two very pretty women. Blandine felt a flare of jealousy until she decided they must be Drummond's sisters.

She would meet them back in England. *Nan, Kate,* Edward would say gallantly, *I would like you to meet my new wife, Mrs. Edward Drummond.*

Please, please, m'ladies, call me Blandine, she would say in her best English, curtsying. And they would. It would be a great thing, the beginning of a deep friendship among the three of them. She always wanted sisters. She had but one, and lost her.

She caught herself. *Nan? Kate? Blandine, what are you thinking?*

An interior door led into the man's best chamber. Such a rare luxury, in the colony, a room dedicated only to sleeping. On the bed, she saw the bearskin robe, the one she had given him, flung over a feather mattress. The place smelled of bear and wine and tobacco and spices and the human male. Delicious.

She recalled seeing a perspective tube erected on the dwelling-house's roof, with a ladder leading up to it, so she went back outside (leaving everything exactly how she found it, except for turning one of the wig stands the opposite way to the wall).

Blandine wondered at herself. What was she doing? She climbed to the roof. The perspective tube was one of the smaller ones, a spyglass, really, the kind that Drummond said were mostly for military men to use. He had it mounted on a tripod and aimed into the town.

She bent down and put her eye to it.

An opaque blankness. She adjusted her gaze, and then the image popped into view. She could not tell exactly what she saw at first. With a sinking in the pit of her stomach she realized what it was.

Her dwelling-house. Her windows. Her rooms on Pearl Street.

Drummond had been spying on her.

Drummond hurried along the canal, crossed a bridge at Brouwer and headed down the street toward Blandine's dwelling-house. He felt upset and worried about what he had just seen through the glass.

Actually, the sight had been so strange, so unexpected, that Drummond mistrusted his own eyes. Standing on his rooftop, playing his spyglass over the ships moored in the East River road, he had suddenly swung around, on impulse, and searched out the two-story clapboard house on Pearl Street where Blandine van Couvering rented rooms.

A whim, really, nothing more. He had been thinking of the woman, and the spyglass simply represented a playful way to render her closer.

Bending himself to the eyepiece, he adjusted the aim until he fixed on what he wanted. But as Blandine's home swam into view, he found he had focused on something very different than a common unpainted Dutch dwelling-house. Standing in the backyard of the place, gloomed in by shadow, a figure stood motionless. Its tall, shapeless body was indistinct, but its face was clear enough, even to Drummond's sight from a quarter mile away.

Not a face at all, but a mask with blank eyeholes and a cruel slash for a mouth.

Drummond had never seen one before, but he felt sure he was looking at the witika.

Tall, towering, beyond any human stature. The being seemed to float without walking, moving forward.

Taking the rungs of the ladder three at a time, Drummond rushed downstairs, through his ground-floor rooms and out into the late afternoon hubbub of the street.

Halfway down Pearl Street, he met Antony and the river indian Kitane, coming along the other way.

"Is she home?" he demanded of the giant, nearly frantic.

Antony shook his head. "I don't know where she went," he said slowly. Distress appeared on his face. He was uncomfortable not being sure, for once, just exactly where Blandine van Couvering was.

"She told me to take Kitane home," Antony said, gesturing to the native.

"I saw something, I just saw something," Drummond said. "At her house."

"When?"

"Now!"

"You were there?" Antony asked.

"No," Drummond said. "Or, yes. I was looking through the perspective tube."

Antony pulled a long look at Drummond.

"It was the monster, the goblin thing," Drummond said.

"You saw the witika?" Antony said.

Kitane let out a moan. As much as any man with Lenni Lenape blood can pale, he paled. Then he bent at the waist and vomited over Drummond's shoes.

"By the bowels of Christ!" Drummond shouted.

"He's sick," Antony explained.

"No joking," Drummond said.

"He thinks he's being stalked by the goblin."

Drummond stomped the cruller puke off his feet. No one paid the trio any mind. The colonists had seen many men empty their stomachs in the street before. It was a common-enough occurrence.

One person who happened to be passing by did notice him. "Mister Drummond?" said his old *Margrave* shipmate Gerrit Remunde.

"We have to—Let's go!" Drummond said. He ran off toward Pearl Street, not waiting to see if Antony and the stricken Kitane would follow, leaving Remunde looking puzzled.

He found Blandine's dwelling-house empty, its mistress not at home.

In the yard behind her rooms, nothing. The afternoon shadows had cast themselves farther across the garden, that was all.

"The beast has taken her," Drummond said.

"No, no, she was just here with Kees," Antony said.

"Kees Bayard?"

"We were together not fifteen minutes ago, and then she sent us out."

Drummond and Antony searched the premises. The rooms, and then the garden. Kitane didn't help. He stayed seated on the back steps that led from the yard to the door into Blandine's *groot kamer*. He still looked queasy.

Antony and Drummond walked the yards, the paths behind the yards, the little narrow alley leading down toward the shore. Nothing. They returned to Blandine's garden empty-handed.

Antony stared at Drummond strangely. He didn't have to say what he was thinking.

"It was here, I tell you," Drummond protested. "It was this house, this yard. Look!"

He pointed northeast across the settlement. He could pick out his own rooftop, where the brass perspective tube propped on its tripod reflected a glint of the setting sun.

"Tell me," Drummond said. "Did Kees Bayard have time to dress himself up as the witika?"

"The witika is no man," Antony said. "No natural man, anyway."

Drummond paced the yard again, then bent down to examine the ground.

A series of impressions marked the soil along the edge of the yard, pushed an inch deep into a soft loam of the garden.

"Well, it wasn't the beast," he said, loud enough for Kitane to hear. "Or if it was, the creature wears European shoes."

22

Four dark-haired, dark-eyed children sat on the backless bench, their feet swinging well above the floor. Aet Visser had a small chamber off the *groot kamer* of his house, a waiting room of sorts for his orphans and their minders—anyone who needed to transact business with him on a given day.

Blandine had seen these particular legs dangle here before. Visser told her that they were all members of one family, fathered by a white colonist and an indian woman, then abandoned when the couple moved far up the river, never to be seen again. Her brusque dismissal of Kees (Blandine was afflicted with cruel second thoughts) coupled with Edward Drummond's baffling betrayal of her privacy had rendered her wholly out of sorts. Woebegone as she was, Blandine felt as though she should be sitting on the bench with the children. Bad little girl, bad!

The door to Visser's *groot kamer* remained closed. She wanted badly to see him. As ridiculous as she knew him to be sometimes, with his slurring, stumblebum ways and his too-rosy complexion, she needed him. He was the one she turned to, as close to a parent as she possessed since her own had perished.

Visser had maps pinned up on the walls of the antechamber. She always liked to peruse them, although she had little idea where on the globe the lands depicted lay. The soft greens and pinks and blues of the maps inflamed her imagination. She had often thought of commandeering a ship, any ship in the harbor, embarking for whatever realm to which the journey would take her.

Do it. Do it now. Get far away from this little settlement, so close and suffocating.

"Do you like the pictures?" said the handsome little boy at the end of the bench. He was probably about eight or nine.

"I do like them," she said. "Very much."

Next to him sat three girls, in descending order of years, with the smallest only about two or three. At this toddler's age Blandine had been safe in the arms of her mama, singing and waddling around in her warm wool jumper and insisting that she be able to fry the doughnuts in the kitchen alongside her mother. She was a big girl!

Blandine extracted a wedge of marzipan from her pocket and broke bits of it off to give the children.

"What is your name, sweetcakes?" Blandine said to the smallest.

"Tha-bean," the toddler said.

The biggest boy laughed. "She means 'Sabine,'" he said. "She don't talk too good yet."

"That's all right," Blandine said. "We will just call her 'the Bean.'"

"That's what we do call her!" the boy said. He leaned across to nuzzle his sister. "Our little bean."

"My name, Blandine," Blandine said to Sabine, pointing to herself. "Your name, Sabine. Sabine, Blandine."

The child gurgled happily.

Soon she had the girl on her lap. They sang a silly song together that Blandine knew from her own toddlerhood, about birds in the air and fish in the sea. Or rather, Blandine sang, and the little one mouthed an occasional word.

> *Dik-duk, dik-duk*
> *Ain't that how my little chick clucks?*
> *Kiss-kiss, kiss-kiss*
> *Don't my fishy-fish go like this?*

The blistering winter air had rendered the toddler's cheeks chapped and pink. The Bean gazed up at Blandine with her finger in her mouth, mesmerized and content.

Then Visser came out of the inner room with Lightning at his side. The orphanmaster appeared startled to find her there, although it was a regular-enough occurrence.

Aet Visser often seemed surprised, as though reality sprang events on him from wholly unexpected directions. Lightning pushed past Blandine without a word. He chucked the baby, who recoiled from him, and vanished out the door.

Standing behind the orphanmaster in the inner chamber was his servant, Anna, like Lightning another half-caste native.

"This is Anna," Visser said. "Anna is my helpmate, my house servant."

Blandine looked at Visser strangely. She had certainly met Anna many times before. Didn't Visser remember? Had his mind become totally addled by drink?

"I know Anna, Aet," Blandine said.

Anna smiled and nodded and gathered up her brood of chicks from the backless bench in the antechamber.

"Kiss-kiss, fishy-fish, kiss-kiss!" yelled the oldest boy in a mock-aggressive tone.

"Paulson," Visser said, calming the boy. Then, to Blandine's astonishment, he swept the toddler girl up into his arms, bussed Sabine's cheeks with kisses and deposited her in Anna's arms. She had never known Visser to be so demonstrative with his charges. His usual posture was one of affable remoteness.

"Anna takes them home for me, poor things," Visser said, a little embarrassed himself by his display. "Corlaers Hook. We heard the parents died from the hot sickness. No other family. Terrible times."

Blandine well knew Anna's story. An orphan herself, Anna had come under Visser's care very early in life. She now lived north of the town on the East River shore, from where she traveled each day. When she was not cleaning Visser's rooms, she took care of the four orphans Blandine had been regaling with nursery rhymes. They traveled to Corlaers Hook and back with Anna.

"Good-bye now," Visser called as Anna and the children left. "You will come tomorrow to clean house?"

Anna looked back over her shoulder, giving him an odd look, as did Blandine. Visser acted very strangely today. Perhaps it was not a good idea for her to come.

"I'm so glad to see you," Visser said. "I was just heading out the door to the Imbrock woman's wassail. Would you like to accompany me?"

"I don't know that I am in the mood for crowds," Blandine said.

"Nonsense," Visser said, bustling around for his muff and cloak. "You will know everyone there."

"That's what I'm afraid of," Blandine said. "All the familiar faces, with familiar tongues wagging in their mouths."

"Never mind, never mind," Visser said, ushering her out the door and closing up his dwelling-house behind them. "Saint Paul puts it this way, 'gossips and busybodies, saying things they ought not to.'"

Visser lived in the far corner of the colony. His makeshift dwelling-house, a crumbling heap of logs and clapboards, appeared ready to tumble into the East River. It had been in that state as long as Blandine could recall. Visser had lived in the place for twenty years, and rarely lifted a finger for its upkeep.

"You've had a bad day, dear," Visser said as they set off along the Strand. "I can tell."

As they passed through the town, Blandine declined the necessity of stopping at her home to change into party costume. "I will not stay," she said.

"The Imbrock boy will be there," Visser said. "Her orphaned nephew, one of my wards, actually, and the one who . . . you know."

"Was taken," Blandine said.

"Yes," Visser said. "Our only witness and, I'm afraid to say, never the most intelligent boy in the settlement." He lowered his voice. "I believe his wits are addled."

Sacha Imbrock kept her residence on the opposite end of Pearl Street from Blandine, just around the corner from Stuyvesant's Great House. She liked to think of her home as the pale reflection of the governor's great glory. The irregular bricks that clad its exterior walls showed almost black-red, demonstrating that they had come from the first brickyards in New Netherland, thus establishing the Imbrock clan's primacy in the pecking order of the colony.

December robbed the front garden of its color, but the canes still displayed plenty of thorns. Acclaimed within the community, assailed by a Puritan few as a frivolous gratuity, Sacha Imbrock's famous garden plot grew only roses, red, pink, white, yellow and flame orange. One or another of the blooms showed all summer long.

Visser mounted the shallow stoop with Blandine and lifted the heavy knocker, shaped like the head of a horse. The door swung open. For the first celebration of the Advent season, Sacha had decorated the front of the house with cedar boughs. Rushing Christmas, she knew, but she couldn't resist their soft needles or their fragrance.

The initial assault upon a guest's nostrils came from a huge ham that had been smoked, covered with dried fruits and baked all afternoon in the oven by the side of the hearth fire. Now it was given pride of place on the groaning board that greeted Blandine and Visser as soon as they walked in. Pink, fat-beaded slices taken by the other guests had reduced the joint by half. Daffodil-yellow butter lay mounded on the long oak table next to the ham, with crusty, slash-topped bread ready for the eating.

On the sideboard, smoked oysters and trout and hard crackers and onions and pickled pullet eggs.

Aet Visser lit up like a child in a candy shop. He hustled forward, not to the food but to the punch bowl. First things first.

The Imbrock main hearth-room opened onto a stairwell and another chamber, its curtained bed pushed to the wall to enlarge the space. The result was an irregular rectangle of perhaps forty English feet, peopled now with two dozen couples, assorted children and several specially hired servants.

Word was the director general might come, if only were it not that he suffered a slight stomach bloat.

Seated ladies balanced small china plates atop their jewel-toned petticoats, delicately biting on cubes of Holland gouda with white, mouselike teeth. Women as well as men brought long-stemmed pipes languidly to their mouths, an activity that showed off the polished gems with which they adorned their fingers.

The centerpiece of the evening, without a doubt, was little Ansel Imbrock himself, the witika survivor, trotted out by his aunt Sacha like a prize pony. The adults chattered questions at him and hung on his tongue-tied, yes-and-no answers.

Had he been ill-used? Did the witika feed on him? Was the beast terrible? Did its eyes shoot fire? Did it display its brazen nakedness?

Yes, no, yes, yes, huh?

Visser had his own reason for attending the gathering. Through his sources around the director general, the orphanmaster heard that Ansel had made an absurd charge against Visser. He was supposed to have led the orphan boy up the river to meet the witika. Since he, Visser, had a solid alibi for the time in question, Ansel's claim had tarnished the veracity of the whole story.

"I still want to know why the boy might have cooked up such a charge," Visser said to Blandine. But when they approached the crowd of partygoers around Ansel, the orphanmaster's nerve failed. He hesitated.

"Another time," he said, withdrawing back toward the *groot kamer*.

Blandine hung on Visser's arm as they circumambulated the room, punch cups in hand. Blandine noticed most of the guests looked rather quickly away when they saw her. Sacha Imbrock had not readily welcomed them at the door as she did other guests. At last, Blandine and Visser fell silent in a corner. He drank and gorged on punch and ham. She watched the people who were covertly watching her.

"Don't know if it's frostier inside or out," Visser said, taking a drink of his punch.

The matronly partygoers talked behind their hands about Blandine. Her rejection of a marriage proposal had instantly made the rounds. Who was she to throw over a man like Kees Bayard?

Martyn Hendrickson approached them, evidently the only guest with the confidence to do so.

"Miss Blandina," Martyn said, bowing. "Visser."

"Mister Hendrickson," Blandine said.

"What a story the boy has," Martyn said, nodding his head to where Ansel held court.

"Fantastic," Visser said, his mouth full.

"Yes, we plan to speak to him very soon," Blandine said. "To find out the particulars of his tale."

"I would be quick about it, if I were you," Martyn said. "He's about to disappear upstairs to bed."

"The poor boy must be completely worn out," Blandine said. "I wonder at his aunt parading him about."

A fiddler began to stomp out a rustic Scottish reel.

"Would you join me for a country dance?" Martyn asked.

The younger couples among the crowd eagerly took to the *groot kamer*'s cleared center space. The fiddler sang with a reedy voice:

> *I live by twa trades, sire, I live by twa trades*
> *If you ask me what they are, I say the fiddle and the spade*
> *The fiddle and the spade, sire, the fiddle and the spade*
> *One is for the landlord, the other is for the maid.*

As she and Martyn performed the steps, Blandine caught whiffs of her dance partner's French perfume mixed with body odor and the smell of brandy. The dissipated life. In spite of her reflexive dislike for Hendrickson, she felt sorry for him. All that glorious possibility, wasted.

"Where is your man tonight?" Martyn asked.

"Perhaps with his uncle," Blandine said. "They are very closely tied."

"No, no, I mean your English man," Martyn said.

Blandine colored. "I could ask you where your lady is, but I have the idea she may be down by the Strand," she said.

He laughed. "Miss Suzy does get around." And he spun Blandine in a circle that made her petticoats fly.

Aet Visser, too, had taken a partner, dancing with the hostess. But perhaps *dancing* was too fine a word for the man's wild flailing. Other guests broke off to watch him, unable to choke back their laughter.

As she left Martyn and came off the floor, Blandine thought of Kees. She recalled with fondness his childlike enthusiasm for dancing, and hoped she would not see him at tonight's wassail. Ordinarily she would attend a party like this with him. She imagined Kees coming into the Imbrock house, crossing the great room with Lilith Camber on his arm, or perhaps Maaje de Lang. Bitter, bitter, the betrayals of men.

Here came Maaje herself, pushed by others to be bold enough to approach her.

"Blandine," she said, ignoring Visser. "You are without Kees tonight?"

"And he is without me," Blandine murmured. Maaje, her courage all used up, simpered, turned and ran.

A smattering of applause broke out around the stairwell. They were sending the boy Ansel upstairs to bed, baffled and sheepish from all the attention.

"He will not sleep tonight," Visser prophesized. "I know him. He's something of a mooncalf."

Blandine's visions of Kees had unsettled her.

"I must go," she said.

"D'ye mind if I stay?" Visser said, his mouth crammed full of cake.

"You're ridiculous," Blandine said. "But you're good." She kissed him on his reddened, grizzled cheek.

Outside full dark had fallen, a pre-solstice winter dark, cloudy on this night and unilluminated by stars. Blandine proceeded along Pearl. She had never seen the town so emptied. It wasn't yet eight o'clock, but it felt like midnight.

Again the feeling crept across her that she had had in Beverwyck, of someone watching. She tried to shake it off but it only came on stronger. Every shadow in every doorway gave birth to a man.

In the harbor off the wharf, the carcass of an enormous porpoise floated, bumping up against the pilings of the pier. Waterfront rats jumped on and off the fleshy corpse, grabbing a morsel, leaping away, guzzling it down, going back for more. Much like the Imbrock sideboard.

Nary a soul around. She couldn't understand it. The Advent season normally featured much visiting and crowded streets, even late into the evening.

Blandine felt a hand on her arm. She startled and drew back. "Miss Blandina," a voice from the shadows murmured.

Martyn Hendrickson, her dance partner from the wassail.

"A dreary affair," he said. He wouldn't let go of her arm. "I had to leave. And you, I think, they drove away."

"I hate them sometimes," Blandine said.

"I hate them all the time," Martyn said. His sour breath washed over her.

"Heading for the Strand?" she asked.

"This way," he said, retaining his grip on her arm. He pushed her into a tiny alleyway that the settlers called the Box.

I can surely handle Martyn Hendrickson, Blandine thought to herself. If he doesn't break my arm.

"Demons abroad," Martyn hissed. "I would not want you harmed by them."

A tower of cooperage and wooden crates blocked their way. "I can take care of myself," Blandine said.

"Ah, yes, you are your own woman, aren't you?" Martyn said. "Nevertheless, the problem with looking for demons is that you very well might find them. Hmn, Blandina? Always looking into this witika business?"

She thought of Pim, warning her off the Africans. Kees, telling her to leave her concerns about missing orphans alone. Visser saying that her fears would be assuaged. And now Martyn.

She wrenched free, stepping backward to the street.

Martyn leaned toward her, and she flinched, but it was only to buss her cheek.

"Come by the house on Market," he said pleasantly. "I'll have the servants make sure you get a bundle of tea."

Martyn slipped past the heaped-up barrels and disappeared down the dead end of the Box. Blandine thought she knew every nook and cranny of the island, but evidently, Martyn Hendrickson knew a way out that she didn't.

A shaken Blandine hurried on her way, looking behind her repeatedly as she went. But Pearl Street remained deserted.

She approached her dwelling-house.

There, in the dim corner beside her stoop, a figure slouched, huge, taller than any man. As Blandine stepped back, it lunged forward. She choked off a shriek.

Antony. "I'm back," he said. "I saw Kitane safely home."

"You startled me," Blandine said. She realized the encounter with Martyn had thoroughly jangled her nerves.

"You have a visitor," Antony said.

Kees, Blandine thought. Come to renew his plea.

23

Edward Drummond waited for Blandine in the *groot kamer*. He jumped to his feet when she came in. He had been sitting in front of the fire, which he had let die to embers.

"I'm sorry," he said quickly. "Antony allowed me to come in."

Blandine crossed to her *kas* and put up her shawl. She didn't know how it would sound if she tried to speak, so she remained silent. Her heart and mind each pulled in several different directions of their own.

"I had to speak with you," he said.

"Drummond," she began. Not "Mister," not anymore.

"Please," he said. "Hear me out."

She hesitated, and then sat beside him by the hearth.

"I understand that you think me a superficial sort of man," he said. "That maybe I have tried too quickly to express my feelings for you, and you resented that."

"It would help if you did not try to tell me what I think or feel."

"What I want to say, if we could set all that aside, the misunderstandings that can develop between a man and a woman, what possibilities I might feel and you reject—"

"Drummond!"

"—If we could set all that aside," he said again, "there is a thing going on here, in this town, in this colony, and it's something important that needs to be dealt with."

Blandine's heart fell and rose at the same moment. Here she thought for a fleeting moment that perhaps she was going to get her second marriage proposal of the day, and instead the man was proposing only that they "set all that aside." All what?

But there were indeed strange happenings in New Amsterdam, events distressing and confusing, and her heart rose at the thought of someone else, some paladin arriving to help her deal with it.

"I saw something this afternoon that made me think you might be in danger," Drummond said.

"What was that?"

"A figure in your garden, in disguise, some sort of man or monster, very strange."

"You were here in my garden this afternoon?" Blandine asked, already knowing the answer.

"No," he said.

"Then how . . . ?"

"I happened to be looking through my spyglass," Drummond said.

"Your spyglass," Blandine said. "You happened . . . ?"

"I have one mounted on the roof of my house," he said. "To see the ships of the harbor, that sort of thing."

"Or to see through the windows of the women in the town. Were you spying on me, Drummond?"

"No! I mean, that's not what's important."

"That's the kind of thing we shall set aside, is that it?"

"Don't you see? Someone or something was in your garden! Today, this afternoon. And it looked like . . ."

"The witika," Blandine said.

"Or someone who meant you to think he was the witika," Drummond said.

Blandine leaned over and, elbows on her knees, stirred the embers in the hearth. The flames rose and illuminated her face. Her postures, thought Drummond, can be so like those of a rough-and-ready man, but her features . . . It was an intriguing mix.

"There are a lot of things going on right now, things you might not know about," she said. "Did you hear the African community is missing three children? They have disappeared. No one knows where they've gone. No one seems to care."

Drummond matched her with revelations of his own. He said, "Do you know Aet Visser believes one of his orphan children has been switched for another? And that the scene that the Imbrock orphan described seeing in the woods, the picture your director general painted so graphically from the pulpit on his day of penitence and fasting, is very close to the scene of a killing that happened in the north?"

"The Jope Hawes murder," Blandine said.

"Exactly," Drummond said. "There are a lot of pieces of a puzzle lying around and we seem to be the only ones interested in picking them up. How many children have died now? Three? Four?"

"I know of four gone for sure, either dead or disappeared," Blandine said.

"Maybe there's more."

"Maybe more."

They were silent for a long moment, both staring at the embers. There were cities revealed there among the coals, fiery foreign hells, countries of the damned.

"I propose we act together," Drummond said. "Let us make an alliance of two. I know what you must think of me. But stopping these killings is far more important than our opinions of each other."

Blandine could only feel that Drummond did not know the first thing about what she thought of him. And she realized her upset of earlier in the day over his intrusion on her privacy was hypocritical. How had she found him out? By trespassing on the privacy of his rooms.

"Blandine?" he said.

"I'm sorry, what is your first name?" she said. Another lie. She knew it well. Why was she acting this way? The man had come to her in good faith.

"Edward," he said.

"I think I am not yet worthy of your first name," Blandine said.

He seemed taken aback. "What do you propose?"

"I shall be Van Couvering to you, no 'Miss' necessary, and you shall be simply Drummond to me," she said. "I also propose that I make the alliance of two some hot cider."

"And we leave all that other business aside, Van Couvering?" Drummond said.

She looked him in the eye. Was there a hint of smile there? "We leave it aside," she said. She extended her hand.

They shook on it.

Ansel snuggled in bed with a pressed rose against his face. The dried flower was spindly, fragile, like a spider's web. It still smelled faintly of summer.

His auntie had given him many things. A home not the least. A toy boat. A picture book. But he remained an orphan. She had not been able to give him love, and for that he had to cast his mind back to the few years he spent with his mother. The memory of her faded like a pressed rose. He was left with a dim, half-remembered shape entering a room. But the soul of her, the feeling of her, stayed with him.

Mommy, Mommy.

Anse loved to smell his aunt's roses, the scent of which overwhelmed him during the season, going into or coming from the dwelling-house's front door. He was a sensitive child, and spent much of his time down at the Strand, dreaming over the voyages he would make someday. He never spoke to his aunt of such things, believing her to be a bit stern when it came to little boys such as him.

Aunt Sacha had an older son whom she did love. Rik Imbrock lived at home still, serving his apprenticeship, barely and only occasionally, to a shoemaker. Rik had a reputation for roughness. In battle with the Munsee he once drop-kicked the severed head of an enemy high over a breastworks like a Shrovetide football. Or so he said.

Anse tried to stay out of his way. Rik never seemed to smell the front-garden roses.

The boy laid the pressed rose beneath his pillow and squeezed his eyes shut. He could hear the voices of the adults, downstairs, the pounding feet of the country dance. The endless song of the fiddler kept going 'round and 'round.

> *Turn and turn again*
> *Now the handsome man, now the pretty maid*
> *We end as we begin*
> *Put down the fiddle and pick up the spade.*

Sleep would not come to Ansel Imbrock.

Behind the clouds, the blank sky of a new moon. The grounds of Petrus Stuyvesant's Great House lay in shadow.

For Lightning, since he was, or felt himself to be, a ghost, the task was quite easily done. The iron fence around the director general's residence proved no problem. He floated up and over it in a moment. He crossed the frozen grass, shuffling his feet to obscure his prints. He pressed himself flat between the face of a stone wall and a line of close-planted yew trees, a space no other human being would even notice existed.

Lightning's trespass represented mere boastworthy stuff. Proposing the scheme, the master cautioned that the Stuyvesant house was the most closely guarded in the colony. Lightning had not blanched.

"All the sweeter," he said.

It would be a coup, they both thought, and a mystery that would strike terror in the hearts of every person in the settlement, to sneak brazenly past the director general's domestic fortress with ne'er a how-de-do.

Lightning made the boy's yard. Inside, fiddle music, dancing, the vile recreations of the European long-noses. What he would have liked to do was walk through the door of the party and stride to the center of the floor. In all his half-breed glory. Maybe remove his hat for added effect. That would silence them.

He tested the stability of the rose trellis that ran up the side of the house. A few seconds later, he had scampered up it and was tugging at the bedroom sash.

As stealthily as mist, he entered the darkened room. Padding across it, he approached the sleeping figure.

Who proved, to Lightning's surprise, to be fully awake.

"Mommy!" the boy managed, and Lightning quickly fastened his hand to Ansel Imbrock's mouth.

It had been the master's idea. Yes, we first let the boy go, to bring back a report to the settlement, to frighten the colonists near to death. But then, how about this? We go back and steal the same boy! They would crap their pants!

In spite of himself, Lightning had laughed out loud. He noticed that the master said that "we" would resteal the boy, when really he meant Lightning would.

The master said, completing the joke, that he would be downstairs dancing as Lightning was upstairs kidnapping.

As it turned out, the boy proved so fear-stricken that he struggled not at all. Stiff as a board, in fact, which caused problems of its own. Halfway down the trellis, the wood laths gave way under their weight. Lightning thought the crash would reveal them, but the fiddle music covered all.

In the streets, a single late-night pedestrian straggled by, too stewed to notice that Lightning hauled a kid under one arm. The settlement barricaded itself in at night. Out of fear of the witika. Out of fear of him!

He poked through a loose log in the palisades wall, far away from either gate, reunited with his pony cart and carried Ansel Imbrock up the island to the Place of Stones.

His captive did not survive the journey.

Part Three

The Place
of Stones

24

It was Christmas season, and the boys at the Red Lion were telling director-general jokes. The knives gleamed in the rafters, with the pipe haze in the air making the gold in the hafts look like silver, and the silver in the blades look like gold.

Pim said, "So Milady Pukeface is doing a little country dance with the director general, see, at a holiday party or the like, and she says, 'Is it hard to dance with that leg of yours?' And Stuyvesant says, 'Which one?'"

Such "which one?" jokes were fast gaining currency in the colony. They would be lost on anyone not living under the iron hand of Petrus Stuyvesant, and they always had an identical punch line.

Rik said, "They was in bed, in the middle of their rut, and his girlie-love says to him, 'Oh, M'lord General, it's so long and hard!' And Stuyvesant says, 'Which one?'"

"That guy," said Martyn, "I'd like to take him down a peg or two."

Always well-hated not only in the settlement but in New Netherland as a whole, Stuyvesant in the winter of 1663 engendered outright hostility. Discontent veered toward open rebellion.

The man was just so damned high-handed. Stuyvesant's sins were manifold, chief among them a relish for draconian modes of punishment. For the theft of cabbages, he had a man's ears sliced off, "the better for him to resemble the bounty he stole." The gibbet, stocks and whips of New Amsterdam all saw steady use.

Add to that a prickly religious intolerance. The director general ordered a Quaker to hang suspended by his arms with heavy logs attached to his feet, afterward having the man chained to a wheelbarrow and whipped for days with a bull pizzle. Stuyvesant persecuted Lutherans and Baptists equally, refusing to recognize any religious entity other than the Reformed Church.

He taxed, demanded obeisance, conscripted troops. The Dutch in Patria had recently managed to throw off a yoke of tyranny, kicking out their Spanish overlords and establishing the Republic after eighty long, torturous years of war and resistance. That example lay fresh in the minds of the Dutch colonists of New Amsterdam. If their countrymen back home could do it, why couldn't they?

Ludwig Smits said, "The witika snatches Stuyvesant from his bed and drags him off into the woods. The beast proposes to eat M'lord General for dinner. 'I usually begin with a leg,' the witika says. And Stuyvesant says, 'Which one?'"

Ross Raeger heard the jokes, and knew what they meant.

"Stuyvesant is finished," Raeger told Drummond. The two of them sat in the little cubby off the Lion's second-floor stairwell landing. The holiday festivities in the taproom below seemed to have taken on a quality of desperation. A man had only a single throat down which to pour brandy. Much the pity.

Drummond agreed with Raeger's analysis. A politician, he thought, could survive unpopularity, scandal, mutiny, being caught with his hand in the till. Humor, no. Satire was the great killer of power.

"If we dance in here—" Raeger began.

"When," Drummond interrupted.

Raeger nodded, smiling. "*When* we dance in here, Stuyvesant will exhort the citizens to fight, brave Dutch stalwarts against the invading English. And he'll propose to give them a good stiff leg up their arse if they don't. To which they'll respond—"

"Which one?" Drummond said, and both men smiled.

Raeger had called Drummond over to the Lion for a coded letter, received from England on *Sea Serpent*, concealed inside a shipment of window glass. They were perhaps the only two people in the whole colony not talking about the Imbrock snatching: the poor orphan taken, terrorized, escaped, only to vanish again, disappeared from his very bed with the cream of New Amsterdam society wassailing just one floor below.

Drummond puzzled through the code in the letter Raeger presented to him.

"The king proposes to give us to his brother," he said.

"Us?" Raeger said.

"America. All land between the Connecticut and Delaware rivers."

"And New Netherland?" Raeger asked.

"The thorn is to be removed from the lion's paw." The letter, written in a simple cipher of transposed Latin, addressed Drummond personally, from Clarendon via his spymaster, George Downing. King Charles II grants colonial land rights in America to his brother James, Duke of York. Dutch rights to said lands negated.

"It's happening, then," Raeger said.

"It is," Drummond said.

"Do they deign to say when?"

"Well, you know how it works. The king puts his '*Carolvs Rex*' to a piece of paper in the Privy Council, and it's up to others to carry out his wishes."

"You and me, in other words," Raeger said.

"We are mere foot soldiers in a very large army," Drummond said.

"What would be your guess?"

"I don't know how and I don't know when," Drummond said. "If you put a pistol to my head and made me speculate, I'd say an invasion flotilla from England arrives here this summer."

He thought, suddenly, of Blandine van Couvering. What would she do when New Amsterdam went English? And how would she respond to Drummond's own role in an English takeover? Would he and Blandine— new allies—become enemies?

"I'll be out of a job," Raeger said morosely. "Maybe I'll stay on."

"In the king's hands, this town will boom," Drummond said. "I've never seen a better natural harbor anywhere."

At the end of Clarendon's letter, a two-word addendum: "*Crawley mort.*" So the regicide Drummond had tracked down to a Catholic town in Jura was no more. No details given, but he could imagine the scene. Three or four black-garbed assassins (there never seemed to be any shortage of such men) slipping into William Crawley's apartment at dusk. A struggle, the man overpowered.

Strangling was Clarendon's preferred method of dispatch, in order that the death-warrant signatories might experience some of what the executed king might have felt, pressure at the neck. Drummond often wondered how much the second Charles himself knew about the extermination of the regicides. Probably very little. He was, after all, the "merrie monarch." Clarendon did not think it necessary to trouble the king with the messy details of revenge carried out in his name. It just . . . happened.

And Drummond, did he feel guilt? After all, as the finger-man, he had fingered Crawley. Common law had it that he was as culpable as the men who actually did the deed.

But he felt surprisingly cool about it. Drummond once styled himself a Cartesian, and he saw the events in which he took part as a mechanical process, pure and ineluctable as the escapement of a clock. The moment Crawley placed his seal on Charles I's death warrant, the process began (this happened, then this happened, then this . . .), which led to Drummond's visit to Jura, which in turn led to those lean and hungry men making *their* visit.

Thought of the regicides made Drummond consider a task he had left unfinished.

"I have to go back to New Haven Colony for that damned trio of judges," he told Raeger. The crown never sent Raeger anywhere. They were content to have the man impersonate the role of a tapster, and post regular reports to London on the dispensation of the colony's troops.

"You can go by water this time, can't you?" Raeger said. "I don't think the harbor will ice in for a few weeks yet."

"I am relieved not to make the journey overland again," Drummond said. "The last time nearly killed me. I thought I would be eaten by bears."

Raeger said, "An unobtrusive little coastal sloop, you should be able to make New Haven in a day."

"After Christmas," Drummond said.

Carsten Fredericz made Blandine wait. She had come to the home of Miep and her parents on a simple holiday courtesy visit, but upon arriving had been treated coldly. Greeted at the door by Carsten, who then vanished and left Blandine standing alone in the family's great room.

The Fredericz dwelling-house had been enlarged, in the manner of many homes in the colony, with a second great room, the "best chamber" built directly on the other side of the chimney, doubling the size of the living space. In spite of indian attack and plague, horrible weather and failed crops, notwithstanding its own internal divisions, New Netherland thrived beyond anyone's expectations.

Blandine heard furious whispering from behind the best-chamber door. Carsten and his wife, Blandine thought, debating the suitability of their daughter associating with such a controversial figure as Blandine van Couvering. This after they had previously begged and begged Blandine to take their addle-minded daughter on as an apprentice.

The door of the best chamber swung open, and greeting Blandine was not Carsten, nor Miep, but the mother, Meike. "Miep won't be able to come out," she said.

"Ah," Blandine said. "I wanted to see her. I have a small Christmas gift for her."

"She is indisposed," Meike said. Blandine tried to imagine how a little snip of a girl like Miep Fredericz might qualify for the regal term *indisposed*. She noticed the mother could not meet her eye.

"Is she ill?" Blandine asked gently.

Carsten thrust himself into the room. "You'd best leave now," he said. Meike placed her hand on his arm, restraining him.

"It's just that I have a present for her. May I leave it?"

"No gifts from the likes of you!" Carsten said, almost shouting.

"Please, Carsten," his wife murmured. "Be civil."

Blandine tightened her blue shawl around her shoulders. As Aet Visser observed, a cold wind blew through the New Amsterdam colony, both outside and inside the dwelling-houses. She turned to go.

"I also have her wages," she said.

Carsten struggled with himself, cupidity and the question of appearances battling it out. "Wait," he said. "Perhaps . . ."

"I would wish to count her out the money myself, in person," Blandine said, and she stepped out through the front door, closing it behind her.

The Fredericz family lived on Tuyn Street, so Blandine turned alongside the canal to head toward her own home. High tide filled the ditch with seawater from the East River, and down below her a few merchants pulled their boats into the narrow canal, one maneuvering a barge piled high with hay. Blandine proceeded quickly, walking into the sharp wind off the harbor.

"Miss! Miss!" a small voice called from behind her.

Miep. Blandine allowed herself an inner smile. Cupidity had won out after all.

Blandine and Miep took mulled autumn cider together at the hearth in Blandine's rooms, the girl stammering and hesitant. "They told me to come right back," Miep said.

"After you collect your wages," Blandine said.

"Yes," Miep said. She savored the cider, though, so warming after the chilly walk through the settlement.

"Do you know the Godbolt children, Miep? George and Charles, Mary and Ann?"

"Georgie. They call him Georgie."

"All right," Blandine said. "You went to school with them?"

"The boys are nice enough," Miep said. "But the little girls are rude."

"It's usually the other way around," Blandine said. "And William, the orphan they keep as a ward, do you know him?"

"No."

"No?"

"He is impossible to know," Miep said. "He doesn't speak."

Blandine leaned over to the hearth and poured Miep another helping of cider.

"I should go," Miep said. "They said . . ."

"If I told you of a way to help William, would you do it?"

The girl looked at her doubtfully. "I don't believe what Mama says."

"What does Mama say?" Blandine asked.

"She says you truck with the Devil."

"You and I both understand that can't be true," Blandine said. "You know me well enough, don't you, Miep?"

"You treat me better than they do," Miep said petulantly. "At least you believe I can do things."

She seemed on the verge of tears. Blandine took Miep's head and laid it on her shoulder, petting the girl's hair.

"Tell me, Miep," Blandine said. "Will you help William Turner find out about his real parents?"

* * *

When the *schout* read the prisoner lists, he cited Corporal Jeffrey Shire as convicted of public drunkenness, sentenced to "ride the wooden horse" for an afternoon, two o'clock to close of parade, in the concourse to the north of the fort. The horse in question wasn't an animal at all, but a wooden rail made to wedge uncomfortably up the guilty man's crotch and carried by six husky soldiers.

Stay astride the "timber mare" long enough, and you would feel yourself half split in two. The tailbone would sometimes shatter, and at any rate, sitting down with any comfort would prove impossible for weeks. Shire had a heavy musket tied to each leg for extra weight, a fitting touch, since he had discharged his own firearm several times in the course of a drunken night of revelry, thus disturbing the public peace.

Director General Stuyvesant, his nephew Kees Bayard and Kees's friend the resplendently wealthy Martyn Hendrickson gathered together with other colony worthies to witness the commencement of Corporal Shire's punishment. Not for any enjoyment they might get from the spectacle—Stuyvesant, at least, never seemed to derive joy from any experience whatsoever—but merely to add to the sense of public humiliation.

The punishment took place in a location worthy of spectacle, directly below the towering earthen ramparts of the fort, in front of the elegant housefronts of Stone Street and Market Street.

"He should be shorn, he should be shorn!" called out Stuyvesant, seeing Shire's straggly hair spill down over his shoulders. The *schout* had one of his boys scramble up the horse, a good twelve feet high, and scrape the man's head with a dull razor.

"Taking it well," Martyn said, smoothing his doublet. He wore his own hair long and wavy, but due to his family's standing in the colony, no one dared criticize him. "At least he's not whimpering."

Stuyvesant paced, his false leg sounding an uneven rhythm on the packed dirt of the parade ground, leaving an odd track in its dirty covering of snow. "He's a soldier," he said. "Pain for a soldier should be mother's milk."

The director general knew the intimate contours of pain, thoroughly and indelibly. In an engagement with the Spanish on the Caribbean island of Curaçao, almost a decade ago now, a papist cannonball screamed through the air to tear off his right leg. He leaned on his sword, staring downward. Nothing remained but tatters and bloody shreds, no foot, no shin, just a tangle of dangling, threadlike nerves, veins and arteries.

He sank his stump into the sand of Blauwbay Beach and woke up a few hours later on a surgeon's table aboard his flagship. What followed were agonizing months—years, really—of recovery, learning to walk again with the ridiculous peg they fashioned for him, every step pure torture.

So don't talk to him about pain.

Newly shorn and properly righted, Corporal Shire felt his timber mare hoisted by six strong men, quick-marching around and around the parade ground. By the tenth round, he began to let out short, propulsive moans on the downstroke of each stride. Blood showed on his trousers.

"He bleeds like a woman," Martyn noted.

"Uncle," Kees said, "there may be more barbering to be done in your jurisdiction."

"Yes?" Stuyvesant said. He made ready to leave the parade ground, where dozens of spectators had now gathered to jeer at the corporal. Shire knew many of them. He didn't blame them. He would have jeered, too, were he in their place. But Stuyvesant certainly didn't have time to see the man endure the whole four hours of his punishment.

"A long-haired Englisher," Kees said, "by the name of Drummond. Needs to be cut down."

"Drummond?" the director general said. "Why do I keep hearing that name?"

He looked around. "Godbolt!" he shouted, summoning the man from where he stood with a group of scarlet-heeled grandees. George Godbolt hustled over.

"Weren't you talking about one of your countrymen by the name of Drummond?" the director general said.

"Yes, M'Lord General," Godbolt said, bowing his head to show his deference.

"A papist, I think," Kees said. "Or at least, definitely of the English royalist faction. Wears his hair like a lion's mane, imitating his High Mightiness."

"*Ex more,*" Stuyvesant said. "No crime in that."

"Against none but fashion," said Kees, and Godbolt laughed.

Stuyvesant did not join in. "I've made inquiries," he said, "and Drummond seems to be a simple grain merchant. Enterprise is to be encouraged in the colony, by landsmen and foreigners alike."

"A grain merchant who has never made a trade," Kees said.

"He does nothing but sit and toy with his glass lenses and perspective tubes," said Godbolt. "He has a spyglass mounted upon the roof of his dwelling-house."

"Has he?" the director general said.

"For what the purpose? We have to ask ourselves," Godbolt said.

Interesting, Martyn Hendrickson thought. He himself had often wished for the ability to focus on people's activities without their knowledge.

"As you, Godbolt, can attest, we have many English friends," Stuyvesant said. "At times I feel my own countrymen turn against me, claiming no responsibility for the settlement's defense beyond that of their own single homes. But the English residents in my jurisdiction I can always count upon. In the late Esopus war, I asked for volunteers and got four Dutchmen and forty Englishers."

Godbolt stared at his feet. He had not been among the forty.

"There are Englishers, and there are Englishers," Kees said. "All I suggest is that Drummond's activities warrant looking into."

"This is perhaps a private affair between you," Stuyvesant said. Kees's mother, the director general's sister, had complained of Kees being thrown over by the Van Couvering girl for this Drummond fellow.

"He is in constant communication with factions in New England," Kees said.

"Is this true?" Stuyvesant asked, his interest pricked at last.

"I could shed some light on this." Martyn smiled. "Soon after he arrived in the colony, Mister Drummond made a journey up the North River and stopped for a visit to our patent. He spent a night with my brothers on the estate, went to Beverwyck and then continued on east, to New England."

"Why wasn't I told about this?" Stuyvesant said.

"It didn't seem important at the time," Martyn said. He examined his fingernails. "Drummond said he needed merely to purchase some horseflesh, and our plantation proved the most likely place to do that."

"And he went on to Massachusetts?"

"New Haven Colony, I think," Martyn said.

"Tell me why a grain merchant would visit New Haven," Kees said, "where they grow no wheat, and import none to make beer."

"I want to add in one other thing, if I may, M'Lord General," Godbolt said. "Full moon last, November third, on the night of the day that Ansel Imbrock was first taken, this Drummond was seen coming in through the land port at dawn. At dawn, M'Lord General. He came from parts north. He carried with him some equipment, or perhaps weapons, in concealing boxes."

Corporal Shire shrieked in pain as one team of carriers dropped the wooden horse to the ground, with another team immediately taking it up again.

"Thank you, gentlemen," Stuyvesant said. "I must take this all under advisement."

I will put a runner on him, the director general thought. One of the Pavonia indians, perhaps. This man Drummond needs looking after. Stuyvesant turned his back to leave the parade ground just as the screaming corporal rode by.

The gentleman in the scarlet heels proceeded through the settlement to the wharf district, where he entered into the mazelike, chockablock neighborhood of huts and cabins bordering on the pier warehouses.

He passed along the back of a teetering clapboard dwelling-house that was originally two floors but which was now collapsing into one. Lashed to the leeward side of this structure, scaling up a moldy, weathered wall of rotting wood, a stairway led to what was left of the upper story. The winds off the river smelled strongly of decay, and the whole effect was one of enduring poverty and neglect.

The gentleman knocked at a board-and-batten door at the top of the stairs and entered without waiting. Inside all was gloom and damp. A woman sat bent over a rickety table at a window. Another form, older, more decrepit, could barely be discerned beneath the covers of a moth-bitten bed in the opposite corner.

"Do you have them?" the gentleman asked.

"They are finished," said the woman at the window. She was young, although you could barely see it, bundled as she was against the winter cold. Beneath a knitwork cap her eyes shone clearly, gray and alert. Only a few sticks of firewood lay beside the smoky fire in the hearth.

With fingerless leather gloves she lifted a small box from her table. His eyes fell on the gobs and dabs of color on a palette that lay before her, next to the handful of brushes that seemed to be all she had to conduct her business. Spread around the room, laid out on every surface, drawings on planks of wood.

These painted portraits, likenesses of the good citizens of New Amsterdam, served as the only amelioration of the depressing atmosphere. The gentleman recognized a few of his acquaintances, figured among the art. They had been commissioned for a few stuivers each from the petite, ragged woman standing before him, the colony's lone portraitist, Emily Stavings.

In any other part of the world, it would be considered outlandish for a female to render pictures of people, landscapes, anything. Women simply did not enter the trade. But here on Manhattan the Dutch gave women freedom to become artists alongside men, just as they were encouraged to act as merchants or ship factors. For Emily, portrait-painting was not a vocation so much as a calling.

The gentleman opened the box Emily gave him. Inside, fitted into an ingenious series of slots, pieces of glass gleamed in the dim light. The gentleman eagerly attempted to extract one and pricked his finger in the process. He swore an oath.

"Yes," Emily said. "I have cut myself, too. You have to hold them like this, do you see?"

She held one of the glass lozenges by its edges. The gentleman had himself provided the small transparent rectangles to her, each one inch by three, not lenses but window glass. She would never have had been able to afford the precious material herself.

The gentleman took the shard from her, crossed to the window—parchment, he noticed, not glass—and held it up to the fading afternoon light.

An image of a demon stared out at him.

"Very fine," he said. "You have the detail exactly." Some blood from his pricked finger smeared on the miniature.

"I had difficulty getting the paint to stick to the glass," Emily said. "I finally discovered if I mixed the pigment with glue, that would do."

With increasing excitement he went through the slides one after another. "Some would say you have this business almost too well. As though you have met up with Old Scratch himself, perhaps bargaining for your soul."

Emily shook her head. "I merely executed what you told me." It had been the strangest commission she had ever received, on a surface she had never tried. She could not understand to what use the final product might be put.

With a shiver she recalled the gentleman coming to her with the job. She welcomed the work, any work, and was extremely adaptable as to subject. She could not afford to be picky. These were like miniatures, and she had done miniatures many times before.

What troubled her was the trance that the gentleman entered into when he described the pictures he wished Emily to paint upon the individual pieces of glass. In a spill of words he described fangs, glaring eyes, fierce claws. His respiration became rapid, his eyes glazed over.

But he had promised her a full guilder in advance, and another upon completion of the work. Not seawan, either, but real coin. Now he seemed quite happy with the result, and carefully reinserted the slides into their slotted box.

"You will come to see your pictures displayed?" he asked.

"Oh, no," Emily said. "I have Mother." She indicated the lump of blankets on the bed.

"Perhaps it is better," the gentleman said. "You will speak to no one about this."

A command, not a question. Emily reached out and patted the man's breast, smiling a desperate smile. "Is there anything else I could do for you?"

The impulse seemed an inexperienced stab at the coquettish, the effect, the exact opposite. The man reached hurriedly into his purse. "Thank you, no. I must leave."

"I don't know if you saw," Emily said. "The image of the Lord Christ Our Savior?" She tapped the open box, indicating the last painted-glass slide in the bunch.

"Yes?"

"I rendered him with your face."

He gave her two guilders instead of one. She looked at the gold in her hand and impulsively reached out to embrace him, smearing his cheek with an awkward kiss.

The gentleman appeared horrified. Grabbing his little box, he fled down the rickety stairs as though he were pursued by the very demons Emily had painted upon the rectangles of glass.

25

Aet Visser liked to visit the work yard on High Street, behind Missy Flamsteed's taproom on the Strand. He'd pass out dried fruit, talk with his wards, attempt to convince the ones who were not under his authority to come inside the fold. Sometimes he brought his strange half-indian companion, Lightning, with him, other times other men in scarlet heels.

Tibb Dunbar, also known as Gypsy Davey, made himself scarce during such visits. He counseled his High Street followers to do the same.

"They ain't no friends of ours," he growled, talking about Visser, Lightning, adults in general, scarlet-heeled or not.

Not all boys listened. An orphan child named Dickie, sickly and meek, newly arrived in the colony, did not know enough to wipe the dirty snot off his face, much less how to negotiate the perils and pitfalls of a parlous world.

Dickie was seen leaving the work yard with a gentleman who some said was Aet Visser and who others swore was the half-indian Lightning. It didn't matter. The two of them, the orphanmaster and his shadow, who all the orphans called "the Crease" for the ugly runnel on his head, were thick as twins.

"They probably promised him a Christmas gift," Tibb Dunbar said, taking a deep suck on his pipe. "We won't be seeing little Dickie again."

And they didn't.

Sinterklass—Santa Claus or Saint Nicholas—came to New Amsterdam in early December, arriving with a ship that sailed all the way from Patria laden with toys and other gifts. Children laid out their shoes on the hearth the night of December fifth. The next morning, they would find them filled with nuts, sweets and, for a fortunate few, gold coins.

Sinterklass himself rode slowly down the Broad Way and along Pearl Street on a stolid white mare, fairly gleaming in his long, draping robe, pearly beard and tall red bishop's hat and miter, brandishing a golden crosier with a curled top. He had apples for everyone, hard candy, frosted nuts.

But these treats were only a precursor to the grand feast celebrated the following day, December sixth, when wealthier colonists served roast goose and potatoes and *kool slaw* drenched in vinegar and melted butter. Sinterklass was the patron saint of children, doling out gifts to the well-behaved, though everyone got their share regardless of how naughty they had been.

Each child knew the story of the three little orphans during a terrible famine, how a malicious butcher lured them into his house, slaughtered and carved them up, then placed their remains in a barrel to cure, planning to sell them off as ham. Saint Nicholas resurrected the three boys from the barrel by his prayers, bringing the orphans magically back alive through the power of faith.

The spirit of the season ruled New Amsterdam between the Feast of Sinterklass on the sixth and *Kerstydt*, Christmas, on the twenty-fifth. The director general, who made clear his disgust with any drunken carousing during the holidays, yet made his Great House ablaze with candles and invited colonists in to dance in the entry hall.

But the mood this year was on the whole muted. Murder dampens the spirit.

Young Peer Gravenraet had only recently reached the age when he could be about outside after dark, at least in his home neighborhood of Beaver Street. The family lived in a new three-bay house overlooking the canal, with two proud chimney stacks. Passing his twelfth birthday gave the son of Femmie and Aalbert Gravenraet the freedom he coveted. During the day, his parents allowed him the run of the settlement, river to river, palisade to strand.

And then, suddenly, just this holiday season when it would have been so great to roam wild, the newly earned freedom was withdrawn. His mother sat him down.

"Peer, my darling, your father and I are going to say, just for now, that you must remain close to home," Femmie said.

"Why, Mother?"

Femmie looked at him sharply. He was not yet of the age where he could ask why.

"There are evil doings in the colony, things you know nothing about," Femmie said.

Things Peer knew nothing about? Of course, he knew everything about everything. His mother didn't know half what he knew.

"Children have gone missing," Femmie said. Yes, yes. The Imbrock boy, so stupid he wouldn't be able to find a button on a shirt.

"An indian demon is abroad," she continued. I know all about that, too, Peer thought smugly. The witika. Whoo-ooo! Peer owned a penknife. He'd like to see the witika try anything on him.

Then Femmie said, "A witch lives within the palisade." Hello. What's that all about? Peer needed to know more, much more, such as what was the woman's name. A witch! He'd like to get some of his friends together, they would go make a visit, toss some stones at her window, get her to show her long-nosed face.

Kidnappings, demons, witches. That was that, as far as Femmie and Aalbert Gravenraet were concerned. Peer's roaming privileges were curtailed.

"It is only for now," Femmie said, attempting to tamp down her son's tendency toward rebellion.

He thought to argue. I am not an orphan, Peer could have told Femmie. The witika takes only orphan children. So how am I in danger?

He knew what would happen if he raised that objection. A hard-knuckle rap on the head, and an admonition not to talk back to his elders, who knew better than Peer did.

It seemed all the mothers had conspired to rein in their children. Peer's friends had the "talking to" also. None of them had the freedom any longer to go abroad after dark.

"Mother?"

"Yes, Peer?"

"May I still go to the Kerstydt Eve pageant? It is just down at the Stadt Huys. I told Rem we would go together."

"You will go with me and your father."

No appeal. Peer would not be allowed to dash freely through the meeting-hall after Roose van der Demme. No horseplay. He'd be under the thumb—and within reach of the hard knuckles—of his parents.

"There is to be a fright show of the Devil," Peer said.

"Who told you that?"

"The crier said it."

Oyez, oyez, Peer heard the town crier call that noonday, *a Christmastide entertainment in the Stadt Huys, come one, come all, at evening drumbeat.*

"Well, maybe there will be, and perhaps good boys who behave may see it, in order to have some sense scared into them. But no roistering about. Promise, Peer?"

"I promise, Mother."

So it was not until Christmas Eve that young Peer ventured out of doors after dark. The sky over the great bay to the west held the last fading light. Stars winked on overhead. Crowds of settlers streamed toward the Stadt Huys. Snow settled on the peaked rooflines.

Peer blew out his breath, experimenting with the various ways it frosted in the cold air, and tugged his parents forward. He was overjoyed to be out. He had the feeling of urgency, of a great event unfolding.

Hurrah for Christmas! He is born!

No wind, but the colonists beside Peer still cupped their hands around their tapers as they proceeded down Beaver Street, merging into another current of people at Pearl. The men wore heavy fur muffs and the women warm capes with close hoods. As families left their dwelling-houses to make their way to the Stadt Huys, Peer could see inside their rooms, a flickering golden light of many candles.

Dogs ran wild, snuffling the new snow and barking at the holiday commotion. The Stadt Huys loomed above Peer, a thousand stories tall.

First, the carolers. A Christmas hymn. Then a Bible homily, "Joy in Our Hearts," Isaiah 9:2–4, Titus 2:11–14 and Luke 2:1–16. A segment of a passion play, acted out by characters in costume.

"The time has come," intoned Wilhelm Ruden, dressed as Lord Jesus, "for the lamb to return to Jerusalem to accomplish that which has been foretold."

As the Christmastide pageant proceeded, the great Stadt Huys meeting-hall became close, its air clogged with tobacco smoke and human exhalations. Three-legged stools had been arranged near the mammoth hearth, where a yule log the size of an ox smoldered.

It seemed as though all of New Amsterdam were there. The women's cloaks dragged on the floor as they composed themselves, and the men sat squarely, their hats in their laps. Most were a bit sleepy, having over-indulged on the day's slices of venison, stews of hare and roasted sweet potatoes, with well-crusted bread and rich, dense cheeses to accompany it all.

Aet Visser, for one, drank too much gin at the Lion before meeting with Anna to escort her and the children to the show. To Anna's dis-comfort, Lightning accompanied Visser. Kees Bayard stood at the back of the hall. Martyn Hendrickson leaned against the wall beside him, his glittering eyes surveying the audience.

In the crowd, Martyn picked out Polish laborers and Swedish arti-sans. A small clot of Africans, attending with a few friendly Canarsie *wilden* from Long Island. The Godbolt family. Martyn could see the girl Hannie, the one who had relayed stories of the witika in the clearing in the woods. And Maaje de Lang, accompanying the soon-to-be-wed Elsje Kip. Off in the far corner, looking typically supercilious, Edward Drummond, sitting so as to display his green-stockinged legs.

Set thy best foot forward, recalled Martyn, thinking of the "which one?" jokes current in the colony.

Beside the Englisher, Blandine van Couvering, veiled and hooded, since at present she was in bad odor in the community. A face that pretty, thought Hendrickson, should not be obscured. Her figure, too. Strong as a pony with good little muscles.

Also in the audience, orphans. They had been much on the colony's mind lately, and the room was full of them. The twins, Sebastian and Quinn Klos. Waldo Arentsen, a little towheaded boy. The silent one with the Godbolt children. Tara Oyo sitting among the Africans. Dirty-faced Laila Philipe, beside her fellow foster-child Geddy Jansen. Yes, and the child-rogue they called Gypsy Davey.

The passion performance finished up, with Wilhelm-as-Jesus pro-claiming, "If any would come after me, he must deny himself, take up his cross, and follow me. For whoever wants his life will lose it, but whoever loses his life for me will find it. What good is gaining the world, if you lose your soul?"

Well, thought Martyn, the good is, you have the world.

Dominie Johannes Megapolensis assumed his place in front of the audience. "Satan!" he shouted. The chatter of the crowd immediately died.

"The Devil," Megapolensis continued in his stentorian tones. "Beelzebub. Lucifer. Accursed Dragon. Old Scratch. Old Harry. Foul Spirit. Master of Deceit."

The dominie glared around the huge hall, raising his arms. "I would like to introduce you to the Evil One tonight, since this is the black night before the birth of him who slays all evil, Our Lord Jesus."

"Amen," murmured members of the audience.

"Please snuff your candles," Megapolensis said. "Go ahead. For the Prince of Darkness will only appear in darkness."

The room dimmed as one after another the tapers were extinguished. The women blew out their candles, whereas the men pinched the glowing wicks between their spit-wet fingers. Claus van Elsant, funeral caller principally but the colony's jack-of-all-trades, went around to each of the hall's oil-lamp sconces and cupped them out.

The only light came from the hearth, and the embers of the dying yule log, which had been burning since mid-December but was now nearly consumed. A child whined and was shushed. The muffled sounds of two hundred human souls could not fully dispel the darkness.

They were already frightened, and the show had not even begun.

"Have you seen him in your dreams?" the dominie intoned, a voice in the night.

The black dark, complete. Suddenly, against the white plaster wall that faced the hearth, a shimmering image. A crimson-colored face, black scowling eyes, horns growing from the scalp like knife blades.

A woman—Gertrude Pont—screamed. Low moans.

The image flickered out. Darkness again. A frightened murmur rose from the crowd. Had they just seen what they thought they had seen? Had the Old One actually appeared among them?

Now, in another place, another monstrous image. A man, a Dutch man in a waistcoat and breeches, materialized, and crouched on his back, feasting upon the man's brains with long, venomous fangs, a teeth-gnashing demon.

More moans, a scraping of the three-legged stools upon which the burghers sat with their wives, children whimpering helplessly.

"Jesus save us!" came the cry.

"He stalks among you!" shouted Megapolensis.

In the darkness, a few skeptics. Martyn Hendrickson and Kees Bayard exchanged knowing smiles, their teeth gleaming.

On and on it went as panic rose in the hall, one fiendish image after another. At each display, wails rose and fell like sirens. One of the brave bachelors present bent over and vomited. Audience members stumbled over one another in the dark, trying to find the exit.

Gradually, the images changed. The skin color of the demon went from red to green. The monster got gaunter, hungrier. Taller, with longer hair.

It was Hannie who blurted out the name first. "The witika," she shouted, and soon the whole crowd took up the cry. Wives fainted, plummeting to the broad floorboards without their husbands being able to help. The whelps, Tommy van Elsant, Peer Gravenraet and their friends, turned into sobbing babies. They blundered for escape.

"Hold!" said the dominie. "Courage! Courage! For the Prince of Peace doth come."

But it was too late. Shrieking, weeping, rushing out alone or dragging their loved ones with them, the residents of New Amsterdam performed a wholesale retreat from the Stadt Huys fright show.

The dominie was there to announce the last of the images, the last of the glass-slide paintings by Emily Stavings, projected upon the wall by the new invention of the magic lantern.

The magic lantern. Just a lens with a light behind it, but if you have never encountered it before, wondrous, frightening.

Jesus finally appeared, yes, the Son of God displayed on the white plaster wall. With a familiar face. But the glass upon which the image was painted quickly cracked.

"Light! Light!" called Megapolensis.

He, too, rushed out of the room, a shepherd pursuing his flock.

Claus van Elsant lit the wicks of the oil lamps. Their faint glow reil-lumined the hall.

Only five people were left in the room. The funeral caller, labori-ously completing his job of relighting the lamps. Martyn Hendrickson and Kees Bayard, observing the room-clearing enterprise with evident satisfaction. Tipped stools and knocked-over chairs everywhere.

Near the door, observing the other two observers, Blandine van Cou-vering and Edward Drummond. When Kees saw Blandine with the other man, his face went pale and his thin smile vanished.

Blandine nodded to Kees and led Drummond out of the hall.

Outside, in the street, Peer Gravenraet held tightly to his parents. He wished he could have climbed into his mama's arms.

The settlers hurried to their homes, still struck by fear over what they had seen. The panic affected them differently. Some wept. Others chattered or giggled self-consciously. But they were all eager to dive into warm beds and duck their heads under their feather coverlets, anxious to drown themselves in the black sea of sleep.

Beaver Street lay deep in shadow, so when Peer's foot kicked the foot that lay in his path, he did not at first think what it was. But Aalbert erupted with a "God's faith," and a neighbor couple, the Nattersons, pulled Peer away from the grisly find.

A child's foot, chewed ragged at the ankle.

"Witika," Femmie said, stepping back from it.

"Call for the *schout*," Michael Natterson said.

Peer buried his face in the folds of his mother's gown.

26

"How many of them have died?"

Blandine and Edward stood on the New Bridge over the canal, a common meeting place for wealthy burghers, but deserted this Christmas morning after the fright-show hangover from the night before.

Antony sat a few feet away, squatting at the bridge steps and tossing stones into the canal. Across the river the hills of Breukelen rose, iced by snow sugar.

"How many? Would you like an inventory, Drummond?" Blandine asked.

"It might help, Van Couvering," Drummond said.

"Died or just missing?"

"Both."

"All right," Blandine said, beginning to count on her fingers. "Piteous Gullee."

"No, first the Hawes boy, up north."

Drummond tamped tobacco into a Belgian-style pipe and lit it. At Raeger's behest, he had taken up smoking. The aroma floated over to Blandine, triggering an intense desire to indulge, which she fought back. Below them in the canal, the tidewaters flowed in, creeping up the ice-crusted ditch a little at a time.

"Then there's the scene described by Hannie de Laet and Hans Bontemantel," Blandine said.

"The young lovers. Let's just say, in that instance, victim undetermined."

"I guess that could be the place where Piddy was killed," Blandine said.

"Or some other child, unknown."

"There's Bill Gessie and his sister, Jenny, who never came back. And Ansel Imbrock, taken but not killed, then retaken. Then this new one."

"The random stray foot," Drummond said.

"Definitely a child's."

"And fresh."

"Ugh," Blandine said.

"I mean only that he or she had been recently killed. Who is missing in the past few days that we can match with a stray foot?"

"I haven't yet confirmed with Aet. But that's five, or six, depending."

"You forget one," Drummond said.

"Who?"

"I don't know for sure. But there is the situation of William Turner. The Godbolts' ward."

"That's just a question of identity, isn't it?" Blandine said. "Not murder."

"But say Aet Visser is right. Say William Turner is not William Turner. Doesn't that leave us with another missing child? If the real William does not live with the Godbolts, then where is he?"

"So we have . . ."

"Jope Hawes, a Dutch son with two parents living," Drummond said.

"I heard tell that the father died. But after the son's murder," Blandine said.

"Two orphans taken, both Dutch. Perhaps a third."

"Three African children," Blandine said.

"Were any of them orphans?"

"Yes, all of them."

"And all under the age of ten," Drummond said.

"Well, the Hawes boy was twelve," said Blandine. "And finally William Turner. That makes seven."

"Orphans and Africans," Drummond said. "Can you think of what they might have in common?"

"I can," Blandine said. "I have thought about this. They are both highly vulnerable in the colony."

"But perhaps it's just a crime of opportunity," Drummond said.

"Isn't that the same thing? Do you mean that Africans and orphans both get around more than other children?"

"Out and abroad? Working? Less supervision? Lax guardianship?"

"One might think so," said Blandine archly, "unless one knew how closely held children are within the African community."

"I apologize, Van Couvering."

"Don't mention it, Drummond."

She had to admit that he looked gorgeous this morning, leaning on the balustrade of the canal bridge, in a cobalt cloak and casually unbuckled boots. The man was annoying, but she could yet feel herself coming around.

"It's troubling," he said.

"I don't think that quite says it, Drummond."

"No, I mean that these five, or six, or seven or however many, are only the ones we have any idea of. What we don't know is what's truly terrifying."

They both fell silent.

"Do you have children, Drummond?"

"No," he said. "I had a wife and an infant, too, both dead in childbirth. I yearned for that baby."

"I'm sorry, Drummond," she said.

"And you, Van Couvering?"

Blandine shook her head, gazing out on the East River. "I'm an orphan."

"Last I knew, orphans might bear children," Drummond said.

"I mean that this is what I have in common, sir, with some of the victims."

"I take your meaning to be that if I don't myself have offspring, why should I care that someone is murdering those of this colony? Do you seriously ask that?"

"Children die in New Netherland all the time," said Blandine. "Murder rarely comes into it. I merely consider your incentive here."

"You play *advocatus diaboli*," Drummond said. Devil's advocate—an apt formulation, given the imagery of the fright show the night before.

"I am being accused as a witch, Drummond, because I am paying too much mind to this matter. You would do well to look to yourself."

Drummond extracted a small metallic item from his doublet and passed it to Blandine. A miniature pistol.

"Tap action," Blandine said briskly. "I'd say forty caliber. Is it French?"

Drummond looked at her strangely. "Good Lord, Van Couvering, is there anything you do not know?"

"Papa was a gunsmith," Blandine said, smiling. "It's a pretty piece."

It was indeed French. Filigreed silver, with its thumb-style applewood stock checkered with inlaid silver wire. The pistol had, she noted, a sliding safety. It fit neatly into the palm.

"You have a pocket in your muff?" Drummond asked.

The muff Blandine carried was gigantic, still not as big as Drummond's, but made of beautiful silver fox fur.

"Put it in there," Drummond said.

"A loan," Blandine said.

"A gift," Drummond said.

"I'm not sure I can be taking gifts from you, Drummond. That might put us on a whole other level, could it not? Next thing, you'll step up to a ring."

"All right, woman, a loan," Drummond said, exasperated. "You know who gave me that? Look at the engraving."

Blandine examined the barrel jacket of the tiny pistol. "*Charles Rex,*" she read.

"The king," Drummond said.

"I know that," Blandine said.

"In recognition of my service to the crown."

"Oh, I am a republican," Blandine said, making to return the pistol. "I cannot possibly take such a priceless royalist piece."

"Shush," Drummond said, pushing the gun back at her. "The king directed me to give it to a woman someday, and now I have."

"Well, in that case," Blandine said, and she slipped the pistol into her fox fur muff. If nothing else, she could trade it for at least a half dozen beaver pelts.

"Now that that's settled," Drummond said.

"Yes," Blandine said, "now that it's settled, what next?"

"I knew a man in Holland, a lens grinder, a very fine man," Drummond said. "He told me something that stuck in my mind. He said that everything a human being does is necessarily entirely insignificant. But it is very important that he do it anyway."

"All right, we're important," Blandine said. "Where do we start?"

"I should think we should start at the beginning, don't you?"

"Jope Hawes," Blandine said.

Drummond proposed a trip to the north, to the Hendrickson patent, but this time approaching from the direction of Connecticut. "I would like to speak with the Canaan landsman who discovered the Hawes boy dead."

"Then go on to talk with the mother," Blandine said.

Visions of an intimate sleigh ride up the frozen Fresh River naturally occurred in Drummond's mind. He and Blandine, under the single bearskin.

"If we go," Antony interjected, "I can drive the sleigh."

Drummond's vision abruptly vanished. A merry company. Just the three of them.

Perhaps, he thought, they might stop off at New Haven first.

"I have accounted for all of my charges but one," Aet Visser reported to the director general. "His name is Richard Dunn, and he came in on *Sea Serpent*, his father dying on the crossing. His mother dead in Plymouth, before they ever departed for the new world."

"The foot may be his?" Stuyvesant said, a look of distaste passing over his face. He sat behind his official table in the audience room at the Stadt Huys, the morning after Christmas.

"The foot may be his," Visser repeated stupidly, looking a bit rumpled and carelessly shaven after the punch cups he had downed the day before. He felt intimidated in the presence of *Mijn Heer* General. As, he supposed, he was meant to feel. "At any rate, if it's from one of my wards, I can't imagine whose else it would be."

"An English child," the director general said. "He was placed where?"

"With Missy Flamsteed, at the Jug," Visser said.

"He lodged at a tap house?"

"A mere stopgap, *Mijn Heer* General," Visser said. "Missy Flamsteed often takes my wards on a temporary basis. She sleeps them in her back hearth."

"We cannot have loose body parts littering our streets, orphanmaster."

A sad child, Dickie Dunn. Visser saw him only briefly, when *Sea Serpent* docked. Sickly from the voyage, grief-stunned by his father's death. He had relatives in Portsmouth, or Bournemouth, or somewhere, and no possessions or inheritance. Visser had planned to ship him back to England as soon as possible.

"A quiet boy," Missy Flamsteed said, when Visser questioned her in the wake of the shocking Christmas Day discovery. "Stayed near the chimney heat and crapped himself silly for the first few days he was here. Had to keep putting porridge into him."

If the youngster strayed at all, she said, he strayed to the wharf, looking out at the sea (actually, since this was the East River, staring across the anchorage to Breukelen), morose and pining. A shock to the system, this transition from old world to new. Some folks just could not accomplish it. It didn't help that Dickie Dunn was all of five years old.

Someone or something haunted the docks of New Amsterdam, Stuyvesant was convinced. First the Imbrock boy, taken, the first time at least, from wharfside. And this latest, Dickie Dunn, who could not have ventured away from the Strand.

"You are convinced it was Dunn?" the director general asked Visser.

"With a high degree of certainty," Visser said. "Always with the proviso that it will turn out, indeed, an orphan who was targeted. A terrible business."

"Naturally, suspicion falls upon you."

"What? *Mijn Heer* General!"

"The Imbrock child told us you took him into the forest."

"He was confused," Visser sputtered. "I was known to be with the dominie that day."

"You deal most prominently with the parentless and abandoned, after all."

"My wards are my special chicks," Visser said, enormously flustered. His hands shook. "I would never do anything to harm them. On the contrary, I do everything I can to protect them, curry them, favor them."

"Yes," said Stuyvesant, sounding not entirely convinced. "If we hear otherwise there will be grave consequences for you. I might wonder, also, what you and George Godbolt have got cooked up together with this orphan ward of his, William Turner. Is there anything I should know?"

"I offer you my resignation, sire," Visser said, hanging his head, abject and groveling. "Effective immediately."

The director general duly noted Visser's disheveled hair atop his skull, and then waved him off. "No need for extremes. It's just been some muttering on the part of half-wits in the community. Orphans disappear. And you are the orphanmaster. The people love to mutter."

"I assure you, I am guiltless."

"No man is guiltless, Aet," Stuyvesant said. "You are stained with sin as are all men born of women. *Vitiis nemo sine nascitur,* Horace tells us, no man is without faults."

Visser would have continued to protest, but the director general held up his hand. "You are using the Englishman Edward Drummond as a liaison of some sort," he said.

"Drummond?" Visser was nonplussed.

"*Posthac,* you are to discontinue any and all official relations with the man," Stuyvesant said. "I don't care if you are friendly with him in the course of your private life, although I will say there have been mutterings about him, too, and not by half-wits, either. As far as your official duties as orphanmaster are concerned, Mister Drummond is off-limits."

Visser left the presence of the director general frightened and mystified. He felt, as he often did, as if he were in over his head. How much did Stuyvesant know?

He could not glean, he could not scan, he could not plumb. *Cogito ergo caput meum dolet,* he said to himself, imitating the director general's idiotic predilection for Latin phraseology. I think, therefore my head hurts.

Visser badly needed a brandy. Perhaps some roast pork stuffed with prunes. He headed down Pearl Street for the Red Lion.

He had not taken twenty steps before Martyn Hendrickson fell in beside him, wearing an extravagant cloak and his broad-brimmed cavalier hat.

"Been to see the one-legged wonder?" Martyn asked.

"Yes, I was summoned," Visser stammered. He felt unaccountably as if he had been found out in some transgression.

"Had a good little talk, did you?" Martyn asked.

Visser left off answering as they crossed the canal. "Did you?" Martyn demanded.

"We did, a very brief one."

"About what?"

"What?"

Martyn stopped Visser abruptly and guided him, a little roughly, off the street into a stable yard. "I asked what the goddamned substance of your conversation was."

"Nothing of import," Visser said. He hesitated. "Well, *Mijn Heer* General did appear distressed about body parts showing up discarded on the streets of the settlement."

"A messy business, that," Martyn said. "Put the fear of witika into every household in town, didn't it?"

"You contracted to hire out the youth in question, I believe," Visser said. "Richard Dunn, called Dickie."

"Did I?" Martyn said. "There are so many we employ, I lose track. Did you happen to mention my contracting the Dunn boy to Monsieur Stuyvesant?"

"No, no," Visser said hurriedly. "I would never . . . A private business, surely, a contractual agreement, confidential to the parties involved. A man's servants are his own affair."

Martyn nodded. "That has always been my opinion. I wonder if you yourself might need a little more household help."

"Me?"

"Your growing family," Martyn said. "Perhaps I could send brother Lightning over to help out."

"That won't be necessary."

"Are you sure? It would be no problem for me to do so. Your pretty little half-breed wifey has her hands full."

Martyn swept his cloak aside and casually rested his hand on the hilt of his parrying dagger, carried in a leather sheath on his belt.

A weak feeling ran through Visser's gut. His senses became acute. He smelled the manure of the yard as though it were smeared in his nostrils.

"Really, Martyn, please."

"No?" Martyn said. "No need for Lightning to strike, so to speak?"

"No, no."

Martyn stared at Visser for a long beat. The horses in the nearby stalls snorted and wheezed. "I'll bid you good-bye, then," he said. Martyn stepped backward onto Pearl Street and strode off.

Perhaps, Visser thought, no pork dinner at the Lion. He had lost his appetite.

There will be a fire. Gaze into a campfire, and you share a view common to all humans of all ages who ever looked into one. The Maid of Orléans stared into a fire. Caesar. Moses. Embers are eidetic. Flames are the original shape-shifters.

So, a fire. In a lodge, in a cave, in the open air. Around it, the gathered clan. Close to the warmth, seated in a position of respect, the sachem, the singer, the vision woman, the one we've all come to hear.

At this fire, for this song, the singer changes. At times it seems to be one of the chiefs, Quesqakwons, perhaps, or Mattahorn, maybe the great Tamanend. At one moment you clearly see it is Hawsis, the old woman. But then the shape shifts and you are not sure who or what you are looking at. A mountain lion. A coyote.

Suddenly it is Kitane seated at the fire, the others waiting on his words. He looks to the sky, stares into the flames and begins to sing.

The twin sisters, Nanabush and Bachtama, hated each other from the start and fought even in the womb. Their battles were such that their mother, Arwen, died in giving birth. Their father, the wind god, enraged with grief, attacked his newborn daughters, who had no choice but to defend themselves. They killed their father in the fight, thus rendering themselves orphans from birth.

Struck by loneliness, Nanabush wandered across the sky-bridge from her home in heaven to stalk the forests of earth. She incarnated herself as the dog, the coyote. Her sister, Bachtama, when she came hunting after Nanabush, incarnated herself as the lion, the catamount.

Nanabush and Bachtama found the woods, meadows and rivers of this world splendid and incredibly bountiful, but wholly devoid of gods. Bachtama was forced to create a suitable husband out of the mud of the river bottom. She bore a devil, who instantly mated with its mother to create a race of humans. Nanabush, looking on with jealousy, created a mate of her own out of the ice of a glacier, coupled with it and gave birth to a demon. It forced itself upon its own mother and Nanabush gave birth to a rival race of humans.

The lion-devil-mud children of the orphan sister Bachtama and the dog-demon-ice children of the orphan sister Nanabush battled for supremacy back and forth across the earth. One of Nanabush's sons, the arrogant Witika, proposed a strategy to vanquish the rival clan forever. He directed his sisters and brothers to open wide their mouths and eat everything in sight, consuming all the game, all the maize, all the squash and cranberries and ramps, everything edible that ever existed.

Witika's strategy worked. A new god, starvation, ruled the world. Bachtama's children became bereft and solitary, which is the reason the catamount cries at night. But after everything edible was consumed by Nanabush's children, they had nothing left to eat themselves, and they, too, fell under the dominion of the new god, starvation.

At this, the great god Manitou, looking down upon earth from heaven, had pity. He stomped on the bellies of Nanabush's children, and they disgorged all the beasts of the forests, the fish of the waters and the fruits of the earth. And Manitou cursed Witika with eternal exile, sending him off to wander alone, afflicting him with an appetite that could never be sated.

But Witika is a coyote's child, so he turned Manitou's curse back upon itself. When he eats, he eats only the flesh of humans, and he shares his affliction, this hunger for human flesh, with all who encounter him.

Master and slave lounged in the Place of Stones. A wet, spattering snow blew in from the river, so they sat just inside the mouth of the cave. Lightning built a fire on the lip outside, and the fat flakes dropped into it, hissing. Behind them, the bones, showing white as the cave-throat dark swallowed them.

"He was easily taken?" the master said.

Lightning grunted. "They are all easily taken," he said. "Didn't I creep into the very house of one, while you yourself feasted below?"

The master disliked Lightning's boastfulness, but the trait seemed to run in his Esopus blood. At least, the man was half Dutch, or half

German, or half whatever it was that randied the Sopus woman who birthed him.

Lightning took off his hat and vigorously scratched his head. He had seated himself below his master, leaning back against a cairn of stones and bones, so he gave a rare good view of his scarred scalp.

The master looked on with fascination. The scalping scar, he noticed, seemed to have faded somewhat, yet remained heavily mottled with purple and red. The skin still layered the indian's skull with extra tissue, waxy and uneven, as though the flesh had bubbled and then solidified. The crease looked like it could channel rainwater.

Perhaps a wig, the master thought. Weren't wigs supposed to be *au fait*?

Out loud, he said, "I appreciate the getting of a white child."

"I serve my master," Lightning said.

"I had forgotten, really, what white flesh tastes like, and I've often wondered if I could discern the difference, set side by side."

Lightning bent forward to the fire. He snapped open his Barlow—a prized possession—and sliced from a buttock that hung on a crane hook above the flames a small crescent of human flesh. Then he reached over and did the same from a calf section that lay athwart the stones of the fire ring.

"No, no," the master said. "They are of not the same vintage, and I will be able to tell which is which from the taste."

"This one, the black, has been frozen in snow, just thawed this morning," Lightning said. "Do you want me to blindfold you?"

The master laughed. "I don't ever feel at home," he said, "unless it is here in the Place of Stones with you."

Lightning fashioned his staple-wool scarf—another prized possession, and one he customarily used to affix his crumpled felt hat firmly to his head—into a covering for his master's eyes. Lovingly, he tied it around the man's skull.

He was helpless now, thought Lightning.

"All right," the master said. "First one, then the other. After, I will tell you which is which, and you tell me whether I am right."

A collop of flesh from the ham. The master chewed thoughtfully. Then one from the calf.

"They taste the same," the master said. "Like the smoke of the fire."

"You must guess."

The master tasted again, one after another. "This is the white child," he said, holding out a scrap of flesh.

He was wrong, Lightning noticed, fielding the scrap. The one the master had extended to him was from the little African girl.

"You are right!" he cried, and the master stripped the scarf from his eyes and laughed. The two pieces could be identified from small flaps of skin still attached to them, one darker, one lighter, but Lightning easily switched them so that the master was fooled into thinking he had guessed rightly.

"I knew it," the master said giddily. "The one has a flavor more of . . . well, I can't explain it, I just knew."

Lightning pushed what remained of the two slices into the master's mouth. He never partook, himself, but the master consumed human flesh with an enthusiasm bordering on gluttony. Lightning had never before seen the witika madness settle on anyone so completely.

Usually, normally, among the Lenape and their Algonquin cousins, the madness killed. From self-loathing, or from the effects of the poisonous diet. Yet the master thrived. Perhaps the Dutch were different. The Esopus had another name for them, in addition to swannekins. *Moordenaars*, meaning "murderers."

Looking at his master now, chewing away, Lightning recognized the expression on the man's face. Not disgust, not nausea.

Bliss.

27

Blandine and Antony turned out not to accompany Drummond on his post-Christmas jaunt to New Haven. It was probably better that way. Drummond had once seen, at a cattle-market fair in the Mitte quarter of Berlin, a juggler who kept four live cats and a screaming piglet up in the air at once. Marking king-killers for death with Blandine van Couvering on hand struck him as the more difficult task.

So, he would travel by coastal from New Amsterdam to New Haven, conduct the king's business privately, then rendezvous with Blandine and her giant at Fort Huys de Goede Hoop, "Fort House of Good Hope," the Dutch holdout trading post at Hartford, in the heart of Connecticut. Afterward, they'd proceed northward by sleigh to Jope Hawes territory.

New Haven, January, in the bold new annum of 1664. A low town of a few stone buildings, thatch-roofed wood-framed houses and many log huts. Chimneys were held together not with mortar but with clay. At least, Drummond thought, the residents were not living in earthen pits, as he had seen in Hartford and other hamlets in Connecticut.

The Puritan response to the new world consisted of prayer, sweet pudding and the stocks. The pudding was quite good, but the other two elements were strained from overuse. In place of the shining city on the hill, the New Haven Colony had thrown down a tight-as-a-pinprick theocratic harbor village.

Drummond had had his fill of Puritan religious fervor and spectacles of public punishment in the Civil War. The New Haven Colony did not agree with him.

Except, perhaps, the waterfront. The harbor was quite good. Coastal shipping generally made a stopover at New Haven on the transit between Boston and New Amsterdam. Although nary a taproom or sporting house marred the town's sanctity even on the wharves, more secular travelers could find rooms and convivial atmospheres at several dwelling-houses in the harbor district.

At one of these, a wooden-framed structure with a generous public room, Drummond met with Tunny Beechman, Ross Raeger's man in Connecticut.

"You are going to have to cut your hair," Tunny said. "They'll mark you right off as a royalist if you enter a meetinghouse with locks like that."

"I'll tuck them under my hat," Drummond said.

"Which ye will remove at the meetinghouse door," Tunny said.

Since the only communal gatherings in the town took place in one of four meetinghouses that were less like churches than public halls, Drummond had proposed to go around in disguise. He needed to gain entry to the community, and community in New Haven meant the ceaseless, droning prayer meetings.

A few times before, in England during the war, going incognito, he had worn the mockingbird clothes of the Puritans—black fustian tunics with plain white linen yoke collars. This would be trickier. The New Haven settlement was small, fewer than three hundred souls. Residents knew one another. They were suspicious of outsiders, even of their Puritan brethren from Plymouth and Boston. If he carried out his plan, discovery would be a very real threat.

"You could be hung," Tunny said cheerfully. "At the very least, the stocks. They ain't comfortable." He rubbed his neck as if recalling a personal experience with the wooden traps of New Haven.

On his initial trip to the colony in October, Drummond had marked out the Puritan elders most likely to be harboring the trio of regicides lately sighted in the town. Now, on this second visit, came what Drummond referred to in his mind as "the Touch," a delicate maneuver that was a central strategy of his particular brand of spycraft.

"How you going to get them to bite?" Tunny said. They were closed in his upstairs boarding room. Using a leather-stropped razor and a scrap of diaper to mop the blood, he shaved Drummond's head.

"I'm going to say I've found the regicides," Drummond said.

"But you ain't found them," Tunny said, plowing a furrow in Drummond's skull.

"No, I ain't found them," Drummond said, wincing.

"So how can you say you have when you ain't?"

"Well, Tunny, I guess I'm going to lie," Drummond said.

The heavy snow of the New Year lay on the town like a curfew. The holiday spirit did not seem much abroad. The only real life came from the wafting scent of yeast out of the bakeries.

When the drumbeat sounded that sunup, Tunny and Drummond presented themselves at the meetinghouse for morning prayer. As opposed to midday prayer, evening prayer or midnight prayer. The New Haven colonists were a very prayerful people. All the getting done of God's work made Drummond wonder if there was any time left over for the works of man. When did the religious caterpillars get the opportunity to build houses, harvest crops, make pudding?

"Goodman Allerton," Tunny said to a hawk-faced elder at the door of the meetinghouse, "may I present to you Harry Fossick."

"Of Maine," Drummond said, greeting the man in the Puritan style, with an open hand rather than a bow.

Allerton gave him a wordless, parsimonious nod and entered into the hall. Drummond endured an interminable service, during which blood from Tunny's scalping trickled down the back of his neck. The sermon's theme: accept Christ as thy savior now, in this world, or meet him in the next world as thy judge.

Evidently personal talk was for after the service, not before. Goodman Allerton sought Drummond and Tunny out as the presbyters flocked out of the meetinghouse into the chill morning air.

"Mister Fossick of the district of Maine," Allerton said to another elder Drummond had seen leading the services. "Goodman Remmick."

"I give ye best wishes for the New Year," Drummond said, again restraining his all-too-royalist bow. "I am down from the Sagadahoc Colony."

"For what purpose?" Remmick said. He had more meat on his bones than his fellow elder, but Drummond still felt himself confronted by two hunch-shouldered crows.

"Worship, and a little trade," he said. "We have so few manufactories in the north, and the settlers of your colony are known for their industry."

"The Maine district is much afflicted by French papists, I believe," Allerton said to Remmick, as if eager to curry favor with a superior.

"Please see that you enter the lists with our sheriff," Remmick said.

"I will," Drummond said. "Oh, and I wish to see the two judges of the English king who are in town, the colonels, Goffe and Whalley. And perhaps a third judge, the man Dickwell, Dickson, something like that?"

The Touch.

Drummond might as well have slapped Remmick and Allerton across their faces. Remmick recovered first. "You are mistaken," he said.

"We harbor none of the judges here," Allerton said.

"But I've been told where to find them," Drummond said.

Remmick glared furiously at Tunny. "It was not me, sire," Tunny said, practically groveling in front of the eminence.

"Who informed you of this, Goodman Foster?" Remmick demanded.

"Fossick," Drummond corrected him. "One of your local mocking-birds perched on my window sash and chittered in my ear."

Remmick appraised him coolly. "Do animals speak to you often, Mister Fossick? I believe the last case we had of that here, we hung as a witch."

"Her corpse spoke after death," Allerton said. "Confessing her sins."

"Have I offended?" Drummond said. "I am heartily sorry. I merely seek to keep good company with the men who removed the vile Roman, the first Charles, from besmirching our land with his papistry."

Settle down, he told himself. *Don't overdo it.*

"England's corruption is beyond the death of one man to remedy," Allerton intoned, but Remmick placed his hand on his cohort's arm.

"Good day, Mister Fossick," he said icily. The two Puritans hurried off.

Drummond watched them go. "How did I do?" he asked Tunny.

"I believe I'll have to go to Boston for a few weeks," Tunny said mournfully. "Did you call him 'sire'?"

"I did not," Drummond said.

"I think you called him 'sire,' sire. Or acted as though you might. That gave you dead away. You make a very poor Puritan."

"Thank you," Drummond said. He gazed at the square patch of black that was the back of Goodman Remmick, receding down the street. "That man's stare could stop the hands of a clock."

"Boston," Tunny said. "Maybe for a few months."

We will make them flee to their stoat hole, Drummond told Tunny.

He had boys on alert to follow Remmick and Allerton. According to their later report, Remmick went directly to his dwelling-house, but Allerton made a stop before going to his. He spoke to a laborer, a pitman at a woodlot named John Meigs, who immediately mounted a horse and made for the western district of New Haven. Meigs proceeded to the home of a Puritan minister, John Davenport.

The regicide colonels, Goffe and Whalley, left Davenport's house "in blistering haste," according to the report of one of the boys. The colonels stopped at the home of a Mister Jones, took mounts and met another man, whom Drummond considered to be Dixwell, the third regicide. The three spurred their horses into the wilderness, to the West Rock Ridge a mile from the town. There they repaired to a cave.

"A cave?" Drummond asked.

"Yes, sir," said the little harbor ruffian whom Tunny had employed as a tail. "Quite a nice cave it is, too," the boy added. "Furnished with several cots and a chest of drawers. I could be at home there."

The child looked as though he only occasionally saw a roof over his head. Parentless, no doubt.

"You didn't give yourself away, did you?"

"No, sir," the orphan boy said, a wry miniature adult. "I pretended to be a mere passing urchin. Which wasn't difficult, since that's what I were. They didn't want me near the cave, see, but I went. Then they cast some stones to shoo me away, so I peels down my pants and showed them my backside."

Drummond laughed. "Admirable discretion," he said. He pushed a coin into the ruffian's dirty palm, and immediately had three other wharf rats, none of them over the age of ten, clamoring for remuneration of their own.

Should he trust the word of urchins? In the past, he had found them surprisingly reliable, but Drummond thought in this case he should see for himself. He rode out to West Rock Ridge and peered through his spyglass at the three regicides. They paced and argued in front of a smoky fire at the mouth of their cave. Not a cave at all, really, but an immense riven rock.

Through the glass, he saw the face of Whalley, the Puritan general.

Drummond recognized him from the field at Worcester. Older now, but then, who wasn't?

Satisfied, he left New Haven Colony, mentally composing his message to Clarendon. *Inveni eos.* I have found them. Rendered in cipher, thus:

Bgoxgb xhz

Afterward, in a few months, say, given the vagaries of cross-ocean travel, the lord chancellor's stranglers would come.

On the clear green ice of the Fresh River at Hartford, a cutter sleigh waited, triplet-hitched, with a cargo box behind. A collection of desultory flakes hung in the air, not falling but floating. Back in New Amsterdam Drummond had heard Raeger call it "dandruff snow." Hoarfrost lent a white, shimmering patina to every surface.

As well as the three horses he had harnessed, in the Russian style, to the sleigh's shaft bow, Drummond attached his old friend the roan by a hemp-rope line to the back of the sleigh. He had picked up the horse from where he boarded it on his last trip to the New Haven Colony.

Having spent the intervening weeks in lazy, stabled contentment, munching on oats and dried apples, the beast now stared dolefully at him, recalling the sluicing rain of the Mohawk Trail, as if to say, "What new hell have you invented for me this time?"

Drummond stamped his feet on the snow-covered planks of the river pier. He was there, but where was Blandine? He left word with the Dutch traders at Fort House of Good Hope that she and Antony should meet him at the Fresh River docks.

He wore a wig that resembled his old hair, so that Blandine would not be taken too much by surprise by his appearance. He fretted. There was a point in most enterprises, he knew from experience, where aims appeared ludicrous and the prospects of success dim.

She came down from Hartford town, dressed in a riding habit she had ordered direct from London: a red wool gown and jacket with buttons of brass and a brocade waistcoat. Over it she wore a mink cape. In a mink-trimmed riding hat, her face pinked by the cold, stamping the planks of the pier herself with elk-skin boots, Blandine van Couvering looked ready for adventure.

"Lord," Drummond said to himself, "never did someone who wanted to be a man so much embody a woman."

Antony trailed behind her, obscured by the stack of woolen blankets he carried that was almost as tall as he himself, and burdened with a canvas *voyageur* pack as well.

And Kitane. The Lenape wrapped his upper torso in the pelt of one of the forest lions of the new world, of the kind Drummond had glimpsed watering itself on the North River's shore during his first trip into the American interior. He wore heavy leather leggings, a red-felt cummerbund and the same kind of elk-skin boots that Blandine had on. He, too, had a pack slung over his back, off which a couple of bear-claw snowshoes dangled.

Only three passengers could fit comfortably on the upholstered bench seat of the sleigh. What would the Lenape do, trot alongside? Drummond did not put it past him. Kitane looked incredibly hale. Gone was the hangdog pallor of their previous meeting. The expression of the proud trapper had returned to his face. Beneath the catamountain hide, his naked chest displayed its fierce bird tattoos.

"We are four?" Drummond asked, as the trio trooped down the pier toward him. "Is there room?"

In answer, Kitane leaped from the pier onto the ice, sliding smoothly across it like a skater. He spun around and hopped atop the buckboard cargo box at the back of the sleigh. The Lenape stroked the nose of the tied-on roan, and the horse nickered.

"Greetings, Drummond," Blandine said.

"Van Couvering," he said. "You come with a suite of courtiers."

"Ah, yes," she said, coming to him hand outstretched. "My retinue. I try to discourage them, but they insist on following me around."

They shook hands. "I have the bearskin," Drummond said. "Why ever did you bring so many blankets?"

"For trade, Drummond, for trade," Blandine said.

Drummond drew her aside. "The last time I saw Kitane, I had to clean the man's puke off my shoes. Is he all right?"

"He is much stronger," Blandine said. "His witika fear has mostly left him."

They both looked over at the Lenape, sitting serenely on the cargo box.

Antony approached Drummond. "You've yoked three together," he said, gesturing at the trio of horses, stamping the ice in front of the sleigh. "How does that work?"

"The two side ones we harness in breast collars," Drummond said, helping the man by sloughing off a few layers from his tower of blankets. "The middle animal trots and the outer ones canter. I saw it done in Muscovy, it works quite well."

What the arrangement gave them, most of all, was speed. Antony settled his pack and took up the reins in the center position of the postilion. Blandine and Drummond sat on either side of him. The silent Kitane hung on behind.

They set off at a clip that Drummond did not think possible to maintain. The sleigh runners sliced the windswept river ice with a thin, hissing cut. He reached back and untied the roan to let it trot along at its own pace. The horse swung abreast to match its gait with the three white-stockinged bays they had in harness.

As they flew up the river, the ice changed from green to blue, to a milky white, then to a cloud color that resembled the eyeballs of the horses. Antony artfully steered them clear of any open or soft spots in the river ice. The sleigh blasted through patches of snow, which blew upward and swirled madly in their wake.

The bearskin Blandine had given Drummond, draped over the two of them but folded behind the back of Antony, lent the journey an intimate feel. Blandine did not talk. Drummond sat starboard in one corner of the seat, the continent-sized expanse of Antony's back took up the middle, and she sat to port. The sun broke out even as the snowflakes still levitated magically, motelike, in midair.

"Festive," Blandine said, laughing at the small, multicolored snow-bows that sparkled above the frozen river. But that was all she said until, an hour later, this: "Drummond, I think your hair is bleeding."

A cut Tunny had inflicted on Drummond's scalp had reopened under the drubbing it was taking on the journey. He doffed his hat and took off his wig.

"Drummond!" Blandine said.

Antony looked around and almost crashed the sleigh. Kitane, too, was interested, leaning over the back of the sleigh to take the wig from Drummond's hands, examining it carefully.

"Hast that always been your hair?" Blandine said, slipping into an extra-formal kind of speech.

"I had myself shorn in New Haven," Drummond said.

"Lice," said Antony.

"A business decision, purely."

Blandine looked closely at Drummond, as though trying to glean the truth behind his words. "You resemble a convict," she said.

"Escaped from New Haven jail," he said, smiling.

"And what was your crime?" Blandine asked.

"Oh, impure thoughts," he said. "I'm afraid I failed miserably as a Puritan."

They made the cascade rocks that blocked the river at Windsor, its splashing waters arrested into icy shapes, huge mid-current boulders glistening as though they were sheathed in glass. There, a broad track diverged around the rapids.

Antony led the sleigh horses, Kitane stayed stubbornly atop the cargo box, and the roan ranged freely to the lip of the surrounding forest. It bucked and danced, friskily kicking at the snow, apparently deciding the trip might not be so bad after all.

Blandine and Drummond walked together in the track of the sleigh. "Do we make a mistake?" Drummond asked her. "I don't have any understanding of what we'll find at the other end, neither Canaan nor the Hawes place."

"Oh, no," Blandine said. "This is right, this is where to start, at the border of New Netherland and New England."

"Your people and mine," he said.

"New England is so well settled and prosperous," she said. "Antony remarked upon it on our trip from New Amsterdam to Hartford. So many farms, so much ambition, so much enterprise. I have heard Boston now numbers five thousand souls. I fear you will snow us under."

"The Dutch are no strangers to ambition and enterprise."

"I wonder, though," Blandine said. "Will I be allowed to conduct my trade under the rule of the Stuart king? I've heard that in English law, a woman cannot sign her name to contracts or represent herself in court. Is that true? She becomes a vassal of her husband? And if she has no husband, she has the same legal status as an infant child?"

"I suppose it is true," Drummond said. "I never thought about it."

"Because you are a man," she said. "You are not an indian, so you care not what happens to Kitane, nor an African, so Antony gets none of your concern."

Good Lord, thought Drummond, *is this the way it's going to be?* "Van Couvering, if you are going to take our time together as an opportunity to strip the hide from my back, I think it will be very trying for me."

"I only point out that an English takeover of New Netherland would ill benefit me as a woman. We ourselves, I mean the Dutch, have two kinds of status in marriage, called *manus* and *usus*. *Manus* is more like your English common law, no rights for the wife, she is chattel of her spouse. With *usus*, the wife retains her independent status, she legally is her own person, not subsumed under her husband. If I ever marry, it will only be *usus*."

"How could you ever find a man bold enough to accept such terms?" Drummond said lightly.

Blandine looked sideways at him. "I shall use a pistol."

Drummond laughed. They mounted a rise and saw Antony and Kitane ahead of them with the sleigh, waiting on the blue sheet of river ice above the Windsor rapids.

28

S tuyvesant sat in his Stadt Huys audience room surveying his New Haven visitors. Misters Allerton and Remmick were worthies of the Connecticut Colony, no doubt, but men toward which the director general of New Netherland had every reason to harbor suspicion. Here were the Englishers among those who were massing upon New Netherland's borders, intent to steal his American empire away.

Mid-January, 1664. The men had made a long, snow-blanketed trip south to visit the director general, which only increased their sour mood.

"I shall come straight to the point," said Remmick, the one with close-cropped gray hair. "Is New Amsterdam in the practice of harboring assassins within its jurisdiction?"

The director general's *schout*, a Belgian Walloon by the name of Bernard de Klavier, stirred at the thought of lawbreakers in his bailiwick. Stuyvesant made a barely perceptible movement with his hand to still his lieutenant.

"We are a settlement of peaceful, law-abiding citizens," the director general said. "And we repulse any criminal incursions from outside our lawful borders."

A dig at English pressure on New Netherland. Remmick ignored Stuyvesant's sally. "A man recently appeared in our colony, representing himself as a goodman believer from the Maine district," he said.

"Which he was most assuredly not," said the other New Haven man, Allerton.

"An Englishman?" Stuyvesant asked.

"A gentleman imposter, going about illegally under disguise," Remmick said. "He slipped away before we could properly question him. The dockside caitiff who aided the man decamped from town, too. But our investigations traced back the assassin's trail. He began here, in New Amsterdam."

"An assassin, you say. Did he attempt murder? We are always willing to help a neighbor keep the peace, provided said neighbor respects our sovereignty."

Again, another dig. New Englanders, some from Connecticut as well
as others from Massachusetts Bay, of late habitually made forays into
Dutch territory, claiming huge swaths of Long Island, Westchester and
the northland for their own.

"Your so-called sovereignty is not the question here," Remmick said.
"The question is rather will you give help yielding up a homicide!"

"Do not come into my chambers and raise your voice," Stuyvesant
said. "Have you a name for the miscreant?"

"He said his name was Harry Fossick, which is another indication of
his subterfuge," Allerton said.

"I don't understand," the director general said.

" 'Fossick' means 'to seek out' in our English language," Remmick
said. "An alias, for certain."

Abiit, excessit, evasit, erupit, quoth Stuyvesant. His guests put on
that pained expression of the unlearned in which the director general so
delighted. "He has left, absconded, escaped and disappeared?"

"Yes," Remmick said.

"Tell me," Stuyvesant said. "Is this man tall, shapely, with a good leg
and a mop of curly dark hair?"

When his New Haven visitors departed, the director general left his
chair and turned to the *schout*.

"Edward Drummond has rooms in the town?" he asked.

De Klavier nodded sharply. "In Slyck Steegh, on this side of the
canal."

"I think he is due for a visit."

"Yes, *Mijn Heer* General." The sheriff turned to go.

"De Klavier?"

"Yes?"

"If the man were not to be at home, all the better. Conduct a search,
and don't be pretty about it, either."

Kitane perched on the back of the sleigh. Snatches of conversation blew
in the wind from Drummond and Blandine, sitting a few feet in front
of him on either side of the bench. What he heard distressed him. They
appeared to be telling him to cannibalize the orphanmaster.

"Eat Visser," he heard, over and over, the words snatched out of the air and inserted like a pair of iron nails into Kitane's ears.

"Eat Visser," they said. Was it meant for him? A command? Or were they worried that this was what Kitane might do? The man Visser was fat enough, it was true. The corpulent orphanmaster would provide anyone interested with several meals. But the Lenape didn't believe that Blandine, at least, would intend the man, or Kitane himself for that matter, such monstrous harm.

The old witika madness still dogged him, kept at bay only by the constant lash of his will.

Blandine and Drummond were indeed having a conversation about the orphanmaster, his trustworthiness, his secrets. Yet what the Lenape at their back heard as an insidious suggestion was merely the two of them pronouncing the man's name, Aet, in the English manner, to rhyme with *beat*. They didn't realize that each time they said it represented a small trigger for Kitane.

Toward the end of the day, as the sleigh approached the territory of the Massachusetts Bay Colony, without a word Kitane slipped off the cargo box. Antony pulled in the reins to halt the progress of the horses, thinking to pick him back up. But the Lenape simply bent down, tied the small, circular snowshoes onto his feet and set off at a quick march into the forest.

"What is he up to?" Drummond said.

"Don't worry about him," Blandine said. "He goes to do a bit of business for us."

"William Turner?" Drummond said.

"Or the boy Rebecca Godbolt swears is William Turner," Blandine said. "Kitane will ask among the natives about the trade of a boy last spring. If we can unlock that mystery, perhaps the fate of Piteous Gullee and the others will open to us, also."

"So what will he ask?" Drummond said.

"If any of his tribal cousins can tell him about European captives, taken and then swapped as hostages," Blandine said. "The Godbolts obtained the boy they switched for William Turner somewhere."

"Very good," Drummond said. "Very, very good. Van Couvering, you are a wonder."

The man had already disappeared into the woods. His tracks led forward and then disappeared, swallowed by a boundless wilderness.

The remaining three sojourners overnighted at an inn in Springfield, where Blandine did a rollicking trade in blanketry. In the morning they pushed west along a tributary of the Fresh. The sleigh proved more and more troublesome. Trees blocked their passage up the increasingly narrow river.

After a particularly harrowing time dragging the sleigh up the river's bank, around an obstacle and then back down onto the ice, only to be faced with another downed tree around the next bend, Blandine and Drummond conferred.

"Antony," Blandine said, "we want you to take the sleigh back to Springfield and proceed from there to Hartford. I'll give you money for passage back to New Amsterdam."

The big man let a sullen look cross his face, as he always did when Blandine suggested they part company.

"We'll take two of the bays and the roan," she said. "Can you make do with one?"

He didn't answer, but began to unhitch the harness from one of the two outside sleigh horses.

"That's the one I'd take, too," Drummond said. "She's got the best head on her."

Antony didn't respond. "We shall reunite at the Red Lion," Drummond said, "as if there we had hidden our gold."

The giant stayed silent, so Drummond tried again. "In mid-month there will be a full moon, and we will take the perspective tube out on Mount Petrus."

"I know when I am being talked down to, Edward," Antony said. But he appeared to cheer at the prospect of another bout with the mountains of the moon. "Diana," he called the world he saw through Drummond's apparatus, and told Blandine it was a land of freedom that he often visited in his dreams.

They parted. Drummond bear-hugged Antony, and was bear-hugged in return, an experience that resembled being closed into a tomb and lifted by a tornado.

Drummond rode the roan and Blandine took the bay gelding, with the other bay, a mare, relegated to pack duty. They reached Canaan at dusk and lodged in one of three farmhouses clustered in a small grouping next to a millrace and an ice-choked waterfall.

The man of the house, Jonathan Pynchon, appeared stunned into speechlessness by the appearance of two strangers out of the snowy wilderness. But his wife, Betty, was chatty and welcoming. Blandine warmed to her immediately.

"Oh, you've come about the Hawes boy," Betty said, as soon as Blandine broached the subject. "A terrible business, that."

She turned to her husband. "Jonny, send Gar over to fetch Enoch Woods."

"Now?" Jonathan said.

"Give the boy a lantern," Betty said, pushing her ten-year-old son, Gar, toward the door of the cabin. "If he gets lost, it'll be only one less mouth to feed this winter."

She laughed gaily and turned back to Blandine. "Enoch's the one who found the body at Bitterroot Spring. He's the one you'll want to speak with."

The dinner the Pynchons were able to lay out was humble but bountiful: trout, chestnuts, a ham, elderberry jelly and the oddly named *wentelteefje*, a kind of egg-soaked Dutch toast that translated as "turnover bitches." A feast in the midst of the wilderness.

Both the taciturn Jonathan and the equally mute Enoch Woods became considerably more animated with the administration of generous drafts of the house's excellent hard cider. As did Blandine and Drummond.

"The body lay in a very violent posture," Enoch said, detailing his discovery of the Jope Hawes murder.

"Bitterroot Spring, a dependable fresh watering hole, now ruined," Jonathan interjected. "Five miles west of here, across the supposed border of New Netherland."

Enoch verbally elbowed his host aside. "The body was split open like a citrus orange. Its entrails trailed out and were festooned on the branches of the trees overhanging the spring. It lay faceup, but its bottom was twisted around so that its buttocks showed. Half-moon bite marks all up and down the flank."

Enoch, not yet out of his twenties, appeared much older than his years. A wen disfigured his forehead. By the light of the hearth fire, his face became animated only when he talked of the murder. Enoch always referred to his discovery as "the body," never naming Jope Hawes.

"The family paid quitrent to the Dutch patroons," Jonathan said. "They was freeholders, but the patroons claimed the land to be part of New Netherland, though no one has ever surveyed the border, so we don't know."

"Hawes was a fool to pay rent," interjected another neighbor, Jack Nelson, newly arrived. The arrival of strangers in the settlement excited universal interest, and the Pynchon cabin became increasingly crowded.

"I was told there were indian signs around the scene," Drummond said.

"Aye, that there was," Enoch said. "The totems and fetishes they use in their heathen worship. That doll they all keep in their lodges."

"A willow circle, with a cross laid over it?" Blandine asked.

Enoch nodded vigorously. "Yeah, they had that, a number of 'em, tossed all around the body. But the chillingest thing were the face left stuck to a tree, looking down at ye like a spirit out to steal your soul."

"The boy's face?" shouted Jonathan. "They took off the boy's face?"

His wife shushed him and took away his flagon of cider.

"Not the boy's, not the boy's, you muzzy fool," Enoch said, equally inebriated.

"A mask," Blandine said quietly.

"That's it," Enoch cried, stabbing his finger at her.

But it was Gar, the ten-year-old, who provided the real gem of the evening. After she had shooed all the guests home, Betty was up in the sleeping loft with Blandine, putting Gar and his two sisters to bed. After Bible verses, Gar reached out and took Blandine's hand.

"He knew the Hawes boy," Betty said.

"I met him every year at the harvest carnival up in Taconic," Gar said. "I missed him a lot at this year's fair. He were a crack shot, a real crack shot. His daddy were sick, so Jope fed the family. He got two little sisters, just like me."

Then he added, almost as an afterthought, "The Hendricksons hated him."

"Why do you say that?" Blandine asked.

"Because I know it," Gar said. "They was always saying he was poaching, though how you can poach on your own rented land, I don't know."

"He got in a disagreement with the patroons?"

"Disagreements, hell, they was fights," the boy said.

"Gar," his mother warned.

"They was!"

"Watch thy tongue," Betty said.

"The fights were about poaching?" Blandine said.

Gar shook his head. "About them being behind on rent. Hendrickson said, 'I'll toss your family off this land,' and Jope says, 'I'll kill ye if ye do.' He wasn't a boy to back down."

"I don't like to speak ill of anyone," Betty said. "But the Hendricksons are unpleasant people, what I've seen of them. They are frantic about English encroachment on their patent. They have been here to Canaan, one or the other of the brothers, many times to complain of it."

"My daddy says, if they had their way about it, the Hendricksons would declare war on Massachusetts and Connecticut both," Gar said.

Blandine wished the family a peaceful rest. She and Edward slept in two great chairs pulled up in front of the hearth.

"Good night, Drummond," Blandine said.

"Good night, Van Couvering," he said in return, listening to her breathing until he fell asleep himself.

Blandine and Drummond reached the Hawes place as the five o'clock sun disappeared. Beneath towering cedars, the forest seemed to hold more light than the sky. Throughout the long, frigid day, the trail offered rocks and slippery leaves beneath powdery snow that at times reached the bellies of their mounts. The horses made their way, plunging through the drifts, snorting by the end, in a lather, desperately needing a break.

But stopping was not an option. Shadows already dropped, spider-like, from the cedars, elms and oaks. There was no horizon, no landmark to guide them. They must reach their destination by full dark or freeze.

Drummond grew up riding. Blandine demonstrated a competence, but found the journey something of a trial. She sat on the horse not *damensattel*, but in the French manner.

"You ride astride," Drummond said, then immediately felt foolish for stating the obvious. "I could rig you a pommel if you wish."

Blandine shook her head. "I've often thought that if things made any kind of sense, men would be the ones to ride sidesaddle."

He shut his mouth for a while after that, having to think about it, forcing himself to believe that she had said what he thought she'd said. When they got on a wide trail leading west, Blandine pulled her bay alongside the roan. She looked over at Drummond.

"You're grinning," she said.

"Am I?" Drummond said. He performed an expansive gesture with his arm. "This wilderness. It answers."

All Betty Pynchon in Canaan had said was "Ride west along the stream. Diverge at the laurel thickets. Continue through some miles of cedars, then tall oaks until you reach the spring. The house, if you can call it that, will lie half a mile from the spring, and you can follow the brook directly to it."

Drummond's surveying compass showed them the westerly direction of their route. Rasped cheese and leaden bread had been their sustenance on the trip, along with a flask of apple brandy Enoch Woods bestowed upon them as they left Canaan.

Following any directions at all was difficult in the snow-blanketed landscape, especially with the blue shadows coming on.

Riding side by side, they spoke little. Finally, Blandine broke the silence. "So, Drummond," she said, "are you ever going to tell me what brings you to the new world?"

"Not wheat?" Drummond said.

"No, not wheat. I thought we had established that. You act a role."

"And you wonder who is the puppeteer."

"Oh, I think I know," Blandine said. "The second Charles."

"Yes, the second Charles," Drummond said. "It is no great mystery."

Feeling a relief no longer to withhold secrets from her, Drummond told of his work for the king, that he had been sent to New Amsterdam by the Earl of Clarendon, with the twofold purpose of tracking the regicides in Connecticut and gathering intelligence about the town's defenses.

"You misled me, then," Blandine said. "You came here to do the colony wrong."

"Forgive me," Drummond said earnestly. "You well know the Dutch cannot maintain their hold."

Whenever someone presented Blandine with a sin, a tragedy, an occurrence they would see pumped up into a catastrophe, whenever a trade went bad or she was swindled somehow, she always brought herself back to reality by thinking on her sister, Sarah. "A child did not die," she would say to herself, and whatever seemed horrible before suddenly appeared less so.

"Are you going to kill these three judges of the king? The regicides?"

"No," Drummond said. "But someone will."

"How can you stand that?"

"I've been a soldier," he said. "It's like what they say about being a priest. Once a soldier, always a soldier. You obey orders."

"And if the orders are bad?"

"I've been careful not to let that happen. I think I've been on the right side."

"Everyone always thinks they are on the right side," Blandine said.

They fell back into silence again, Blandine struggling with whether she could accept Drummond for what he was, learn to forgive.

Bitterroot Spring, when they finally arrived at it, proved an outcropping of sharp, erect gray boulders, where the body of young Jope Hawes had been discovered six months before. Blandine and Drummond now stood near their ultimate destination.

Blandine knew that too much time had passed for them to find signs of the murder at the spring, but she wanted to see the place anyway. The two dismounted and paced the site, Blandine lifting her heavy skirts above the snowpack. Her high elk-skin boots kept her dry at least to her knees.

"A bad place to die," Blandine said.

Drummond was about to respond, "There is no good place," but held back as a hawk passed over them, flying pell-mell through the woods, effortlessly dodging the overhanging branches and screaming its cry of *"Kree! Kree!"*

"Let's go, Drummond," Blandine said. It was only getting darker. "There's nothing for us here."

They pulled up to the Hawes homestead as the woods went inky black. From their point of view at the edge of the clearing, the cabin seemed abandoned. A small, half-collapsing barn looked as though it were fleeing from the house, heading back into the forest.

No one around. No fresh tracks in the snow.

They led their horses into the barn's musty darkness, finding a listless little pony inside so emaciated she appeared more like an oversized goat. Feed looked to be scarce in the rick, and strewn on the dirt floor were layers of filthy straw. A kicked-over empty bucket showed next to one half filled with water. When Drummond extracted a bundle of carrots from the canvas pack on the spare bay, he made sure to give a few to the pony.

Standing before the door of the cabin, which was as small as the smallest dwelling in New Amsterdam and built of rough-hewn logs, Blandine realized that there was indeed human life inside. The faintest yellow light shone through the cracks in the shutters that covered the little window to her left.

Drummond and Blandine looked at each other. Just as Blandine lifted her hand to knock on the door, it swung open. Backlit by the faint glow of the fireplace coals stood a child of perhaps five, with dark eyes and hair almost as fair as Blandine's. A colorless blanket enveloped her body, and on her feet were creations that resembled not shoes nor stockings as much as bandages.

"We don't know you," said the girl.

"That's right," said Drummond. It was nearly as cold in the room as it was outside.

"No, we don't know you," the girl repeated.

"Might we come in, miss?" offered Blandine. "Just for a moment."

The child stepped toward them into the doorway.

"Mama is sick," she said.

Blandine and Drummond peered into the room. Two stools stood in front of the hearth, one cockeyed with a broken leg. The floor, like the stalls of the barn, had yellow straw cast across its length. A small table stood by the left wall. What the interior displayed most were rags, mounded in piles on the table, cast off along the wall and cascading dangerously toward the hearth.

The cabin walls had begun their existence as white plaster, but had been discolored by smoke from the fireplace, which apparently had a dysfunctional flue. Even standing at the open door, Blandine suppressed an urge to cough.

"Perhaps we could help your mama," said Drummond.

The girl stepped slowly backward, toward the smoldering hearth, and admitted the two visitors.

"Who is it?" said a form on a bed to the right of the fireplace. It was impossible to see her features in the darkness. There appeared to be a pile of rags atop her not unlike the ones scattered around the room. An older girl sat at the edge of the bed.

Blandine removed her gloves. The tips of her fingers felt frozen.

"Who is it?" said the mother again.

"They didn't say," said the little girl.

Drummond and Blandine stepped toward the woman. "I am Edward Drummond, and this is Blandine van Couvering."

"I don't know you, do I?" whispered the woman. They were close enough now to see her features, which were pinched and gray and seemingly soiled with the same soot that hung in the air of the house.

"We haven't met," said Blandine. "We are here to talk with you about your son."

"Mama is tired," interjected the girl at the edge of the bed. She, too, wore a ripped, dirty blanket and bandagelike wrappings on her feet.

"I know, dear," said Blandine. "But we need to speak for just a few minutes."

"It's all right," said the woman. "I am Kitty Hawes. It's not my son you are speaking of, it is my nephew, Joseph. We called him Jope, because when she was little that's all my youngest could pronounce."

A tiny light flickered in the eyes of Kitty Hawes as she looked at her daughter. She paused. "A wicked world it is."

"We're sorry for your loss," Blandine said, crossing the small, cluttered space to stand next to the bed. "We don't wish to bring up painful memories, but we need to know how it happened."

"You don't bring painful memories, I live with them every day," Kitty Hawes said. "I remember Jope leaving out that door carrying our musket as though it happened just before the moment you came in."

Drummond let his gaze wander around the room, inventorying the fireplace crane and trammel, the several cook pots laid on the bricks, all as barren as the kicked-over bucket in the barn. Apart from a long rope of onions hanging off the summer beam, nothing of sustenance appeared anywhere in the cabin.

"What are you called?" he asked the youngest girl in a soft voice.

She looked at him suspiciously. "Laura."

"A pretty name. What is your sister called?"

"Evie." Laura stared at him some more, then suddenly broke out in a smile and jumped several times in place. A heartbreaker.

Drummond turned back to Blandine's conversation with Kitty Hawes.

"Can you tell us anything about when he was found?" Blandine asked. "We have heard some of it from the Hendricksons, and from Enoch Wood. But it all sounds so wild."

"By the time the landsman brought me Jope's body," Kitty said, "it was difficult to even look at him. He had these . . . pieces taken out of his flesh. But I washed Jope and wrapped him and my husband and I were about to lay him in a grave by the barn. Then the Hendricksons sent over a pine coffin, bless their souls."

"I was interested to hear you say he was your nephew," Drummond said. "We were under the impression he was your child."

"Oh, he is not my son," Kitty said. "Jope is my husband's brother's boy. He was living with us because both of his parents had gone to their graves. Vomiting blood. Same as Matthew, my husband, not three months ago."

She coughed and held a discolored square of linen to her mouth.

"An orphan," said Blandine, sotto to Drummond. He nodded.

Blandine had mouthed the word quietly, but feeble as she was, Kitty Hawes heard it anyway. "We never liked to see it that way, Jope an orphan," she said. "He was as close to Matthew and me as any son could be. My girls loved him as a brother."

Laura crept over to Drummond's side, taking his hand in a filthy one of hers.

"Since he passed, and my husband passed, there is no one to till our acreage," Kitty said. "Girls ain't old enough. Strong enough."

"I am too strong," said Evie.

"Evie," said her mother, "go put some of that samp on for supper."

"I'm hungry," Laura said.

"I know you are, honey," said her mother. "Help Evie now. You can go outside and bring up a turnip from the root cellar."

The two girls drifted off to their chores, Laura holding on to Drummond's hand until the last moment.

"I didn't want them to hear this," said Kitty Hawes. "It concerns Jope."

She sat up in bed and held the stained cloth to her mouth, controlling her coughing.

"There were things. Things around him."

Blandine looked over at Evie by the fire.

"They brought the items back to us along with the body. But I burnt most of it. They weren't fit to be near good people such as us."

"What do you mean?" Drummond said.

"Things written on stones. Bones. And something I saved." She stopped, reached down along the wall under the bed, and pulled out a totem figure.

"A sort of dolly," she said. "But not the kind my girls would ever play with."

Kitty Hawes handed the corn-husk doll over to Blandine.

"The heathens keep 'em in their lodges for protection, or maybe they worship them. Matthew told me it was to them the mother spirit. This one has that blackish paint on it. The work of Mahicans, maybe, or Quinnipiac. We see them sometimes, crossing our land."

She fell back on the rags that served as her pillow. Evie came over from the hearth.

"She needs to rest," said the girl. "Can I give you some corn mush?"

"We're fine," Blandine said. "We have food ourselves, and perhaps we can share some with you."

Drummond and Blandine walked to the door. Coming in at the same time was Laura, holding the small globe of a purple-topped turnip. "You won't go," she said stoutly.

The repast they all shared that night held little cheer and smaller savor. Blandine managed to find two pieces of hard candy secreted in her kit. She shared the treats with Laura and Evie. The girls received them as manna from heaven.

"Happy Christmas," Blandine said.

"Happy Christmas," the girls murmured in concert, sucking on the sugar.

Blandine masked her emotion by doing what she did whenever she didn't know what to do. She cleaned. The cabin did not give up its dirt easily. Drummond read to the girls from the New Testament, the welcoming of Jesus by the children on Palm Sunday. The only book in the house.

At the end of the night, as Drummond prepared to go to bed in the barn, Laura refused to let him leave. She had been resting in his lap all evening.

Standing on her tiptoes, holding on to Drummond's cloak, she put her tiny mouth to his ear. "Mister," she said, "might you need a servant? I can cook, and clean, and I'm so good at taking care of Mama."

Drummond kissed the top of her head and took himself out to the barn, which with four horses in it seemed to offer warmer possibilities than the dwelling.

The girls curled up together like puppies, lying amid the rag piles that seemed the family's only asset, on the bricks in front of the dying embers of the fire.

Blandine slept in bed alongside the clammy, corpselike body of Kitty Hawes, turning her face away to avoid the woman's cough. She woke in the night to find Kitty clinging to her. The corn-husk totem doll had somehow migrated from beneath the bed to lodge alongside Blandine's ribs.

29

"We had visitors," Ad Hendrickson said to his brother.

"Aye," Ham said. "The Englisher."

A long pause. The brothers were in the *groot kamer* of their northland plantation house. They had closed up the rest of their rambling manse, relegated the servants to the barn and retreated for the winter into the single large room.

"You see he don't come here to visit us," Ad said.

"No, he don't dare."

Pauses in conversation between Ad and Ham customarily grew to great dark gulfs, through which sea dragons swam. A report had come in from their indian friends (the Hendricksons still had a few, those they hadn't exterminated) about trespassers on the eastern perimeter of their patent, along the contentious boundary with New England.

An English gentleman and a wench, on horseback.

Drummond.

Other reports had come to the Hendricksons throughout the fall into Christmas, troubling accounts of the witika business afflicting the capital to the south. Ad, especially, didn't like it. He had dispatched brother Martyn to New Amsterdam to keep him out of trouble, not to send him into the midst of more.

Ad had no use for the city. He construed the Hendrickson patent on the North River, its plantation and woodlands, its livestock and tenants, as a self-contained realm. Petrus Stuyvesant might make noise about being governor of all of New Netherland, but his authority meant little here. The estate comprised the Hendrickson duchy, an independent principality, and it weren't no republic, neither. Besides, the peg-leg had his hands full with all the wickedness of New Amsterdam.

Ad stirred the fire in the hearth. Ham liked to keep the *groot kamer* cold, freezing, in order to save on firewood. He assumed his usual seat in an upholstered, thronelike chair along the wall, as far from the chimney

as he could get. But Ad, at forty years old, felt the first touch of the bony
fingers of age. A hardwood fire felt good on a dark winter day.

Ham rose and crossed to the chamber-stool lodged near the outside
door. He unbelted himself, squatted and evacuated noisily with several
sharp cracking blasts. The chimney draft drew the stench into the room,
but Ad paid it no mind. His brother's smell was as familiar as his own.

The Hendrickson clan started out in the new world four decades
before as a single-room family, and here they were back to it again.
From a miserable cabin (Ad kept it maintained, two leagues to the west,
nearer to the river, as a memorial) they rose to the largest house in the
North River highlands. Losing their mother and father at the start of
the struggle and forging ahead in spite of it. Tearing their patent out of
the unbreached wilderness by sheer force of will.

It was Ad and Ham that did it, really. Little Martyn was useless, a
weepy child, always burbling about missing his mama.

"I knew Mister Drummond was a problem when he first came to us on
his way to Beverwyck, jawing on about the Hawes boy killing," Ham said.

"Now this business to the south," Ad said.

"We should have shut him up in the smokehouse when he turned
thirteen," Ham said. He didn't need to name Martyn.

Ad said, "Fed him through the smoke hole."

"He gets antsy, we close the hole," Ham said.

The brothers laughed together silently. Ad again stirred the fire.

"I sure get tired cleaning up after him," Ham said. "I used to wipe his
little infant ass, but I thought that would be over when he growed. Is he any
good for anything besides spending our money and causing commotion?"

"Nay, for nothing but that," Ad said.

A long pause. Flames flared in the hearth and showed Ad's face.
Across the room, Ham remained in shadow. The brothers both knew
they loved their baby brother with a depth of emotion that veered toward
mania, but neither of them would have confessed it upon pain of death.

"When are we thinking of going down there?" Ham said.

"This week," Ad said.

He retrieved a cleaver from a pin on the chimney and crossed to the

pantry closet to cut slices of beef for their noon meal. Ham went outside
to get the beer, kept frosty cold in a bank of snow.

"I want, I want, I want, I want, I want!"

It was the kind of January day when the frozen ground temporarily thawed, men unbuttoned their waistcoats and the round sky above
brimmed with deep azure. Hausfraus bared their necks and shoulders to
the hot sun as they vigorously swept their stoops, stopping occasionally
to chat with their equally energetic neighbors. Oxen pulling carts full of
wood or stone to building sites seemed to haul their loads lightly in the
mildness of the day, flanks steaming beneath their yokes.

"I want . . ." The little girl stopped and put her finger in her mouth.

"Yes, Sabine, what is it you want?" Aet Visser had promised Anna,
Sabine's mother, to take the child with him for the morning.

"The play place!"

Anna, the woman Visser introduced to everyone as his servant, had
work to do. As always. When she wasn't cleaning Visser's home, she had
the job of stringing seawan for Frederick Philipse, the well-fed merchant
who had barrels of shells and beads stashed in his cellar on Stone Street.

The Dutch, from a waterlogged country, did not much favor cellars.
But such understories proved viable in New Amsterdam, and several of
the finer residences possessed them. Anna would sweep and polish the
Philipse storeroom, cleaning its smooth floor of paving stones and bright
whitewashed walls until not a speck of dirt survived.

The casement windows, installed up high to let in light from the
street, she washed to a transparent sparkle. You barely needed a candle
to work in the space, it was so little like a basement.

Here were dozens of wooden casks of seawan. Anna's job was to
count out and then string the beads, purple with purple and white with
white, on durable twine imported from Amsterdam. Her elder children
helped her, separating the finer shells from the not so fine. But Sabine,
at three, was only a nuisance.

Visser picked up the little girl at Philipse's Stone Street mansion
at nine o'clock that morning. The other children, Paulson and Abigel
and Maria, plunged their hands again and again into an open seawan

barrel, dribbling the beads out of their fingers to hear the sound they made.

Visser pretended to let Sabine carry the leash of the little dog Maddie, and they walked out about the town.

"Pow," Sabine said, using the nickname that had evolved when the children were forbidden to call Visser Papa. "Can we go? I want to!" She jumped up and down, holding his large hand in her own two and pulling him in the direction she wanted to head.

Pow and the Bean.

Visser patted the brandy flask in his waistcoat. He had worries about being seen drinking on the street, and also about being seen with Sabine. It was natural enough for an orphanmaster to accompany an orphan. But Visser was convinced that a person of only mild aptitude would be able to glean, at a glance, his paternal relationship with Sabine.

People would surely know a father and daughter when they saw them. Then a can of worms would be opened in Visser's private life that could not easily be closed back up. What kind of orphanmaster would he be, with a family of four bastards and a common-law wife?

On Market Street, just around the corner from Philipse's dwelling-house, lay a property that had once been used by a family of colonists who had no funds to build a real house. Instead, they dug a hole in the ground and lived under a roof of bark and thatch for the five years they tried to make a go of life in New Amsterdam.

Since the family returned, disconsolate, to Patria, ownership of the property had been under dispute. As a result, no dwelling-house had been erected there, even though Market was now a street of fine homes. The roof of the pit-house had long since decayed and fallen in. Between two handsome residences sat this eyesore, a round-shouldered depression in the stony ground.

The pit made for the perfect play place, as far as Sabine was concerned. But Pow was the only one to allow her there. She jumped, one step at a time, two feet on each step, down the flight of slate stairs that led to the pit's hard-packed floor.

Once there, the Bean busily began to take handfuls of wet earth from the sides of her "house." Roots, pebbles and the random grub filled the muck, just the right consistency for making into pies. Visser sat at the bottom of the steps, only a slight headache marring the pleasure of watching the Bean assemble her feast.

He wondered at how a man of his advanced age—he was nearing fifty—came to be caring for a toddler. "By the usual method," he muttered to himself.

"*Koeckjes,*" the Bean said, presenting a mud confection to Maddie, then pushing a handful of patty-cake soil toward Visser's mouth.

"Come here," said Visser. "I'll give you a cookie, all right." He grabbed her and tickled her until her bonnet fell off. Then he gave her what they, in the Bean's family, called "whisker love," rubbing his rough beard across her soft cheeks.

"Pow!" she protested, laughing helplessly. "Pow, no!" She wrapped her arms around his neck and held on, Maddie yapping all the while. When the Bean escaped to scamper back across the dirt floor of the pit, Visser removed the brandy from his pocket and raised it to his lips.

"Ho, down there," came a voice from the street.

Visser quickly replaced the stopper on the brandy bottle and laid the vessel on the ground beneath the folds of his cloak.

"Visser!" came the voice of Martyn Hendrickson from above. Sabine sat on the ground, still shaping her feast of mud, her skirts a filthy puff in a circle all around her.

"Hendrickson," said Visser. "What brings you out?"

"Exceptional day, is it not?" said Martyn. "That sky is a robin's egg."

"Have you been spending much time away from town?" Visser said. He remembered Martyn's menacing, hand-on-dagger conversation in the stable yard. They had not seen each other since.

"Lying low," said Martyn. "Pretty thing she's turning into."

Visser winced. "The dog?"

"The child. Which one's this?"

"Sabine," said Visser. Thinking he was calling her, the Bean toddled over into Visser's arms and turned her rosy face up to the man towering above.

"Hello, Sabine," said Martyn. "Hello, little girl."

Sabine smiled and put her mud-caked finger to her mouth. Visser batted it gently away.

"I have cookies!" the Bean said. She pronounced it, with her usual lisp, as "tookies."

"I wish I had a little baker like you," Hendrickson said, smiling.

To distract the man from his interest in the child, Visser fished out the bottle. "Can I tempt you with a pull of cognac?"

"For now, no. I am off for parts north. *Hunter* awaits me at the pier." The Hendrickson family's river sloop.

"Another day, then," Visser said.

"You have your hands full, Visser, do you not?" Hendrickson said. "All the poor orphan boys and girls, and just one of you."

"God's work," said Visser.

"Ah, God," Hendrickson said. "He's gone and died and made us all into his orphans, hasn't he?"

Visser blinked up at the man.

"Difficult to keep them all alive and prospering, I guess," said Hendrickson, allowing his vague smile to remain in place.

Visser could not respond to that. He pulled the Bean close.

"I did have another shipment," Visser said.

"Ah, yes, *Eenhoorn*, the *Unicorn*," Martyn said. "I wondered that you didn't come to me when it docked. I thought maybe you were angry with me."

"Oh, no," Visser said.

"Good specimens?"

"One or two you might be interested in," Visser said.

"Keep us in mind for them, will you? My brothers always need willing hands for the estate, and I myself—well, you know my needs."

"I will wait on your return," Visser said to Martyn. "When will we have that good fortune?"

"Oh, you'll know it when you see me," said Hendrickson.

Per usual, thought Visser. But Hendrickson's departure gave him an idea.

Martyn started to go. He stopped and turned briefly back around.

"She really is adorable," he said, smiling down at the Bean. "Grow her some, and then bring her to me."

Stone Street remained the prime address for the burghers of New Amsterdam, but the Hendrickson place gave Market Street a particular cachet all its own. The colony's joiners, turners and housewrights had been kept busy on it. Riven shingles covered most of the upper story, but a new addition featured the settlement's first slate roof, as well as decorative cornices and a series of window-sash embrasures that were at least four feet broad.

The wonder of it was that the dwelling-house stood empty much of the time. Ad and Ham seldom came to town, and Martyn, well, Martyn was a flibbertigibbet, a cuckoo flitting from nest to nest, gone even when he was present. He would as well pass out over dice in the Mane as sleep in his own bed.

And the three brothers were all there was, the father crushed by a falling tree on the estate up north, and soon after the mother dead when Martyn was three. The boy entered a rheumatoid fever delirium and woke up a week later to find his dear mama gone and buried. The tragedy marked him. His brothers always said Martyn became a different child after that, weepy, angry, unpredictable.

For years, he ran from his sorrow. Even as a child, he slept away often. Ad and Ham never knew where he was or what he was up to. When Martyn turned twenty, they sent him on a tour of Europe. He returned with new costumery and revised manners, but never said a word about his experiences to his brothers. To them, Martyn remained remote, unpindownable.

So the Hendrickson town house stood grand and lonely, its hearth fires attended by servants, its floors swept and its linens changed, usually for no one.

Visser liked to visit. He would ascertain that the hosts would not be present, then rap upon the garden door to gain entry. Several of his orphan charges found service work at the house over the years, and he conducted his forays under the pretense of checking up on them.

It did not hurt that the empty house kept an excellent larder. All servants and no masters lent the premises an air of holiday, and his orphans fed and beveraged Visser well. He liked being served. He habitually avoided any brush with the cookstove himself. Anna cooked for him, or he took his meals at the Red Lion.

This day he saw Hendrickson ride away from the pit toward the canal and the river docks. He hustled the Bean and Maddie back to the care of Anna and left quickly, trailing apologies, fare-thee-wells and half-explanations. Then he returned to Market Street, passed by the pit and continued down the street to the hulking wooden monster that was the Hendrickson dwelling-house.

"Halloo!" he cried, coming into the little vestibule that gave onto the town house's great room.

Myrthe and Nicole, a matched pair of German cousins, fifteen years of age, their mothers, sisters, both dead in an indian massacre, interrupted their prattle to greet him.

"Sire," both girls exclaimed at once. Visser habitually forgot their last name. Mueller, that was it.

He strode into the center of the room to admire its spaciousness. Oh, the habits of the rich! He liked how the gold wood of the pine floorboards gleamed beneath several coats of naval varnish. He liked how the mantel was not of rude fieldstone but boxed in by a green-painted wooden frame braced with stout pillars. He liked the cushioned chairs, made easy by stuffing the upholstery with overgenerous amounts of horsehair.

Everything spick and span. His charges evidently did their jobs well. They now brought him coffee. Coffee!

Someone was cracking the whip, Visser had no idea whom. Not Martyn. The man could not run a household if his life depended upon it. He needed taking care of, and could take care of nothing himself.

"*Mit schlag*, sire?" Myrthe said to him, offering the cream she had just whipped that morning.

"Certainly," Visser cried, extending his cup. "Do they treat you well here?"

"Oh, yes, sire," Myrthe said, dishing up a fat, oily dollop of *schlag* into the orphanmaster's coffee and then curtsying. "Very well."

"I'm glad of it. No one getting too familiar with ye?"

Myrthe blushed. "No, never, sire."

Servant rape was a problem in the colony. Visser had encountered cases before, and wouldn't countenance the practice, sending for the *schout* whenever circumstances warranted. Martyn, drunken, decadent Martyn, might be a prime suspect for it, if his brandy habit would ever allow him concupiscence.

"The new best chamber is finished," Nicole said. "Would you like to see it?"

"After my coffee," Visser said. "Go ahead about your duties, child. I would not draw you away from them. I will show myself the new room on my own. It is just through there?"

"Yes, sire," Nicole said. The two cousins drew self-consciously away from Visser to the opposite end of the room, where they made elaborate motions of polishing plate.

Invigorated by the coffee and settled by a stomach full of pastry delicacies, Visser strolled through the echoing chambers of the Hendrickson house, examining the cloth, thumping the plasterwork. He entered the new room, part of yet another addition.

A new chimney, a new hearth! Manganese tiles from Delft framed the fireplace, each maroon-and-white square depicting a scene of *wilden* in the new world. Visser bent his head to examine the images. Someone's idea of the American indigenes, to be sure, but nothing close to reality. Nobody ever got the natives right. From Visser's experience, they were not to be got. Except for his Anna.

"Put your hand on the wall just there and push," Nicole said. She had entered the room stealthily behind him and startled Visser.

"What?"

"That panel, there," the girl said. "Push it."

Visser did so, and the wall yielded with a click and then swung outward.

"A secret chamber," Nicole said. "The housewright said we are to go inside there in case of indian attack."

"It is the only room we don't clean," Myrthe said, coming in behind Nicole, "because we dasn't enter."

"I'll go in," Visser said.

"Oh, no, sir," Myrthe said. "No one is allowed."

"Go to your silver cleaning," Visser said, employing his voice of command. The two girls hesitated, then left.

He opened the door wide and stepped inside the secret room.

A sharp metallic smell hit his senses. The place was small, five feet by ten, extending back along the side of the chimney stack. The only light came from a narrow horizontal window at the top of the far wall.

Wishing for the full effect, Visser swung shut the door panel, closing himself in. Crocks of water lined one side. A wooden *kas*, or wardrobe cabinet, stood crammed at the far end, its double doors fastened with a bent and varnished stick.

Visser never knew what made him slip the stick aside and open the doors of the cabinet. He was naturally curious, especially in other people's houses, where he spent a good deal of his time. But this went beyond idle curiosity. Some sense of the place gave him a feeling of urgency.

Inside the wardrobe were linens, lengths of cloth. But stuffed into a bottom back corner was a disheveled heap of garments for children, shirts and pants and jackets. They were wrinkled and stained, and gave off the dead smell Visser encountered when he first gained access to the secret chamber.

He reached out to touch the fabric of one coat, and found it stiff with dried blood. Black confetti flecks came off on his hand.

That was not the horror of it, though. The horror of it was Visser recognized many of the clothes.

30

Miep Fredericz and young Ann Godbolt were not the best of friends. Though they sat in the same classroom, two years separated them. But when Miep hooked her arm through Ann's outside the schoolhouse and whispered in her ear, Ann began to consider her quite nice.

"I think the schoolmaster is sweet on you," said Miep. "After lunch I saw him staring."

Adolphus Roeletsen, a gangly Flemish import of twenty-six who had been known to go head to head with the director general on Latin phraseology, possessed two qualities that were a boon to misbehaving students: bad eyesight and a distracted sensibility. He barely saw his students when they sat before him, let alone favor one of the girls in particular.

But Ann Godbolt, rather full of herself at the advanced age of thirteen, believed every word Miep said. In fact, she wished to hear more on the same theme.

So Ann invited Miep to visit her home when the school day ended. The Godbolt family lived on the corner of Beaver Street and the Broad Way, and their crisp clapboard town house abutted a small shop whose door stayed open most of the day, the better to entice potential shoppers with the fragrance of the smoked pork within.

A favorite game of the two Godbolt girls, Ann and Mary, was to peek out the glossy black shutters of the upstairs windows and, when passersby ignored their family shop, to drip soapy water onto their heads.

"Miep!" Mary whispered, holding the water jar. "Come!"

Miep Fredericz looked around the corner parlor on the second floor while the girls engaged in their pranks. There was a baby's cradle on rockers, and a bed with dark blue curtains all around it.

She felt like a spy, and relished the feeling. Her assignment from Miss Blandina—to find all she could of what the Godbolt children knew about their foster brother, William Turner—at first troubled her, then tantalized her.

Blandine's standing in the community had plummeted since Miep had worked for her in the fall. "You are to have no more business with her," Carsten Fredericz van Jeveren told Miep just after Christmas.

"Why, Father?" Miep asked.

"Do what I tell you, d'ye hear?" Carsten barked, saying no more.

But the school-yard children knew. Blandine van Couvering, they gossiped to one another, stood accused of witika witchcraft. The particulars were vague, but the children embroidered their own fanciful details. Blandine ate orphans. She liked their stewed eyeballs, Paula Kertemann suggested, most of all.

Miep remained aloof. Loyalty was her lodestar. She alone knew Miss Blandina. She alone would help her, save her from the gossip and scandal, pull her out of the burning flames at the stake. If her mentor found it necessary to know more about the Godbolt ward, William Turner, Miep would oblige.

It was time to put Miss Blandina's plan into effect. Miep pulled from her pocket a netted bag Blandine had given her, stuffed with honey balls, peppermint sticks and chewy golden toffee.

"Ann, Mary," Miep called. "Would you like a candy?"

Ann and Mary left off their soap-water game as if jerked by a chain. They were usually forbidden anything sugary.

Miep's bag proved bottomless. After Ann and Mary crammed their cheeks full, Georgie and Charles tumbled into the room. The boys didn't have to demand their share. Miep gave it freely.

The Godbolt children sat sucking and munching, their backs along the wall, while Miep stayed in the center of the room, like the conductor of an orchestra.

"Where's the other kid?" Miep said. She found herself smiling foolishly in her nervousness, but the thought of Miss Blandina made her soldier on. "Is he still at school?"

"Don't know," said Georgie. At six, he was the youngest. His teeth had gotten stuck in a toffee bit and he drooled a fat teardrop of brown-colored spittle as he tried to work the piece loose.

"William," said Mary, her mouth full, too. "Don't even think about him. He wouldn't want any candy anyway."

"Ask William, 'Do you want some candy?'" said Ann. "You know what he'd say? Nothing."

The Godbolt children all laughed.

"He don't say nothing!" Georgie crowed. Miep stepped forward and stuck a peppermint stick directly into his open mouth.

"He's a mute," said Mary.

"He's dumb," said Ann.

"You know, I had a funny feeling when I saw him this year at school," Miep said. "He looked different to me."

The Godbolt children turned sullen, silent. They glanced sideways at one another. All their licking, sucking, chewing and chomping slowed.

"William is a very nice boy," said Ann. "As nice as can be."

Mary glared at the other children. "William has become a part of our family," she volunteered.

Charles said, "I like him. I really do."

Georgie said, "Me, too. Especially the new William." He held out his peppermint stick, admiring the way he had sucked it into a point at the end.

Miep said, "Especially what? The new William?"

Ann said, "Go get washed up, Georgie, your face is a mess."

Mary said, "Yeah, Georgie, go away, you're annoying."

"But I'd just like a little more candy wandy," said Georgie, sensing Miep's interest in his remark. Georgie liked attention, and didn't usually get it in the hurly-burly atmosphere of the Godbolt household.

Miep steeled herself. She took a caramel out of her bag and waved it in front of Georgie. "Tell me about the new William."

"He's a bad boy I like who's nice to me," Georgie said, taking the caramel. Ann, sitting beside her little brother, kicked at his shin with her pointed silk slipper. Georgie just giggled.

Miep found herself stumped. What would Blandine have her do? Her mind felt thwarted, dim.

"Is it a secret?" she suddenly said. "I love secrets. I can keep a secret."

"Mama told us never to tell," Ann said.

"I promise," Miep said.

"Mary," Ann said. She pulled her sister and Miep into the empty hallway, away from the boys.

"Wandy, wandy!" Georgie called after them.

"All right," Ann whispered. "Do you pinkie-swear not to tell?"

Miep held out the little finger of her right hand. Ann and Mary held out theirs. The three girls linked pinkies and pulled. The pact was sealed.

"The orphan boy William came to us a lot of months ago," Ann said.

"In the spring," Mary said.

"Then he went away," Ann said.

"He went away?" Miep said.

"We lost him," Ann said. "No one knew where he went. Our parents were frantic."

"They loved William," Mary said. "And he was going to give us a lot of money."

"Real money, gold money," Ann said, relishing the tale. "He had a 'heritance."

The three girls had their heads together, their mouths a few inches from one another in the dark hallway.

"So what happened?" Miep asked.

"We got a new William," Ann said. "A different William."

"He came from the Sopus indians!" Mary said, glorying in the outlandish detail, raising her voice. Ann shushed her.

"See, if we're all quiet about it, we'll get the 'heritance anyway," Ann said. "No one is to know. Not Petrus Stuyvesant, not the schoolmaster, not the orphanmaster, nobody."

"We'll be rich!" Mary said, again too loudly.

"We're already rich, booby," Ann said. "We'll be richer. When we go to Paris, France, Miep, I shall bring you back a ribbon."

"Thank you," Miep said, smiling.

"Have you any more caramels?" Mary said.

Just then Miep saw Rebecca Godbolt come to the bottom of the staircase below them. She held a slab of bacon in one hand and a cast-iron skillet in the other.

Miep motioned to the girls, and they stepped back out of sight toward the best chamber.

"Pinkie-swear," whispered Mary, kissing Miep on the cheek. Miep nodded, crossing her fingers behind her back.

"Children," called Rebecca, "do I have to do everything myself?"

* * *

Lightning enjoyed entering homes whose occupants were not present almost as much as he did when they were home and asleep. He liked the sense of intimacy, of prying out people's secrets, of touching private objects.

His master had instructed Lightning to salt the home of the pretty Dutch she-merchant with witika items. The willow-stick totems, a lodge doll and one of the deerskin masks. Lightning chose a mask he had crafted and rejected as unworthy for ritualized use. He carried them all in his kit bag when he slipped over the woman's garden wall, through her yard and past her back door into her chambers.

Also in his bag, a bit of mischief that would help doom Blandine van Couvering to be burned at the stake as a witika witch.

His master liked to keep garments from their kills. It was a stupid quirk of his, Lightning realized. But Lightning had quirks of his own, and he felt indulgent toward those of his friend.

They had to force the she-merchant and the Englisher off the trail somehow. And the best defense was to attack. This the master taught Lightning.

Pawing through the she-merchant's *kas*, Lightning found lace frillies, rigid underclothes that kept milady's figure from spilling out, numerous handkerchiefs. He took a couple of the latter. More than anything, Lightning liked to present himself as a European, a swannekin gentleman of the most impeccable costume. The nose-cloths might help that effect.

Lightning's secret dream was to join the promenade at *kermis*. Dressed as a dandy, the linen square stiff in his breast pocket, he would mince, he would quick-step, he would parade. In his vision, the woman beside him showed up indistinct. Perhaps Lightning could be allowed to promenade on his own, to the wonder of all onlookers.

Yes, Lightning was half Sopus indian. But he was half German, too. Wasn't Germany a well-recognized part of the continent of Europe? Yes, he was a vile bit of rape spawn. But couldn't a fellow rise above his beginnings?

From within Blandine's *kas* he extracted a linen gown of light apricot, slipping it on loosely over his shoulders. Swannekins sometimes wore women's clothes at *kermis*, didn't they? Everything was upside down. Lightning brushed his fingers against the fabric and brought them to his nostrils, inhaling the Van Couvering girl's scent.

Lightning looked around the room he had broken into. He would have all of this someday. The dwelling-house. The garden. The comfortable bed with its goose-feather mattress. Perhaps Lightning could even possess the she-merchant's rooms themselves, with all their furnishings, after he watched her sizzle in the flames at the stake.

"Witch!" he would shout out, adding his voice to the others.

What a surprise the meddling girl would have, when she returned to New Amsterdam to find all fingers pointed at her. Witch!

The master would take care of bringing the witch-hunters down upon Blandine. The Van Couvering woman was the one, the master would say, she made the witika appear. She murdered the children herself. Look in her rooms. You will find the evidence there.

The Walloon *schout*, De Klavier, would search Van Couvering's rented dwelling-house on Pearl Street. Lightning thought he might take a table across the way, at the Red Lion, to watch the fun.

Thoughts of the Red Lion made Lightning hungry, and he took an onion from a wreath above the hearth. He sat down at the table, dreaming over how it would be—the search, the discovery of incriminating evidence, the hated she-merchant branded as a witch, the instigator of all the orphan-killings in the colony burned at the stake.

Contemplating these thoughts, Lightning bit into the onion and ate it like an apple.

The nights were the worst for Aet Visser.

After Anna and the children left for their lodgings up at Corlaers Hook, he found himself alone in his hodgepodge of a dwelling-house. He couldn't stand it. Insomnia plagued him. He would oftentimes bolt out of the house and wander the dark precincts of the settlement. He would have climbed out of his own skin if it were possible.

On many of these black wanderings, Visser wound up in front of the pit-house on Market Street, the place where Sabine loved to play.

Beside the pit-house, on the eastern edge of the lot, lay piled an old mound of dirt, an excavation from the original pit. Weeds had grown over it with the years, a frowzy green beard of dock, chickweed and henbit. In the winter the mound became a ten-foot-high hump of frozen snow. An unremarkable feature of the settlement, except for one attribute that drew Visser to it.

From the small height of the dirt mound, it was possible to keep an eye on both the front entrance and the back garden door of the Hendrickson mansion, just down Market Street. From atop the dirt and slush of the mound, Visser could surveil the house where Martyn Hendrickson (occasionally) spent his nights.

What was Visser doing? Why did he watch? He tormented himself with random imaginings. He explained the clothes he found in the secret room at the Hendricksons' in various ways. Adias and Abraham were the real witika killers. Or perhaps Martyn had been secretly deputized by the *schout* to look into the orphan-killings and was keeping the clothes as evidence. Any innocent explanation would do.

Otherwise—if there were no innocent explanation for the clothes in the *kas*—then the only alternative explanation was that he himself, Aet Visser, the orphanmaster, charged with guarding the interests of the colony's parentless children, had instead fed them into a monstrous, murderous, unthinkable plot.

So he watched. Some days and most nights, he would find himself standing partially concealed by the small knob of dirt near the pit-house. He did not feel the cold. Or rather, he understood that the cold represented a measure of his penitence.

What was he looking for? Certainty. He groped toward an awful truth that he both needed to know and was desperately afraid to discover. Hoping, and hoping against hope. He and Martyn Hendrickson were thick as thieves. If Martyn was guilty of monstrosities, well, then, so was Aet Visser.

He watched Martyn come in from his evenings in the Red Lion, his nights at the sporting houses of the Strand.

This particular night, Martyn entered the hulking mansion, closed the door and lit no lamps inside. Visser peered at the house as though his gaze would penetrate the wooden ramparts of Fortress Hendrickson. He always experienced a sense of relief when Martyn was safely at home. Visser could see both doorways. Martyn could not leave without the shadowy midnight watcher spying him.

So Visser was stunned out of his wits that evening when, after seeing Martyn enter his home and stay there, where he could do no one harm, suddenly the man's voice sounded behind him.

"It's Mister Visser," Martyn said. "Out for a breath of night air, orphanmaster?"

Beside Martyn, smirking knowingly, stood Lightning.

"Martyn," Visser said. "How did you . . . ?" He must be seeing things. He had witnessed the man just now go into his house, had not seen him come out, yet here he was. A man could not be in two places at once. Unless he were a wizard or devil of some sort.

"Come along with us, brother," Lightning said.

"Yes, do," Martyn said. "We're off to the hunt."

A hunt? At night? Perhaps, Visser thought, they were headed to the whorehouses of the Strand. "I have an appointment," he said, stammering out the words.

"Break it," Martyn said.

"No, no, no, no," Visser said.

"No, no, no, no," Lightning mocked him.

"Well, go along, then," Martyn said. "Go to your odd late-night assignation, at a time when no one has meetings. As long as your rendezvous is not with the *schout*. It's not with the *schout*, is it, Visser?"

"No," Visser said, his mouth quite dry.

"Because if you talk to the *schout*, we might have something to say to him, too."

"About you and my beautiful sister," Lightning said.

"Please, Martyn, no—I am silent as the grave," Visser said, groveling. "Anna is my . . ."

"Your what?" Martyn demanded. "We let you have her, Visser, but we can take her away, too."

Visser stood shamefaced, his neck bent like a whipped dog.

"Are you our man?" Martyn asked.

"I'm your man," Visser said, his voice a whisper.

"Good," Martyn said. "*Au revoir*, then."

The two men strode off together, not toward the Strand but to the north, toward the palisade wall. To the hunt, whatever they might mean by that.

31

Weary and travel-battered, Blandine and Drummond returned to New Amsterdam in the dead cold of early February. The East River roadstead proved clogged with jumbled floes of ice. They disembarked their sloop at Hell Gate and proceeded toward town along a well-trampled footpath through the snow.

They spoke about what new evidence they had gleaned on the winter trip to the north. "He targets orphans exclusively," Blandine said.

"He? Do we know he's a he?" Drummond said.

"No woman, whether she be *wilden*, Dutch or English, could do what has been done to those children."

"Perhaps, but I was thinking more 'they' than 'he.'"

"Granted," Blandine said. "It might be more than one."

Not a soul appeared to them on the path. The surrounding *bouweries* looked deserted also, the smoke from a few lone chimneys providing the only sign of life. "What about the witika?" Drummond said.

"What about it?" Blandine said.

"Do we think it could be an indian demon doing all this?"

"You mean Kitane, while he's possessed."

"No, I mean a creature nine feet tall that can walk on water," Drummond said. "The monster we saw in the fright show on Christmas Eve."

Blandine said, "I don't believe in haints, sprites, ghosts, devils, sea monsters nor anything else used to scare children or childlike adults."

"Nor witches," Drummond said.

"Not witches either," Blandine said, smiling painfully.

"Nor any god," Drummond said.

Blandine was silent. Even though she didn't believe in ghosts, she could still scare herself by imagining bumps in the night.

Drummond said, "What man knows orphans? To kill or kidnap orphans, one has to know which child is one, and which is not."

"I know you mean Aet Visser," Blandine said. "But he put you on to the Godbolts, trying to ascertain if they had switched out William Turner. Would the real killer have done that?"

"We don't know what happened to William Turner, or if anything did," Drummond said.

"Kitane is in the northland, trying to turn up the facts of that," Blandine said. "He could be waiting for us in the settlement."

"Aye," Drummond said.

They could see the palisade wall of New Amsterdam before them to the south as they trekked along the river.

"Piddy we know disappeared," Blandine said, once again going through the sad litany of victims. "Ansel Imbrock, we know. The Gessie kids."

"Dickie Dunn," Drummond said. "The missing-foot boy."

"Let's concentrate on those," Blandine said.

"They've disappeared, yes," Drummond said. "But if they have indeed been killed, then where are the bodies? *Habeas corpus*, as the director general might say."

The odd sense of a deserted community continued as they came to the boundary of New Amsterdam. Approaching the land port at the East River end of the palisade wall, they found it closed and fortified.

"Halloo! Halloo!" Drummond tried, but no one came. This was decidedly strange. Even in winter, the land ports normally bustled.

"What's happened?" he said.

"The English invaded and rounded up the Dutch," Blandine suggested. "Sent them all back to Patria."

"Who will make the doughnuts now?" Drummond said. "Have you ever eaten English cooking?"

"Come on," Blandine said. She led Drummond west along a narrow path running below the wall. Two hundred yards along this track, Blandine pushed in a pair of the palisade logs, which swung easily aside to admit them to the town.

"Very clever," Drummond said. But he noted the position of the gap, in order to be prepared if his compatriots in the English army ever needed to breach the colony wall.

They found themselves in town, near Smit Street, which ran south and would lead them readily to Drummond's quarters in Slyck Steegh.

A brittle winter sundown lengthened the shadows in the settlement. No one abroad. A plague? An indian attack? Drummond couldn't fathom it.

A solitary soul did see them as they made the corner from Smit onto Slyck Steegh. A block away, coming up from the wharf district, a single figure, indistinct in the late afternoon darkness. The figure halted, shouted an unintelligible cry and ran away.

Blandine shook her head and laughed. "Welcome home," she said to Drummond.

"Stop and sup with me," Drummond said, when they reached his rooms.

"I think I would rather go straight on," Blandine said.

"We shall say good-bye, then," Drummond said.

"Good-bye, Drummond."

"With affection," he said, and bussed both her cheeks in the French style. Her skin felt soft and warm.

Drummond watched her go. He mounted his stoop and was about to unlock his front door when he found he could just push it open. Walking in, he realized instantly something was amiss.

His rooms had been tossed. Seriously. Every item of furniture overturned, every possession thrown to the floor. Drummond crossed to his best chamber and realized the intruders, whoever they were, had done the same there.

Thieves? He could ascertain nothing that was stolen, though much was destroyed. A ransacking, not a plunder.

But where were his papers? They, whoever "they" were, had taken them from the leather document case he kept hidden behind the bricks of the jamb stove.

He was discovered as a spy. The London letters and his orders from Clarendon and Downing were in code, of course, but codes could be broken.

Drummond had an impulse to call Blandine back, but when he went out onto the street, she had already made the turn onto the canal and was gone.

A sickening thought stabbed him. His workshop.

He rushed through his rooms, out the back entrance and into the yard. Full dark had not yet fallen, so even before he reached it, he realized the plunder had been applied to the outbuilding, too. He extracted his Scottish pistol from his belt.

His heart falling, he entered the low, rectangular room. Formerly neat as a pin when he left it a month ago, it was now a shambles. As Drummond stepped forward, glass crunched underneath his feet. Stunned by mounting anger, tears in his eyes, he cataloged his losses. His perspective tube, smashed. His glass-making apparatus scattered to the floor, wrecked. Every instrument that could be bent, busted or mangled, was.

The workshop's generous windows had been mostly broken, also. He looked through the frame of one of them to the top of his dwelling-house across the yard. At least they had not thought to dismantle the spyglass affixed to his roof. Its proud silhouette showed black against the fading sky.

As he stood there amid the wreckage of his life, Drummond heard shouts, voices. An alarm of some kind was being raised from the direction of the wharf. Still overcome with emotion, he crossed to his rooms, stepping over his scattered possessions to make his way to the open front door.

They met him there, at the bottom of his stoop, a dozen men, soldiers, burghers and the *schout*, De Klavier. Godbolt. Kees Bayard. Standing off to the side, the half-indian, Lightning.

"There he is!" Kees shouted, and the whole group rushed forward up the front steps. Drummond stumbled backward, aiming his pistol, at the last moment raising it upward and blasting the door lintel as the men filled the doorway.

Showered with dust and splinters of wood, his attackers retreated as quickly as they came, stumbling over one another in their haste to get out of the line of fire.

It would have been comical if Drummond had been in the mood. A mob of cowards. He reloaded his pistol, righted an overturned chair and sat down facing the open front door. He could hear them gabbing among themselves in the street.

"Drummond!" a voice called up. "We have you surrounded. Surrender yourself!"

De Klavier. Drummond had met him many times when the man shut the Red Lion at curfew. The more limited the authority, the greater the pomp.

"Don't you have a taproom to close?" he shouted out. "Someone to levy a fine against who has spat upon the director general's stoop?"

More voices in hurried conference. The square of his doorway glowed,

they had ignited a torch. A musket discharged, a man screamed, the gab
of voices rose to a pitch.

In his heart, Drummond knew there was nothing for it. What would
he do, hold out against the whole town? Make his escape over the rooftops like a Paris musketeer pursued by a jealous husband?

He decided not. He placed his periwig atop his head. "I'm coming
out," he shouted.

The voices outside suddenly stilled. Whispers.

De Klavier. "Throw out your pistol, first."

Drummond did so, then advanced on the door, stepped through and
stood looking down from the top of his stoop.

Three militiamen trained their muskets at him. The muzzle ends looked
huge to Drummond, bottomless, as if they were tunnels he could step inside.

"Put up your weaponry, gentlemen," he said. "I will come peace-
fully, and you don't want to hurt anyone else among you." One of the
guardsmen lay on the ground, nursing a bloody wound to his right foot,
accidentally self-inflicted.

De Klavier rushed up the stoop, finding his courage against an
unarmed prey.

"Edmund Drummond!" he shrieked.

"No," said Drummond calmly. "You've got the wrong man."

The *schout* halted, momentarily confused. "What?"

"My given name is Edward. If it's *Edmund* Drummond you want, I
advise you to look elsewhere."

The militiamen were on him by then, and they bound his arms and hustled
Drummond off the stoop down to the street. De Klavier rushed to catch up.

"I arrest you in the name of the Dutch West India Company for
treasonous acts against the jurisdiction of New Netherland," De Klavier
announced, finding his footing at last. "You will be conducted to Fort
Amsterdam and thereby be imprisoned."

"In Latin, man, in Latin," Drummond murmured, and the *schout*
again looked confused.

Kees Bayard leaned in close. "You will hang," he said.

"And she will still not love you," Drummond said. Kees smacked him
across the face.

The crowd surrounding Drummond grew rapidly. There was something about torchlight that emboldened the citizenry. "Traitor!" they shouted at the prisoner as he was borne away, following after him to yell "Spy!" "Intriguer!" and "Murderer!" also.

Well, spy, yes, Drummond thought. Intriguer, maybe, whatever it meant. But where had that "murderer" come from? Was he to stand accused of every crime in the colony?

He worried about Blandine.

Down Slyck Steegh to the canal, alongside the canal to Pearl, down Pearl toward the fort. The members of the mob wore heavy doublets. He had neglected his in the ruckus at home and was left in his white linen blouse, open at the throat.

The cold air stung him into that state of alertness he had experienced before only in battle. Some part of him knew the fiercely aware condition represented the only time he was truly alive.

If Drummond were more daring, he would have launched into an English marching song, perhaps "When the King Enjoys His Own Again." But he feared his voice would crack if he tried. He satisfied himself with a crooked smile.

The crowd swelled to dozens strong. Drummond felt as though he were at sea, propelled along by an enormous wave. Past Blandine's dwelling-house and the Red Lion opposite. He stared desperately at both, attempting to discern if Van Couvering, and perhaps Raeger, had been taken also.

But in the foul cell into which they tossed him, a log storeroom in the keep of the fort, Drummond found that the only other inmate was Antony Angola.

"Hello, Drummond," Antony said.

"Blandine?" Drummond asked.

"Fled away," Antony said. "The last I heard, she headed for sanctuary in the Reformed Church, across the yard from us."

"She is here?"

"Not within shouting distance, if that's what you mean. Under the protection of the dominie, for now. They don't want her, Drummond. At least, not yet. You and me, we are to be hanged as traitors."

"You?"

"For my association with you," Antony said. "And for my skin color," he added.

During Drummond's absence in the northland, witika panic had gripped New Amsterdam ever more tightly. The town crier told of another orphan disappearance.

"One of ours again," Antony said. "A little African girl. Not that anyone cares too much."

If one included the mystery of William Turner, the killings or disappearances now numbered eight.

"While you were gone, the colony went up in arms with witika fear," Antony said. "The land ports closed and the militia summoned."

The director general declared another day of prayer and penitence. The settlement's Jews were in hiding, Antony told him, in fear of the ancient specter of blood libel, the idea that Jewish rituals involved the sacrifice of abducted Christian children.

Also, this: a pattern of frost appeared on one of the windows of the Stadt Huys. The frost picture had been construed as a representation of the witika demon, a warning to New Amsterdam to repent of its manifold sins.

Some of the boys of the town had been caught chalking the witika sign up on the facades of public buildings, houses, even across the paving blocks of Stone Street.

"The parents are going crazy," Drummond said, "and the children see it all in terms of a prank."

Later, after they had talked half the night, the giant attempted some genial consolation.

"Worry not, my friend," Antony said to Drummond, rubbing the rope-burn scars around his massive, treelike neck. "I've been hung before, and it don't hurt much."

32

I n the deserted meeting-hall of the Reformed Church built within the confines of Fort Amsterdam, Blandine sat with Johannes Megapolensis, the dominie of the colony and thus the chief religious authority of New Netherland.

"I shall not give you to him, child," Megapolensis said. "Him" being the director general. The dominie and Petrus Stuyvesant had been at loggerheads from the first day of Megapolensis's installment, and the witchcraft charges leveled at Blandine represented another battle in their long war.

"I grant you full sanctuary," Megapolensis continued. "But you must do me one thing."

In the chaos of the previous evening, Blandine fled to the church not knowing where else to go. She and Drummond both had been blindsided on their return to New Amsterdam from the northland. He, evidently, had been taken as a spy. She stood accused as a witch.

Hysteria screamed through the colony like a fireball rocket. Rumors exploded. Amid the insults hurled at her by angry crowds, Blandine heard a jumble of strange reports and half-facts. Much had been made of her coming back into the capital at dawn the day after the orphan Ansel Imbrock had been taken the first time.

In the panicked town, enough suspicion fell on Blandine that her dwelling-house had been searched. Witika totems turned up in her rooms, an indian lodge doll, the circle-and-cross willow fetishes, a deer-skin mask.

And—the kicker, the killer, the discovery that damned Blandine as a witch—the bloody jacket of an orphan child.

Could that be possible? The evening before was a nightmare. As soon as she left Drummond's and proceeded toward her dwelling-house, she had been attacked. She was besieged by a mob, many members of which seemed ready to burn her right then and there. She escaped only by taking out the muff pistol Drummond had given her and firing it in the air.

"What would you have me do, dominie?" she asked. But she already knew the answer.

"Confess your love for Jesus, child," Megapolensis said. "Attest to me that you accept Christ as your Lord and Savior. Fall upon your knees before God."

Yes, yes. They all wanted her to do that, ever since she had been orphaned. Before that, it had not been an issue. She went to church with her parents and believed the fables and fantasies that had been presented there. She was a good girl.

What happened to her? How had she lost her faith? It wasn't that question that tormented her, but others. Why had her parents sailed without her to Patria on their doomed, fateful voyage in *Blue Hen*, taking her little sister but not her? Why had she not insisted on going along?

Instead, she begged them rather to let her stay behind. She was fifteen, and old enough to be on her own, she argued. Her secret reason was that she was in love with Kees Bayard and wished to tease out his love for her. The voyage to Patria—for trade, and to have Sarah christened at her parents' home church in Amsterdam, with their relatives around them for the ceremony—did not seem as vital to Blandine as a backward glance from a handsome boy.

So her parents died, and Sarah drowned alongside them. Innocent Sarah. It was impossible for Blandine to measure her love for her sister.

But love proved a weak thing. It failed to save Sarah. Blandine misjudged the cruelty of the world, a random, coldhearted realm that could snuff the life of such a one in the black seas off Goodwin Sands. She would give anything, a thousand glances from a thousand boys, she would stay forever chaste, simply to have her little sister back in her arms again.

No, no more God for her, thank you. The New Amsterdam dominie— a different one, not Megapolensis—had spoken with her at the time of her sister's death, consoling Blandine in her grief, telling her the ways of God were not to be understood by mere humans. In her thoughts Blandine responded that on the contrary, clearly it was God who did not understand human ways. Why give her the capacity for love and then rip out her heart?

Back then she rooted through the scripture, trying to find solace, an explanation, anything, a shred of text that would give her a reason for Sarah's fate. She found little that was of any use. Job helped. *While thine eyes are upon me, I shall be gone.* But nothing really answered.

"God needed her," the old dominie told Blandine.

"I need her!" her heart cried out.

She did not decline the mystery of existence, the great day that dawns, the light that fills the world. But that mystery no longer wore a human face, a kindly grandfather who dwelt in the sky. It was, rather, a terrible severalty, an all-ness, equally joyous and crushing.

"You've been absent from our church," Megapolensis said now. "Perhaps for this reason the people are suspicious of you, and label you a witch."

"I did not keep those things that they said were in my dwelling-house," Blandine said. "The garment and the witika totems. Whoever told you they were there lied, or someone put them there to slur me."

Blandine had two visitors in the church that morning. A stammering, fearful Miep, who told her what she had learned from the Godbolt children and then said she could never see Blandine again, rushing out of the meeting-hall in great haste. And Aet Visser, acting very nervous and strange.

"The clothing," he said. "The clothing they found in your rooms. I know whence it came."

Blandine had trouble comprehending what he was saying. "You mean, you recognized it. It came from your orphans, the ones who have disappeared."

She understood that much already. She learned it when they branded her a witch and an orphan-killer.

But how had Visser seen it? Was he present during the search of her rooms? The orphanmaster appeared entirely beside himself. He fussed, restless, picking at the skin of his hands and face. He rose from the church pew and sat back down. It was more than just worry about Blandine's fate. She felt sure that something else was bothering Visser, some tremendous load bending him double.

"Oh, God, Blandine," he kept repeating, over and over, near tears. "Oh, my dear Lord."

The man, Blandine realized, was terrified.

"Is there something you have to tell me, Aet?" she asked.

But there wasn't. Visser hustled from the church that morning, and Blandine was alone in the wood-vaulted meeting-hall until noon, when the dominie came to speak with her.

"One word from you," Megapolensis repeated now, "and I will throw all my authority behind an effort to stanch these ugly accusations and rehabilitate you in the eyes of the church."

Blandine nodded tiredly. Somewhere in the fort, not twenty rods from where she sat with Megapolensis, Drummond and Antony were being kept in a small cell. She knew what was coming, and she prayed—was *prayed* the right word?—that she had the courage to face it.

"Child?" Megapolensis said gently. "Do you accept Lord Jesus Christ as the light of the world and the only path to salvation, without whom wait the everlasting flames of damnation?"

Blandine remained stubbornly silent. Sarah's round-cheeked little face floated in her mind.

"I beg of you, save yourself from hell," the dominie said. "Glory is yours for a word."

Blandine said, "I wonder if you could tell me, dominie, who organized the fright show in the meeting-hall on Christmas Eve?"

Megapolensis appeared disconcerted. "You ask that?" he said. "At this, the most crucial moment of your young life?"

He seized Blandine's hand in his and looked directly into her eyes. "If I cannot entice you with an eternity in heaven, perhaps I can make you realize what this mortal life holds for you. Do you know what they do to witches, child?"

"What you will do, you mean," Blandine said.

"They will strip your clothes and march you naked through the streets," Megapolensis said. His eyes had a faraway look, as if he imagined the scene.

"The mob will fling mud and filth at you. You will be shorn of that lovely silken hair of which you are so vainly proud. They'll bind you to the stake beside the gibbet near the fort. Then the *schout* reads out your charges and excommunication."

"Who ignites the flame, dominie?" Blandine asked.

"You will hear the damning sentence," Megapolensis continued, brushing her question aside. "Death at the stake."

But she insisted. "Who strikes the first spark?"

"Child!"

"Who does it, dominie? Are you afraid to say?"

"I do!" Megapolensis shouted. Then, more quietly, "I light the fire."

A silence. Blandine closed her eyes. A weariness took her, so deep that it was like sleep.

She heard the voice of the dominie. "I will start the flames at the outer edge of the pyre, so that the heat will come on you bit by bit, until it invades your whole body."

Blandine heard Megapolensis get up and stride in the aisle of the church. "You will weep and howl and scream your repentance then, as your flesh burns, but it will be too late. Too late!"

Megapolensis let his voice go low. "And let me tell you this, Blandine"— he returned to her, and bent his face to hers once again, until she felt his breath—"those fires in which you will perish are but a feverish instant when compared to the eternal pits of hell."

Blandine opened her eyes and turned to the dominie.

"Credere nequeo," she said. I cannot believe.

Megapolensis gazed at her for a long time. He felt sorrow, because he knew he had failed. He understood Blandine well enough not to bother asking if she were sure, if she had not better reconsider.

He stepped back from her. "Then I cannot help you," he said. "The Lord have mercy on your soul."

Dominie Megapolensis walked from the pew where they sat together to the back of the church. He threw wide the doors of the sanctuary and, with a sweeping gesture of his arm, cast Blandine out.

Ross Raeger heard the tumult in the streets and felt the more disgust for it. Deeper disgust, anyway, than that which was the habitual cast of his mind. There had been a lot of mob action this month, frightened chickens running in circles, baa-baaing sheep following one another so closely their noses became manured.

The witika was bad for business.

Raeger felt unsure of himself. He was an agent of the crown, yes, but at the same time he was what the Dutch called a *weert*, an innkeeper. Lately he detected the mundane concerns of the innkeeper taking him over. Riot might be good for an English agent, but it was bad for a *weert*.

He retrieved his pistols and went to the front door of the Lion. Another day, another mob.

This one, though, was different, and what Raeger saw alarmed him. Gaping, red-faced men shoved Blandine van Couvering down Pearl Street before them. The women in the crowd contented themselves with jeering, but the men wore more excited expressions on their faces. One of them, Aalbert Gravenraet, tore at the lace of Blandine's open-necked gown, ripping it from her shoulders.

She was trying to get to her home, Raeger realized. Why had she left the sanctuary? The frenzy over witchery, he was convinced, would soon die down. No one could take seriously this maiden being in league with the Devil, no matter what sort of witika nonsense they discovered in her dwelling-house.

But the street mob seemed to take Witch Blandina very seriously. The rabble screamed the word at her repeatedly. The girl looked determined but frightened, pushing on for the haven of her own rooms.

She wasn't going to make it. A man—Raeger recognized him as a cobbler fellow who liked to go on drunken tears—pushed Blandine backward and tripped her at the same time. She fell.

Raeger strode into the frenzy of mob members and fired one of his pistols over their heads. Nothing. No reaction. He couldn't believe it. None of them seemed to respect his firearm. They were too far gone. The cobbler pulled Blandine to her feet and rubbed street muck into her face.

Raeger fired again and managed to get to Blandine. He slammed the cobbler with the butt of one of his pistols, and the man staggered away, bleeding.

Down the street, a drumbeat. The militia approached, with De Klavier at the fore.

Raeger used the distraction to usher Blandine quickly to the Red Lion. He pushed her inside and slammed shut the heavy oak door.

"Judas Priest, woman!" he shouted. "They aim to murther ye!"

"Well, I shall not die with a dirty face," Blandine said calmly. She crossed to the tin basin on the taproom counter and splashed water on herself.

The men in the taproom, drinkers and drunks, Dutch citizens all, stared at the apparition who appeared before them. They knew Blandine by sight as a frequenter of the Lion. But here was another woman altogether. One not so demure. The witika witch, wild-haired and dirtied, her purple, lace-trimmed gown torn open so that her breasts half spilled out.

"Whoever harms this woman answers to me!" Raeger shouted, hurriedly reloading his pair.

The men in the taproom looked baffled. Where was their mild-mannered jokester *weert*?

A furious pounding at the street door of the Lion.

"Anyone don't want to get caught in an insurrection," Raeger said, "leave by the Mane." He jerked his thumb toward the casino chamber at the back of the taproom. No one moved.

More pounding. "What d'ye want!" Raeger shouted.

"It's the *schout*," De Klavier called. "Open this door."

"In whose name?" Raeger said.

"In the name of the director general," De Klavier said. "Open up, Mister Raeger, or it will go badly for you!"

"Have ye a warrant of search?" Raeger said. "I am by my rights to ask ye for a warrant."

"Open this door!" De Klavier roared.

Raeger turned to his clientele, two dozen males, rough and ready but uncertain what their next move would be. Raeger knew they would not fight to protect a witch. But they would battle to the death to push back against the dictatorial, overweening ways of Petrus Stuyvesant.

"What do ye say, men?" Raeger said. "*Mijn Heer* General would like to stick his foot up our asses. How do we answer him?"

"Which one?" the men chorused, surging toward the door just as the *schout*'s ax came through it, crashing it half down.

Many of Raeger's customers brandished pistols of their own. Others pulled down blades from the Red Lion's fabled rafters, to be put to use at last.

The Red Lion partisans were outnumbered, but De Klavier and his militiamen were attempting to squeeze through the narrow gap of the doorway. A militiaman stuck his musket through the splintered oak of the door, fired it, was fired back upon, and the taproom filled with billowing smoke.

"Give me a pistol," Blandine said, showing up at Raeger's side.

"Get yourself upstairs," Raeger said, pulling up his gun to keep it away from her.

De Klavier's men smashed the street windows, looking for other ways to gain entry. The Lions tossed the taproom benches across the windowsills to blockade them.

"Go!" shouted Raeger, pushing Blandine toward the stairs to the tavern's second and third floors. "They see you in here, I canna hold them back!"

Blandine still hesitated. "Do it, woman!" Raeger pleaded. It was impossible even to see the stairs with all the powder smoke. At the window, hand-to-hand combat.

She went.

Raeger pulled down the big-bladed silver partizan ax from its prized place in the rafters. As Blandine mounted the stairs, he furiously chopped at the newel post with the ax. She gained the landing on the second floor, and the stairway began to sway under Raeger's furious assault.

A few more full-swing chops with the partizan, and the whole flight of stairs tipped to the side, falling toward the center of the taproom with a splintering, ripping sound.

"Look to yourselves!" Raeger yelled, and a few of the Lions had to jump away as the stairway crashed down.

Blandine stood at the top of a flight of stairs that now dropped off into the smoke-filled air. Then the steps from the second to the third floor started to waver and swing, teetering wildly.

"Head upstairs!" Raeger shouted to her. "All the way!"

His men were busy hauling the shattered flight of stairs across the taproom to block the front entrance. Blandine disappeared around a bend in the stairwell, heading for the third floor, just as the second set of steps crashed downward, practically from under her feet.

"Arrgh!" snarled Raeger. It turned out he was not an agent of the crown after all, nor a mild-mannered innkeeper. He was a pirate.

When the musket ball caught Raeger in the side of the head, a wound that threw him wildly backward, he went down dreaming of mutiny.

The Red Lion's third story stood almost as high as the chestnut tree towering in the yard behind, so high no one could possibly reach Blandine.

Raeger, his head wrapped in a theatrical bandage, his eyes blazing with the headache the gunshot wound had given him, had a rope threaded up to Blandine and tied a bucket to it. He sent her beer and vittles, as well as bulletins about the situation down below.

Impasse [Raeger wrote]. *Peg-leg's troops not getting in, Lions not getting out. We are besieged. Enough provisions to last weeks. Many convinced the witch flew to the rooftop on her own.*

Blandine drank the beer, ate the cold chunks of sturgeon and the bread slathered with honey butter and sent back a note of her own.

Drummond? Antony?

Raeger's reply: *Not hung yet.*

Near dark-fall, the wind rose and a freezing sleet began to spatter from the skies. Outside the window, the big chestnut tree's branches thrashed in the black rain.

The roof gables dropped steeply on both sides of her tiny garret room. A bed, a chamber pot, a single chair. Blandine could see out back, over the yards to the fort, but not toward her own dwelling-house across Pearl Street. Crowds huddled in the lee of the fort, gesturing up toward her aerie.

She was safe, she was the lady in the tower. No one could get to her. She didn't know what to do, so she cleaned the room. The evening waned, darkness closed on the settlement. The storm barreled in from the west.

Stretched out on the woven-rope bed, wrapped in her blue woolen shawl (retrieved somehow from her rooms, and sent up via the bucket), Blandine made fierce plans in the dark. Suddenly she saw a dim shape float in the unglazed window, passing toward her through the rain-lashed shutters. She sat up, afraid.

No one could get to her.

But Kitane did.

The Lenape slipped through the window to crouch on the floor in front of Blandine. She had last seen him weeks ago, snowshoeing off into the woods from the sleigh on the Fresh River.

"Miss Blandina," he said, his body wet and gleaming. "Anything new with you?"

Blandine laughed with delight. "You go away from me and, as you see, I get myself in trouble."

"We will get you out," Kitane said. He laid out on the floor a loaf of sweet cornbread, a wedge of black wax cheese and a knife. The blade he had taken from Canarsie friends in Hell Gate. The food he had purchased from his new favorite New Amsterdam bakery that afternoon.

"I bring you greetings from Drummond and the big one," Kitane said.

"Drummond? How? They are in prison, no?"

"Yes," said Kitane, shrugging. "The two of them are held in the fort. But it is no big thing to get in and out of the swannekin's castle."

The unimprisonable Kitane had indeed crept noiselessly into the keep in the early morning hours. He held a hurried conference with Drummond, who, as far as the Lenape trapper could tell, seemed unconcerned at the prospect of being executed. The Englisher asked most urgently about Blandine.

During daylight, Kitane lay low on the quiet North River shore. He ventured out once, to the bakery. The possibility of becoming mesmerized with witika fever lessened, Kitane figured, the shorter time he spent on the streets, as did the likelihood of fingers pointing, accusations leveled, nooses tied. Still, there was always the whisper of fear that he must keep guard against, trailing him, circling his mind.

Blandine knew that Kitane was better, stronger, healthier. She could tell that from his clear eyes and the way he sat, erect and calm. Almost his old self.

"And the task I gave you, how did that go?"

"The thought of you greased my footsteps through my journey." Kitane smiled ruefully. "There were a few I could have eaten along the way. Some who deserved such a fate. Swannekins and my own people both."

Kitane was the avenger, still, but his revenge did not require the smashing of lives. When he began to talk, the cadences of his voice lulled Blandine back to the snowy reaches of the north.

"You know that I visited my brothers the Esopus when I left you," said Kitane. "After the war there are only a few of the tribe left, fewer than thirty, and most of these are women and children. The great war between the swannekins and the Sopus warriors ended the clan and sent refugees downriver to Pavonia. I spoke to some of the wives."

"You followed them?"

"Down the Mohegantuck, yes." The North River.

"Did they know of the boy William Turner?" Blandine said.

"During the war, they said, three families from farms along Esopus Creek were taken prisoner," said Kitane. "Two of them had whole families of children, five or six. But one couple had a single son."

"What happens to prisoners of war?" asked Blandine, remembering her experience on the banks of the river with Mally and Lace.

"Usually they are roasted. But the Esopus kept these people in their own lodges and made sure they were healthy, because they wanted to trade them back to the Dutch."

"And my people wanted the captives back," Blandine said. Sitting on the bed, she took her hair down. It fell almost to her waist, giving off gleams of gold even though the night was pitch dark with the storm.

Kitane had a prickly feeling in his mouth, almost like nausea, but equally resembling appetite. He pushed it back and took up his story. "The Dutch did not move fast enough to ransom the hostages. The pox came again through the village, and it moved faster."

"I remember refugees from the plagues and wars in the north," Blandine said. "They streamed through the gates of the city. It was the first contagion of summer, but it lasted."

"Many didn't make it to the town," Kitane said. "They died where they walked."

"War and pestilence," Blandine said. "'Behold a pale horse: and his name that sat on him was Death, and Hell followed with him.'" There was nothing like a nonbeliever to quote the Bible. When Blandine was little, she enjoyed the drama of the language and the strangeness of the stories. But now the Word was just words.

"The clan tried to isolate the ailing ones, Esopus and swannekins, in lodges away from the cook-fire," Kitane said. "But their loved ones insisted on tending them, and then they would sicken themselves."

Blandine had known some of the Esopus people, close allies of the Lenape who came to trade in Beverwyck.

Kitane gazed out her window. A peal of thunder, then a streak of silver cut across the night sky. This swannekin sky-castle struck him as rickety, ready to fall. Voices from the taproom down below. More flashes, more thunder.

Lightning, Blandine thought, so odd in winter. Comets, plagues, portents. The dominie was going to have a lot to chew on in his sermons. That thought naturally led her to the man called Lightning, with his dead eyes and creased scalp. Was he out there hunting for her along with the rest of the colonists?

"When the pox scourge ended, and the war was over," Kitane said, "only one of the swannekin hostages was left."

"A boy," breathed Blandine.

"He was young and small, but healthy. The clan expected that he would stay on with them."

"As sometimes happens," Blandine said.

"As sometimes happens," Kitane agreed.

"This was the beginning of autumn," said Blandine.

"Then a strange thing occurred," Kitane said. "A man and a woman came on horseback to the Esopus. They led a third horse, a sagging, elderly nag. To this horse they had strapped two pony kegs and a string of hams and sausages."

"Traders," Blandine said.

"The sausage man and woman went into the lodge of Memewu, the clan's last surviving leader. They stayed only a short time. The women of the lodge prepared meals, and brought in to them a roast fish and some ash corn."

Another crash of thunder. "What do you think happened?" Kitane said, looking at Blandine.

"The man and woman rode away from the camp with the boy."

"And the horse, the hams and the kegs stayed behind," Kitane said. "I guess Memewu judged the boy not worth much."

"If the animal was so broken down, why would anyone want it?"

"Meat."

"And the barrels held rum?"

"One did," Kitane said. "The other, seawan, blue glass, from Holland. Still good for trade."

"When did this exchange happen?"

"The month of the goose moon," Kitane said.

October. The pieces fit with what Miep told her in the church that morning. William Turner gone, disappeared. The new boy, the Esopus plague survivor, claimed by the Godbolts, the pork dealers.

The question remained, what happened to the real William Turner?

Kitane stood by the window, next to the curtain of freezing rain falling outside. In a moment he would part that curtain and climb into the dark. Blandine had the same feeling again, a certainty she and Kitane came from different worlds. At that moment, the Lenape was probably listening to the whispers of the mice that lived in the walls of the Red Lion garret. Whispers that Blandine could not hear.

She rose to her feet and crossed to him. Blandine would have liked to do something, make some gesture, throw her arms around him, comfort him somehow, extend a warm hand from her world to his.

She would have, if she were not sure he would instantly flap away into the night in response, soaring through the storm like some kind of immense moon moth.

33

The next morning, in the anteroom outside the audience chamber of the Stadt Huys, Lightning huddled with Martyn Hendrickson.

"I was there when they grabbed Drummond from his rooms," Lightning said. "I wanted to convince them to hang him right then, but they took him to prison in the fort instead."

"Did he weep?" Martyn asked.

"He grinned," Lightning said, his face darkening. "Something very strange happened. When Drummond first appeared in his doorway with his cocked pistol, he was shaved nearly bald. The next time we saw him, only moments later, he had grown long, curly hair. The man must be a devil of some sort."

"A wig, Lightning. He put on a wig."

"You have told me about these things, but I never have seen one," Lightning said. "It looked like his real hair."

"Was he wounded? Did he fall when the mob mistreated him?"

"Do you think I myself could obtain a wig?" Lightning asked.

Martyn rolled his eyes. The man could not be dealt with logically. He was too much concerned with the hideous mottled scar atop his head. To distract Lightning from his new obsession, Martyn directed him through the infernal catechism.

"Who sits on a throne in heaven?" he asked.

"Lucifer," Lightning said. The questions always soothed him.

"Who sits in hell?"

"Father Jesus Christ the Lord Our Savior," Lightning said.

That "father" was extraneous, but the answer was close enough, Martyn decided. "What does God do?"

"God sleeps," Lightning answered. Then he said, "How much does a good wig cost?"

Martyn gave up. From now on, he knew, wigs were all he would hear about from the damned half-indian. The man was manic. Martyn would have to get him a wig somehow. Perhaps Drummond's. He wouldn't be long needing his.

Martyn headed into the audience chamber, and Lightning made to go with him, but was stopped by the militiaman guarding the door.

"Are you a witness?" the militiaman asked Lightning.

"He's with me," Martyn said.

"Europeans only allowed, unless they are witnesses."

Lightning's face darkened, but Martyn only shrugged. He passed from the anteroom into the audience chamber, leaving his protégé behind.

In the chamber, they were hearing the Africans, Lace and Mally and Handy, talk about their latest missing child. Tara Oyo, the girl's name was, they said, six years old. She had been found, stripped naked, facedown in a rotting litter of leaves, missing a haunch and the fingers of her left hand.

The director general gave the Africans a scolding. "Why let this child wander alone?" Stuyvesant asked.

"She wasn't wandering, she had to work, and she was going—" the man Handy said, but Stuyvesant cut him off.

"It seems your community is lax about attending to its children. You must pray over it, and search your hearts to find if you are not as much to blame as the demon that took her. *Quae nocent, saepe docent.*" What hurts, instructs.

"Sire—" the woman Lace said, but again, the director general interrupted.

"We have heard enough about this instance," he said, dismissing the Africans. They stood, not knowing what to do, but finally turned and passed Martyn on their way out of the audience room.

The director general and his citizen-advisors, the Nine, had convened to sort out the witika madness that gripped the colony. The Nine were what passed for representative democracy in New Amsterdam. Stuyvesant would just as soon keep his own counsel, but unrest in the streets was such that he had to admit some burghers and leading citizens into the governing process.

Convening the Nine, Martyn knew, was a sop. In his experience, advising the director general was like trying to get a stone to absorb water. The words ran off and soaked into the earth.

But the exercise was often entertaining. George Godbolt was there, Kees Bayard, the *schout*, De Klavier, Aet Visser, Chas Pembeck, the Company tax official, the schoolmaster, Adolphus Roeletsen, the powerful patroon from across the river in Pavonia, Michiel Pauw, the *burgomeester*, Rem Fuchs. And finally, Martyn's own brother Adias Hendrickson, making a rare appearance in the capital.

A collection of enfeebled idiots, as far as Martyn was concerned, even though on occasion he had himself numbered among the Nine. Nine ninnies, his brother not excepted. Friend Visser, he noticed, looked ill, slack-faced. The orphanmaster avoided Martyn's gaze.

"I now convene this body as a correctional tribunal," Stuyvesant announced. "We shall take up the business of the imprisoned spy Edward Drummond."

"Hang him," Kees Bayard said, immediately. For weeks, he had been pressing his uncle with the case against Drummond.

"And the African, too," George Godbolt said.

"No, no, not the African," Kees said.

The director general rapped his knuckles on the grand polished-mahogany table behind which he sat. "Gentlemen," he said, "let us consider the evidence. First the evidence, then the hanging."

He shuffled some papers on the desk. "Thanks to the diligence of our *schout*"—nodding to De Klavier—"a great deal of material was recovered from the spy Drummond's chambers. Included were coded messages in Latin."

A look of immense satisfaction passed over the director general's face. Petrus Stuyvesant loved Latin as a harsh mistress. He gloried in always being the smartest gentleman in the room, the smartest in the colony and among the smartest (he qualified carefully) in the world.

"I have personally broken the code on these messages," he said. He waited for the proper level of awe to settle upon his tribunal.

The effort had taken Stuyvesant many hours, laboring alone in the night, picking away at the scribbles taken from a leather box found in Edward Drummond's best chamber. Letter by letter, word by word, a frustrating work requiring ferocious concentration. The director general loved every second of it.

He did not divulge all of what he found in the coded messages. The English were moving against him, that was certain. He already knew that, but he had not grasped how far their plans had developed. They had spies everywhere, in the capital, at Fort Orange, in Wildwyck, on Long Island. Drummond's papers drew a noose around the director general's neck.

Among the documents there were sketches of every major building and thoroughfare in New Amsterdam. A diagram of the fort. Lists of English settlers. Also uncovered were plans against the New Haven regicides.

"These papers reveal Edward Drummond to be a paid assassin of his High Mightiness, the king of England, and an agent of his papist schemes," Stuyvesant said. That much he was willing to make public. "He has come to our jurisdiction to wreak havoc, on the trail of the judge-commissioners who lately condemned to death the former king, Charles I. He journeyed recently to New Haven Colony for the purpose of tracking the regicides who find safe harbor there, exposing them to the sitting king's murderous fury."

The director general rose to his feet, or, as the wags would have said in the Red Lion, his foot. "Edward Drummond is a murderer," he announced sententiously. "These documents represent his confession. He is condemned to hang."

He looked around the chamber. The Nine tripped over themselves to agree. "Aye," said Kees Bayard.

"Aye," De Klavier said.

"Aye," Godbolt said.

Ayes from Pembeck, Roeletsen, Pauw, Fuchs.

Visser, silent, abstaining. The worst circles of hell, Martyn thought acidly, were reserved for those who do not decide which side they are on.

His brother spoke up. "I don't scruple at hanging the man," Ad Hendrickson said. "But I wonder what connection he has with this witch business."

"The witch and the spy are in league," Martyn said, drawing a stare from Stuyvesant. When one of his brothers was present, Martyn was allowed in chamber only as a silent observer.

"That is a lie," Kees Bayard said, gamely defending his old love. "Blandine van Couvering is the target of a campaign to make her appear guilty."

Martyn decided he would have to deal with Kees Bayard directly, sooner or later. The man had labeled him a liar in public discourse. Dueling was disallowed in the colony, but Martyn had picked up a taste for it during his sojourn in Paris. And there were other ways.

"Drummond and Van Couvering were clearly seen entering the settlement at dawn after the Ansel Imbrock kidnapping," De Klavier said.

"Perhaps she has bewitched him," Godbolt said.

"She is innocent!" Kees burst out.

Stuyvesant sat heavily back down in his chair, rapping for order. He addressed his nephew directly. "Personal connections have no place in this chamber," he told Kees. "You must sacrifice your own petty concerns for the good of the public. I myself have sacrificed much"—here he stamped his wooden leg on the floor, as he often did for effect. "You need to show you are ready to keep a clear head or recuse yourself from this deliberation."

"Yes, Uncle," Kees said, cowed.

"Yes, *Mijn Heer* General," Stuyvesant corrected.

"Yes, *Mijn Heer* General," Kees said.

"We could call for testimony from the militia sentry at the land port," De Klavier suggested.

"Which one?" the director general asked. A barely suppressed titter passed through the assembly. Stuyvesant had pronounced the punch line to his own joke. *Human beings can be so cruel*, thought the director general. He felt fury rise in him.

"The disposition of the case of Blandine van Couvering is a religious matter," Stuyvesant said coldly. "It was resolved not by this body but by myself in concert with Dominie Megapolensis."

He paused, and once again stood. "Just before this meeting, the dominie and I made a finding of *actus reus*, wrongful acts. Blandine van Couvering will be burned at the stake for perverse and sundry high crimes, murder, kidnapping, the eating of human flesh, depravity and consorting with the Devil. May the Lord have mercy on her soul."

Kees groaned audibly, but the rest of the Nine fell silent. Aet Visser put his head in his hands. Only Ad Hendrickson spoke up.

"All right, all right," he said, impatient. "What I want to know, is she convicted of this witika mess? Will there be no more disappearing orphans? Has the lawful pursuit of this matter closed?"

He seemed to be addressing the assembly, but he was staring openly and sternly at his brother.

"So we shall have a hanging and a burning," Martyn said lightly. "Perhaps they can be arranged on the same day."

"*Ipso lex,*" said Stuyvesant. By the power of law, he meant, but the schoolmaster, Roeletsen, spoke up.

"If I may, *Mijn Heer* General, you mean *ipso iure*, since that is the ablative—"

"Good God, man!" Stuyvesant cut him off.

"How about the witch's African?" Ad said. "As I understand it, you hung him once already, and yet he still lives."

"A stouter rope," Martyn suggested.

In the street outside the Stadt Huys, shouts, cries, raised voices. Martyn at first thought the public had somehow become aware of the sentences against Drummond and the witch, just passed down by Stuyvesant and the Nine, and the shouting expressed their approval.

The call of the town crier floated up to the third-floor audience room. "*Oyez, oyez,* the prisoners have escaped! They have escaped!"

34

In the event, departure from Dutch captivity proved relatively simple to pull off, which Drummond should have known, judging by the state of the rotting wicker gabions stacked along the fort's parapet. The citadel had been allowed to fall into a general state of disrepair.

While their jailer slept that early morning, Antony managed to pry loose a log at the back of the cell. They both squeezed through the space, Antony having a much harder time of it than Drummond. The wall gave out to an adjacent passageway which had, at the end of it, a barred window that was easily forced. They climbed the earthen ramparts and then faced a thirty-foot jump to the parade ground below.

"I'm not doing it," Drummond said. "We'll break our necks."

"Snowbanks," Antony said, and he leaped off. Plummeting downward in the dawn dark, the giant plunged into a massive snow pile and disappeared completely. Drummond peered down. A white snowman struggled out of the hole made from the fall and waved up at him.

"Well, all right," Drummond said, and jumped himself.

Blandine, too, found her extraction from the siege at the Red Lion a fairly straightforward matter. Taking her shawl and all the extra clothes she could gather, she rode the rope down while standing in the bucket, twirling queasily for the whole thirty-foot drop. Raeger greeted her in his first-floor taproom headquarters.

"It's time for ye to leave, wench," he said, lapsing into pirate talk. "They are stacking the faggots and pounding in the stake. If ye stay on, ye'll see yourself roasted to a smoking char by nightfall."

"I shall leave then," Blandine said. "Though I will dearly miss your company."

"I remain here to fight the good fight for the people's rights," Raeger said. "Due process, protection against unlawful seizure, enforcement of the writ."

"Aye, and iced beer," Blandine said. "Don't forget that."

"You were liking that style, were ye, up in your attic aerie? We kept it in the snow, back of the Mane."

"I was getting used to it, although tepid is fine, too."

The Lions, Raeger's valiant customers and loyal troops, slept every which way in the taproom and the casino chamber. If the director general's militiamen thought to rush the place at that moment, Blandine thought, they would have an easy time of it.

Raeger bundled her out of the Lion through the Mane, and handed her off to Kitane, who led her through backyards for the whole of the block to emerge into the deserted market square.

Neither of them spoke. The early morning streets were empty. A rattle watch came by, crossing Brugh Street. The man didn't see their two shadows, passing quickly to the north, edging along the fort toward the parade ground.

There another pair of figures awaited, one overlarge, one regular.

"Hello, Drummond," Blandine said.

"Miss Blandina," Antony said. Kitane stood beside Blandine.

"Once more, the four of us," Drummond said.

The light had broken fully with the sunrise. In order to avoid the land port, they sought to pass around the palisade wall along the rough shore of the North River.

There were numerous hitches. They had to conceal themselves for an hour in a shed in the Company gardens on the settlement side of the wall. The Broad Way became more peopled during that time. They knew how easily recognized Antony's profile was.

Finally they made the circuit around the wall. They crept through the fields north to Little Angola and Mally's cabin. Lace was there, also.

"They were going to burn you, girl," the normally stern Mally said. "I saw the blood in their eyes."

According to plan, a sleigh waited at Mally's. But another snag: no horses. "They coming," Mally said.

Every moment, Blandine knew, meant they were closer to being recaptured. Antony and Drummond had concealed their leaving by heaping bedclothes in their cell to resemble sleeping forms, but soon enough that ruse would be uncovered.

"I should go," Drummond said.

"Horses coming, I told you," Mally said. "Have faith."

"Well, no, I was thinking, if we are marooned here, I could just dash back into town for a bit."

"What?" Antony said.

"Drummond!" Blandine said.

"I need to retrieve something," Drummond said. "A thing I forgot."

"What is it?" Mally said.

"You are not going back there," Blandine said. "We just escaped!"

But Drummond was not to be deterred. "Really, it will only take a moment. I'll be back by the time you have the horses hitched."

"For pity's sake, Edward," Blandine said, forgetting their agreement about using last names only.

"It will be fine," Drummond said. To Antony: "Remember, hitch the horses three abreast, the two outside—"

"—with breast collars, I know," Antony said.

"Then we'll be able to outrun anything," Drummond said. He left by the side door and slipped off to the south, toward the palisade wall of the settlement.

"That man," said Mally, "is either plumb raving crazy or just down-right insane. That's the only two choices he's offering to us."

Blandine fretted out an hour. The horses came and were hitched to the sleigh in the same style of triplets that had served them so well on the trip up the Fresh River. Antony packed the few belongings Blandine had taken from her time in the Red Lion tower. Lace and Mally loaded foodstuffs and other supplies.

"I'll go find him," Kitane offered.

"No, no, he'll come," Blandine said. "He said he would, and he will."

"Unless he's captured," Antony said, tightening the traces on the sleigh horses. The beasts shifted their weight back and forth, breaths wreathing in the frosty morning air, eager to get going, two buckskins and a spotted perlino. Kitane had thieved or bartered them from where he did not say.

As Antony finished, Drummond approached, coming not from the south, the direction they expected him, but from the north.

"We should go," he said. "As I was leaving I heard the town crier call my name. I am absconded, he was shouting."

He had been detoured, in town, by an unfortunate encounter with his old *Margrave* shipmate Gerrit Remunde, who came out of nowhere as Drummond slinked down the backstreets of the settlement, trying to avoid notice.

"Mister Drummond!" Remunde called. "We want to have you for dinner!"

Drummond took off. He had to run the long way around to lose the man.

Still a little winded, Drummond tossed onto the bench of the sleigh the crucial item he had returned to town in order to fetch: the bearskin Blandine had gifted him with, many long weeks ago in Beverwyck.

Blandine tried to look stern. "That was foolhardy," she said.

"The pelt is devilishly warm, and we have a cold journey ahead," Drummond said. He turned to the giant. "Antony, my friend, let's away."

But Antony remained standing apart. "I don't go with you," he said.

"What?" Drummond asked.

"I am too easily seen," Antony said. "If I pass by, everyone remembers. You will do better without me."

"Nonsense," Drummond said. "We need you. Hop on."

"No," Antony said. "I'll be fine here in Angola. Lace and Mally will hide me."

Blandine put her hand on Drummond's arm, and he realized the arrangement was something she and Antony had worked out while he was in town.

Kitane, too, would stay behind. No grand good-byes from him, simply a quick fade into the back alleyways of Little Angola.

"Safe journey, Blandina," Antony said, tears streaming down his face. "You take care of her, Edward."

Drummond shifted over to the center of the sleigh bench and took up the reins.

"Better days," he said.

"Better days," Antony said.

"God watch over you," Mally said. Lace just waved, overcome by emotion.

"We shall meet again in the taproom of the Red Lion," Drummond said.

"As if there we had hidden our gold," Blandine finished the phrase for him, and they set off.

Immediately, they made a mistake and ran into trouble. Drummond intersected the Broad Way to head for the ice of the North River, but that brief crossing displayed their sleigh to the land port two hundred yards to the south.

They were visible to the settlement but for a moment, though it turned out to be enough. Their pursuers were onto them at once, three sleighs of militia, assorted private cutters, streaking out from the settlement like hounds to the hunt.

"Drummond!" Blandine said, looking back over her shoulder.

"I know," Drummond said. "I see them."

He sped down the lanes of the *bouweries* north of the palisade wall. A hayrick lay athwart their path and he veered away. The shoreline of the river showed ahead of them, dropping off sharply to the ice. But the horses took the jump easily, and the sleigh soared for ten feet before crashing crazily onto the hard blue surface of the frozen river.

"Judas Priest!" Blandine swore, bouncing off the bench with the jolt. She had taken up Raeger's signature curse during the battle of the Red Lion.

Three hundred yards behind them, on the ice, a squad of sleighs swung onto their trail. But Drummond was right. Their pursuers harnessed only two animals in tandem per sledge. The new innovation of the troika, so impressive to Drummond during his recent sojourn in Russia (tracking a regicide who had hidden there), provided their sleigh with an extra advantage.

The far-off bang of a musket, and a puff of white smoke appeared above one of the sledges to their rear, but the distance was much too great.

The surface of the river proved perfect, made for velocity. The sleet of the storm the night before had frozen flat as a pancake. They raced, drawing slowly away from the sleighs behind them. Four hundred yards, five hundred, a half mile. The sledges on their trail dropped out singly or by twos and threes, stopping and turning around.

All except one. Every time he looked behind to check the pursuit, Drummond noticed the small cutter hitched with a single horse. Far from falling back, the cutter was gaining on them, not quickly, but bit by bit.

They thundered on, the horses frothing, tiny speeding figures dwarfed under the blue, larkless vault of heaven. At the top of Manhattan Island, Drummond swung wide to avoid the open water at Spuyten Duyvil. The cutter followed.

Much more of this, Drummond knew, and the horses would be blown.

"He is only one, Drummond," Blandine shouted at him over the crash of the runners on the ice.

Drummond had an idea who whipped that cutter forward, and he was unsure what kind of firepower the man carried. He did not want to risk himself or Blandine in a direct face-off. They would try to outrun their lone hound.

He took a route that led him nearer to the shore, around a patch of open water. Another mistake. The cutter chose a different route, swinging around toward the middle of the river. That turned out to be the quicker path. When Drummond and Blandine finally got past the water and back onto glaze ice, the cutter had pulled close.

Martyn Hendrickson held the reins of the sled in his teeth, aiming a pistol that exploded with a sharp, echoing report. The ball flew closely by them, making a noise between a whistle and a hiss. The cutter hurtled onward, the black charger at full gallop.

"It's Fantome," Blandine shouted. "Kees's horse. The best in the colony." In one of Raeger's chatty notes to her while she was barricaded in the tower, the Red Lion's proprietor informed Blandine that Kees had, a week before, forfeited his prized horse to Martyn Hendrickson at a game of dice in the Mane.

Lost his girl, lost his horse, Raeger scribbled. *Upset at both.*

The enormous, night-black stallion blew out flecks of white foam from his nostrils but still strained at the harness. Magnificent, Drummond thought. Just our luck.

"Shoot him," he told Blandine.

"No!" she shouted.

"Shoot the damned animal, Van Couvering!"

She drew the little palm-pistol Drummond gave her from her muff. Blandine banged off a shot, not at the horse, but at the sleigh driver. She missed.

Martyn was upon them, seemingly unable to reload in mid-ride, but wielding an evil-looking bullwhip. He lashed out with the whip, and it snaked above Drummond's head, stinging his cheek with a deep cut. Drummond steered the sleigh away from shore toward the center of the river. But the cutter swung to the other side. Martyn readied the whip once again, this time aiming for Blandine.

"Where are your pistols?" Blandine shouted to Drummond.

The whip came down, but its snapping tip missed Blandine and wrapped around the rail of the sleigh. The leather lash ran itself taut, tangled at the other end in Fantome's harness. The tension yanked the cutter off center. The little sleigh tilted over on an angle, riding a single runner, and ran wildly off course.

The whip broke, and at the same moment the cutter overturned, with Hendrickson clinging to it. It spun crazily across the river surface toward a soft spot on the ice. The frozen surface buckled, giving way, plunging the cutter, its driver and the stallion into the black water below.

As Blandine watched, the little sledge sank out of sight, and Fantome surfaced, screaming, scrabbling madly at the edges of the hole into which he had fallen.

There was no sign of Martyn Hendrickson.

Blandine grabbed the reins from the bleeding Drummond. She drove the sleigh onward, up the frozen river, out of reach of the settlement and all pursuit, beneath the blue, enclosing sky.

35

T hey left the river in late afternoon at a frozen, mazelike marsh, its reeds dry and yellow-brown and covered in mounds of snow. Unhitching the sleigh and stripping the harnesses from the horses, they each rode a mount and used the spare third horse for the pack.

Blandine, at least, had a sense of safe haven, of leaving their pursuers far behind. No one knew where they were. Drummond was not so sure. A spy left unhanged tends to look back over his shoulder.

They climbed the hardwood hills on the river shore to where, in a grown-over meadow with a faint track leading to it, stood a cabin constructed of peeled cedar timbers. Built by Blandine's parents, rented out to tenants, the structure had been abandoned in the first Esopus war.

This was thirty miles from New Amsterdam, on land purchased out of the family's earnings from a shipload of musket parts from Patria. Willem van Couvering had the idea that the cabin would serve as a base for fur-trading, not willing to believe that beaver, once so plentiful, had already been trapped out along the river, all the way up to Beverwyck.

Big plans. The Van Couvering family would have a dwelling-house in New Amsterdam, a *bouwerie* a short league beyond the wall and a fur-trading cabin thirty miles farther upriver in the northland. But before they could enjoy all that, the parents would just make a quick dash across the sea to get their youngest daughter christened.

The cabin stood empty for years. Blandine had no idea what kind of shape it was in. She knew her father had constructed it to last. She had helped him build the place, in fact, to the extent of her ten-year-old abilities, toting nails to her father when he called for them.

Now, as Blandine and Drummond approached, the buckskin geldings they rode foundered in the high-drifted snow, so they dismounted and led them. Blandine climbed the icy stone stairs to the front porch, trying the door. It wouldn't budge. Drummond came beside her and they both put their shoulders into it and pushed. It swung open.

Inside, a single great room, with every surface shimmering in the last afternoon light, dusted with delicate rime frost. Spidery ice crystals covered over the casement windows. Abandoned as it was, fallen down and long unused, the place yet resembled a fairyland. The interior glowed white.

Blandine and Edward walked through the room with hesitant steps, as though they did not want to break its spell. Wherever they stepped, they left prints in the powdery layer of snow on the floor, drifted in from one of the cracked windowpanes. A circular staircase in the Dutch style wound up to a second-story loft.

A winter stillness, glistening, unbroken. Everything was ice.

"It's like . . ." Drummond said, and instantly regretted speaking as Blandine reached out and put a finger to his lips.

"Shhh," she said.

Holding hands like children, they walked through the place.

"I'll make a fire," Drummond whispered, thinking it was something he could do. Both of them were frozen to the bone.

Blandine merely nodded, passing through the house and into memory. She should have been exhausted from their journey up the river but felt not at all tired. She climbed the staircase. It had been designed, she knew, to bring mother and father and little Blandine and baby Sarah up to two small bed chambers. Back then, the house had been full of chairs and tables, rugs and beds and pictures.

As the evening came on, the snow shimmer inside the cabin faded to silver. The domicile never had much light inside, despite its glass windows, and now the blanket of winter outside rendered its rooms grayer and more hushed, like the inside of a satin cave.

She returned to the first floor. Drummond had a fire in the hearth. He had laid out the bearskin.

Blandine approached Drummond as he fed in more wood, the yellow flames crackling, hissing, heating the air. He looked back at her over his shoulder. She smiled awkwardly and commenced the complicated procedures that a fully clothed woman of the day required in order to strip naked.

She removed her silk stockings, reaching deep under her costume and pulling them off singly, her legs smooth and bare. The string laces of her maize-colored bodice came next, loosened at the back with her arms reached behind her waist, and then drawn through their eyelets. As the piece's tight fit went slack, Blandine took it off. She stood in her gown of ivory linen.

She did not speak during this. In her thoughts, she begged Drummond not to be awkward, not to overplay it, and especially not to vaunt his experience over her lack of it. She was a moral woman, he was a gentleman. Nothing in that precluded what they would do this night.

Again Blandine reached around behind herself, undoing the three cloth-covered buttons that held her gown in place. She shimmied her waist to release it. She did not like him to see her hands trembling, so she held them close as she opened her lace-collared chemise.

Underneath, the underbodice, her stays, which she unhooked, uncovering herself to the waist. Slipping her palms alongside her hips, she allowed the last layer, her petticoat, to drop to the floor in a cloud of emerald. She took a final ribbon from her hair, letting the heap of blond tresses fall down her back, and finally stood unclothed before him, pale, shivering in the still cool air, the firelight playing on her skin.

By the end of the first week, Blandine found herself able to talk in an ordinary, less love-struck fashion. Not about anything important, but more along the lines of "Pass me the salt, darling," and "Has the bucket of snow melted yet for water?" Whether it was she who spoke or he, Blandine often could not tell, their two voices seemed melded into one.

Many of their days involved the green petticoat. Edward knew that the best emeralds are those that display an elusive hint of blue within them, and he thought the petticoat brought out the color of her eyes, blue within the swirl of green. So he requested it often.

She watched the whip wound on his cheek slowly heal. "Dashing," she murmured. "Ladies love a scar."

"I do not care for the plural," Drummond said. "I care only for one."

No one beyond Antony and Kitane knew where they were. Their pursuers might be searching for them, but here they were removed from fear. Somewhere, deep in their thoughts, they knew they would eventually have to face whatever was brewing downriver.

Not now. Not here.

Mainly Blandine drowsed in Edward's arms as the fire roared, and touched his face and his chest as though she had never touched a man before.

Which she had not.

Outside the casement windows on the cabin's first floor (they didn't bother with the second), the two of them could see the horses they had taken up the slope from the river, tied beneath a narrow shelter beside the tumbledown barn. There was still hay in the barn from the old days. That and the withered apples they gathered, ferreting them out from under the drifts around old trees in the orchard, kept the horses in fairly good spirits.

For five weeks, Blandine and Drummond stayed inside, tended the fire and made love often, every day, and during stretches of blizzard several times a day. Blandine unearthed her father's ragged copy of the tragedies, and they read to each other from *Lear*, *Othello* and the Scottish play. Mally had packed them provisions, and they cooked simple meals, *hutspot* with potatoes, carrots and onion, toasted cheese, slices of Lenape-style dried venison, smoked herring, a cracked-wheat bread, risen over the coals.

Drummond had succeeded in secreting among his things a surprise delicacy almost unknown in New Amsterdam: a cone of white sugar. They took slices of dried pear, moistened them with brandy and dipped them in the sweet, crumbled granules, lounging on the bearskin before the hearth.

No more Van Couvering and Drummond. He addressed her as Blandine, as he always had in his mind, or sometimes "Ina," while she, relishing his given name, called him Edward. In his more idiotic moods he cooed at her as *"la petite souris,"* the little mouse.

He had removed his waistcoat for good, it seemed, as she had tossed away her gown. She went about the place dressed in his white linen blouse, unbuttoned and untucked—there was nothing in which to tuck it—barefoot.

The weeks tripped by. They had only three conversations of any note.

* * *

The first:

"After the attack, I changed my thinking," Blandine said during one noontime meal before the fire.

"The Mahican attack, you mean," Drummond said. "Berry-picking." She had told him some about it, but not all.

"I realized that I had never really thought about things before. I just accepted what people told me."

"They always want you to take what they say on faith," Drummond said. "The spiritual is the most important area of life, and they don't want you to think too hard about it."

"I felt during those days as though I were spinning out of control," Blandine said. "I would walk along the Strand, look out at the bay and realize how much I loved the beauty of the world. It nearly choked me sometimes with emotion. The world is beautiful even for a coyote."

"Even for a mole," Drummond said.

"For a worm."

"A gnat."

"For a rock!" said Blandine. "Even for that stone in the hearth! Yes! But then I would look at the explanation I was being given for all this gloriousness, and I just refused."

"Credere nequeo," Drummond said.

"That's right," Blandine said. "What I told the dominie."

He picked up her mass of hair as it fell over her shoulders and held it to his face. He wished he could protect Blandine from everything the world was going to hand her, but knew that was impossible, that ultimately she would have to protect herself.

"There is a man," Edward said. "His name is Benedict Spinoza. He's a lens grinder in Holland."

"He is who you read?" she said. *A Short Treatise on God, Man and His Well-Being.*

"He puts into words what you are talking about. He knows the glory of the world cannot be contained. It must be infinite. It can't have a human face."

"I know!" said Blandine. "It must be everything, all things. I thought that myself, and then I thought how dangerous that kind of thinking was, and I tried to stop."

"Bento Spinoza's thought is so dangerous that they tossed him right out of his community."

"Like us."

"Like us," Edward said.

Blandine's eyes shone, staring into Edward's face. "I really felt alone," she said. "I never considered that anyone believed as I did."

"Once you do begin to think about it, though, it becomes obvious," Drummond said.

Blandine nodded. "Difficult, but obvious," she said. "You're right."

"After Worcester, I, too, lost my faith. My boots had waded in blood up to the ankles. The god held up to me to believe in seemed so . . ."

"Petty and small," Blandine said.

"Yes. When you see men being smashed by cannon fire, you can't believe again. A god who gives a damn in any way whatsoever about human pain and hopes and predicaments just begins to appear ridiculous."

"What I found myself thinking was, no god at all," Blandine said. "Or a different kind of one. I didn't know if it could even go by the name of God."

Edward said, "The god my soul needs is huge and unbreakable. Spinoza's god. That's what I see out here in the new world. And their old-world god just turned out to be small and soft."

Blandine snuggled her body up against his. "Like you," she said. "Small and soft."

He laughed. "Like your breasts."

"My breasts aren't small!"

Edward said, "Nor am I, if you'd just do your job."

She did.

The second:

"The question to ask about crime is always, *qui bono?*" said Edward. "That's how the constable is trained." They had walked outside to take some air that afternoon, looking over the vast iced-in river below, congratulating themselves, with the impossible satisfaction of lovers, on their good luck and good taste in each other.

After their walk, they returned to a still warm cabin and a hearth with dying coals.

"*Qui bono?*" Blandine said, poking the embers with a heavy stick from the woods outside. "My Latin . . . *Qui*, I know. That means 'who.' But *bono*? Good? 'Who is good?'"

"Who benefits? Who gains from the crime?" Edward said. He pushed a fresh log into the fire, and rubbed his hands together.

"Ah. Well, the killer benefits. Or killers," said Blandine.

"Yes, but how?" Edward said. "These are strange, chained-together murders. I have never heard of killings that go forward serially. What links them? How could anyone gain by slaying orphans?"

Blandine thought she knew. "There is a thrill from killing, isn't there? Isn't that enough? You've killed, haven't you? Is there a thrill to it?"

He did not hesitate. "Yes," he said.

"What is the thrill made of? What does it mean?"

Drummond thought back to his battles, the bitter defeat at Preston, the bloody Worcester, the engagements of the Russo-Polish War, the Anglo-Dutch campaigns (his people against hers), the Northern War.

" 'Not me,' that's what killing means," he said. It was his turn to poke the fire. "That's it right there. If you are the killer, that automatically means you are not the killed. It feels like power. At least, I think that's how the human mind works."

Blandine said, "So our killer, he wants it to be not him. Where does that lead us?"

"He doesn't want to be a dead orphan?"

"Which might mean he's an orphan, alive," said Blandine. Herself an orphan.

"Visser always calls himself an orphan," Edward said.

"That's just more of his nonsense," Blandine said. "Technically, I suppose it's true, but he told me his parents lived to old age."

"Could you imagine him using his wards as catamites?"

"Abuse them sexually? Certainly not."

"He keeps a secret family."

"Pish-posh," Blandine said. "If Anna and her brood are a secret, it's an open one."

Edward pulled a long look at her.

"What?" she said.

"You don't want to believe it's him," Edward said. "You're being blind."

"You forget that, unlike you, I actually know him."

"If you know him so well, tell me this," Edward said. "How corrupt is he?"

Blandine put her thumb and finger out, about an inch apart. "Not totally, but neither is he pure. Like he says, he lives in the real world."

Edward laughed. "I'm not sure I would describe New Amsterdam as the real world. It is more like a dog pit at the fair."

"Visser himself called New Netherland a *narrenschiff*, a ship of fools," Blandine said. "But I know what you mean."

The orphanmaster possessed a few traits that argued for him as a murderer. First and foremost, to Drummond's mind, was the man's conversance with, and proximity to, the settlement's orphan population. To be able to kidnap them, murder them, perform whatever ghoulish acts upon them that had been done, the guilty party must necessarily know which children of the colony were parentless and where they all were placed.

How many orphans were there in New Amsterdam? What had Hendrickson said? Two hundred something. Every one had come through Visser's hands in one way or another.

There was also Visser's general dissolution, his inebriated mental state, his habitual companionship with Lightning, surely the kind of man Drummond could readily believe was involved in the orphan-killings.

"You must leave off your foolish sentiments about the orphanmaster," he said. "If you allowed yourself to see things clearly, you'd conclude he is the one."

"I don't want to live in a world where a man like Aet Visser kills children," Blandine said.

"Why, because he's jolly? Because he tells a good joke?"

"Because he's all I have," Blandine said softly.

Edward was going to push it some more, but a look at Blandine's face made him back away.

The third:
The third conversation you shall not be privy to.

Their only visitor was Kitane. Riding an ancient-looking mule he garnered from the Canarsies, he'd come bringing foodstuffs and news of the colony. The Lenape seemed to pass through the woods effortlessly, even in the high snows of winter.

The first time, they were surprised. In late afternoon, a rap at the window.

Blandine nearly jumped out of her skin, which was, coincidentally, all she wore at that moment. She wrapped herself in Drummond's cloak and the two of them met Kitane at the door. He stood before them, his moccasins saturated with snowmelt, the cat hide draped loosely about his torso.

After greetings, they drew him into the warm cabin. "Have some for me?" he asked, indicating the plate, mounded with Drummond's sugar, that lay carelessly on the hearth bricks.

"Of course." Blandine pushed the sugar toward him. "Now tell us everything. Do they still search for us?"

"Not so much. The director general, he has other problems."

"How is Antony?"

"Still hidden in Little Angola," said Kitane.

"So he remains at the capital," Blandine said. "But how long can you hide a giant?"

"He is all right for now," said Kitane. "The African people shield their own."

"He is well cared for?"

"He asks about you," Kitane said.

"This is the longest we've been apart since first we met," Blandine said.

Kitane ate well when the food was served, from the provisions he brought—venison strips and farmer cheese, crackers and greasy pemmican, loaves of bread, only slightly stale. Blandine and Edward contributed the last of their sweet butter, which they kept fresh in a crock of snow outside the cabin's front door.

"There is this, too," Kitane said. He presented them with a schoolroom lesson board, a piece of slate in a wooden frame. "It comes from the boy, William Turner."

Edward peered over her shoulder.

"*Drumin? Ubi es?*"

Drummond had been a schoolboy once. " '*Drumin*,' that's Drummond. *Ubi es?* Where are you?"

Blandine turned to Kitane. "Where is the boy? With the Godbolts?"

Kitane nodded. "They don't let him out of their sight."

Blandine rubbed out the message on the slate, but there was no chalk to send a response. Drummond pulled an ashy stick from the fire and presented it to her.

Soon, was the first word she thought to write. Then *courage*.

Kitane finished scooping sugar into his mouth. His moccasins dried by the fire, his pack empty of the supplies he brought to Blandine and Edward, he tucked the message slate into his kit and set off.

The Angolan known in the colony as Handy had hunted prey both in Africa, far back across the green sea of time, and here on Manhattan Island, in what everyone called the new world.

He himself, Handy thought, was in no way new, an old man who did not know his years. Forty? Fifty? Sixty? The young ones of Little Angola called him Grandfather, though fortune cursed him with childlessness.

Boys and girls who were not his own came to his garden on Company land along the North River, visiting him while he was on his knees, tending his potato plants.

Can I help you, Grandfather? Can I, Grandfather? the children chattered. What they meant was that they were hungry. Handy allowed them to reach deep into the hills of peaty dirt and pull out the firm, round, spud-golden treasures beneath.

Were the children aware of how their presence mocked him?

I am nobody's grandfather, child. I am Handy Kimbarata, born a prince, whose line will end with my own death in a strange land.

The air still held some winter on an early April morning when Handy set forth with his scattergun across the island toward the Kollect Pond, glad for having thought to wear the single pair of woolen socks he owned. After stopping a moment to chew on a hunk of molasses bread, his breakfast, he swung through a ravine that cut between two rocky hilltops.

Directly ahead, the Kollect's surface gleamed through the trees. Frost on the rotting leaves of the ravine showed him the trail of a coyote.

He had followed the animal's footprints before, tracking them to the north bank of the Kollect, where birch trees sprang out of a carpet of moss on the shore of the pond. This day, the track again led into the reeds and vanished. No sign. Handy swore under his breath, invoking an old Bakonga imprecation, untranslatable, about monkey entrails.

Handy once watched, arrested in place, as a coyote ripped through a pen of baby lambs. The animal fled before he could take a single forward step. They were quicker than wind.

This is your day to die, coyote.

Handy crossed over to stalk the watery southern edge of the Kollect, which was fringed with reeds. The pocked crust of half-frozen mud first crunched, then sucked at his feet as though it would pull him down.

Easy, fool, Handy said to himself, fall in the pond and you've got a cold walk home. He followed a narrow winding path that curved into the frigid water. The inlets of the Kollect here were topped with thin, fragile panes of silver ice.

He spotted the coyote. Not twenty yards away. Leaning down to the water and lapping. He could see the animal's delicate pink tongue. Handy moved carefully to raise his firearm.

A flash of brown-gray fur. The coyote disappeared so quickly Handy almost felt he hadn't seen it at all. So he ran, cracking the ice and sloshing through the shallows, to get to where the animal last was. Let off a shot through the trees, the slope rising just there.

He saw flesh poking from the ice for a moment before his mind allowed him to understand what it was. Greenish and blood-black, rising out of one of the small cracked floes. He stepped forward. Something—a gnawed arm?—thrust above the surface. This was what had drawn the coyote back again and again.

Unsteady, feeling as though an awful dawning were being prepared for him, Handy took a step forward and fell to his knees, slopping the icy water over himself.

He didn't feel the cold.

The body was half-encased, imprisoned, caught where it lay, the glossy ice translucent. He could clearly see her face turned upward to the sky, wide-open eyes staring.

Piteous.

Part Four

The Crown Province
of New York

36

The adult colonists of New Amsterdam did not know the truth, and neither did their children, the ones in households with a mother and father and warm circles of relatives within which they comfortably lodged, safe and secure.

The governing officials of the colony did not know the truth, the director general and *schout* and *schepens* and *burgomeesters* and the Nine (with one exception: the orphanmaster knew).

The common men in the settlement were likewise all unknowing, the bricklayers, scavelmen, drunkards, apothecaries, cartwrights and saddlers. The women did not know, either, the she-merchants, godmothers, midwives, bakers, gossips, the sewing *klatsches* and guests at the caudle parties.

But the orphans knew. Tibb Dunbar knew it first. The indentured servants, the trash pickers, the gutter muckers, the street urchins, the children unloved and abandoned eventually came to understand. In their long days of labor, scrubbing floors and cleaning the jakes and throwing garbage to the swine, they would at times encounter one another. They exchanged hurried whispers. Intelligence, warnings.

Watch out for a man in scarlet heels. Beware the orphanmaster. Beware the half-breed indian with the stove-in hat. The Crease ain't no joke.

Look to thyself. Step brightly, or ye will find thyself murthered and eaten.

"Be sober, be vigilant," quoth the Bible-schooled among them. "Because your adversary the Devil, as a roaring lion, walketh about, seeking whom he may devour."

They didn't know names. The orphans did not tell tales of witika. They did not fear imaginary goblins. Their experience had taught them that men were the real demons.

So Tibb Dunbar passed the word to Baertie van Vleeck, who told it to Laila Philipe. Laila whispered it to Waldo Arentsen. The Klos twins got it from Waldo, and one of the twins—it was so difficult to tell the two apart—told the orphan who masqueraded as William Turner.

William, observant as he was silent, paid attention. On his way to school, to run errands for Rebecca Godbolt, or to serve his master Drummond—and thank God for Drummond, the only person in this town who had a pleasant word for him—he kept his eyes open.

It is surprising how much a person with open eyes can see that others don't.

William lived through the horror of a frontier war, saw himself stolen by the river indians, then watched his parents die of the small pox as their hostages. He'd been traded for a nag to a cruel English couple and locked away in an attic for days at a time. Not to speak of being constantly pinched, poked and punched by the Godbolts' natural children.

Through the fall and winter, he watched and waited. Everyone shrieked about the witika. Spring, he decided. Springtime was when he would make his move.

Time to be a hero, the boy said to himself, as the spring winds of April thawed the woods. Track the bad man, uncover the evidence, stop the murders. He was only a small child. But the adults seemed to be unable to do anything about orphans disappearing from the colony. He felt that it was left up to him.

William stashed provisions, clothes and an extra pair of shoes in a hidey-hole in the Godbolt attic.

"William," Rebecca Godbolt commanded, "fetch a string of onions for dinner." William would do as he was told.

On this day, the day they called Good Friday for reasons William could never understand (why was the day they murdered Our Dear Lord Jesus called "good"?), he pleaded a stomachache. Mixing dried bread with smashed-up maize, watering the recipe, he managed to concoct a passable batch of vomit to spill beside his bed.

"*Ewwww!*" Mary cried when she stumbled through his alcove and almost stepped in the mess. "Mama, Billy made sick!"

Rebecca bustled in, felt his forehead for a scant two seconds and tut-tutted how much of a bother William was. She ordered her other children to stay away.

Rebecca Godbolt had been trying on her warm-weather costumes all morning to see if they still suited her figure. Easter approached, a day for finery to be displayed and admired. She didn't have time to clean up an orphan's vomit.

The family banged out the door for Good Friday services, lending William a full four-hour head start. He knew where to find his quarry, Lightning, the half-indian all the orphans called "the Crease," for the ugly groove in his forehead.

William picked up the trail at the usual place, behind the Red Lion. He hid around the side, by the cistern, so he could see the comings and goings as freely as if it were a meeting-hall. The Crease wore ordinary European clothing, a shirt and waistcoat and pouchy breeches. When he left the Lion, exiting out of the Mane in back, William waited until he was a block gone, then followed.

The half-indian loped west on Pearl Street over to the fort. William crept along behind him, hunching behind stoops and pressing himself against doorways so as not to be seen. Together, they moved into the market square and north through the parade ground, past the fine houses of the Broad Way and Stone Street.

In the Company's gardens, the mounded earth still slept at this, the very beginning of spring. The Crease never halted or even slowed down.

Private Christen Christoffelszen Cruytdop manned the Company's west land port on the palisade wall. When the Crease reached the sentry, Cruytdop simply waved him through. He saw the half-indian nearly every day, since the man often ventured down to the taprooms around town, sometimes not returning north until after curfew.

He let Lightning through, but stopped the orphan boy.

"Halt, you," barked Cruytdop, stepping from his post. The child came nearly up to the sentry's chest, but not quite.

William took a piece of slate in a wooden frame from around his neck, where it hung with a length of twine. "*Godbolt,*" he wrote in chalk.

Cruytdop would not have been able to pass any rigorous literacy test, but he was aware of the Godbolt family, primarily because his young wife, Wanda, favored their sausage shop. Cruytdop looked annoyed by the chalkboard. Couldn't the child speak?

"Your business?" Cruytdop said.

William again bent over the board. "*Cloth*," he wrote. Another word Private Cruytdop could read. He knew that residents of Little Angola, just north of the wall, frequently were paid to finish sheets and towels for the denizens in the settlement.

He was afraid the boy would begin to write again, something to stump him this time. So he finally waved him by.

William could no longer see the half-indian he trailed. Lightning had gotten too much of a lead in the time William was stuck with the sentry. The Broad Way turned rustic once past the palisade wall. Here were fruit orchards, small *bouweries* and the strip of properties that made up Little Angola.

Running along, William caught sight of the Crease. The half-indian was hustling now. Tall, ancient pine trees towered over the lane. William hid behind one, then darted forward to the next one.

When the road turned into a trail, slippery with April mud and strewn with gray rocks, William got a second wind. The trail twisted, climbed up and down hills, crossed rock formations.

Would they be reaching some destination soon? William wondered. The youngster had trod too many miles already. He walked on.

"Do you have a gun?"

William was startled nearly out of his shoes. Somehow, the Crease had materialized, squatting on a big boulder just beside the trail. William had been following him, and now suddenly the half-indian was there in front of him. He stared down at William, negligently holding a flintlock pistol in his right hand.

"Do you have a gun?" Lightning asked again. "Because I have one. Do you see it?"

William nodded. He would have been struck dumb even if he weren't already mute.

"Good," the Crease said. "You are so eager to follow me. My pistol will show you the way. Come along."

After the shock of his covert visit to the hidden room in the Hendrickson manse, Aet Visser lost his direction. He no longer understood what he was supposed to do in life. His orphanmaster duties seemed meaningless or, worse, downright evil. He spent his days wandering the settlement, avoiding those citizens he knew, which turned out to be, just his luck, an overwhelming percentage of the colony's population.

During that dark time it seemed to Visser that New Amsterdam had the atmosphere of a coffin, sealed in, confining and brutally contained. There was no way out. The settlement's triangular boundaries had two sides cut off by water and a third closed in by a palisade wall.

Still, there were places where a not-too-particular man might lose himself. Visser shunned the Red Lion in favor of the Jug, Missy Flamsteed's tap house on the Strand. There he could drink in obscurity, content to languish in the shadows, unbothered by the other waterfront drunks.

Visser did not call the Orphan Chamber to sit during all of January, nor in February, nor, so far, for the first weeks of spring. He officially postponed the proceedings once, then again, then did not even bother to post a notice. The orphanmaster simply failed to show up for his own court.

The director general, who normally kept a tight grip on every administrative matter in the colony, found himself too distracted by his main worry—the insolent incursions against New Netherland by the English settlers of Connecticut and the Massachusetts Bay Colony—to notice Visser's dereliction.

Visser did not walk the streets, he skulked them. He crossed the settlement not via Pearl or Stone but through the *quartier perdu* of Tuyn Street. He habituated alleys and lanes. He slipped through the palisade wall and wandered north.

Where was he going, exactly? Everywhere he went, he discovered himself there, and that ruined everything. The only real relief would have been to take on a new self and crawl out of his old one.

He kept coming back to Martyn, dissolute, unhinged, brilliant, wealthy, self-obsessed Martyn. The man's watery death upon the ice of the North River had not removed Martyn from Visser's thoughts.

Domineering guilt wore on the orphanmaster. Among the bloody garments secreted in the cabinet, Visser recognized a shirt of Ansel Imbrock, a torn doublet of Dickie Dunn. The thought of so many orphans dead or disappeared, and his own part in it remaining hidden from public view, tormented him. When he made his discovery in the *kas*, he should have run outside screaming.

Alarm! Alarm! The witika killer is found!

Why had he not?

Because Martyn and Lightning held a terrible secret over Visser's head.

Visser had thought that Martyn Hendrickson's death might give him a measure of relief, and for a brief moment, it did. The night after the settlement rocked with the news of the favored Hendrickson son's drowning, Visser slept soundly for the first time in months. He woke up late and resolved to convene the Orphan Chamber that very day. He even shaved.

Humming to himself, he set off to greet the morning, what there was left of it. He met the *schout* heading down Long Street toward the Stadt Huys.

"De Klavier!" he cried.

"Well, Visser," the *schout* said. "We have not seen much of you these past weeks. Have you been ill?"

"A Lenten penitence," Visser said airily.

"Yes, I thought you looked off your feed," De Klavier said. "How are your bowels treating you?"

"A disciplined fast is just the thing," Visser said.

At that moment, Visser caught sight of Lightning, slouching against the sun-warmed stone of the Stadt Huys. His carefree mood evaporated. The half-indian might appear a casual lounger to the passing colonists, but his gaze bore into Visser like hot iron.

He read the message clearly in Lightning's eyes. *Martyn is dead, but you are not released.*

Visser stepped back from De Klavier. "I have business," he said, and abruptly hustled off. Not in the direction he had been going, De Klavier noticed, and not the way he had come, either. He fled up Smit Street and disappeared into the anonymous neighborhoods of the settlement.

What was that all about? De Klavier had not a clue. He thought the orphanmaster's cheese might be slipping off his cracker. The witika had everyone rattled, and of course, it would be natural that Visser would be most concerned of all, his wards disappearing into thin air as they had been doing.

Visser had been so convinced that Martyn's death freed him from his bind. Convinced, too, that the orphan-killings would end, that the witika business was over.

But it was not to be. He had forgotten Lightning. Visser resumed his aimless wanderings on the backstreets of the settlement.

Ad and Ham Hendrickson tended to avoid appearing in public, but they made an exception for their brother's funeral. Which was not a real funeral, since no corpus had been recovered. But one afternoon during his wanderings, Visser heard the funeral caller sound his mournful droning cry as the procession for Martyn Hendrickson wound through the streets.

"God, who works in mysterious ways, in his infinite wisdom has called home to glorious heaven, where he shall sit among the hosts, friend Martyn Hendrickson, a family man, grandee, commissioner of the Nine, captain of the colonial militia, patroon, citizen, paragon, whom all shall mourn. All mourn Martyn Hendrickson. Good men must die, but death cannot kill their names. All mourn Martyn Hendrickson."

Visser watched the procession from a distance. At its head, Van Elsant, the caller—the *aansprecker*, the funeral inviter—was immediately preceded by a young, formally dressed boy hired for the occasion. As was the custom, black crepe streamers flowed back from both their cocked hats.

The boy was an orphan, Visser noted, but one whom he'd had no part in hiring out. The life of the colony had begun to pass the orphanmaster by. Step out of harness for a moment and they begin to forget you. The worse you feel, the worse treated you are.

Ad and Ham Hendrickson, Stuyvesant, Godbolt, Kees Bayard, all the leading lights of the colony took their place in Martyn's funeral procession, wending across town toward the Doden Acker, the graveyard. Not to a freshly dug grave this time, just to a cenotaph. Such monuments usually marked sailors dead at sea, their bodies unrecovered.

Martyn's death changed not a thing. All Lightning had to do was whisper a single word to remind Aet Visser he remained forever bound.

Anna.

An orphan girl Visser was officially pledged to protect as orphanmaster, but who was now his clandestine common-law wife.

Visser's relationship with Anna began in shame and darkness when the girl was thirteen. He was the lust-gripped client, she was the child whore, run by her brother.

There can exist a special innocence of the ruined. Anna Weiss grew up enduring furious assaults, physical, emotional and spiritual, first from her twin brother, Lightning (when he was still known as Gerald Weiss), then from Lightning's friend Martyn Hendrickson. The two friends brutalized her, and when they'd had enough, sold her to be brutalized by others.

Visser stood at the end of a long line of customers. But a light broke. He saw within this ravaged, beautiful child a stubborn blamelessness. He fell in love with her.

Extracting Anna from her brother Lightning's clutches required massive applications of money—the greater part of his illicit earnings as orphanmaster. For years, Martyn and his alter ego Lightning tormented Visser by threatening to expose the sordid details of Anna's past.

Martyn demanded that Visser supply the Hendrickson family with cheap orphan labor. It had all come down to that terrible moment in the secret chamber of the Hendrickson mansion. Through Anna, Visser was still bound to Martyn. He couldn't speak, couldn't confess, could never tell what he had found stuffed into the corner of the Hendrickson *kas*.

Martyn's sway continued from beyond the grave, in the malevolent form of his shadow, Lightning. As soon as Visser stepped forward to make a clean breast, it would be the end of him, and more important, the end of Anna. He would be disgraced. She would be driven from the colony, perhaps back into prostitution. Their children would be scattered, indentured, lost.

Once he gave in to blackmail, Visser could find no way to extricate himself. He twisted like a rat being shaken by a terrier. If Martyn had been guilty of terrible crimes, Visser was, too.

When he wandered the back alleys of the settlement, it was with a hellhound nipping at his heels. Every morning, Visser would decide once again not to convene the Orphan Chamber that particular day. Instead, he burrowed down Tuyn Street, sticking to the margins, avoiding any direct intercourse with passersby.

He was headed nowhere, and he would soon reach his goal.

"We've had a lot of activity here lately," said Lightning, sitting cross-legged on the ground before the fire ring. "As you can see."

Lightning worked his flint and had a blaze going more quickly than any man William had ever seen. In a cold hearth, it usually took William himself a full ten minutes of striking and striking, metal to flint, in order to start a fire for the Godbolts.

Beyond the flames of the fire, William could see the black opening of a cave. The walk up the island had taken half the day. The afternoon shadows lengthened. They were somewhere high on a hill, surrounded by rocky promontories. Far below, the mumbling of a creek.

William sat on a fallen log. This was a bad place, he knew. The air smelled of rotten meat. The first flies of spring made a sound like an angry thought inside his head.

He is the one, William thought, looking at Lightning. He saw him clearly, a man in halves, European and indian, the two halves fighting. Him wanting you to believe he was a swannekin, when really anyone could see what he was.

The Crease. That's what Tibb Dunbar called him.

Why am I still alive? William felt cold fear as well as another thing, a boldness that lay atop his panic. Damn him, he thought. Damn his ugly creased skull straight to hell.

He recalled the word written on the slate Kitane had carried back to him from Drummond and Blandine. *Courage.*

Lightning had made William quick-step all the way up the island, at first at the point of his pistol. But soon enough, the half-indian shoved the weapon into his belt, and the two continued walking together as though they were a father and son out for an Easter holiday hike.

Somewhere up the island, they scaled a steep rocky cliffside and came to a clearing where the ground was covered with dark, oval stones. Upon their arrival at the place, the Crease showed William around, gesturing proudly to the cave a number of times, bending forward at the waist like an usher in a church. He babbled.

"The parts of the whole need a place to go," the half-indian said. "The master will come to see what is choice and what is not. It is his decision, not my own."

William nodded as though he understood, when he did not.

"My master knows many things about the night, and about children," said the Crease. "You should meet him. He is the true orphanmaster."

He pronounced the name.

If William had not been certain before, he now knew beyond doubt the Crease was crazy. The man he named as master, Martyn Hendrickson, was dead. Everyone knew that. Yet Lightning spoke of him as if he were present, perhaps asleep next door, in the cave.

William noticed some small objects arrayed on the ground around where the Crease squatted, items that he kept touching and manipulating and piling one on top of the other.

"The relics here are utmost holy," said the half-indian. He abruptly fell to laughing as though he were watching a clown at *kermis*. "Yes, we have witika fever here. This is where to catch it. We all have witika fever!"

A wave of nausea crashed over William, and he folded his arms and stared down at the ground. Saliva flooded his mouth. He didn't really want to know what the half-indian held in his hands.

"I like your silence," said the half-indian, approaching the voiceless boy on his hands and knees. The man was deranged. "I like you. I might like you too much, but that choice is my master's. He's the one who decides the deed. I merely advise and collect the afterbirth. Relics, icons, the essential leave-takings. That's me."

The Crease reached out with a gentle hand and patted William on the knee. The boy stared at the stars painted along his jawline.

William tried not to show he was cringing. He thought of how he would find out what he needed to know.

He took out his chalk. "*William Turner?*" he wrote. "*Orphan.*"

"Can I hold that?" said the Crease.

Lightning gently removed the slate from around William's neck. "You really don't speak?" he asked.

He leaned forward and pinched a portion of William's flesh, just above his left elbow, twisting it so viciously that the skin abraded and bled. Tears came to the boy's eyes, but he did not cry out.

Lightning nodded, as if satisfied. "Now, William Orphan Turner," he said. "That is a story." He narrowed his eyes as though they could burn through the mute child.

"After the one up north, the Hawes boy, the master's brothers got a little peevish with us. Sent us down here. But you know when you get a taste of something, and want a little something more? Like . . . ice cream. Have you ever had ice cream?"

William shook his head.

"Well, no matter. A thing you like, you want some more, right? That's natural. So we found a little African orphan girl. The master did it."

He waited for some sign of understanding from William, but the boy kept an expression of confusion on his face. "You are asking where William Orphan Turner comes into it, aren't you? Very simple. He saw it. At the Kollect. He was going for water. He saw the master, and I saw him see. Now, do you see?"

Again, William shook his head. He reached for the slate but Lightning held it away.

"He witnessed the master doing the black girl, don't you understand? So little Billy Turner had to get done, too. And afterward, when we learned he was an orphan, too, well, we took that as a sign. We didn't think it was a coincidence. Not one orphan, but two!"

An object hung from a nearby tree branch, swaying slightly. It resembled one of the hams in the Godbolt attic. Lightning pointed to the haunch of meat.

"Do you see the tasty?"

William nodded, barely.

"The master calls it the 'divine carcass.' The cadaver of God. He can be clever with words, though he is sometimes very stupid with other things."

Lightning rose smoothly to his feet, unfolding his legs as though they were made of spring steel.

"Wait," he said. "Wait, wait. I kept a souvenir of William Turner."

He turned and strode into the cave. William heard him rooting around in there as though it were a wardrobe closet.

"Aha," he called out, and returned to William at the fire. Holding out a two-inch bone to him, Lightning smiled broadly and gestured for the boy to take it.

Clean and dry, boiled white, the finger was jointed into three interlocking bones. A signet ring rode on the knuckle like a quoit.

"Have it, it's yours," the Crease said. "And now, my master has requested my presence. I promised him I would be back by nightfall."

In other words, the Crease was telling William that he had an appointment with a dead man.

He crossed to a leather box that lay on the ground next to the cave mouth. He bustled busily with his back to William. Then he turned, tugging a hairpiece into place on the crown of his naked head. The periwig, light brown and curly, reached just below his shoulders.

"Well?" he asked, flipping the luxuriant hair with the back of one of his hands. "Not at all like a Sopus, is it? More like a European."

William nodded slowly. The man looked as though a shaggy billy goat had crawled atop his skull.

Lightning leaned toward him conspiratorially. "I know you won't say a word about all this, because you ain't the talking type." He had a good laugh over that.

Then, quite unexpectedly, he was off like a panther down the rocky cliffside, wig hair flapping like a pennant, disappearing into the late afternoon woods. He left William alone, unshackled, alive. The boy couldn't understand it. But then, nothing Lightning did made any sense.

When William was sure the Crease was gone, he opened his left hand, the one that clutched the finger. Around the slim bone rattled the heavy gold signet ring, a large "WT" initialed on its bezel.

"William Turner," the boy said out loud.

37

After another exhausting day of wandering alone, Visser approached, with a measure of relief, his own home, in a private lane off Long Street near the East River land port. Anna would have dinner for him. Loud and rambunctious as they were, the children would manage to soothe his jangled nerves. He would nuzzle the Bean and be renewed.

Lately, his family had been staying more and more with him in his ramshackle dwelling-house. He no longer saw the need for the propriety of sending them up to Corlaers Hook each evening. Propriety, for him, had vanished behind that secret door in the sprawling dwelling-house of his patron.

Good Friday. Or perhaps it might already be Holy Saturday. The days merged together for Visser. The drumbeat sounded so often, calling the colonists to worship in this sacred season, that he was unsure what day it actually was.

In High Street he passed the ragged artist Emily Stavings. He had always meant to ask her who had organized the appalling fright-lantern show of Christmas Eve. The paintings projected were clearly hers. No one else in the colony was capable of executing anything nearly so handsome.

But Visser passed Stavings by without stopping. In all his recent wanderings he determinedly avoided speaking to people, if at all possible. He had cut many good citizens that way, people he once accorded his friends.

He trudged up the short rise in the lane that led to his door. His domicile, a fantastic warren of additions, chambers and sagging hallways, shone with a welcoming glow in the springtime dark.

"Anna!" he called upon entering. "Children!"

No one at home.

Flee, Visser thought. *All is discovered*. The *schout* and the director general would be in his chambers, asking, "When did you first discover the bloody clothes of the murdered orphans?" "What was your involvement?" And, "Why did you say nothing about it?"

He had a brandy bottle hidden in a cubby in the vestibule, and he fortified himself with that before he went inside. As he passed into the great room, he stopped cold.

The *schout* did not lie in wait. Nor Petrus Stuyvesant.

Sitting in Visser's parlor chair was the dead man.

Martyn Hendrickson.

Resurrected. He looked paler than normal, blue-lipped, as though the cold of the North River still hung on him.

"Ah, Visser, you've come at last," Hendrickson said, his wet boots steaming from the heat of the hearth.

"You are dead," Visser stammered.

"It's Eastertime!" Martyn declared, laughing. "He is risen!"

Opposite to Martyn, in the matching hearthside chair, sat Lightning. Held tightly in the half-indian's lap was Visser's little fur ball of a dog, Maddie.

Lightning wore not his customary ancient hat of collapsed black felt, normally forever affixed to his head, tied in place by a scarf in winter and a piece of rope in summer. It was indeed strange to see him out of it, so identified had he become with its display.

Instead, the half-breed wore the most outlandish periwig Visser had ever seen, a curly monstrosity that would have been right at home in Fontainebleau.

But Visser had no thought of Lightning. Not right at that moment.

Sitting on Martyn's lap, fussing contentedly with a lace ribbon, was the Bean.

"*Guten abend*, Pow-Pow," Sabine said. "*Wie gehts?*" She barely looked at him, so caught up she was in her ruffle.

Martyn, on the other hand, stared at him fixedly.

"Well?" Martyn said. "You've been asking around about us, haven't you? Poking your fat red nose into our business. And here we are."

With a kind of marveling pride, Martyn revealed the story of his resurrection. How Fantome had struggled to gain purchase on the edge of the crumbling ice, which kept breaking away under the horse's hooves. How the heroic charger finally managed to haul itself up on the firm, frozen surface.

And how Martyn himself, submerged for a good ten minutes beneath the water of the North River, had been dragged out by the stallion only because his body was tangled in the traces. He lay more dead than alive when Lightning, rushing up the river on a run, discovered him.

But the icy water shut down Martyn's body. His blood retreated to his brain, keeping it nourished. And by a miracle Lightning was able to revive him in front of a fire at the Place of Stones, a half hour after Martyn died in the river. The half-indian conducted the corpselike body home to the big house on Market Street, where Martyn's brothers, Ad and Ham, further thawed him out and kept him away from the eyes of the world.

"Jesus did not do better with Lazarus," Martyn said, reaching across to slap Lightning on the knee. "And look! In return the good Lord granted our handsome friend a full wealth of hair."

"Sabine," Visser said. "Come to Pow."

The child, still fixated on her bit of lace, obediently began to squirm off Martyn's lap. He held her back.

"I think not," Martyn said, smooching at the Bean's neck. "She is a cherry so delicate it must be plucked only with the lips."

"I warn you, Martyn—" Visser began, but Lightning rose abruptly to his feet. Maddie fell to the floor with a yelp.

"I need to know one thing," Martyn said. "And you will tell it to me straight off."

He stared, his eyes boring into those of the orphanmaster. Visser dropped his gaze. "I want to know where that fucker Edward Drummond is, and his whore Blandine van Couvering."

Blandine and Edward rode south on the Post Road toward New Amsterdam.

The morning sun woke flights of bluebirds, fat buds at the ends of tree branches and the gentle exhalations of spring. The vast highland valley of the North River lay before them, most of its trees still denuded by winter. But if you looked at the hillsides slantwise, Blandine noticed, you could catch the first hint of yellow-green. The sloppy trail spattered her gown and Drummond's doublet with mud.

"Do we know what day this is?"

"No," Drummond said.

"It may be Easter Sunday," Blandine said.

"Aye," Drummond said.

They were riding into a trap. Either that, or the messages that reached them through Kitane were true.

In New Amsterdam, and in New Netherland as a whole, the political winds had shifted. The estrangement of the Dutch citizenry from their director general, thrown into high relief by the Battle of the Red Lion (Raeger capitalized it thus), had recently become complete. An increasingly marginalized and desperate Stuyvesant turned to the English residents of the colony for support.

To curry favor with them, the director general promised Drummond a new trial. A proper English jury trial, it was said, independent from government influence, six men brave and true.

As for Miss Blandina [Raeger wrote], she is guaranteed a full ecclesiastical hearing. The witika fever in the settlement has cooled somewhat, though an Africanus orphan disappeared this spring. Some say this is proof positive of Miss Blandina's innocence, that the witika struck again when she was gone. Come home, you two, and we'll kick over the tables and haul down the staircases once again. This place makes no sense without you.

They debated.

"We can't stay in this fairy castle forever," Blandine said.

"We can't?" Edward said.

They took the Post Road south at the first melt. The chorale of spring peepers sounded in the low wet marshes at the side of the trail, the insistent song of the immature little frogs swelling to such a volume that it became almost alarming.

Blandine, at least, did not look overly happy about heading home. Drummond thought it was more than her worry over an uncertain reception at the other end of their journey.

"You are ill at ease," he said. "I used to see you this way often, but . . ."

"Not lately," Blandine said.

"No, not lately," Edward said. "Lately you've seemed content."

He wondered if he should hazard a guess. "You are upset with the two of us," he said. "You think that by our time away from New Amsterdam we have shirked our commitment to ferreting out the truth of these murders."

"For our own pleasure," Blandine said.

"And putting aside the fact that if we had stayed in the capital, we would have both been executed."

"Hmmn," Blandine murmured, as if it were a small thing.

Drummond said, "It is not like we haven't been thinking about the killings."

"Like worrying a bad tooth," Blandine said.

"And what are your thoughts? If not Aet Visser, who? Who would you propose?" They had been over and over this, increasingly so in the past few days, since their decision to return to the capital.

"In my dark moments, I think it is all of them."

"All?"

"A whole cabal," Blandine said. "The director general and his nephew. George Godbolt and Aet Visser and Martyn Hendrickson and every damn well-fed burgher in the settlement. I see them get together for a kind of horrible children-killing sport."

Edward looked at Blandine oddly. "I hope your dark moments are few," he said.

A face peered out from the recesses of Blandine's mind, its outline becoming clearer and clearer. A handsome face. She wasn't sure, and would not want to say the name before she was certain.

Raeger survived the Battle of the Red Lion and emerged a hero to the rebellious Dutch populace. He sent a sloop to meet Drummond and Blandine at the Tappan Zee, where the river ice had broken up enough to allow travel by water. The ship couldn't take the horses, so they hobbled them and would send a groom up for them later.

"Aye, Easter it is," said their captain, Jeremy Stroose, when they asked after the day as they boarded *The Republic* on the morning of their rendezvous.

"Good of you to come on a holiday Sabbath," Drummond said.

"Oh, this river's my church," Stroose said. He swung the sloop out among the ice floes of the middle channel.

Soon, visible along the North River shore of Manhattan Island, came the familiar *bouweries* and Company farms, the reed beds where the Mahican canoes had long ago been beached, a fleeting glimpse of Little Angola. Blandine felt herself gripped with a sharp pang of missing Antony.

They passed the boundary of New Amsterdam, marked by the palisade wall, after which there appeared in quick succession the Company gardens, the fort, the gallows.

"I guess the director general has been busy," Drummond said grimly.

A body hung in the gibbet.

High tide. Stroose had an offshore wind and brought them in close to the settlement, cutting alongside the shoreline, the sloop throwing off white froth from the prow, dashing at the waves as though its inanimate timbers could feel joy.

"Oh, my God," Blandine said, staring at the hanged man, swinging at the end of the rope just a dozen rods away from them.

Blandine recognized the body. She moaned and dropped to her knees.

As the town drums beat the glad tidings of Easter, Aet Visser wandered far from the church meeting-hall, along the wall at the northern limit of the settlement. He traversed the street below the palisade several times without noticing just where he was.

At one corner, he encountered Tibb Dunbar. The ragamuffin froze upon seeing Visser. A quick moment passed between them. The boy he knew as Gypsy Davey recognized who the orphanmaster was. And Visser saw a look of naked fear cross the orphan's face.

"No, Davey, no," Visser murmured, reaching out. But the boy ran, vanishing into a walk between two dwelling-houses along the wall. Visser leaned up against an orchard fence and wept.

His own chicks feared him. He had let them down. In his soul, it was as if he carried with him an immense stone, a weight so heavy it threatened to force him to the ground, drag his body into the earth, send him straight down into a fire-and-brimstone netherworld.

He had kept his mouth shut about his own complicity in horrendous crimes. A voice inside him would shout, *But you didn't realize! Your complicity was mitigated by your ignorance!*

Visser provided Martyn with the orphans of New Amsterdam. He received money for the service. But he had done so with the best of intentions, thinking to place his wards as servants in the many Hendrickson holdings. He had no way of knowing what their fate would be.

He had beaten back his suspicions and entered into a foolish delusion, accepting the strange nightmare of indian demons and supernatural murder as an explanation for the events that had late afflicted the colony.

Why? He was a coward. Since childhood he had been yellow, a character flaw that he had tried and failed to correct. Trembling before authority, being swayed by convenience, physically unable to face fear, going along to get along. Ugh! How life had dirtied him!

But that wasn't it, was it?

The reason for his silence did not come truly home to him until he saw his three-year-old darling sitting in the lap of the monster, Martyn Hendrickson. He would do anything to save the Bean from ruin. Anything at all, even pretend ignorance toward evil.

His crimes had to be laid against that tally: the Bean, kept safe and happy, maintaining her existence of innocent joy. Visser was her bulwark. If the world ever knew of his involvement in the witika business, Sabine would be tarred with his brush. He would take on the sins of the world in order that she remain unsullied.

Contemplating these dark, desperate thoughts, Visser wandered through the colony, unaware of his surroundings, down across the parade ground, around the fort, past the *moolens*, to arrive inexplicably at the foot of the town gallows.

It had often happened like that. Visser would trudge all day long, avoiding all eyes, unmoored, wandering like Odysseus, only to find himself drawn again and again to the gibbet.

It had become an object of fascination for him. The wind from the bay blew strong here at the edge of the shore, bringing the smell of the sea, somehow fresh and decayed all at once.

At his back, the *moolens* spun ceaselessly, creaking out the message that, so said Dutch tradition, the noise of their turning made: *work harder, work harder.* In counterpoint to the stern Calvinist squeak of the windmills, the seals populating the rocks off the island's point barked joyfully.

The gallows structure itself had been constructed for hard service, built to last out of island oak harvested from the great stands that greeted the colonists when they first arrived. The wrights framed in massive eight-by-eight beams, crossed with nailed-down two-inch-thick milled planks, creating something like a civic monument. Looming above the structure, blocking any view of the settlement to the east, the ramparts of the fort.

The mechanism of the trapdoor in particular intrigued Visser. He took repeated tours underneath the apparatus, marking the hinges and the throw-chock, which connected upward to the hangman's handle.

The thirteen steps (Visser had counted them many times), likewise sturdy, rose from a stone landing laid at the platform's south side. Thirteen being the traditional number, as were the nine loops of the knot that tied the noose. The business end of the hangman's handle, visible on the platform beside the square outline of the trapdoor, was worn from use to a fine, smooth finish.

The director general liked to leave the rope in place as a symbolic caution to sinners. Occasionally, during his darker moods, Visser slipped the noose around his neck. Just to try it out. Just to see how it felt. He imagined that the rough hemp coils smelled of the condemned.

A long parade of prisoners had marched here. Mount platform stairs, step, step, step (thirteen times), cross planks, bow head to accept noose, last words, hood slipped down, darkness, drop, sudden wrenching snap, silence.

On this morning, the bright joyous day of Easter renewal just beginning, Visser could hear the barely audible strains of the congregation, singing hymns in the meeting-hall of the Reformed Church inside the fort. A solo air. A psalmody. Then Visser recognized the ancient Dutch hymn:

> *Blijf met mij, heer*
> *Als't zonlicht niet meerstraalt*
> *Blijf met mij, heer*
> *Als straks de avond daalt*

Abide with me, Lord, as the sunlight shines no more, abide with me, Lord, when soon the evening falls . . .

It seemed everything pointed him one way. Martyn holding the Bean in his lap. The fear in Gypsy Davey's eyes. Even the bay's blue-lit waves trended in a single direction only.

Visser found that he had indeed mounted the thirteen steps, that he had indeed slipped the rope around his neck. Though he had never tightened the noose around his neck before, he often wondered how that would feel.

He snugged the rope, took a last look over the bay and reached out to pull the hangman's handle.

38

"It couldn't be him," Blandine said. "Tell me it isn't Aet Visser."

"Why would they hang him?" Drummond asked. "And on Easter Sunday? It doesn't make sense."

"They must have done it on Good Friday," Blandine said bitterly. "The director general likes to leave his bodies to rot a little, send a message."

They arrived at the wharf ahead of the news. After Stroose docked *The Republic* at a finger pier on the East River, Blandine and Edward disembarked and hurried down the rough-plank causeway to wharfside.

At the moment they took their first steps on New Amsterdam soil in two months, the town crier's call rose from the opposite side of town. His echoing voice floated on the still Easter air like a curse.

"*Oyez, oyez*, the orphanmaster is dead. The orphanmaster is dead. Discovered hung by the neck at the town gallows."

It was all so confusing. Obviously, it had indeed been Visser dangling dead at the gibbet. Just as obviously, the hanging had not been carried out by the town authorities. And if the director general had not ordained the hanging as punishment for some heinous crime, who had?

The realization dawned only slowly. Drummond walked with Blandine up the canal to his rooms on Slyck Steegh. They proceeded in silence. She did not weep, but her face wore a suffering, shocked expression.

On the streets, along the waterfront, on New Bridge over the canal, the residents of the settlement paraded in their Easter holiday finery, gossiping volubly. The women wore their best gowns, looped up high to display the riotous colors of their petticoats. In Blandine's unsettled mood, the effect seemed that of a circus in a cemetery.

No one paid the least attention to the two returned exiles. Edward and Blandine passed through the crowds as ghosts. The words *Aet Visser* and *suicide* flew from the lips of the colonists. Someone said, "One is risen, and one is fallen," and someone else laughed at the Easter witticism.

Blandine felt dislocated. Coming back to New Amsterdam represented a treacherous-enough transition for her, without adding to it the distress of Visser's death. Old feelings of loss and abandonment welled up in her. She had lost her first father, and now she had lost her second.

They turned off the canal to the quieter side street. Drummond mounted the stoop to the front door of his rooms. Nine weeks previous, he had been hauled down those same steps as a traitor and a spy. It seemed another age. The buttonwood tree on the street in front of his dwelling-house, bare then, now showed tiny green buds.

Raeger had Drummond's front door repaired, the bullet hole in the lintel fixed, the disorder of the rooms righted, the mounds of broken glass swept up from the floor of the workshop. Raeger saw to it that the Swedish landlord had been paid his monthly twelve-guilder rent.

But as Drummond and Blandine entered, the hearth was cold, and the rooms displayed a suspended, out-of-time feel. As they wandered through the place, Blandine finally wept disconsolate tears over Aet Visser. She sat down, rose up abruptly, ventured out into the yard, came back inside again, Drummond always at her side.

Blandine found herself unable to make her brain work, not willing to understand what she was doing there. Why? She asked herself over again. Suddenly more tired than she had ever known herself to be, she sank down upon Drummond's big bed in his best chamber and, after crying for a restless half hour, dropped into sleep, watched over by her lover.

Dreams of falling, drowning, losing control. The witika swooped over the thatched rooftops of New Amsterdam like a leather-winged bat.

She woke to pounding on the front entrance door. The room was dark. Drummond wasn't there. The bearskin had been thrown over her, so their paltry few goods from the sloop had been delivered to his dwelling-house. How long had she slept?

Out in the great room, voices. Blandine recognized De Klavier and the dominie, Megapolensis. Drummond's voice, too, bringing her comfort.

"It is better that this whole scandalous affair has ended," De Klavier said.

"Has it ended?" Drummond asked.

"Obviously, Aet Visser preyed upon his charges," Megapolensis said.

"His death was his confession," De Klavier said.

Blandine rose and appeared, sleep-tousled and disheveled, in the doorway of the best chamber. "There's nothing obvious about it," she said.

Drummond crossed to her.

The dominie appeared upset, embarrassed. "Miss Blandina," he said.

"They have come to read us our indictments," Drummond said.

"We might have met you at your ship's docking," De Klavier said. "But this unfortunate incident with the orphanmaster disturbed our preparations. On Easter Sunday, too!"

Megapolensis took a sterner tack. "I wonder that you are bold enough to show yourselves in sin together," he said. "This is no way to present a defense in an ecclesiastical court, nor in any other, for that matter."

Edward put his arms around Blandine and kissed her tenderly. She was puffy-faced from sleep, her eyes red from crying, but he didn't see it. Instead, he thought, is a woman ever more beautiful than when she just awakes?

"You bring shame on you both, but especially upon you, Miss Blandina!" Megapolensis said. "I can no longer stay in this room."

"You must," Drummond said. "You must stay in order to congratulate me and give Blandine your best wishes."

"What?"

"The banns were read in the Dutch church at Esopus Sunday last," Drummond said. "You shall no longer address her as 'Miss.'"

"You are married?" Megapolensis said, clearly stunned.

"We will be, if you will do us the honor," Drummond said.

For once, Megapolensis was without words.

De Klavier looked nonplussed. He had come to upbraid the accused spy, to inform him of his pending retrial for treason, and instead found himself pounding Drummond on the back and bussing his intended on her cheek. She really was quite the loveliest maiden in the colony. It would be a pity to burn her.

Megapolensis found his tongue. "My hearty congratulations!" he said. "Of course I shall officiate the vows. I am happy, happy, happy for you!"

"I'm afraid our joy is mixed with grief over Mister Visser's death," Blandine said.

"No, no," Megapolensis cried. "Don't you see? The man was clearly plagued by guilt for his offenses. It is as the *schout* said: self-authorship of one's death is the surest admission of culpability one could possibly provide. His confession removes all shadow from you, Blandine! Your trial now becomes purely *pro forma*. I have no doubt you will be cleared of any involvement in witchcraft or devilry."

"Aye, but you shall still have to stand trial," said De Klavier. He attempted to reassert the severity of his office. He turned to Drummond. "As shall you."

Drawing a document from his waistcoat pocket, De Klavier assumed a stance of formal attention. "Edward Drummond, the ruling of the director general is, ye shall not depart the jurisdiction, ye must present thyself every day, once a day, to the *schout*—that's me—if ye engage counsel, to inform the office of the director general. We shall expect you to make no discourse with the general public to inflame opinion, nor confer with criminal associates."

Drummond wondered if Raeger would fit into that last category.

"How about a wedding ceremony?" he asked. "Might that be allowed?"

When De Klavier and Megapolensis left, Drummond uncorked a bottle of brandy and poured a few fingers into a pewter tumbler. He and Blandine shared the drink.

"Hungry?"

She shook her head.

"We could go to the Lion," he said.

"The Sabbath," she said. "The taproom hearth is left cold. By order of the director general."

"Well, anyway, I have to speak with the *weert* there, an interesting man, a pirate, I think, in his former years."

Blandine's laugh turned immediately to tears. "Why did he do it?" she cried.

"Darling," Drummond said, wrapping her in his arms again.

"I want to go to my dwelling-house," Blandine said, speaking with her face buried in Drummond's chest. "I want to go home, retrieve my things, and then come back here to stay with you the night."

"Then that is what we shall do," Drummond said.

* * *

Tibb Dunbar sank his teeth into Peer Gravenraet's left earlobe and wouldn't let go, no matter how many times Peer punched and punched at Tibb's face. Blood from the two boys mingled and flew. Tibb tried again to hook his leg around Peer's and bring him down.

The Coney Boys were challenging the High Street Gang, and each group had put forth their champion. Just off New Amsterdam's wharf district, in the little one-block lane between High Street and Slyck, the gladiators met, Tibb and Peer, a bout, they both swore, to the death. The ring of combat involved two tight semicircles of spectators, the Coneys on the town side, the Highs on the wharf side.

Peer Gravenraet's standing among the Coneys had soared with his Christmas Eve discovery of the severed foot, to the degree he took his rightful place at the head of the gang. The Coneys recruited their membership from the well-dressed boys of the settlement, those who were all familied up, the ones who like as not had a few strings of seawan in their pockets.

The High Streets were from a more ragged class. They took their name from the address of the work yard behind Missy Flamsteed's tap house, where many of them spent long hours at cutting firewood, stall-mucking and vittle preparation.

Requisite for membership in the Highs: orphanhood.

A few of the High Streets were indentured to the families of the Coneys. When Saint Nicholas came at Christmastime, the High Street boys were the ones who did not find gold coins in the shoes they had laid out on the hearth the night before, nor candy nor wooden soldiers either. They woke the next morning to find just their same old shoes, cold and empty.

Trouble brewed between the two bands all fall, with running battles continuing through the winter and into the spring. The Coneys delighted in taunting the Highs with their victimized status. They would scrawl the circle-and-cross witika sign on the facade of the Jug, the unofficial headquarters of the Highs. Being caught at such a prank meant a thorough pummeling by members of the orphan gang, but the dare was worth it.

The Coney Boys scared themselves silly telling witika stories, but took great pleasure in the fact that it was always orphans that the indian demon targeted. They were safe, they were coddled in the stronghold of parents and relatives and friends, not like the dirty urchins who were consumed, one after another, by the voracious monster.

"Witika take you!" was one of the jeers the Coneys leveled against the Highs.

It had come to this, Peer "The Rat" Gravenraet versus Tibb "Gypsy Davey" Dunbar, man to man, hand to hand.

There is no dirtier street fighter than a twelve-year-old. "No eye gouging," the Coney Boy Denny Bayard had announced at the beginning of the battle, after which the contestants came together. Both immediately went for the eyes of the other.

The left eye of Tibb Dunbar had, in fact, swollen shut, but he fought on just as well with one. He liked torso shots, and he was wearing his opponent down. Peer tended to go for the face.

Two adults came down the lane from town, but the gangs were so avid that they ignored the intrusion until Blandine and Drummond were upon them. They waded into the melee, though, and dragged the boys apart.

"Leave us be!" Peer shouted. The Coney Boys booed, but didn't dare advance on the formidable Drummond. And they would never hit a woman.

"Peer!" Blandine cried. "You're bleeding!"

"The *schout*!"

De Klavier approached, advancing up the lane from the direction of the wharf, calling out, "Here now! Here now!"

The two gangs scattered. De Klavier managed to snag one, a girl, Laila Philipe, age ten, but the rest artfully eluded him. "Little snip," he snarled.

Dragging her by the neck, the *schout* approached Blandine and Drummond on the former field of battle.

"The imps," he said. "You two are in the middle of this?"

Drummond laughed and bowed. "Innocent bystanders," he said. "Although I'd lay my wager on the orphans."

Blandine said, "Let her go, De Klavier. That's Laila Philipe. She has a fine foster family and her guardians will be worried about her."

De Klavier let up on his grip, and Laila instantly vanished down the lane toward the wharf.

Mortal enemies Tibb Dunbar and Peer Gravenraet happened to flee in the same direction, slipping into the yard of a chandler's shop and hiding amid the cooperage there. Breathing hard, bleeding, they stared at each other in the darkness.

"Happy Easter, rabbit," Tibb said. The Highs always called the Coney Boys the Rabbits. Likewise, the Coneys customarily referred to the Highs as the Lows.

"Glad tidings, low boy," Peer responded.

Fast friendships have been formed before in the euphoria that follows a good fight. An ear-tattered Peer extended his hand to a punch-stunned Tibb. Tibb took it. Both boys started laughing at once, and they shared a good one together, wheezing, coughing and spitting chips of teeth and gobs of blood.

Thus began the alliance of the Coney Boys and the High Street Gang.

Blandine's rooms had the same lost-in-time air that Drummond's displayed. Lace and Mally were in to restore order after the searches of the witchcraft tribunal, and during the mistress's exile up north they continued to come, at Antony's insistence, to keep the place tidy.

Miss Blandina would return, Antony always thought. Things would go back to the way they were before.

When Blandine did come back, she knew nothing would reverse time. "I don't want to stay here," she murmured, as she and Edward passed through her cold, empty chamber. Dusk had fallen. They lit candles, but the light only weakly pushed back the dark.

"We said we would stay the night at mine," Drummond said.

"I want to go everywhere with you," she said. They embraced. "London, Batavia, the Barbados."

"*Cain-tuck-kee*," Drummond said.

Blandine laughed and nodded. "Yes! *Cain-tuck-kee*. We'll open the first entrepôt west of the mountains."

"I'm told you hold a plot of land up in Beverwyck," he said.

"I do!" she said, smiling.

"First things first," Drummond said. "Get your things together and we'll go home."

"It won't take long," Blandine said.

"Let me go across and see if Raeger is at the Lion," Drummond said. He left her alone.

In her *groot kamer*, Blandine fingered the things she left behind. The scattered items seemed alien to her, as though they belonged to another woman altogether. The gowns, scarves, linens, combs, pins, slippers, tabards looked helpless, forlorn, disowned. She decided she didn't need any of it. How we weigh ourselves down!

But a small curio that Aet Visser had given her, a scrimshaw figurine he got off a ship captain, that she would keep. Blandine wondered it was not confiscated as evidence when the witch-hunters searched through her rooms.

If she had but gazed outside the casement window of her *kamer*, Blandine would have seen a figure standing, staring in. She busied herself packing. The masked shadow floated closer. Towering, spectral. If there hadn't been a wall and a window separating them, she would have smelled the Devil.

And indeed, she sensed the beast before she saw it. A prickly sensation at the back of her neck forced her to turn and look.

The witika.

"Edward?" Blandine whispered. But Drummond was gone.

The figure outside moved. With an eye still on the window, Blandine looked hurriedly around the great room. Her muff pistol, she thought. Where was her fox-fur muff? Back at Drummond's.

The cloaked shape mounted the steps from the yard, swung open the door and stepped into the room facing Blandine. She could not grasp how enormous the witika was. It stood filling the room, the top of its vacant-eyed deerskin mask practically grazing the ceiling. No man was that tall. No man was eight or nine feet, not even Antony.

Blandine made a move to flee, heading for the doorway that led out onto Pearl Street, but at the same moment Lightning crashed into the room from that direction.

As he reeled past Blandine, the half-indian grabbed her hair. She shouted with the pain of it. The two of them staggered across the floor and slammed into the opposite wall. The witika loomed beside them.

Lightning held a blade to Blandine's throat.

Drummond rushed in after Lightning with two cocked pistols, one in each hand. He fired at the witika, the boom sounding enormous in the closed room, the muzzle flash brilliant. White, sulfurous smoke filled the air.

"Drop your pistol!" Lightning shouted. He drew the dull spine of his knife across Blandine's neck as a threat, then reasserted the sharpened blade so hard that the pressure drew drops of blood. His lavish wig trailed down to swing over Blandine's face.

Drummond could not get a clear shot. In view of the knife at Blandine's neck, he let his unfired weapon fall to the floor.

The witika had unaccountably vanished in the smoke. Dead? Fallen? Disappeared?

"Now you—" Lightning began, but Antony hurtled into the room, bellowing past the disarmed Drummond to tackle the half-indian. Thrown back, Lightning released Blandine, but turned his knife on the giant, stabbing Antony deeply in the chest, pounding away with his blade. Antony's huge body bent at the waist and collapsed.

Blandine picked up Drummond's pistol and shot Lightning in the head, sending him instantly to the floor. His wig lay in bloody disarray, with his scalping scar once again visible. A great gout of blood fountained out from the middle of the crease, where the ball Blandine fired had bored a smoking hole.

39

Governing such a contentious jurisdiction as New Netherland put the director general in mind of Julius Caesar, felled like a dog by multiple stab wounds on the floor of the Roman Senate. Stuyvesant likewise felt himself under assault on all sides. His foes were always evident, and every friend eventually revealed himself only as the wearer of an affable mask, hiding an enemy within.

This morning, the news from Long Island, bad. The Dutch towns of the west end were forcibly taken by Connecticut. The news from the northland, bad. The Massachusetts Bay Colony asserted its claim to all country north of the forty-second parallel of latitude. Fort Orange and Beverwyck fell into that territory, as well as a huge portion of the Hendrickson patent.

And now, this. His *schout* had arranged the audience.

Appearing before the director general in his chamber at the Stadt Huys, the accused witch Van Couvering, the English spy Drummond and a young male-child with a fantastic story to tell. Or not to tell, since every indication had it that the boy was mute.

His name was Jan Arendt, but he had been masquerading as a servant-ward of the Godbolts named William Turner.

"*Mijn Heer* General, the case is complicated by the fact that the God-bolts seem to have disappeared," De Klavier said.

"What do you mean?" Stuyvesant demanded.

"Their dwelling-house is empty, they themselves, the father, George, and the mother, Rebecca, all their children, are not to be found."

"Don't be obtuse, *schout*," Stuyvesant said. "Find them."

"I have searched, and I regret to say that I have not been successful," De Klavier said. "There are some indications they decamped during the night, abandoning many of their possessions."

"Where did they go?"

"Rhode Island, my sources tell me," De Klavier said. "Providence."

Of course, the director general thought. They'd take anyone up there in that open sewer of a colony, thieves, misfits, traitors. Providence was a sink into which all the dregs of the new world ran.

Godbolt. The director general had begun to count on the man. He appeared to be God-fearing and trustworthy. Stuyvesant had made him a friend, an ally.

"*Et tu?*" he murmured to himself. The only thing Godbolt left behind, evidently, was the knife in the director general's back.

And the child. "Who is this boy?"

"A Godbolt ward," De Klavier said. "An orphan."

Stuyvesant felt like seizing his head and pulling out a few strands of his rapidly graying hair. Orphans! He was beset by them, bedeviled, hounded! What had he done against them? How could they, the lowest of the low, bring down the director general of a great colony? He felt like the man who stuck his head in a *bijenkorf*, a beehive, stung all around.

De Klavier pushed Jan Arendt forward and the orphan boy laid his grisly little find in front of Stuyvesant. Bleached-out human finger bones, adorned, if that was the word, by a signet ring.

"It seems—this is difficult, *Mijn Heer* General," De Klavier stammered. "Godbolt seems to have committed a fraud. He replaced a ward of his, William Turner, with this one here, whose real name is Jan Arendt."

Stuyvesant sighed. "George Godbolt did this. Who I recently elevated to the post of *burgomeester*. One of the Nine."

"Yes, *Mijn Heer* General."

"Why?"

"The original orphan boy William Turner was victim of the witika, or rather, of Aet Visser—" De Klavier began. He faltered.

Edward Drummond spoke up. "There was an inheritance involved," he said.

The director general turned a cold eye on the man, wondering that he had the temerity to show up in his audience chamber. In the messages confiscated from Drummond's rooms, Stuyvesant had decoded the Englisher's opinions of him. Vile, hurtful sentiments, cynical in the extreme.

No one saw the good, they saw only the bad.

"William Turner had expectations of good money from his family in England," De Klavier said. "George Godbolt wished to be executor of that estate. When he lost William Turner, he faced losing control of thousands of English pounds. So he sought another supposititious child to take the young heir's place."

"Fantastic," Stuyvesant said. The evil of which his fellow humans were capable should have long ago ceased to amaze him, yet once again, he found himself amazed.

"And this . . . relic," he said, gesturing to the finger, which pointed back toward him accusingly.

"We have not been able to retrace the path to where this boy Jan says he discovered it," De Klavier said. They had searched the rocky outcroppings farther north on the island, but found nothing as bizarre as a cave full of bones.

"*Mijn Heer* General, we wish to adopt the boy," Blandine van Couvering said, speaking for the first time. "The lack of an orphanmaster in the colony has thrown issues of guardianship into confusion. So we came directly to your excellency to petition for relief. We know the boy. Mister Drummond, Edward, has had him in to work for him. We will take him under our care and give him our name."

Stuyvesant thought about the nasty business of the recent violence in Blandine van Couvering's rooms. A man killed, another stabbed. Riot and anarchy. The lady seemed positively to attract disorder. The suicide of Aet Visser had mooted the witika witchcraft accusations against her, but the director general still believed that she was, as the book of Job said, born unto trouble, as sparks fly upward.

"You are betrothed, I hear," he said.

"Yes, Your Excellency," Blandine said.

The union of a spy and a witch, Stuyvesant thought, appalled. *O tempora, o mores!* The manners and behaviors of his colonists made the director general shudder. If God did not call fire down upon the sinful inhabitants of New Amsterdam, then apologies were owed to the cities of Sodom and Gomorrah, since this settlement outdid them in wickedness.

But after all that, one could not say otherwise but that Miss van Couvering graced the colony with her beauty. His nephew, Kees, had been a fool to lose her. The finest example of Dutch womanhood, yet she set herself against the director general and his kin. Why?

Well, Stuyvesant needed a new orphanmaster, since his last one hung himself for reasons depraved and unaccountable. Van Couvering would now no doubt be exonerated at her ecclesiastical trial. Perhaps she could be fully rehabilitated. An orphanmistress? It had never been done before.

"You realize that you might be marrying a condemned man," the director general said. He could not get himself to say Drummond's name. "This person's trial has yet to be conducted."

De Klavier said, "The director general has graciously assented to empanel a special jury for Mister Drummond, in the English manner."

"I am optimistic, *Mijn Heer* General," Blandine said.

"And you, sir," Stuyvesant said to Drummond, "you are a killer of king-killers? One of the Earl of Clarendon's men?"

"I'm an Englishman," Drummond said.

"Yes, you are," Stuyvesant sneered, showing his disgust.

He slapped both hands on the table in front of him. What did it matter? Jan Arendt or William Turner? What did he care? He had more pressing matters to which to attend. He had wasted too much time on this foolishness as it was.

"You, boy," he said to the orphan. "I guess we should call you not William but Jan. Do you wish to be taken in by this lady and this gentleman?"

Jan nodded solemnly.

Returning from his terrifying adventure at the bone-filled cave, after having been absent from the Godbolt household for two full days, including Easter itself, Jan had been Bible-beaten to within an inch of his life by Rebecca. He stood it as long as he could, and then he spoke up.

"I know what happened to William," he stammered out.

Rebecca arrested herself mid-swing, the Good Book balanced above her head. She stared down at the child she had been abusing.

"George?" she called out, her voice faltering. She had never heard the boy speak before. Was it a miracle? Or devilry?

"I know that he is dead," Jan said. "I know that I am not he. My name is Jan."

William the Silent no more.

He spoke up in Stuyvesant's audience chamber now, trembling ever so slightly in front of the intimidating man with the false leg.

"I wish to go with Mister Drummond and Miss Blandina," he said, loud enough for all to hear. "My name is Jan Drummond now."

The stars of the dogwood flowers along the canal burst out. The cherry and apple trees in New Amsterdam gardens bloomed with a pink-white tinge. Blandine van Couvering and Edward Drummond pledged their marriage vows on a springtime day made glorious by love, bright skies and the bubbling aroma of fresh-fried doughnuts.

The first of May, warm and clear. Colony matrons, having gone about well-laced and bundled up for the long cold months of winter, felt moved to strip off their stockings, hike up their skirts and let the soft breeze play against their skin. They leaned back on their *stoeps*, twiddling their toes and enjoying the sunshine. Their men, locked in the unending battle of existence, eyed the bare legs of their goodly wives and had thoughts of matters other than profit and loss.

The feast laid out in the backyard of Blandine's dwelling-house displayed all the bounty the colony had to offer. Doughnuts, yes, steaming hot and plunged in Barbados sugar. And also meats, confections, beverages and desserts.

The multiple black clouds that hung over these particular nuptials seemed to vanish with the morning, as though the ceremony had been given a special one-day dispensation by the weather gods. Aet Visser's death, the groom's impending treason trial and his possible execution by hanging, the late unpleasantness with mob violence, murder most foul and sundry hauntings by demons—well, just a puff of wind from the cheeks of heaven had blown the skies clear of it all.

Antony recovered gradually from his wounds. The *schout* oversaw the disposal of the dead body of the renegade half-indian Lightning, his burial unheralded by the funeral caller, his grave unmarked. Blandine scrubbed and scrubbed to clean the bloodstains from the wide plank flooring of her rooms.

The charges against the bride, of consorting with the Devil, had, at last, been laid to rest. Blandine's ecclesiastical trial, officiated by Dominie Megapolensis and featuring an august panel of three local pastors, was a two-hour affair concluded a week before the wedding. The finding? The charges were groundless, baseless, a rude contumely created for reasons unknown by the real guilty party, Aet Visser.

"I always believed in her," said the reigning matron of the settlement, Margaret Tomiessen. "Didn't I tell you that she was as guiltless as a newborn child?"

The other women in her circle, matrons and maidens both, looked to Margaret for direction as to whether a proper lady might attend the wedding celebration. Every person among them, from the acid-tongued Jacintha Jacobsen to a newly *enceinte* Elsje Kip and a fresh-faced Maaje de Lang (what was she so happy about?), wanted desperately to go.

The combination of splendid food and inestimable grist for gossip was just too difficult to resist. Nothing like the spice of scandal to attract the polite and decorous. Luckily, following Margaret's lead, the ladies did not have to defy the temptation.

Margaret said, "I testified at her trial, did I tell you that?" (She had told them that.) "I said I had seen men enter her domicile when she was not at home. Were they Aet Visser and his henchmen? I don't know for sure, so I couldn't say. But there was an opportunity to break into that poor girl's dwelling-house to spread around those horrid demon-indian articles they found there. That's all I had to tell their excellencies."

Conspiracy! Dark doings under the cover of night. A virtuous maiden's honor besmirched. What could be better?

So, with Margaret Tomiessen's blessing, the proper ladies would come to the nuptials, and that meant the men would be allowed to come, and that meant that the whole of New Amsterdam—all those who could fit, anyway—would be arriving at Blandine van Couvering's Pearl Street dwelling-house on this splendiferous springtime day. Across the street at the Red Lion, Ross Raeger threw open his doors for any overflow crowd that might happen by, putting up a groaning board of his own.

As the preparations were being laid for the ceremonies, the prospective bride and groom strolled together through the Clover Waytie, the freshest meadow on the island, where the verdant smells of springtime were strongest.

Together, they inspected a gold ring.

"It's dulled by time and far too big for your finger," Edward said. The white-gold metal of the band, he thought, matched the color of her hair.

"I love it," Blandine said.

It was Edward's own ring, worn by his officer father before him, nicked and knocked about a bit over the years (a Swede's blade bounced off it during the Battle of Warsaw, saving Drummond's finger), but meaningful to him. The ring represented his connection with a family and a past that he had left behind in his teens, as a young ensign entering the crown's army.

Blandine decided she would wear the band not on her finger, but hung around her neck on the fine gold chain that usually displayed the enameled rose her parents had given her when she turned thirteen. The rose she would put away, far back in her *kas*, folded in a scrap of linen. That was then, this is now. She would move on.

"Are you sure?" she asked.

"We will have it worked on by a goldsmith, to size it so that it may fit your finger," Edward said. "Is there a goldsmith in this damned settlement?"

"No, no, not the ring," Blandine said. "I mean, are you sure of us?"

Edward looked at her and was about to laugh. A little late for her to ask that, wasn't it? But something in her expression made him hold off.

"Yes, I'm sure," he said. "Very sure. Sure beyond certainty."

"And the other thing, is it over?"

He knew what she meant. The witika, the orphan-kidnappings, their alliance of two to stop the killings and find justice for the dead.

She wanted desperately for him to say yes. On this day of all days, the ugliness of the world must be beaten back. She could not prevent an image from assailing her at unguarded moments, the towering figure of the deerskin-masked witika, filling her great room, then vanishing abruptly.

What did the apparition imply? Could it be she just imagined it? Aet Visser was dead and gone. If he had formerly been the one masquerading as the demon, then who was this terrifying specter? Visser risen from the dead? An ally of Lightning's?

The violent Easter evening confrontation had been so sudden, so chaotic. It happened in seconds. As time went on, the memory became more faded and jumbled, and she became unsure of what she had seen and what she hadn't.

Blandine told herself that on her wedding day she would banish all such thoughts from her mind. She would be married in the garden where the creature last appeared, a clear rejection of its power and reach. But she needed to turn to Drummond for support. Was it over?

"Yes, it's over," Drummond said.

He put the ring into her palm and closed her hand over it. "Give that to Megapolensis, and let's do this."

The couple persuaded the dominie to perform the ceremony at the home of the bride rather than at the church. An unusual request, one Megapolensis would not generally allow. He had argued against it, telling Blandine that to conduct the ceremony in the Dutch Reformed House of God would dispel any suspicions that might linger about her as a woman once accused of witchcraft.

But he did not argue too long or too hard. The fact was that, as dominie, he himself might well come under criticism for conducting the wedding at his church.

Blandine left Drummond, crossed town and met Megapolensis.

"Here it is," she said, giving him the ring Drummond had given her.

"Good," the dominie said. "Then we are ready."

Megapolensis had come to accept that some of the circumstances of this union departed from the conventional. Blandine's religious conviction wavered. She had no dowry. She had no parents. She would continue to work independently as a she-merchant, trading up and down the river, and as much as she valued a spotless *groot kamer*, being a hausfrau would never be her sole identity.

In Holland, generous fathers-in-law presented their prospective daughters-in-law with a chatelaine, a waist-hung filigree from which suspended objects a wife would need—her household keys, most important, and a scent ball, a pincushion, a needle case and perhaps a small mirror.

There would be no chatelaine for Blandine. Drummond's father, Captain Llewellyn Drummond, had died seventeen years before, in a meaningless skirmish in the English Civil War.

Nor would his mother take part in their nuptials. Judith Drummond lived with Edward's two widowed sisters in a dwelling she had inhabited her whole adult life. Through wars and civil disruptions, changes in governments and social upheavals, Judith remained at Ditchley Gates, the family country house near Durham, waiting for the unscheduled and sporadic visits from her military husband and son. The woman would not even hear of Edward's wedding until a message crossed the sea to reach her, weeks after the ceremony took place.

She herself had no family, Blandine thought, heading back to her rooms from meeting the dominie, and Edward had none present in the settlement. With Aet Visser gone, she had no one to give her away. She had brought herself around to thinking it was better that way. She and Edward were as two innocent children, a pair of solitary human beings, clear of any attachments, no holds on either of them, standing alone together and becoming as one.

"It may be a sad thing to have no relatives here," Drummond said. "On the other hand, we never had them to spoil our courting." Blandine's thought of her parents made her smile, the idea of them dictating how long a *queester*, a gentleman caller, might stay into the evening.

Blandine clung to her fond feelings for Aet Visser. The orphanmaster, she thought, was always one for a punch bowl. His shadow would fall over the ceremony, adding a tincture of melancholy to the otherwise joyous occasion. But she had come to accept this, too. Blandine remained the man's steadfast advocate. She and Edward planned to have an empty place setting at their feast table, a symbol of an absent friend.

She returned home from the church and mounted her stoop. Ross Raeger called to her from in front of the Lion. "A great day," he said.

"Aye," Blandine said.

"It's not too late to change your mind and marry me instead," he said.

Blandine laughed. "I would always smell of onions and beer," she said. "The life of an innkeeper's wife is not for me."

She stepped inside her dwelling-house and closed the door behind her. A jolly fire blazed despite the fine May Day weather, and a fatted side of beef roasted slowly over the flames.

To help her prepare her premises for the party Blandine appointed a *spellmeisje*, a playgirl, Miep Fredericz van Jeveren, who under her expert command had applied soap and water to clean her already spotless *groot kamer*. Miep arranged the bride's basket with green garlands, and would hold her fan and perfumed gloves and veil when Blandine wasn't using them. Mally and Lace were in, too, to spread the cloths on the tables and fold napkins into fanciful shapes, houses and turtles and stars.

Via her trading contacts throughout New Netherland, Blandine carefully provisioned the party, arranging with the cooks of the town to turn out their finest cuisine. There would be local delicacies, of course. Slabs of sirloin, breasts of veal, crisp-skinned turkey and gamey venison in white pastry, all displayed on a plank table beside a whole roast spring lamb and pound upon pound of *fricadelle*, mince meat.

Then there were foodstuffs Blandine obtained from the stores of her ship-trader cohorts, specialties imported from Amsterdam, flavors of Patria. A barrel of pickled herring, whose briny flavor would bring tears to the eyes of colonists who missed their homeland. And of course, the Dutch cheeses. Cumin-seed-studded cheese. Red-wax-covered hard cheese. A green cheese tinted by the dung of sheep.

Drummond insisted on no less than a dozen hogsheads of French and Rhenish wine. Raeger promised to roll twenty half-casks of ale across the street. Delftware platters would constantly circulate, offering shreds of golden tobacco. Finally, for dessert, rosewater-scented marzipan, whimsically sculpted to resemble spring lambs and baby chicks.

She had left nothing to chance. Blandine wanted the stays of her women guests and the belts of the men to be thoroughly loosened by the end of the day.

For all that, she had a persistent worry that no one would come.

Shooing Blandine away from her obsessive checking on the banquet, Mally and Lace fussed over the bride's hair, which she had fixed in sausage curls and pinned to her head so that it half cascaded down the back of her neck. Slipping out of her street dress, stepping out of her everyday underclothes, the bride put on a fawn-colored silk gown over a blue damask petticoat.

She was ready. She felt lighthearted and a little light-headed. Any anxiety she experienced that morning had fled, with joy and exhilaration flooding in to take its place. Blandine rose from the chair where Mally and Lace had sentenced her to sit, erect and unmoving so as not to muss her costume. She crossed the *groot kamer* and stepped out into the garden.

My, what a lot of people had come after all! They crowded into the yard all the way to the garden wall. She heard them shuffle into the great room behind her, too, as she left it. A few scamps had climbed the roof of the sailcloth-maker's shop on the Strand, their view directly down into Blandine's yard. Led by Tibb Dunbar, they stamped and whistled as they saw her come out.

And Edward. Hatless, wigless, standing alongside Megapolensis in a newly tailored blue waistcoat of wool crepe, wearing a cream-colored blouse and a silver lace neck scarf. His brown hair had grown in shaggy, an inch long. He had on brick-red breeches and his usual polished black boots.

Handsome to a fault, Blandine thought. The groom should not out-shine the bride.

"You are very welcome, Miss Blandina," little Sabine said, a rehearsed line she repeated flawlessly. Wearing a fawn silk dress to mimic Blandine's, with a fat lace ribbon in her hair, the Bean curtsied and held up a bouquet of early-blooming forsythia for Blandine to add to the bridal basket. Jan stood beside her, holding her other hand, his form stiff in a tight waistcoat.

The Bean, Anna, all of Aet Visser's family had come to live with Blandine in the wake of his death. They had nowhere else to turn. They had been relying on the orphanmaster's largesse for their living, and were now bereft. Sabine was too young to realize what had happened. She kept asking when Pow was coming back. Anna was stoic, but the older children were inconsolable.

At the bride's approach Lace and Mally released a quartet of trained songbirds, each tied at the foot with a string, to fly over the bride carrying a garland of lilies. Blandine, allowing the Bean and Jan to lead her down a pathway strewn with the sheaved leaves of yellow pond reeds, took her place alongside Edward.

She stood alone, an orphan to the last.

But Edward's secret smile was all she needed. Everything was going to be fine.

She scanned the crowd. Kitane, invited but not present. Where was he? She saw Kees. Kees was there? Beside him, holding onto his arm, a self-conscious, smiling Maaje de Lang. So that's how it went, Blandine thought.

Blandine's attire, the ladies agreed, was more than acceptable. The finest seamstress in town, Geertje Hapje, dove into her stock of fabrics to come up with the perfect cloth. Blandine's gown did not come alive until she stepped outside into the sunlight, the fawn-colored silk glowing, shining, throwing off deep glints of green and blue. The folds of the dress draped almost to the ground in back, but were pulled up in scallops at the front, held in place by silver ribbons.

Underneath the gown, the blue damask petticoat and another of deep-pile rose satin. Her bare, powder-white shoulders were framed by a light silver lace scarf, matching Drummond's, her legs set off by bright white stockings. She had on high-heeled shoes with blue and yellow embroidery and a florette of silver ribbon. Blandine wore no makeup, but bit her lips to give them color.

"Lovely," murmured Margaret Tomiessen. Her judgment echoed through the tight grouping of New Amsterdam ladies like a wave through an inland sea. "Lovely," repeated Lucy Hubbard to Femmie Gravenraet, who passed the word on to others as a sort of communal gift.

Antony, his wounds still swathed in bandages, stood beside the dominie, directly in front of Edward. In the wake of Lightning's knife attack on him and his convalescence, Antony had taken up preaching. He asked Blandine if he could say a few words at the ceremony.

But first, and quite unexpectedly, Jan sang a solo air. His pure bell of a voice quieted the chatter of the crowd.

> *Stabat mater dolorosa*
> *Juxta Crucem lacrimosa*
> *Dum pendebat Filius*

Stabat Mater. The mournful mother wept. A Catholic hymn! Drummond cast an eye over to Megapolensis, but the dominie seemed unconcerned. Either he did not recognize the words, or he didn't care.

Then, Antony. His theme, from Corinthians: the redemptive power of love.

"Though I speak in the tongues of men and of angels, and have not love," Antony said in his strong voice, "I am become as sounding brass or a tinkling cymbal. And though I have the gift of prophecy, and understand all mysteries, and all knowledge; and though I have all faith, so that I could remove mountains, and have not love, I am nothing."

The bride, calm and serene, nevertheless found her eyes again straying over the faces assembled together, watching her, crowding the garden, crammed at the casement windows of her rooms, standing on the rooftops across the yard.

What was she looking for?

A deerskin mask.

Blandine forced herself to stop, to attend to the words Megapolensis was saying over her. Vows chosen by the groom, from the English Book of Common Prayer.

"Will you love him, comfort him, honor and keep him, in sickness and in health, and forsaking all others, be faithful to him as long as you both shall live?"

She remembered to say, "I will."

40

During the sweltering August of 1664, England and the Dutch Republic moved slowly toward war, lumbering along on a collision course like two ships of the line. Which trading empire would gain the upper hand would not be immediately decided, but eventually one stalled while the other covered the globe with its arrogant imperial glory.

The seeds of England's victory were already sown. A little-known act of Parliament early in the century would prove the tipping point. The Statute of Monopolies, passed in 1623, came to be known as the Patent Law and would eventually lead to the spinning jenny, the rolling machine and Blake's dark satanic mills. England would rise on cotton cloth and railroads, while the Dutch Republic remained fat, happy and static.

In the late summer heat, the Countess of Castlemaine, the English king's bewitching mistress, withdrew from court to await the birth of a daughter, her fourth child with the second Charles. Christened Charlotte, the infant later became Lady Fitzroy and Countess of Litchfield. "We know but little of her except that she was beautiful," wrote one nineteenth-century commentator, that she was a favorite of her uncle James, Duke of York, and that she was mother of eighteen children herself.

In New Netherland, in the new world, the balance between Dutch and English interests stood poised to tilt. In the *bouweries* and plantations, the fields of wheat and corn baked under a summer sun, growing toward an abundant harvest. But it was as if the countryside held its breath. The month seemed overhung with event. Dreams disturbed whatever sleep there was.

The Hendrickson mansion remained closed tight, even in the heat. Inside, two brothers continued to hide one of their own.

For a few days at August's beginning, a *longueur*. The trial of Drummond, the English spy, would provide some entertainment in the capital. But the witika fever that had gripped the colony had finally broken. The orphanmaster, author of the crimes, was dead, buried without rites, a suicide. The foul murders of settlement children, the good burghers of New Amsterdam believed, would add no new links to its long chain of horrors. As in other beliefs, they were wrong.

Tibb Dunbar would never have been taken had he not tied on a woesome drunk the night before. He and ten-year-old Juno Brecht procured a three-quarters-full brandy bottle, filching it from the pantry cupboard of a *groot kamer* whose location shall not be identified. The two boys took the liquor to their stomping grounds at the great oak north of the town, and settled in to drink.

Summer on Manhattan. Tibb time, his favorite season, lazy and at the same time brimming with possibility. When the gardens were full, when the stoops yielded prizes left for him by his kind women protectors, when brandy bottles fell out of the sky.

Halfway through the evening, Juno felt the need to splash water on his face, staggered to the East River, fell in and passed out on the shore. He woke with a pleasant headache the next morning, none the worse for wear, and headed to Missy Flamsteed's for a little hair of the dog.

Tibb Dunbar slept off his drunk, dead to the world, the red kerchief draped over his face like a shroud. As demons often did, the witika came to him in his dreams. His legs wouldn't work, he couldn't get away. When Tibb woke, the morning sun blazing down, the day already hot, he thought he still lay in a dream. Something was indeed wrong with his legs. He reached his hand down to feel them and it came away sticky with blood.

"Christ in the foothills," he swore, his favorite oath. He tried to rise and made it up only with extreme difficulty. His left leg proved completely useless. It could not support his weight. The short sailor pants he wore were matted down with half-congealed blood.

"Halloo, Juno!" he called. But his drinking buddy was long gone.

Gingerly, Tibb examined his leg. A deep cut showed behind his knee, severing the cordlike tendons. The lower part of the leg flopped around like a baby's rattle. He could only hobble painfully.

"No mercy," he cursed to himself. "Fetch the pickles." Then he stopped cold, sagging back against the trunk of the great oak.

Ten yards away, down an alleyway of pines, he saw an apparition that proved he still remained in the grip of his nightmare. The witika stood there, motionless, staring.

Tibb was brave, but he was not a fool. He would have run if he could.

"Yaaah!" he screamed, hoping either to wake himself up or frighten the demon away. He bent down painfully, seized a large rock and hurled it toward the witika. From long practice, Tibb's aim was true. The rock smashed into the leering deerskin mask of the demon.

A strange thing happened. The monster instantly collapsed, as if the rock had punctured a bladder-balloon that inhabited its costume.

Tibb could not believe his own eyes. He surely dreamed all this. It could not be real. He hobbled up to the heap of clothes that had just appeared to him as the witika.

A bundle of sticks, propped up to mimic a demon form. A crude mask. A lace collar like a burgher wore. But inside it, nothing, just empty air.

"Huh, just some gummy outfit," Tibb said to himself. "I never did think it real." He laughed with relief.

From out among the alley of pines stepped a second witika demon—a real, full-bodied one this time. It loomed over the boy as though it were tall enough to block the sun.

"Judas Priest," Tibb swore.

The monster held a dagger in its left hand, the blade already bloodied, which it drove into Tibb's neck.

The boy screamed and staggered away.

Bleeding, half-lame, Tibb Dunbar nevertheless made a game attempt at flight. It would turn out later that the orphan boy was a royal prince after all, the child of an English lady and her lord, kidnapped as an infant by pirates, discarded for his colicky bawling on the shores of Prince Maurice's River. Or perhaps that story was only a figment of Tibb's dying dreams.

The witika caught him not too far off. The orphan swayed in place, unable to go another step. Blood pulsed from his wound. He felt the close panting breath of his attacker.

"*Dik-duk*," the witika said, raising the red-stained dagger.

"Nice costume," Tibb said, his last words, his last sneer at the world.

He died unmourned. No one missed him. Or at least, no one of any worth. A troop of urchin street children, what were they?

Drummond holed up in the council chambers of the meeting-hall inside Fort Amsterdam. The summer was proving mercilessly, scorchingly hot, and the room's windows opened to admit a little air off the bay. He sometimes took refuge there, officially to help prepare the defense for his upcoming trial on spy charges, but really (occasionally) to allow himself a short respite from home.

In the three months since his wedding, Drummond found himself a bit marriage-stunned. Nothing serious, and he cherished his new wife beyond anyone in the universe, but there was only so much a man could take. He not only had to become accustomed to living with a woman, but since he had inherited (willingly, joyfully) a collection of foster children, wards and sundry outcasts, he was now the proud father of a new extended family.

On the whole, Drummond loved it. Jan, Sabine, the other children in Anna's household, all provided him with laughter, surprises and a depth of caring that he had not heretofore imagined possible. The relationship that flowered between the Bean and Jan, for example, was a wonder to witness.

It was just a bit sudden, that's all. One minute Drummond was a cavalier on an important mission for a crowned head of state, the next he was gently moving aside hanging pairs of women's stockings to get to the jakes. Blandine would never detect in him a hint of distress over his new circumstances, he made himself careful about that. But once in a while, an afternoon or two a week, he escaped to smoke his pipe in the empty and silent chambers of the Fort Amsterdam meeting-hall.

While the newlyweds lived at Drummond's, Blandine had installed Anna's family in her old rooms across the street from the Red Lion. As a surprise wedding gift, Drummond presented his wife with a new dwelling-house. Well, it was a house in the process of being built, anyway, the housewrights and joiners were still swarming over it, but it would be finished, everyone said, very soon. They had been saying that for a while now.

The structure arose on the site of a former pit-house on Market Street, quite the best address in town if you didn't count nearby Stone Street, and a place, Sabine told him solemnly, where she and Pow used to play.

The ghost of Aet Visser still hovered around Drummond and Blandine's instantly created family. The orphanmaster's financial affairs proved an impossible tangle. The degree of his involvement in the witika business remained shrouded in mystery. The townspeople still referred to him as a murderer. But Blandine, at least, stayed faithful to his memory. She would not hear a word said against him.

She and Drummond liked to climb the ladder to the roof of their rooms on Slyck Steegh and look through his spyglass, the only perspective tube that had survived the violent search of his premises by the town's civil authorities. On full-moon nights, Antony would come over, Jan would come up and they would attempt to re-create the magic of that night on Mount Petrus the previous November.

But many times, during the day, Edward and Blandine enjoyed training the spyglass on the building of their new dwelling-house on Market Street, across town. Looking through the lens and seeing the carpenters at work provided a nice sense of microcosm, as though Edward and Blandine were children again, playing with a dollhouse.

Yes, their new life together was altogether delightful, altogether lovely. Couldn't be better. But Drummond was not such an unfeeling brute that he could ignore the shadow that sometimes passed behind Blandine's eyes. He noticed that, like himself, she occasionally needed time alone. She seemed attracted to the homes of their neighbors on Market Street, and would walk out of a summer evening, traversing the few blocks to the canal and back, thoughtful and unreachable.

With all she'd been through, Drummond thought, Blandine had a right to feel an occasional inward turning. He resolved to be more tender, more attentive. Things would be better, he believed, once they moved into the new place, and left behind for good his old rooms and hers, with their unpleasant memories and associations.

When Ad Hendrickson found him in the meeting-hall council chamber that afternoon, Drummond naturally thought the man had come to discuss some issue surrounding the new house. They were to be neighbors. The Hendrickson town house was just down Market Street from them. Perhaps the construction mess had somehow disturbed the Hendrickson peace, and he had come to complain.

Since their brother Martyn's death, Ad and Ham Hendrickson had done something wholly unexpected. After long being country patroons almost exclusively, they moved into town, taking up residence in their gargantuan clapboard mansion. They still remained somewhat remote, and rarely took part in the communal activities of the settlement. Most surprisingly, they discharged all their servants and lived a monastic life. No one ever saw them.

"Hot," Ad Hendrickson said to Drummond, sitting down after greeting him.

"Very," Drummond said. He had not seen Ad close up, he realized, since his visit to the Hendrickson patent the previous fall. The man looked precisely the same. Thin, bony body types often appeared ageless.

"You get a breeze off the water here," Ad said.

"Yes," Drummond said. "May I offer you a plug?" He pushed a tray toward Hendrickson that had shreds of tobacco piled on it. A fine-flavored batch up from Virginia, very smooth.

"Don't mind," Ad said, took some, and lit up.

A long silence. What the devil? Drummond thought.

"You take these as your own chambers now," Ad said, gesturing around the room.

"Oh, no," Drummond said. "I merely meet my solicitor here once or twice a week, preparing my defense."

"He is not here," Ad said.

"No," Drummond said. "Not today." His solicitor was Kenneth Clarke, a strange, uncertain Englishman, recommended by Raeger. The opening of the proceeding was repeatedly delayed. The imposition of an English trial on the Dutch justice system complicated the process. Drummond had begun to think he would never get his chance to be hanged as a spy.

"Then you take these as your chambers now," Ad said again.

Mentally, Drummond threw up his hands. "Yes, I guess you could say that."

"And how is your defense developing?"

"We won't know until we get in front of a jury," Drummond said.

"A jury," Ad said, a trace of a sneer in his voice. "I never saw the use of them myself. Wouldn't a citizen court be open to suasion and bribery? What is wrong with a punishment tribunal?"

"Well, since the last punishment tribunal I came before sentenced me to hang by the neck until dead, I would have to disagree respectfully by preferring a jury trial this time around."

He'd just about had enough of Ad Hendrickson. Drummond had papers to shuffle and pipes to smoke. Whatever it was the patroon was getting around to, he was taking too long to do it.

"Would ye like an acquittal?" Ad said.

"Ah, a tough question. Would I rather be acquitted than hung? Let me think on that. Uh, yes."

"I mean, would ye like an acquittal?" Ad said.

The man was obtuse, or senile. Then the light suddenly dawned on Drummond.

"You mean . . . ?"

"I could arrange for an acquittal," Ad said.

Drummond had the sense of Hendrickson well enough not to ask him how he might manage such a thing. He had lived his whole life around people of power. They were magicians. They could accomplish feats that other mortals could not comprehend, and do it in ways that remained unknown, dissembled, mysterious.

In a barnyard in Cumbria as an ensign on a Scottish campaign, Drummond had an opportunity, during a stretch of idleness, to observe the behavior of the farm animals kept in captivity there.

The pigs were always the most intelligent, most industrious, most ambitious of the stock. They were always finding a way to escape their pens. They would dig under, dismantle, go over any fence presented to them. Ensign Drummond had to laugh at the passive, dim-witted sheep, who watched the pigs at their furious work. The sheep would stupidly stare, munching on their shoots of grass. Why, whatever could Master Hog be doing over there?

Later, when Drummond got to know the ways of powerful men, he thought of the pigs and sheep in the Cumbrian barnyard. Those in power, the pigs, performed spectacular machinations that the citizenry, the sheep, could only look upon and wonder.

"Do you wish payment for this service?" Drummond asked Hendrickson.

"Pish," Ad said. "I have more money than you could ever dream on, Mister Drummond."

"Then what could I possibly do for you?"

"Leave this colony entirely," Ad said. "Take your wife and your brood, go home to England, go to Virginia or up to Canadee-i-o for all I care. I will sponsor your leave-taking if I must, but I wish you to quit this jurisdiction and never return."

No vehemence informed Hendrickson's tone. He was cold but not angry.

Drummond had a quick vision of Martyn Hendrickson, hounding him and Blandine on the ice-flat river, flung into the freezing waters and drowned.

"You blame me for your brother's death," Drummond said.

"I simply want you gone," Ad said. He rose, tapped his pipe bowl into the tray and pushed the smoldering ashes flat. "I'll give you a few days to think about it. Has the trial date been set?"

"Next week, now, the director general believes. Soon, anyway."

"Out from the noose, into a new life elsewhere," Ad said. "If you consider it well, Mister Drummond, I know you will take my offer. But don't wait too long."

He knocked on the table sharply with his knuckles and went out. Drummond stared at the empty doorway as if it would reveal secrets. He was a sheep, wondering at the unfathomable activities of a pig. Ad Hendrickson had left behind a curious sense that Drummond could feel but not quite put his finger on. Then, suddenly, it came to him.

Drummond did not much play chess. But what had just happened with Ad Hendrickson had the uncanny flavor, he thought, of an endgame.

41

Maddie the dog had disappeared. Sometimes the Bean thought she missed Maddie more than Pow. Other times she thought she missed Pow more than Maddie.

She had dreams. Her saying to Pow, "You've come back, Pow!" Or her saying to Maddie, "Here you are, girl! Here you are!"

It made her feel sad, since Maddie and Pow went away at the same time. Jan told the Bean that Mister Visser took Maddie to heaven with him, and the Bean wondered who Mister Visser was until Jan told her it was Pow. That was better. Pow and Maddie together somewhere nice.

A big girl now, turning four in August. August sixteenth, though she had trouble saying it because of the lisp, and everyone laughed at her when she did. A little girl with a lisp should have an easier birthday, such as May fourth, something like that.

When the Bean walked with Blandine around the settlement, at times she heard a dog barking and thought it was Maddie. Once, when she passed the big looming house on Market Street, just before she got to where the play-pit used to be but now where their new house was going up, up, up, the Bean heard Maddie bark and saw her, too. A flash of white fluff glimpsed through an iron fence all the way in the back garden. There and then gone.

No one listened to her when she said Maddie was there. Jan told her that there were a lot of white dogs. Miss Blandina instructed Sabine to hurry and catch up because they had to go talk to Jacobson the carpenter.

But the Bean felt sure. She knew her own dog, despite what everyone said. One day she would go back to the garden of the big house and find Maddie herself.

"What do ye use the stuff for?" Kees Bayard asked Ad Hendrickson.

He had personally delivered to the Hendrickson brothers a smelly round tar-ball wrapped in a crumbling palm leaf and secured with a length of straw twine. It had come via Amsterdam from far-off Batavia, on Kees's flute ship, *De Gulden Arent*, the Golden Eagle, the only vessel he had left since his recent reversals.

"Rheumatism," Ham Hendrickson said.

"You look fine to me," Kees said.

"Bent double with it half the time," Ham said, sitting perfectly upright.

Kees suspected that the "poppy tears" opium tar he delivered to the Hendricksons was being put to use not as an analgesic but for decadent purposes. The whole Hendrickson dwelling-house smelled of it, a pungent incense that reminded Kees of the spice islands of East Asia.

On those islands, most especially in Batavia, the capital of the Dutch colony of Java, the practice of blending poppy tears into tobacco and smoking the resulting admixture had produced legions of hollow-eyed stumblers. They ranged through the streets of Batavia like ghosts. The smokers indulged to excess. They appeared to Kees to have no sense of restraint.

From his trips to East Asia, Kees knew what an opium user looked like, and neither Ad nor Ham qualified. Yet the chambers of the enormous house on Market Street reeked of the stuff. No one else lived there. Ad and Ham shut themselves off from the world. Kees could not figure it out.

He did not enjoy his visits to the Hendrickson mansion. The brothers lived in squalor. They appeared servantless. Objects, clothing and possessions lay in vast, scattered piles in every chamber. Stale, dried-out dog feces trailed through the halls, though no animal was apparent.

In the *groot kamer* where Kees normally met with Ad, silver plates stacked up, crusted with the remains of food. When the brothers grew sick of dirty crockery they merely tossed it out the window into the yard. The only element that kept the Hendrickson place from smelling like a garbage dump was the floating aroma of opium.

It was not his place to wonder why. The previous February, a timely infusion of funds from Ad Hendrickson had saved Kees Bayard's trading empire from ruin. In return for his investment, as well as a killing level of interest, Ad demanded Kees deliver him occasional packets of opium. Kees felt he had no choice but to oblige his creditor.

Adverse luck dogged Kees. Not one but two of his flute ships went down in wrecks, both fully loaded with merchandise. He lost his prized charger, Fantome, in a gambling reversal. Married life did not agree with him. Mrs. Maaje Bayard, as far as he could tell, was simply a hole down which to pitch money.

The woman was a fool. Kees Bayard had married a fool. He could not believe it of himself, but there it was. He sorely missed Blandine, and fantasized about what a life with her would have been like.

And yet Kees believed Blandine herself was the author of his sour fortune. As his ships sank and his trading failed and he found hair coming off his head in great clumps, he harbored a secret conviction. He didn't tell anyone, not even his new spouse. But what they had said about Blandine van Couvering really was true. She was a witch, and she had cursed Kees Bayard out of spite over their failed romance.

Kees rose to his feet to signal that his business with Ad was done.

"When you send *The Golden Eagle* over, we'll take another one of these," Ad said, pushing at the wrapped ball of opium with his finger.

Kees left, and Ad took out a pouch of Virginia tobacco. He opened the packet of poppy tears by slicing the palm-leaf wrapping with a penknife. With the knife's small blade he cut off a dozen small slivers of the opium tar. Then, on the oak tabletop, he carefully mixed the tar with the tobacco.

"You baby him," Ham said, watching the whole process with open disgust. "Waste of good leaf as far as I am concerned."

"It's the only way to keep him in our pocket," Ad said. "Would ye rather have him running around Judas knows where doing Judas knows what?"

In the curtained and muffled best chamber at the back of the house's second floor, Ad entered to deliver Martyn his dose. Brother Martyn slept much of the day. He reclined on a plump but filthy mattress, the hanging drapes around the bed in disarray. A half-full chamber pot balanced precariously among the bedclothes.

Some sort of fly-specked offal rotted on a plate, a child's red kerchief folded neatly on top of it.

Martyn coughed, nodding, to acknowledge Ad's approach. He clutched the apparatus of his opium smoking, which he took not in the

Dutch style, with a long-stemmed clay pipe, but in a bell-shaped brass bowl imported from Batavia.

Last Easter night Martyn had stumbled home to his siblings, displaying a gunshot wound to his side, bleeding and near death. Ad and Ham nursed their baby brother, keeping him out of sight, exiling servants and shunning outsiders. After all, in the eyes of the community, Martyn was already dead.

"You can't kill a dead man," Ham told Ad, somewhat nonsensically, Ad thought.

Martyn's wound had healed by now. The danger of infection passed. But the tonic he started during his convalescence wholly took him over. The little white dog Martyn always kept with him lay on the bed, its fur matted and dirty. The room smelled of opium and dog piss.

"I'll get up," Martyn said. But he rarely did.

When he wasn't sleeping, Martyn was subject to fits of volcanic anger. If Ad failed to provide opium or suggested he go easy on the drug, Martyn went berserk. He cursed his brothers, they that only loved him. Ad and Ham were deeply hurt by the language of these outbursts.

"I hate the two of you!" was the mildest of Martyn's imprecations. "I'll see you both dead!"

Hard as the elder Hendricksons worked to keep Martyn corralled, hidden and off the streets, he occasionally succeeded in slipping out. Always at night, always alone. His brothers never knew where he went. They were equally convinced that they did not want to know.

Whenever she could, Blandine avoided encountering Kees Bayard on the streets of the settlement. She did this not out of spite, but because her presence seemed to excite the man, sending him rambling into self-conscious, tic-ridden conversation about how well his trades were going.

Blandine knew the truth. Her old friend faced disaster. But their friendship came out of another time. Kees wasn't real to her anymore. She wondered what she had ever seen in him.

She dodged Kees in public, but she was very interested in the goings-on of the Hendrickson mansion. The face of Martyn Hendrickson still floated in her mind's eye every once in a while. Before he died, Blandine felt sure that she was getting closer to the truth about the man. The idea haunted her even now. The dead patroon ventured into her dreams at night.

An ominous feeling passed over Blandine whenever she walked by the brothers' house. Ad and Ham, her soon-to-be near-neighbors, never displayed themselves in the sprawling yards and orchards on their grounds. The plantings grew up thick with weeds. It looked as though wilderness had reasserted its sway in the gardens, entering into the vacuum that came of disuse.

Blandine was not alone. The Hendrickson place was slowly gaining the reputation of something of a spook house among the children and the gossips of the settlement. The orphan boys of the High Street Gang ventured onto the property only on a dare.

In the marketplace, Blandine sought out provisioners, deliverymen, anyone who might have been inside the Hendrickson house. She could not find many. A she-merchant baker, responsible for providing three loaves of white-flour bread to the Hendrickson back door every other morning, had not much to say.

"Ad pays me in coin, old-fashioned stuivers from Patria," the baker told Blandine. "He don't let me inside, but as far as I can see from the doorway, those brothers live in their own filth."

On sleepy summer afternoons, while Edward was away in consultation with his solicitor, the Bean was down for her nap and Jan read quietly out of *The Day of Doom*, Blandine had taken to climbing the ladder to Drummond's roof. She used the spyglass to surveil the comings and goings around the Hendrickson dwelling-house.

There weren't many. This afternoon she saw Kees leave the place and head down Market toward the canal. She kept her eye on the spyglass but saw nothing, no movement in the house. The huge glass panes of the sash windows appeared opaque, like black, vacant eyes. The mud sharks in the sandbars off Turtle Bay had eyes like that.

One day, Blandine thought, after they moved to the new house, she would go and make a call on the Hendricksons. It was only the neighborly thing to do.

*   *   *

Kitane lodged not in New Amsterdam but with his Canarsie friends. The trapper had a superb spring and summer. He managed to retrieve Blandine's product from Beverwyck, three stacks of beaver pelts that rose to his own eye-level, quality winter-fur skins, over a hundred of them, eminently merchantable.

He did not often visit New Amsterdam. Occasionally, his favorite bakery, for sweets.

Late one night he drank too much English milk from a cask the Canarsie had from a Dutch trader, reeled drunkenly into town and stole a coping saw from a blacksmith's stable on Long Street. Kitane then crept into the dwelling-house of the director general near the pier, moving easily past the dozing sentries.

Stuyvesant slept alone. In his drunken state Kitane could not keep himself as quiet as he would have wished, but the director general did not stir. He snored evenly.

Kitane retrieved the peg leg from where it rested next to the curtains of the director general's bedstead. Taking out the coping saw from within his robes, he cut an inch off Stuyvesant's oak-and-silver fake leg. Afterward, Kitane returned the device to its place and let himself out.

42

The trial of an English spy in a Dutch colony, when the two father-lands were already at each other's throat. What were the odds that such a defendant could obtain justice?

Drummond knew he was in trouble as soon as the jury was empaneled. In the back row of the makeshift jury box, along with five other *middenstaaid*, middle-class, New Amsterdam citizens, sat his old shipmate Gerrit Remunde.

Drummond now dearly wished he had been more civil to the man, and not cut him so precipitously on the two occasions Remunde had hailed him in the street. What horrible luck! Remunde stared stonily straight ahead, not looking at the accused standing in the dock—Drummond, bareheaded, unwigged, wearing his blue wedding waistcoat.

He had come to have severe doubts about his counsel, too. Kenneth Clarke appeared constantly distracted by tangents, ignoring urgencies that Drummond thought needed attending to in quick order.

In darker moments, Drummond wondered if it were too late for prayer to save him. A consultation with Megapolensis, perhaps, an admission of faith, knees chafed and bruised in earnest supplication to an all-powerful god. Please, Lord, save me from idiots. The only worthy prayer there was.

The trial court convened on August 20, 1664, a special proceeding with New Amsterdam's first jury.

The charge: spying for the English crown.

The meeting-hall council chamber cooked in the summer heat. Stuyvesant sat as judge, *in subsellio*, as he would say, on the bench. Ross Raeger told Drummond the director general might be losing his faculties, since he fell down twice walking the short distance across town from the Stadt Huys to the meeting-hall in the fort.

"Tumbled like a doddering old woman right there on Pearl Street," Raeger said. "Tripped over his own foot. And don't ask me which one."

"The director general has his worries to distract him," Drummond said. "He feels us breathing down his neck." "Us" meaning the English. Rumors of the crown's move against New Netherland buzzed like wasps around the settlement. Every day, there were more incidents involving incursions into Dutch-held territory from Connecticut and Massachusetts.

"*Oyez, oyez, oyez,*" pronounced the town crier in the court. "All persons having business before the Honorable, the special court of the jurisdiction of New Amsterdam, are admonished to draw near and give their attention, for the court is now sitting. God save the officers of justice, the settlement of New Amsterdam, the colony of New Netherland. God save Patria, and may the truth be told in this Honorable court."

Drummond wondered about that last part. *"Dire la vérité et de sentir la lame,"* isn't that what the French said? Tell the truth and feel the blade.

De Klavier directed Drummond forward to the dock. Stuyvesant read out the formal charge: collecting intelligence for the English against the interests of the New Netherland Colony.

"You, sir, are to be proved a spy," Stuyvesant said from the bench.

Teunis Dircksen Boer, the finest legal mind the Company had to offer, acted as *fiscael*, prosecutor.

"Mister Drummond, are you a member of the clandestine society called the Sealed Knot?"

"It is a patriotic fellowship in support of Charles II," Drummond said.

"I didn't ask what it was, I asked if you were one," Boer said. "But it doesn't matter. These documents will prove clearly your activities on the part of this nefarious organization."

Boer began to read, out loud for the benefit of the court, the decoded messages found in Drummond's rooms. Settling in for a long afternoon in the stifling council chamber, the *fiscael* read document after document, droning on like a schoolteacher.

Blandine sat in the front row of the gallery, a few yards from Drummond, who stood before a section of railing that acted as the dock. Spectators crowded into the council chamber. The opportunity to experience the novelty of an English-style trial proved enticing to the entertainment-starved settlement. As befitted their standing, the *schout*, the *schepens*, the *burgomeesters* of the colony took the special chairs of the council members.

The gallery looked bored. This was all? A pumped-up Company *fiscael* reading, coughing, clearing his throat, reading some more? A pall settled on the jury members. Most important, to Drummond's eyes, was the fact that Gerrit Remunde still refused to meet his gaze.

There were a few sparks. When Boer read Drummond's casual remarks about the women of the settlement ("hardworking, well-educated, clever, an asset we would do well to co-opt") the audience woke up. "Some of them are very pretty," Drummond had added in a needless aside, and a titter ran through the chamber.

But that was it. During Boer's endless recitation, Drummond had a thought of giving up and pleading guilty. Anything to get out of this oven of a chamber.

Kees pushed his way through the spectators to kneel at Blandine's side. "Your man is a spy, a traitor and an assassin, isn't he?"

She looked down at him, trying to keep the pity out of her eyes. "I see him as a soldier, nothing more," she said gently.

"Is a soldier what you want? I am a captain of the militia!"

It was pathetic. Once, she would have felt for him. Now, nothing.

"Blandine," he pleaded, putting his hand on her arm. "Don't do this to yourself. Repudiate him."

"This isn't worthy of you, Kees."

On the bench, the director general threw a glare their way, and several members of the gallery shushed them.

"I did this, you know," Kees whispered, showing both pride and pain. "I told Uncle to move against your man. I did this to you and to him."

"Even if it were true," Blandine said, "I would forgive you."

Kees rose to his feet, turned his back on her and assumed his seat among the grandees in front of the meeting-hall.

The *fiscael* read the documents for another half hour, sweat dripping from his forehead and plopping audibly down upon the pages. By the time he finally finished, the sun slanted into the hall from the west, and the eyes of many of the spectators drooped shut.

Kees Bayard woke everyone up by rising grandly from his seat, saying loudly, "The case is proved," and stalking out of the meeting-hall.

Stuyvesant spoke. "The court stipulates that these documents were indeed the ones found in the chambers of the defendant on Slyck Steegh in the colony. Counsel?"

"We accept the stipulation, Your Excellency," Clarke said. He was about to sit down, but rose back up. "Although . . ."

"Yes?" Stuyvesant said.

"We wonder who is responsible for the decoding and translating of these missives," Clarke said. "The answer impinges on the veracity of the version here read."

"The court had them rendered," Stuyvesant said.

"Yes, but who?" Clarke said. "A court can't translate. There must be a person."

"*Mijn Heer* General did it himself," De Klavier said.

De Klavier was out of order, but Stuyvesant was pleased not to have to make the point himself, so he let it pass.

"You did, Your Excellency?" Clarke said. "You yourself?"

"Yes," the director general said.

"Very well, very good," Clarke said. "We shall say no more about that." And he sat down.

But rose again. "Except . . ."

"Yes?" Stuyvesant said. Drummond could tell by the fire in the man's eyes that he was getting angered, not accustomed to having his pronouncements questioned.

"It's just that . . ." Clarke seemed to stammer and lose his way. "My apologies, Your Excellency, but I wonder, could you inform us of your training in Latin?"

"What?"

"The messages were originally written in Latin, I believe," Clarke said. "Have you learning in that direction?"

Watch now, watch now, Drummond thought, the director general will explode any second.

De Klavier once again stood up and spoke out of order. "The director general is the finest Latin mind in the colony, perhaps the finest in the new world."

"*Ipsi dixit,*" Stuyvesant said, hauling out a Cicero quotation ("he said it himself") from the bottomless depths of his knowledge.

De Klavier said, "The director general attended school in Franeker, in Friesland, if you must know."

"Very well, yes, apologies, of course," Clarke said. "I'm sure the translations are very, very good, very exact, not heir to the outrageous errors that often lurk in translated material, misconstruing and missing the original true meaning."

Drummond allowed himself an inner smile. The bumbler in the black barrister's robe might be worth something after all.

The afternoon waned, the court adjourned and the first English-style jury trial in the history of New Netherland completed its opening day. From the sleepy looks on the faces of the spectators, many would not be returning for day two.

That evening, Blandine asked Drummond, "Would you mind very much, Edward, if I didn't come to see the second day of your trial?"

Drummond smiled and shook his head. "I would be absent myself, if it were my choice."

"Nothing will happen at the tribunal tomorrow, will it?" Blandine said.

"My counsel says no," Drummond said. "Only procedural actions."

"It's just I should see Luybeck," Blandine said.

"Go, go ahead, I will return to you well baked after my afternoon in the oven."

Eberhard Luybeck, the probate judge, had been attempting for the last four months to untangle the mess of Aet Visser's estate. He was the same man Drummond had questioned about George Godbolt's financial condition, back at the beginning of his time in the colony.

Blandine moved about the rooms as Drummond sat brooding. She readied them for the move to the new house on Market Street, and worked to pack their possessions.

Drummond took Blandine's hand as she passed by him. "You can't stop us, you know," he said. "Us" meaning the English.

Blandine walked around casually in her camisole and the emerald petticoat. "I trust you," she said.

The New Netherland Colony displayed the kind of atmosphere that Drummond imagined it shared with the last days of Pompeii. Mount

Vesuvius had been smoking for months now, and the explosion was due. Down from New England, up from Virginia, from across the seas, somehow, some way, the English were coming.

Silence between them. Then Blandine said, "Do you want to know why I trust the English? Because I want Beverwyck."

At first, Drummond didn't understand. She "wanted" Beverwyck? What did that mean?

She came and sat in his lap and laid it out for him. The lands of the north, including the vital trading outpost of Beverwyck, had already been claimed by the Massachusetts Bay Colony. Stuyvesant and the Dutch were too weak to resist the claim.

The English, though, when they came in, would maintain proper borders. The colony—her colony, whatever it came to be named under the English, but Blandine's familiar turf nonetheless—would be able to retain its gateway to the fur trade.

It was a question, Drummond realized, of who Blandine trusted more, the incoming English or the rival Massachusetts Bay Colony.

"Both are English, no?" Drummond asked her. "The crown that comes and the New England colony that is."

"Yes," she admitted. "But our treatment at the hands of one will be very different."

Both were antithetical to Dutch interests, in other words, but one more than the other. In this case, the devil Blandine didn't know, the crown, she preferred to the devil she did know, Massachusetts. A nuanced view of real-world statecraft.

Blandine began to talk about the members of the jury in Drummond's trial. "Three tradefolk, a *handlaer* and an agriculturist," she said.

"And Gerrit Remunde," Drummond said.

"Another trader. Every one of those people know where their coin is coming from. Beaver pelts. Communicate to them this one single point and you will have them well in hand: Petrus Stuyvesant will lose Beverwyck for them."

43

Another stifling day in the council chamber of the meeting-hall in the fort. The spectators were fewer today, and some new ones had replaced the old. The director general, Drummond noticed, did not sweat.

As the accused, Drummond stood again in the dock, shifting his feet from one to the other, attempting not to yawn. He distracted himself by examining the six men of the jury. They appeared restless. After the reading of Drummond's decoded messages, the *fiscael* ended his presentation of the case for the prosecution. Clarke rose for Drummond's defense, embarking upon a complex argument involving the supposed nature of his client's crime.

"This charge of treason," Clarke said, addressing the jury directly, "we must ask, against whom? Against what entity? The Dutch West India Company? Can one be disloyal to a commercial entity the way one can to a nation?"

Drummond thought, I will hang for sure if this is the best he can do. The eyes of the jurymen began to wander.

"Tell me, who has this man betrayed?" Clarke said, gesturing to Drummond. "No country. The supposed secret messages upon which the prosecution bases its case represent not treason but a simple business strategy. The day when a corporation is accorded the same standing as a country, with all the rights attending to that status, will be a sad day indeed."

"Barrister Clarke?" the director general interrupted from the bench.

"Yes, *Mijn Heer* General?"

"The Dutch West India Company enjoys the status of an overlord in this case," Stuyvesant said. "The Company thus has standing to serve as a jurisdiction. All this was argued and answered in pretrial."

"Yes, *Mijn Heer* General," Clarke said, clearly dismayed.

All right, Drummond thought, what else do you have?

Clarke again addressed the jury directly. "As members of the jury, you have the right to direct a summary judgment at any time," he said. "If you believe the prosecution has advanced its argument convincingly, you may do so. Likewise, if you believe the prosecution has not made its case, you may ask that this trial end in a finding of 'not guilty.'"

Something was wrong, Drummond thought. The proceedings seemed to be rattling along somehow much faster than he anticipated. He didn't understand what was happening. A summary judgment? Clarke droned on, but Drummond felt the need to interrupt him.

"*Mijn Heer* General?" he called out, turning to Stuyvesant. "May the accused speak?"

"Stand mute in the dock, if you please," the director general said.

Peter Cuyck, the farmer on the jury, spoke up. "Please, sir, we would like to hear Mister Drummond speak."

"The defendant has the right to make a statement to the court," Clarke said.

Stuyvesant repressed his natural rage at being openly contradicted, and curtly nodded his assent. But inwardly he steamed. *The defendant has the right*? Who has rights? Rights were only what he, the director general, allowed. Nothing more. He could give them and take them away.

Drummond faced the jury. "John Winthrop of the Massachusetts Bay Colony has claimed all land north of the forty-second parallel latitude. That cuts our line just to the north of Wildwyck, gentlemen, and that means the Massachusetts Bay Colony will take Fort Orange and Beverwyck."

Stuyvesant stamped his peg leg on the hollow floor of the council chambers. He could not abide this. Drummond saying "our line," as if he were at one with the Dutch jurymen! "The accused will stick to the facts of the present case," the director general said.

But Drummond continued on in the same vein.

"Wildwyck, Fort Orange and Beverwyck. We need them. John Winthrop and Massachusetts shall not have them. Fort Orange and Beverwyck may be called by different names under the English king, but we will keep those entities within this jurisdiction. You may trade up the river as before."

"Mister Drummond!" Stuyvesant shouted, rising up from his chair.

"If you want to keep Beverwyck, come with us, come with England," Drummond said. "If you want to lose it to the Massachusetts Bay Colony, go with this man." He pointed at Stuyvesant, who had gone apoplectic.

"Stand mute! Stand mute!" the director general yelled at Drummond.

"Your Excellency?" Clarke shouted.

Speaking directly to the jury, Drummond said, "The new colony will be called the Crown Province of New York, and you have the promise of King Charles II that its governors will take Dutch law and customs seriously, including all border disputes."

Drummond looked at Gerritt Remunde and the others. Blandine had given him the key. Internecine rivalries trumped global ones every time. It is a human characteristic to fear a local bully more than a remote god. The traders in the settlement cared little who ruled them, Dutch or English. But they desperately did not want to be cheated via a land grab by one of their neighboring colonial rivals.

Gerrit Remunde stood up in the jury box, begging for Stuyvesant's attention. "Sir? Sir?"

"Sit down!" the director general said.

"Your Excellency," Remunde said, persisting. "We gentlemen of the jury wish to direct the court to do what the barrister suggested"—he gestured at Clarke—"what he called it, a summary judgment, that this man be found not guilty of the charge and freed."

The gallery erupted in chatter. "Not guilty" sounded from several lips.

"Out of order, out of order!" the director general said. Stuyvesant stamped his foot repeatedly, attempting to quiet a council chamber that verged on riot.

After a long few minutes, he finally quelled the disturbance. He stood silent for a beat, glowering.

"Spying is by definition a military matter, and I am the duly authorized general of the colonial militia," Stuyvesant began.

He was shouted down by the members of the gallery, who realized what the director general was about to do. "No, no, no!" they called out.

"Captain of the guard!" he shouted. "Captain of the guard!"

Muskets in hand, four of the director general's paid militiamen marched into the chambers from their post just outside the door.

"Director general, I object to this—" Clarke said, but he was jostled aside by the soldiers.

"This court is dissolved!" Stuyvesant shouted, greeted by more calls of "No! No!" But even the staunchest republicans were not about to risk death by bayonet just to save the hide of an English spy. The spectators moved sullenly out as the militiamen cleared the chamber.

"The jury is dismissed," the director general said, speaking over the tumult. "I hereby adjourn, suspend and disperse this court."

More protests were called out, but sounded weaker. In the chaos, Drummond motioned Raeger over from the gallery.

"Get word to Blandine," he said. "She's at Luybeck's." The *weert* rushed out.

Drummond found himself in the dock, facing the director general as if the two of them were alone. Just Petrus Stuyvesant and his musket men.

One look at the director general's face and Drummond knew he was doomed. Challenge a tyrant at your own risk, and the smaller the stakes, the greater the tyranny. The proceedings lost all semblance of a trial. Stuyvesant meant to kill him.

What had Drummond ever done to the man to invite such enmity? He had just been acquitted as a spy. But still Stuyvesant bore down. This was personal.

Drummond couldn't fathom it. Apart from his trenchant asides in confidential diplomatic messages, he'd had few dealings with the director general. Some of the language he had used might have been a little salty, but was it enough for Stuyvesant to want to string him up? Or perhaps Drummond was being blamed for the Godbolt affair?

Kees Bayard could be behind it. Jealousy being the great motivator in human affairs more often than was recognized.

Stuyvesant rose to his feet. "Having heard the evidence, I am within my authority as director general of the colony and military governor to pronounce the accused guilty and sentence him to hang."

His face twisted into something resembling a smile. *Where is your arrogance now, Englisher?*

"This isn't justice," Drummond said evenly. "It's murder."

"Corporal? Take this man into custody."

As the militiamen moved on Drummond, Stuyvesant called out, "Under shackles!"

The day may have started as a jury trial, but in the end, the director general could do whatever he wanted. Might made right.

Desperation, Drummond thought, assessing the situation that would lead, in perhaps minutes, to his death. The director general had merely underlined the dictatorial nature of his governorship. He had already lost the Dutch residents of the colony. By this action, he would lose those few English residents who remained his allies.

Instead, the impulsive Stuyvesant placed all his hopes in the militia. A hundred men with pikes and flintlock muskets. Twenty cannon on the ramparts of the fort. That was all that was left to him.

But the director general possessed an immediate present advantage. For this particular time and this place, he held the guns, and there was nothing Drummond could do to stop him.

He thought of Blandine. *Nothing will happen at the tribunal, will it?*

"Devilish tricky business," Eberhard Luybeck said to Blandine, tying up a sheaf of documents with a length of twine. The two sat in Luybeck's law chamber near the Stadt Huys.

"I mean, Aet Visser was a wonder, had his finger in all sorts of pies, everywhere in the colony," Luybeck said. "Multiple and sundry partnerships, debts owed, debts outstanding owed to him, some sort of royalty relationship with the director general, a share in a Pavonia acreage with the Hendrickson family, payments to them, funds received from them. He was in court more often than he was out of it, and not just the Orphan Chamber either."

Eberhard Luybeck knew that crucial to survival in the profession of law were estates, and the payments attendant upon death. The best things in life were fees. *Probate!* The word was sweeter to him than any other. It was the teat he suckled for all his sustenance, and therefore he loved it with the pure innocence of an infant.

"I merely need to know if he has taken care of Anna and his family," Blandine said.

"Yes, well, he has, very handsomely," Luybeck said. "There can be no formal recognition of his paternity, of course, nor of the marriage. The woman is half a Haverstraw indian, I believe?"

"Sopus," Blandine said.

"A rare survivor," Luybeck said. "I hear that through the actions of our courageous militia the Esopus clan has for all intents and purposes been extinguished. Anna had a twin brother, did she not? This man recently deceased, Gerald, who went by the name of Lightning?"

What?

Blandine felt too unsettled by the revelation to attend much to what Luybeck was saying to her.

Lightning. Anna. Which meant Lightning was uncle to the Bean and all the others. And that his relationship with Visser was much tighter than Blandine had previously imagined.

"Oh, and there's this that Mister Visser left you," Luybeck said. He slid a sealed envelope across his desk table to Blandine.

A jurisdiction cannot have too many gallows. In addition to the public one, on the shoreline outside the fort, the one Aet Visser co-opted for his own last Easter, Stuyvesant also had at his disposal a smaller military gibbet, erected within the fort and used for cases of desertion, insubordination, dereliction of duty. He had hung a sleeping sentry there in just the last week.

It was to this platformless hanging ground that his militia guards conducted Drummond. The smaller gibbet lacked the spectacle value of the public gallows, but in this case was more convenient. The bailey yard of Fort Amsterdam had not been entirely cleared of the citizenry, and many of the spectators who had been pushed from the court chamber assembled near the open gates of the fortress. They had not yet coalesced into a mob.

Drummond saw Gerrit Remunde among them. The man hailed him across the twenty yards separating them as though they were friends at a party. "Drummond!" he called. Drummond wondered if he was again going to extend an invitation to dine.

The militiamen, their numbers now swelled to more than two dozen strong, did not fear interference. The director general stumped alongside them, pointing the way, commanding and instructing.

"Hurry along, now," he said.

The arrangement at this particular gibbet was simple. The condemned would be made to climb upon a trestle, the noose placed around his neck, the trestle removed.

"Position it so I may kick it out from under him with my own foot," instructed the director general.

Drummond bit his tongue. He did not want "which one?" to be the last thing he said on this earth.

As the militiamen moved the wooden frame in place beneath the noose, Stuyvesant came close to the shackled Drummond.

"Am I a one-legged strutting fool?" he hissed. "Am I a changeable and overweening dictator? Is my Latin a joke? Do I set myself up as a lord?"

Drummond at first did not grasp what the man was saying, but then realized Stuyvesant was quoting Drummond's own words back to him, judgments contained in the coded messages transmitted to London. Cited by the director general word for word, from memory. A deep wound, obviously, now freshly reopened.

There it was. Why Drummond had to die. Because he had insulted his High Mightiness, Petrus Stuyvesant. On purely practical grounds, Drummond wished he had been kinder. The language of secret diplomatic correspondence was not meant for prying outside eyes.

The director general stepped back and made a quick gesture. "Proceed," he said.

The militiamen hefted Drummond, still bound, onto the trestle. One of them, a corporal, leapt up beside him to adjust the noose around his neck.

De Klavier was there, standing below, looking up. "Does the condemned wish to be hooded, or to be given a bowl of tobacco?"

"No to the blindfold," Drummond said. "Yes to the tobacco."

"Get on with it!" Stuyvesant barked. But De Klavier merely carefully lighted a pipe and handed it up to the corporal, who placed it to Drummond's lips.

What could be more delicious than a last lungful of Virginia brightleaf? The August sun shone down. He heard shouts, cries, the echoing music of human voices. Through the open gates of the fort, Drummond could see the blue waters of the bay sparkle and heave.

The corporal jumped down from the trestle.

Edward again had thoughts of Blandine.

44

The letter left to Blandine by Visser was marked, on the outside envelope, with the words *URGENT, FOR IMMEDIATE DELIVERY.*

The request evidently went unheeded by Eberhard Luybeck. Its author had been dead now for more than four months.

Blandine repaired to Drummond's rooms on Slyck Steegh to open it.

April 14, 1664

My dearest Blandine,

By the time you read this I will have taken myself far, far away. That does not mean I am excused from all of my wrongdoing. My heart hangs heavy for the role I have played in the harmful and sinful doings in our community. There are dark secrets in my family that I cannot bear to face. I am the man you know, the man who has tried to care for you and watch out for you lo these many years. But I am something else, too.

I am an auxiliary to evil.

Blandine placed the letter carefully upon a desk table in the great room, walked over to the window and opened it wide. She was not sure she could stand to read on. Visser! She had long had suspicions that all was not right with the man, but looked away out of loyalty. Now she took a deep breath of fresh air, steadied herself and returned to the table.

Instead of going immediately back to the letter, she gazed at an hourglass Drummond had just purchased, part of his melancholy campaign to replace all that he had lost in the disruptive search of his chambers. The glass was a particularly large model, imported from London, about the height of a forearm, with turned oak braces. It contained a mixture of pinkish pulverized marble and eggshell. More to avoid the letter than anything else, she turned the apparatus over.

All those ground-up moments cascading through the glass, set against the crushed humanity of Aet Visser.

> I am sure you know that Anna is much more to me than a helper in my home. She is my helpmeet because she is my wife—though in none but the common-law sense—and Paulson and Abigel and Maria and Sabine are the beautiful children she bore for me.
>
> Anna came into my life as a young girl, an adolescent, when I was dealing with the deaths of her father and mother. The story I told you about my own children, that they were orphaned by dissolute parents, is actually true of Anna and Gerald, Anna's twin brother. The two were left abandoned by their parents' abrupt demise when they were nine, left to wander the wilderness.
>
> As orphans, they both fell under my purlieu. With young Gerald, I failed. He turned wild. He disappeared for weeks at a time. He returned from his wanderings bearing scars, carrying a knife collection that no young man could honorably possess. He took to calling himself Lightning.
>
> With Anna, I did better. I was able to rescue her from the sordid life Gerald had her leading. Eventually our friendship blossomed into love. At thirteen, I knew that she was too young to couple with an aging blusterer like me, but I could not help myself, she was too beautiful.

Blandine felt a hard, burning rock in her chest. The hourglass had descended about a quarter of the way down. Once again, she steadied herself by going to the window, taking a moment before returning to the letter.

> Martyn Hendrickson and Lightning became friends at a young age. I thought little of it. Martyn was an upstanding young man from a well-to-do family. He had an easy way about him, a smile for everyone. I thought he might help Lightning.

I was wrong.

Martyn became Lucifer to Lightning's Mephistophilis. Or perhaps it was the other way around. Each was enslaved to the other.

I don't know precisely what ghastly ungodliness the two have been party to over the years. But I did see with my own eyes the brutal evidence of their engagement in . . . I can hardly bring myself to say it . . . every orphan-killing that has taken place in this colony since last summer.

The evidence? Bloody rags, red-stained clothing, held within the Hendrickson house here in town. And I recognized the garments, they belonged to children who I had responsibility for, who I should have protected.

I can never forgive myself for this. I did not know about the particulars when it was going on, but I knew enough. I hid from my duty. I should have seen Lightning and Martyn for what they were—predators. And I will suffer in hell for my inaction.

Martyn Hendrickson is not dead. He is in hiding, awaiting the chance to perform his next infernal deed. I am convinced he will kill and kill, assisted by Lightning. His appetite for death will never be sated.

Find him. Stop him. Enlist Drummond. Save our children, before he takes them all.

God bless you, and reserve some small portion of your love for this broken old man, who remains, as ever, your friend and servant,

Aet Visser

Then, scrawled at the bottom in a hurried hand, a chilling sentence that looked as though it were added later.

I fear for the Bean.

The hourglass had dropped half its contents into its lower bulb. Thirty minutes had passed. Blandine imagined her mind gripped by a pair of terrible claws. She tossed the letter aside.

Martyn Hendrickson alive. And the Bean in some sort of danger.

Blandine knew exactly where Sabine should be at that moment. Not at home, as she wished the little girl was, especially after reading Visser's tag-end warning. But every morning, Anna took the children to examine the work on the new house.

Blandine passed out of the chamber by the door into the backyard and went to the ladder Drummond had propped against the wall of the house. She scaled it, holding her petticoat aside in one clenched hand, a desperate urgency informing her movements.

From the roof, Blandine could scan the whole town, all the sturdy dwelling-houses, she thought bitterly, sheltering the safe little families. She could see the fort, erected to protect the populace, the church, protector of its souls, the roadstead, where ships arrived with bounty from Europe, and the streets, peopled with the ignorant and unconcerned.

There was Drummond's spyglass, trained as Blandine had left it, upon the environs of Market Street. She peered through the eyepiece and found her focus, first locating the new house, where workmen were framing the walls with pine timbers. Here she and Edward would live with Sabine and Jan.

Sabine! *I fear for the Bean.* What had Visser meant?

And just then, as though both God and the Devil were reading her thoughts, Blandine saw the Bean come dawdling down Market Street, trailing her mother, her brother and her two sisters. As they did every day, Anna and the children visited the new house. They were now leaving to return to their Pearl Street rooms.

In a pink, frilly petticoat and a white summer blouse, Sabine played at scotch-hoppers, tossing a pebble in front of her and getting to it however she might, balancing on one foot.

Blandine sighed with relief. Anna was there. All was well.

But in horror Blandine watched as Sabine stopped by the side of the street to look through a gate into a yard. Blandine shifted the spyglass slightly and realized the child was looking at the massive Hendrickson dwelling-house.

She shifted the glass again, and saw that Anna and the children had turned off Market Street into the parade ground next to the fort. The

Bean stood momentarily alone in front of the Hendrickson gate. Why did she stop? What did she stare at so intently?

In a second, Blandine saw for herself. Something white, bounding behind the fence of the big house in the long shaggy grass.

Maddie. The Bean ran through the open iron gate and down the walk toward the Hendrickson backyard.

"Sabine!" Blandine shouted at the child, who could not possibly hear.

Panicked, her breath coming in frantic sobs, Blandine tumbled down the ladder so quickly she ripped her skirt. She had never moved so fast. She dashed inside the chambers, but only to grab the muff pistol Drummond gave her, kept primed and ready on the desk table near the door.

Blandine rushed outside and over to the canal. The big ditch blocked her path. She could head downtown to take Brewer's Bridge or uptown to take the Little Bridge. Both courses would bring her a hundred yards out of her way. The dark mouth of Market Street lay directly across the canal, only three rods distant.

An incoming tide, but the seawater had not yet flowed up the canal to where she stood. A bottom layer of muck remained exposed. On each side of the deep ditch, wooden buttresses, green with slime and built of raw pitch-treated pine, angled slightly outward at the top. But the walls had gaps between the planks, and support timbers that a desperate person could climb to get to the other side.

Blandine plunged in. She half fell, half climbed down the twelve-foot wall on the near side. The stinking mud grabbed her feet as she crossed, and she almost tumbled more than once. Shells and dying fish lay in her path. A nest of eels writhed.

Going up the other side was more difficult. She grabbed at whatever crevices she could find, picking up splinters in her palms. Thoroughly muddied, Blandine made the top and staggered forward into the eastern end of Market Street.

She immediately encountered Anna, wild-eyed, searching. "Sabine!" she called, and the other children called the name, too.

"Anna!" Blandine called.

"Where is she?" Anna said. "Do you have her?"

Blandine took the woman by the shoulders. "You must take the children and go home," she said.

"No, no, I have to——" Anna cried, but Blandine shook her roughly.

"You must do what I say. Take them home. Keep them safe. I will bring Sabine back to you unharmed."

Anna searched her face, distracted.

"I have a gun," Blandine said, showing her palm pistol. "All will be well, I promise you."

Anna turned and herded the other children away.

Blandine moved down the street to the Hendrickson mansion. She stepped through the iron gate warily. No sound, no little barking dog, no Bean. Was she sure of what she had seen?

"Sabine!" she called.

No response. Blandine walked around the house, wading through the unkempt grass, seeing broken crockery strewn about the yard. When she got to the rear of the house, she tried the garden entrance, the one that led into the new addition the Hendrickson brothers had built onto the original structure.

She pushed, and the door creaked open.

Leaning in, Blandine saw a sheen of glossy droplets splashed near the wall, pooling on the parquet floor.

Blood. He has already killed her, she thought.

One step, then another. She was inside.

The red pool on the floor was fresh. The chambers bore the silence of the tomb. A strange mix of smells: rot, gunpowder, wine, a sharp stench like a tannery, an odd sweet perfume laying over all. A summer cook-fire glowed faintly in the hearth.

Deep within the house, upstairs, a sudden patter of footsteps. They abruptly ceased. To Blandine's left, a steep, curving servant's stairway climbed out of sight. Keeping her palm pistol in front of her, she took the winding stair.

Blandine strained her hearing. She reached the top of the steps. The second floor showed itself even darker and gloomier than the first. The walls were of a fashionable tint, tomato red. Stifling heat rendered the interior tight and claustrophobic.

A hallway, running the length of one wing, led off from the stairs to the left and right. Blandine chose left. Belongings cluttered the way, and she had to step over dirty laundry, spine-broken books, a crushed wooden box. She placed her hand on the wall for balance. The plaster felt hot to the touch. The heat closed around her, slowing her thoughts to a crawl.

Proceeding along the hallway, Blandine finally understood the reason for the inhuman blankness of the mansion's big windows. They appeared as voids when seen from the street because the Hendricksons had covered the glass on the inside with tarlike black paint. Thin, weak beams of daylight seeped through cracks and window-frame seams, but otherwise all was sightless dark.

A rustling noise distracted her. A rat, scurrying away from her, hid itself underneath a spill of papers.

Nothing. More silence. A dog yapped, its bark deadened.

Suddenly, from the other end of the hallway came a child's laughter. Blandine turned to see the Bean, barefoot, stripped to her chemise, running from one chamber to another.

"Sabine!"

She rushed to the other end of the hall, but found herself confronted by a maze of doorways. She called out again. More footsteps, starting and halting.

Something was wrong. She heard a thin, quavering, womanish voice, then another voice, Sabine's, joining it.

> *Dik-duk, dik-duk*
> *Ain't that how my little chick clucks?*

Blandine could not understand from where the sound came. She felt disoriented. The voices appeared to emanate from inside the walls.

A giggle, broken off. Perspiration ran from Blandine's forehead, stinging her eyes. Where could the Bean be?

"Ina? Ina?" called a tiny, muffled voice.

Blandine halted dead in her tracks. "Ina" was the name her little sister, Sarah, used to call her.

She rushed through an open door to find a cluttered, filthy chamber, with an upended *kas* beside a disheveled bed. On a table stood a globe and a bulbous brass pipe. The sickly sweet perfume smell managed to overpower the stench of body sweat and garbage.

She stood still, held her breath and detected tiny sounds of movement coming from within the overturned *kas*. Blandine quickly crossed the chamber and pried open the doors of the cabinet.

Inside, amid a jumble of clothing and linens, trembled Maddie. The dog let out a choked whine.

A movement behind Blandine. A hand with a linen handkerchief clapped itself roughly across her face, an overpowering chemical stench filled her nostrils and her pistol clattered from her grasp.

The world faded away.

Her last sight, before she lost consciousness, was the Bean standing in the doorway of the chamber, grinning in delight, her white chemise marked with handprints of blood.

Drummond could not decide which way to leave the world. He had declined a blindfold, but now he suddenly felt as though he could not bear to witness his own hanging. He shut his eyes. Shouts went up from the settlers near the gate.

Who faces death without complaint?

Sightless, eyes closed, Drummond thought of the Lenape warriors Kitane told him about, captured by Mahicans, impaled on a stick of finely shaped ash, just so, there is an art to it, the spear thrust up the fundament through the body to exit at the shoulder, but missing all the vital organs, in order that the victim doesn't die right off. The speared man is tied at the hands and ankles, hefted horizontal, suspended over a fire to be slow-roasted.

Sightless, eyes closed, Drummond asked Kitane, "So the man is alive? What is he doing while all this is being done to him?"

Kitane: "Singing. Laughing. He calls out your name and remembers a game of stick-and-ball you had. As his skin pops and his fat runs into the fire. Smiling. Crowing."

Even at the bitterest of ends, the warrior maintained his dignity. No beseeching of the great god Manitou to save him. Beliefs don't matter. Practice does.

More shouts rose. Drummond waited for the kick at the trestle.

"Blandine," he whispered. He wondered if she had heard about the impromptu hanging, if she were even now rushing to get to him through the streets of the colony.

Rising yells, a whole chorus of voices. The sound of running feet.

Drummond opened his eyes.

He had been deserted.

Drummond stood alone balancing on the trestle, the noose around his neck. He saw the director general and his troop of militiamen hustling away toward the open gates of the fort.

Had they forgotten to hang him? Was it some kind of cruel joke? Perhaps he was already dead, and this was the afterlife?

The whole crowd streamed from the gates out onto the rocky beach that stretched along the Manhattan shoreline. They moved as one, as though they fled some terror or were drawn by some spectacle.

Among the horde going the opposite way, only Gerrit Remunde walked toward him. "Mister Drummond," he said. "May I help you down from there?"

"I wish you would," Drummond said.

Gerrit mounted the trestle—it shook wildly, scaring Drummond witless for a quick second. His former shipmate gently removed the noose and unscrewed the shackles at Drummond's back.

"What has happened?" Drummond asked, leaping to the ground.

"You'll see," Gerrit said.

They walked together to the gates of the fort. The entire colony appeared to have crowded along the Strand, gaping and gawking out into the bay.

Then two tall ships plunged by, English battle frigates, cannon ports open, marines posted on deck, an impossibly thrilling, throat-choking sight, putting up all sail and cutting through the roadstead waters at a fast clip, only twenty rods from shore.

By a quick count Drummond made forty guns in the first frigate, and another twenty-six in the second. The ships were so close he could see lighted punks in the hands of the gunners.

He looked back behind him at the ramparts of the fort. The director general stood beside a gun crew at one of the twenty cannons he could train upon the bay. Colonists crowded on the rocky beach, directly in the cross fire.

Sixty-six guns of the crack English navy, against twenty in a crumbling citadel designed at best as a temporary refuge from indian attack. If Stuyvesant engaged, it would be a bloodbath, and one that the Dutch would surely lose.

"Drummond," a voice called to him.

Antony.

"It's Miss Blandina," Antony said. "Hurry."

45

Martyn and Lightning created their alliance early on in their lives, when they were both nine, in the wild hills and endless forests of the Hendrickson patent. Stalking the woods, Martyn discovered Lightning (he was called Gerald then) and his sister, Anna, twins born of an unholy night of rape by a brandy-bitten German *handlaer* on a frightened Esopus woman, a child, really, only fifteen.

The young Lightning and Martyn fell in love instantly, bonding over their shared sexual torment of Anna. They became inseparable. Lightning called himself Martyn's slave.

In their early teens, they began in the way a lot of killers start, with small animals. Martyn once found a litter of cats on the plantation, and he and Lightning buried the creatures up to their necks in a wheat field, then watched as reapers came through with long-curving scythes.

They teased each other, goading themselves on to greater indignities. In the second Esopus war, Martyn took a captaincy and Lightning became his aide de corps, officially a scout and unofficially the chief torturer.

Lightning helped Martyn drive his abiding sadness deep inside, so deep it nearly disappeared beneath layers of anger and recklessness. A single old memory remained, the only one he had of his mother, cooing a nursery rhyme over him. Words about chicks and fishes.

In the summer of 1663, Martyn came to Lightning with a proposition. His brothers, Ad and Ham, Martyn said, were upset with the encroachment on their land by Englishers from the east.

Trespassers, outlaws, they deserved to die, Ham said.

What would be good, Ad said, is if we could throw a real scare into the whole of New England.

That was when Martyn first heard the word *witika*.

Have a witika scream down on them, Ham said, they would think twice about coming onto our land.

Martyn didn't know what a witika was, but Lightning did. He

described the demon in detail. During his recital of the creature's appearance, appetites and practices, Martyn found himself strangely aroused.

Later, in the wake of the uproar following the killing and the partial consumption of Jope Hawes, Ad and Ham confronted their baby brother. They insisted they had never been serious. It was all just talk, they said. They looked at Martyn strangely, as if he had somehow transgressed, when all he had done was put into practice what they themselves had proposed!

As the witika furor grew in the northland, Ad and Ham feared that Martyn would be unmasked. They exiled him to Manhattan. Out of harm's way. Lightning went with him.

But a taste, once developed, is not so easily given up. So, Piteous Gullee. And William Turner, the orphan boy who had the bad luck to blunder into some of their doings with Piddy. And Small Bill Gessie, and his sister, Jenny, and on and on to all the others, Ansel Imbrock, Richard Dunn, Tara Oyo, Tibb Dunbar. There were others, too, that didn't come to be known by name.

How they worked: Lightning was the rapist, boys and girls both, it didn't matter. Martyn was always the smasher, the basher, the ripper, the killer, the eater. While he performed, Lightning watched, and vice versa.

Martyn and Lightning were having the time of their lives. And it all got blamed on the witika demon. They had good, hearty laughs about that.

Twenty feet beneath the grounds of the Hendricksons' New Amsterdam dwelling-house, Martyn trudged a dank passageway lined with stone. He had Blandine slung over one of his shoulders and led the Bean by the other hand.

"Come along," Martyn said to the little girl. "Keep up."

Sabine didn't know if she was in the middle of an adventure or a nightmare. She tried to be a good girl and do what *dik-duk* Martyn told her. She snuffled a little. Barefoot on the cool paving squares, she carried the limp form of Maddie.

"Puppy's just sleeping," Martyn told her. "Like Miss Blandina."

He carried a torch in his off hand, illuminating the corridor. A cart sat covered in grime. Its wheels were attached to some sort of line apparatus—the rope led forward, disappearing in the murk of the tunnel.

Martyn dumped Blandine into the cart. "Ooof," he commented to Sabine. "The woman should lay off the desserts a little."

Turning a wheel on the wall, Martyn caused the cart to move magically forward. "Would you like to ride?" he asked Sabine.

She said she would. The passageway ahead swallowed the thin flame of the torch, and the darkness scared the Bean, but the cart proved irresistible. Martyn swept up her and the dog and deposited them next to the sleeping Blandine.

Sabine had never seen a wagon move by itself. It was fun. Martyn walked behind, holding the light. Then he fell back a little.

"Mister?"

Everything faded to black. She twisted around to see the torch getting smaller and smaller. The cart creaked forward.

"Dik-duk," she called, a sob choking her voice. No answer.

"Dik-duk," she said again, despairing.

It was chilly in the passageway. She snugged herself closer to her sleeping friend, burying her head in Blandine's chest.

Martyn let the cart disappear ahead of him. He thought how the Romans described the descent to Hades. A gentle slope down. *Facilis descenscus Averno*. There was a line of Virgil for the director general to mull over. The descent to Hell is easy.

How true it was. Looking back over his life, it all seemed a serene glide to where he was now, with a woman, a child and a dog in a Stygian tunnel, water dripping from the timbers overhead. The three of them could be a family about to receive the judgment of Charon. Mother, father, baby, together and unbreakable, even in the underworld.

Ahead of him, in the gloom, the woman in the cart groggily lifted up her head. Martyn couldn't believe it. She had only been out an hour, and he had given her enough of the sweet vapor to drop a horse. The child began to wail.

Martyn swore. He slipped his dagger from its sheath. The old fury rose in him. He rushed forward, squeezed around the cart and kicked open the door at the end of the tunnel.

Daylight flooded in. They lay concealed deep in the gutter of the canal. A skiff waited for them, tied to an iron ring set into the bulwark, bobbing on the inflowing tide. Martyn transferred Blandine from cart to boat, covering her unconscious form with a bit of tarpaulin. He turned to the tear-stained face of the child.

"Now would you like to take a ride in this little ship?" He didn't wait for Sabine to answer, but lifted her and Maddie into the craft.

Martyn poled them down the Begin Gracht and into the larger Heere Gracht. The green water of the canal slid by effortlessly. No other boats or barges were abroad. To prying eyes, Martyn appeared like any other burgher, heading through town with a load of merchandise to trade. Potatoes, perhaps, or firewood.

He could hear the indistinct sound of men's voices above him. The upper stories of buildings in the settlement would appear and then drop behind, cut off by the green-stained walls of the waterway. Martyn had the marvelous sense of passing through the town in a ghost boat, furtive, untouched, invisible. The canal bridges slipped by, one, two, three.

Sabine crawled under the tarp next to Blandine and, snuffling, fell asleep.

Once he emerged from the canal out onto the East River, Martyn set sail and turned the skiff north.

The extensive grounds of the Hendrickson estate in New Amsterdam stretched north from Market Street across the Begin Gracht to Heere Dwars Street. With orchards, gardens and outbuildings, the property amounted to a small *bouwerie* or plantation within the bounds of the settlement.

Sebastian Klos and his twin brother, Quinn, knew the grounds well. They lodged with a foster family on the canal (one of the good deeds of Aet Visser had been to keep the twins together), only a few rods away from the Hendrickson property. The Klos boys—and practically every other scamp, vagabond and light-finger in the settlement—loved to sneak into the estate and steal peaches.

So the Klos boys understood that the stands of fruit trees were well concealed from thieving outside eyes behind fences and a dense, European-style hedgerow. They knew that at the heart of the orchard lay a paddock, a well-fenced half-hectare enclosure that adjoined the stables and corrals in the back of the big house.

And they knew one final thing, that in the Hendrickson paddock occasionally appeared a magnificent black stallion.

Together, the Coney Boys and the High Street Gang knew everything there was to know about the island of Manhattan. In the blazing summer of 1664, they put their joint efforts into ending, once and for all, the witika plague that had late afflicted the settlement.

"I know where is a cave," said one of them, the orphan Geddy Jansen, whose fishmongering foster uncle had brought her along on his tramps to the northern tip of the island in search of eels.

The Coneys and the Highs knew that William Turner—or Jan Drummond or whatever he was calling himself these days, one of the High Street Gang, anyway—was desperately searching for the location of a cave in the upper reaches of Manhattan, so they communicated Geddy's knowledge.

And when Jan Drummond, in receipt of that knowledge, said he needed a steed to travel to said cave, the Klos twins thought of the stallion in the paddock in the middle of the orchard.

Thus when the allied forces of the Coney Boys and the High Street Gang crept into the Hendrickson estate that hot August day, they weren't after peaches. They infiltrated through hedgerow gaps so narrow that no one but a child would ever realize they were there. Taking as their bywords silence, stealth and cunning, the band of irregulars moved at the behest of their captain, Peer Gravenraet.

Peer would rather have been the brave Achilles, and confront the enemy outright, instead of the wily Odysseus, sneaking and faking and dodging. But a raid was a raid, and the time to strike was now, when the colony was distracted by the prospect of English ships off the shore of Manhattan.

"I want one squad south, watching the house, to make sure we are not surprised," Peer commanded, sending out a trio of scouts.

"Disruption in the harbor," Laila Philipe ran up and reported, breathless from having dashed all the way from the fort. "The English have come."

Laila's column of adolescent Amazons were capable of holding their own in any episode of fisticuffs. With their hair pulled back and their skirts hiked up, they were ready for this fight.

"Good," Peer said. He turned to the boy beside him, the small, normally silent child who first proposed the Hendrickson raid.

"Once we go in, we can't turn back," Peer said, a last-minute fortitude check before committing to the mission.

The boy nodded. Jan Drummond, formerly William Turner, sometimes called William the Silent, known to the settlement as the Godbolt ward, was a child who at times even now forgot his words and reverted back to his old mute ways.

"Are you sure this is what you want?" Peer asked Jan.

"Yes," Jan said.

The gangs moved forward on attack.

46

D rummond followed Antony around the side of the fort, up through the market. The settlement flocked with people headed for the waterfront, but they parted readily for the two men rushing in the opposite direction. It helped that Antony brandished a weapon of comforting size, a man-mountain toting a musket almost as tall as he was.

The firearm that Antony held was an original creation of Blandine's. When she was a teenager, her father threw open his gunsmithing workshop to her, tools and all. He challenged her to build him something. Starting with an ancient Dutch harquebus, Blandine tooled the muzzle to a precise thinness, enlarging the bore enormously.

To compensate for the weakness of the brittle old metal, she banded the barrel with iron straps that she smithed herself. For the firing mechanism, she cannibalized parts from other muskets and pistols lying around the workshop, a firing pan from this one, a hammer from that.

The breech wound up so gaping she had to create new shot, pouring the molten lead into moldings she fashioned via trial and error. Just for giggles, Blandine fitted a squirrel-gun barrel below the shotgun, lending the piece an over-and-under effect.

The result was a monstrosity. Willem van Couvering laughed uproariously when his daughter presented it to him. But he admired the workmanship. "This is just *tour de force* stuff," her father said.

Pretty Polly, Blandine named the gun, in honor of its extreme ugliness. She and Willem took it out along the North River shore and tested it a few times, practicing cutting down trees with the thing. But for Blandine, the making of it was always more to the point than the shooting. She gave it to Antony, knowing that only one of his size could handle it.

Drummond knew instinctively where he and Antony were headed. He realized he had always known where it would really, truly end, after all the false finishes and deceptive cul de sacs into which the pursuit of the orphan-killers had led him.

The Hendrickson brothers.

Right turn onto Market Street, past Drummond's own new dwelling, then ten rods east to the Hendrickson estate.

The gates hung open.

"Where is she?" Drummond asked.

Antony was breathing hard. He had run a long way, and the huge gun he carried was heavy.

"I never saw her. We have to find her. Anna told me she was here," Antony said. He gestured toward the dark clapboarded structure, with its great sightless windows. Above the front door, a pane of green bull's-eye glass.

Drummond stepped through the gate. He went to the front entrance, Antony beside him gripping the musket. The door, he realized as he approached it, was slightly ajar.

No sound from inside. Drummond pushed open the door. Where was a damned pistol of his own? Antony nodded to him wordlessly. They entered the big dwelling-house together.

The first thing Drummond saw was Ham Hendrickson sprawled out on the floor of the great room, the top of his head blown off and his blood spilled into an immense dark pool that spread across the floor to the hearth. A pistol lay beside him. Drummond picked it up, inspected it, saw that it was primed.

Kees Bayard, also dead, the blood flower on his white waistcoat showing a fatal wound to his chest, sat propped against the far wall. His stare was blank. Around him were several crushed poppy-tear tar-balls, their black substance smeared across the floor.

Antony and Drummond moved toward the second room, the parlor, the one built into the addition. All was silence, emptiness.

"Miss Blandina," Antony called.

Nothing.

"We need to check through the whole house," Drummond said, dread rising in him.

"I'll take this wing," Antony said, turning back the way they had come.

Throughout the chambers, utter and complete nastiness, dirt, chaos. An odd, sweet smell permeated the air. In a back chamber upstairs, Drummond encountered a family of feasting rats.

But no Blandine, no Ad Hendrickson. He went back downstairs.

In the second hearth-room, Drummond noticed blood pooling in a corner. He crossed to it, dipped his finger, found it fresh. How could it be there? He looked up, thinking it might be dripping from the floor above.

No, it was coming, somehow, from behind the wall.

He pushed on the wainscoting, heard a click and felt the hidden door swing outward.

A small, sepulcher-sized room. Ad Hendrickson lay sprawled at the opposite end, bleeding from the chest.

"Water," he said.

A faint light filtered in from a high, thin window set into the wall above. Smashed crockery littered the stone floor, which was wet.

"Where is she?" Drummond said.

"It was Lightning, always Lightning," Ad said weakly. "I knew that damned buck was crazy when I first set eyes on him. I should have shot him right then, saved myself a boatload of trouble."

"Listen, old man," Drummond said bending his face near to Ad. "I need to know where my wife is."

"He took her," Ad said. "I tried to stop him."

"Who?" demanded Drummond. "Who took Blandine?"

"My brother," Ad said.

"Your brother," Drummond said, "is lying out there in the parlor room missing half his skull."

Ad winced, the blood visibly pulsing from his chest, flowing in waves to the floor. "I mean my little brother, my brother Martyn."

"Martyn is dead, too!" Drummond shouted. "Talk sense!"

"You foolish man," Ad said. "Everything you know is wrong. Don't ye realize? My baby brother has shot and killed all of us. He's gone mad. He'll kill you, too."

"Martyn," Drummond said.

Ad Hendrickson began to blubber, tears falling to mix with his blood. "But it was always Lightning. He made Martyn what he was. He did it all. Don't blame Martyn. Don't blame the baby."

Weeping, he sagged backward. His face went slack.

"Ad!" Drummond shouted. "Ad! Where is she?"

But he was talking to a dead man.

Antony showed at the door of the little low-ceilinged room. He could not fit his bulk inside. "Where's Anna?" Drummond asked him.

"At the old rooms across from the Lion," Antony said. "Blandina told her to stay there with the children."

"We need to talk to Anna," Drummond said. "I have to find out what's going on."

But as they rushed from the front gate of the Hendrickson estate, they met Jan. The small boy rode atop an enormous black horse.

It had been a day of wonders for Drummond, a day of surviving his own hanging, but perhaps this wonder topped them all, since he recognized the charger as Fantome, the amazing animal he had last seen plunging through the ice into the North River. If a beast could come back to life, anything was possible.

Jan did not dismount. "I know where it is," he said. "I know where the cave is."

The cave full of bones. Drummond knew with dead certainty that was where Martyn would take Blandine.

"Where'd you get that animal?" he asked Jan.

"I stole him!" Jan said. "From them"—gesturing with his chin at the Hendrickson house.

Fantome suddenly bucked and whirled in a complete circle, whipping Jan's head nearly off his body as he tried to hold on.

Drummond leapt up behind him. "You stole him or he stole you?"

Getting astride Fantome was like climbing onto some mythological creature, a griffin maybe, or Pegasus. The horse trembled as though he were about to explode straight up into the air.

"Go!" Antony said. "I'll follow."

He strode out onto Market Street, grabbed a good burgher from his saddle on a staid bright bay and put himself aboard instead. The burgher, seeing the size of his attacker and, especially, the enormity of the musket Antony carried, decided not to protest.

They took off, pounding down Market onto the parade ground, scattering walkers on all sides as they raced up the Broad Way, blowing through the sentryless land port into the open country beyond.

"We did not go far enough before," Jan shouted to Drummond, breathless. The two of them had searched and searched for the bone-filled cave where Lightning had taken Jan. They looked among the towering rock piles of the clearing, halfway up the island. They had found nothing. They could never locate the cave.

But the orphans knew. Geddy Jansen knew.

Jolting along at top speed on the back of Fantome, clutched securely by Drummond so he would not fall off, Jan said, "We need to go all the way to the top of Manhattan."

Twelve miles. Drummond hoped there would be time.

In the town behind them, a fusillade of cannon fire boomed.

"Dik-duk," said Martyn Hendrickson.

"Dik-duk," said Sabine, imitating him. That was a song she liked. The Bean sat on Blandine's lap. Martyn sat atop a sawed-off stump across the fire ring, a couple yards away from them. Behind him loomed the dark and toothless maw of a cave.

Blandine had awakened, groggy, a fetid smell on her clothes, to find herself bound securely and Martyn gazing at her.

"How do you feel?" he asked. She didn't answer. A vicious headache gripped her temples in a vise. But at least Sabine was with her and unharmed.

Martyn spoke again. "Did you enjoy the sweet oil of vitriol? *Oleum dulci vitrioli*, the director general would call the stuff. Effective, isn't it? I discovered it in Germany and have been employing it quite often in my pastimes. The vapor gives one the sensation of death without its bothersome permanence. But the smell affronts the nose terribly."

Like clouds passing from the sky, the effects of the ether lifted from Blandine's mind. She still felt woozy.

"Don't hurt her," she said.

"Who, the little one? Or the mongrel?" He prodded an inert ball of fluff at his feet. Maddie. "Out cold. I might have overdone the dose."

"Please, Martyn, do not harm Sabine. Take me instead."

"Why not both?" Hendrickson said, smiling brightly. A pistol lay among the heap of clothes on the ground beside the dog. Children's clothes, bloody rags from orphans, his trophies.

Lightning had liked bones. Martyn liked garments.

Blandine thought that Martyn had something amiss with his famous green eyes. The pupils glittered, enormous and jet black. He sucked on a short brass pipe.

The stench of Martyn's tobacco sickened Blandine.

"You or the little one, what does it matter?" Martyn said. "I ask you that seriously. Doesn't it seem to you that in this new world of ours, we have been entirely abandoned by God? Long ago I recognized you as a kindred spirit, one who believes as I do, in nothing."

"Let her go," Blandine said.

The Bean rocked in her lap. She clacked together the two human rib bones that Martyn had given her to play with.

The little girl remained in her red-stained dress, while Blandine still wore her torn, muddy gown. Martyn had left Blandine's hands free, but bound her ankles and upper arms. She clutched onto Sabine.

"Put those down, honey," Blandine said of the bones.

"No," Sabine said stoutly.

Martyn laughed. "Oh, let her have them," he said. "They are well boiled. They will do her no harm."

"And you?" Blandine asked. "What harm will you do to her?"

"Let me ask you to imagine something, Blandine," he said. "Journey up the North River to Fort Orange. Follow the Mohawk River to the west. You have done this, I know. Leave the river and go overland for a hundred leagues. You will find yourself in the middle of a trackless forest. Not even the *wilden* go there, their villages have been decimated by plague. It is an empty place, a wasteland."

Martyn ran his fingers through his greasy locks. He took another deep suck on his pipe. Blandine finally recognized the smell from ships on which her goods traveled.

Poppy tears.

"Stand in the middle of such a place," Martyn said, "and pronounce out loud the name Blandine van Couvering. Do you hear angels sing? No. Does God answer? No. Don't you see? No one cares. No one is there."

"So it doesn't matter what we do," Blandine said.

"It does not. Which means we can do anything."

"Betray a friend."

"What is that?" Martyn said. "That is nothing."

"Murder."

"Ah, yes. Your man is a soldier. He has killed many times, has he not? Yet you marry him and continue to cohabit with him. So murder shall give us no difficulty."

"Terrorize a whole population," Blandine said.

"As easily as one would drown a kitten," Martyn said.

"Kill a child."

"Yes! Yes!" Martyn cried, chortling. "Especially that."

"Why 'especially'?"

"Because that is the ultimate sin in the eyes of the world, Blandine," Martyn said. "Once you can do that, you are free. Total, limitless freedom."

"I could see how that would be attractive," Blandine said.

"You say that just to humor me," Martyn said, "but it really is true."

He smiled. *"Dik-duk,"* he crooned to the Bean, and she, still occupied with the bones, said it back to him.

"She is no orphan," Blandine said. "She has a mother."

"Unfortunate," Martyn said. "I shall have to break my rule."

"I am one," Blandine said. "I am an orphan."

"Yes, I know."

"We orphans are special, are we not? So alone, so vulnerable," Blandine said. "I wonder if you cried yourself to sleep as a child."

"Shut your mouth," Martyn said.

"Yes, we are alike," Blandine said, her hands gripping Sabine tightly, her eyes blazing. "Both parentless, both without God. But there you are, and here I am. We are free to make choices, and we have both made them, haven't we?"

"I have tasted white, black and red flesh," Martyn said. "Lightning even found me some yellow flesh once, from a cook's boy on a merchant ship just in from Asia. But do you know what I have never done?"

He waited, clearly expecting Blandine to hold up her end of an insane conversation. She worked silently to loose the bonds that wrapped around her arms, but they only tightened more.

"What I haven't done is . . . eat live flesh," Martyn said.

"Take me instead," Blandine said, begging him.

"A trader to the last!" Martyn said, laughing and shaking his head. "Oh, you know, adult humans are rotten with the sins of the world. Their meat is rancid, most unpalatable. I much prefer the fresh."

"Would it matter if it were the meat of a pregnant woman?" Blandine asked.

"Ah, really? My hearty congratulations. I wondered at your heaviness when I hefted you. And that is an interesting offer. But I can always tear the thing out of your body."

He took up a brand from the smoldering fire and put it to his pipe. "I've witnessed it done in the war," he said, exuding smoke from his mouth, like the Devil. "By both sides."

Blandine could see a change come over Martyn. She had never seen an opium taker before, but she felt him slipping away from her, going unfocused and remote.

Martyn stretched out his hand. "Come here, pretty Sabine," he said languidly. "Sit on my lap."

"Don't," Blandine said.

Martyn rose to his feet. Suddenly energized, he declaimed as if onstage, "Madame, I have seen with my own eyes Lightning pull a man's entrails out of his gut, unravel them and then force-feed them back into that same man's own mouth, making him to chew! And you say to me 'Don't'? Don't? Can't you do any better?"

He pulled down the deerskin mask across his face, and mounted a strange pair of wooden stilts that made him tower over the clearing.

The Bean looked up at him and began to cry.

47

After Peer set Jan aboard the big stallion, the Coney Boys and the High Street Gang began phase two of their operation. They attacked the Hendrickson house with a barrage of stone-throwing.

Children hated the place. The orphans knew without knowing that it had some connection with the disappearances of their own. An ominous air of dread emanated from the mansion. The peculiar brothers who lived there became evil figures in the mythology of the orphans, wealthy but malevolent monsters. The decrepit, shuttered residence took on the nature of a spook house. And a spook house just naturally attracts rocks.

Revolution hung in the air. The Dutch had been swept out, but the English had not yet asserted control. Anarchy quickly slipped its leash and loosed itself upon the settlement.

"Now we have a hope to pepper these devilish Dutch traders," swore a drunken German shiv-man at the Jug. "They have salted us too long. We know where their booty is stored."

Added a menacing Polish sailor beside him, "And we know where the young girls live who wear gold chains."

Peer Gravenraet embraced the innate anarchy of the twelve-year-old, and he loved the tinkling sound of smashed glass. He didn't often get a chance to hear it.

"Let's go!" he said, ordering his troops forward.

"Fetch the pickles!" shouted the orphans, their rallying cry. "For Tibb!"

"For the ones we've lost!" Peer called out sententiously.

It was Sebastian Klos—or his brother, Quinn, it was difficult to tell them apart—who cast the first stone. Soon a dark shower of rocks rained down upon the Hendrickson manse, lofted by the Coney Boys and the High Street Gang.

How did the fire happen? How did stone-throwing turn to arson? No one knows. Perhaps a projectile from the hand of Quinn Klos, smashing through one of the big sash windows, ricocheted into the *groot kamer* where Ham Hendrickson lay dead, felled by his own brother's hand.

The thrown rock tipped over an oil lamp. The lamp spilled its fuel. The wick ignited a flame.

A wood-framed, clapboard dwelling-house is an invitation to the gods of fire, a match waiting to be struck. It took only a moment before the flames rose and the house was beyond saving. An orange-black divinity leapt fully born from the roof, roaring, fattening, ascending.

The Coney Boys and the High Street Gang stood stupefied as angry spouts of smoke and fire billowed from the windows they had just finished breaking.

It was by far the most wonderful sight any of them had ever seen.

A half-etherized Blandine crawled on her hands and knees across the uneven surface of the Place of Stones. Her head throbbed so badly it felt split open. A harsh chemical stench filled her nostrils. She threw up a little, but still struggled forward.

Flat stones littered the dirt of the clearing. Sheep-gray rock formations towered like madness overhead. Just beyond her showed the blank eye of the cave.

She had fought against it, but Martyn had doped her again, covering her face with the foul-smelling handkerchief. Then he untied her bonds and laughed while she staggered drunkenly around the clearing, flailing at him. Another dose from the handkerchief. As Blandine lost consciousness, she witnessed him disappear into the cave, hauling Sabine under one arm.

The fire ring displayed the familiar wooden stakes pounded into a circle, ready to be garlanded by a string of guts. In the still-warm ashes, a set of tiny fingers, laid ritualistically in the shape of a fan.

Blandine clutched at wakefulness, lost it, grabbed at it again. The veins in her temples pealed like church bells. She tried to concentrate, to block out the rush of her own poisoned blood.

She heard gurgling water in the stone-choked creek bed down below. And then, from within the cave, the sound of a woman's voice, soothing a child.

"Hush, little one." Strange female tones, fussing, cooing, tut-tutting. "Now, now, it's all right."

Blandine's mind would not order itself. A woman? A matron? Was it her own mother, Josette's voice? She was hearing things.

"Little Martyn will be all better now," the mother promised.

The woman's high-pitched voice was cut by another, a child's snuffling, hiccupping cry. The Bean.

Blandine rose to her feet and stumbled to the cave entrance.

Strewn on the ground in front were dead ashes and chunks of blackened wood. They crunched under Blandine's bare feet as she crossed the threshold into the stone chamber.

A single step led her out of the sunlight and into a dim subterranean coolness, sharply felt after the heat of the day.

A smell of decomposition. Cluttered on the floor of the cave were bones, hundreds, piled and stacked, sorted into a mad kind of order. Blandine recognized deer bones, those of cattle, other animals. Hooves, antlers, everything in between.

The human bones assembled themselves to one side, arranged into a sort of shrine. Candle wax had dripped onto the dirt below, cooling into dirty lumps. A small-statured skeleton, dressed in children's clothes, posed as if to beckon Blandine forward. A necklace fashioned from human nipples hung around its spine.

She shuddered. Where was the Bean? An unreal silence. The stone walls closed in on her. Blandine forced herself to keep going toward the shadows at the back of the cave. She felt as though she were being swallowed.

From the deep recesses, whispery voices echoed. "Time for a bath," the mother said, her words sleepy and soft. "Shall we take off your clothes?"

"No, no, don't want to," said the muffled, teary voice of the child.

"*Dik-duk, dik-duk,*" the mother's voice sang. "Ain't that how my little chick clucks?"

Then, an answering childlike voice: "*Moeder, moeder, moeder.*" Mother, mother, mother. Or, perhaps, she wasn't hearing right, murder, murder, murder. The voice wasn't Sabine's. How many lost souls were in there?

The dirt floor of the cave sloped downward toward a narrow cleft.

Blandine pressed herself against the wall. Her thoughts were clearing by the minute. The cleft led into another chamber. She had to bend over and crawl on her hands and knees again in order to slip through the cramped passage.

A large space. In the weak yellow glow of a single flickering taper, Blandine saw Sabine, totally naked, crouched upon a large flat rock. A carpet of dark-green moss lay atop the stone. The child had the witika sign drawn in ash across her chest. In the muted light, Blandine caught a heartrending, hope-abandoned look on the Bean's face.

Blandine rose from the passageway and moved forward, touching the rough rocks, approaching the girl. "Hush, little one," she said, unconsciously mimicking the woman's voice she had just heard. "It's all right."

She reached the Bean and gathered her into her arms.

A movement behind her.

The witika demon, its shadow huge on the cave wall.

The deerskin face glared down at her, the blood scabs shining in the candlelight.

From behind the deerskin mask came the cloying woman's voice. "Good boy. Good little Martyn."

The monster loomed tall, spreading out its arms, reaching for Blandine and the Bean.

In one hand it held a pistol.

As though events were happening with agonizing slowness, Blandine saw the thumb pulling back the hammer, heard the click as the pin cocked, witnessed the finger tighten on the trigger.

"Martyn!" Blandine shouted, lashing out with her feet at the candle on the crude stone altar.

Lights out.

Sabine tight in her arms, she rolled sideways. The gun exploded, echoing in the closed rock chamber of the cave.

The muzzle flash strobed the darkness, illuminating the witika apparition as in a dream. Afterward, the cave chamber returned to sudden pitch-black darkness, hung with a gunpowder stink.

Sabine clung to her. Deafened, blinded, Blandine scrabbled forward, seeking the way out, the low passageway cleaved into the rock. Nothing. A dirty stone wall.

Behind them, the demon came on. Blandine could smell him, foul and close. He was right behind her.

Her hand groped forward and found the cleft. She pushed Sabine into it. "Run, now," she said. "Run and don't stop."

Little Sabine wouldn't leave.

"Go, go," Blandine said, and pushed the child away from her again.

A hand seized Blandine's ankle, pulling her backward across the rough floor, into the yawning gulf of the inner chamber.

Drummond, Antony and Jan arrived among the rocky promontories near the Place of Stones, having blown out their horses on the frantic trip up the island. They found themselves at the northernmost tip of Manhattan.

Kitane was with them. They had picked him up in Little Angola, the Lenape trapper leaping easily up behind Antony on the borrowed bay mare.

"It's up there," Jan told Drummond, recognizing the gray rock faces where Lightning had led him before.

The four of them hitched the mounts and climbed to a slot in the crags where they could see the flat, stone-littered clearing and the cave opening beyond it.

"Where are they?" Antony said.

A terrifying vision suddenly presented itself: Sabine, naked, running as fast as her small legs could pump, tearing out from inside the cave and crossing the Place of Stones in a fear-blinded dash.

Drummond moved forward and swept the girl up in his arms. The Bean struggled against him, terror not allowing the child to realize who it was that had her. But she saw Jan and her hysteria receded.

"Jannie," she sobbed.

"Where is Blandina?" Drummond asked. "Where is your Ina, Sabine?"

The child gestured to the cave.

Drummond let Jan have the Bean and turned to confer with Antony and Kitane.

"We come in on three sides," he said. "Give me five minutes to move around to the cliffside there." He gestured to the rock face towering over the cave.

"We should go in now, all together," Antony said. "Every minute could matter."

"I need to know that there's not another way out," Drummond said, and he moved off before any more discussion could delay him.

The witika demon brought Blandine to the mouth of the cave, a dagger pressed at her throat.

"Sabine is gone," Blandine said through gritted teeth. "You'll never get her."

The beast lowered the blade to her abdomen. With a slashing movement, the knife sliced open Blandine's already torn and muddy dress.

She felt the blade, cold against her flesh. The Devil was after her unborn. She pushed away hard, putting all the leverage she had into her elbow.

Martyn Hendrickson tottered and swayed backward on the strange wooden buskins he wore to elevate himself to nine feet.

At that moment Edward Drummond dropped from the gray stone crags above the cave, tackling Martyn.

In her exhausted and half-drugged state, Blandine at first thought the whole cliffside had fallen, a rock slide, an avalanche. But it was Drummond.

The two men collapsed in a heap. As he fell, the blade of Martyn's dagger twisted upward and ended up embedded deeply in his own shoulder. He had inadvertently stabbed himself when Drummond struck him from above.

Blandine had never seen Drummond this way. Fury rode him. He tore off the man's witika mask and flung it away.

Martyn fell back, his face twisted into a sick, red-faced snarl. He panted like a cornered animal. But his eyes looked strangely blank, mesmerized with opium.

Drummond began pummeling him. As his fists smashed into the handsome face, over and over, Martyn reached up with one arm as though to ward off the blows.

Blandine saw the dagger. Martyn groped for the handle of the knife.

"He's got a blade!" Blandine shouted.

Bellowing with pain, the wounded man drew the dagger out from his own shoulder and jabbed it at Drummond.

But Martyn was too weak. It was as though the deerskin mask had given him his power. Drummond merely snatched his wrist, bent the weapon downward and disarmed him.

It was over.

Confiscating the bloody dagger, Drummond got to his feet, stepping back toward Blandine.

"Sabine?" she asked, breathing hard.

From the other side of the clearing came Jan, carrying the Bean in his arms. Behind him walked Antony and Kitane.

At that moment of distraction, Martyn gathered his cloak around him, rolled away from the cave mouth and dropped off a rock ledge. They heard a shriek as he disappeared.

They all rushed to the edge of the cliff. Flinging ropy gouts of blood onto the leaves scattered across the forest floor, the wounded Martyn bounded recklessly down the cliff side toward the stream below.

Blandine turned to Antony and extracted her oversized musket from his grip.

"Cover Sabine's ears," she directed Drummond. She stepped forward, shouldered Pretty Polly and let loose.

The boom sounded huge, cannonlike, but the shot went wide, splintering a birch sapling just as Martyn careened by it.

"Judas Priest," Blandine said.

"I didn't think Pretty Polly could miss," Drummond said.

"She's not herself," Blandine said.

At the bottom of the hill, they could see the once-mighty witika monster flailing away, red heels flashing, stumbling, trying to keep his balance.

"I'll get him," Kitane said, loping off in the same direction Martyn had fled.

"Take a horse!" Drummond called.

"I'm going to run him," Kitane called back.

Kitane had a specific tactic in mind. It was a wartime Algonquin practice, modeled on the way wolf packs ran deer, chasing them tirelessly, switching out members of the pack to give others a rest, finally killing their exhausted prey as it collapsed, tongue lolling out and mouth foaming.

Drummond watched Kitane take off after the fleeing Martyn, down the hillside to the little stream that fed into the North River. Martyn ran panicked and wounded, while Kitane managed to affect a casual, insouciant pursuit. They splashed across the stream at the Wading Place, climbed up the opposite slope above Spuyten Duyvil and disappeared toward the Post Road.

"Will he catch him?" Jan asked.

"I am not sure Kitane wants to catch him," Blandine said. "Not right away. First he must toy with him awhile."

"Like a cat with a mousey," Jan said.

"Mousey," the Bean echoed.

Running, desperate and weak, Martyn groped for a way out. He would scream of an indian attack to the first settler he met, gesturing back to the Lenape madman behind him.

But he saw no settlers. The witika terror Martyn himself engineered had depeopled the landscape.

He ran on. Martyn told himself he did not really mind dying. His life, snuffed. It was a pity, he had so much to offer the world, but there it was.

The torture, the time it would take him to die, he also thought he could face. He had been on the other end of the fist and the blade so many times, he thought it might be almost enjoyable to experience how it felt with the positions reversed.

But the eating, that's what horrified him. He recognized the Lenape trapper who was on his trail. The famous Kitane. He knew Kitane to be afflicted with witika madness the same as he, and Martyn could not suffer the thought of his body being consumed by another human.

Yes, yes, Martyn realized he was being inconsistent, even hypocritical. He had certainly eaten his share. He couldn't explain it logically. It was just that the very idea of his flesh residing in another person's mouth sent him into paroxysms of retching disgust. It made his skin crawl.

Martyn lasted a good while on the run. Several miles. Kitane had seen longer. He had pursued Mahican enemies of his people farther, a dozen leagues at least, twenty-five miles. But Martyn did respectably well for a swannekin, especially with a knife wound in one shoulder. The poppy tears helped dull the pain.

Kitane finally closed on him beside rapids that coursed down to the North River. The Lenape clan that lived nearby called the stream the Nepperhan, the "net-fishing place."

Martyn plunged his head into the water, drank deeply, vomited and passed out.

Kitane woke him with a kick to the side of his head. He toyed with him while the fire got going, a little with the blade, a little with a rock employed as a hammer. As Martyn roasted, bellowing at the top of his exhausted lungs, Kitane idly carved the witika sign on the surface of a stone, where it remains, faintly visible, to this day.

Then Kitane ate Martyn Hendrickson, consuming him, over the course of a few days, down to the tiniest bone.

Epilogue

Ten years after he left it, on his way to London to see to family affairs when his mother died, Drummond journeyed alone to Manhattan. He found the place changed beyond recognition.

With insane industry, his English countrymen built, tore down and recast, transforming New Amsterdam into New York. When they had it, the Dutch sought to make Manhattan over as a facsimile of Patria, with canals, waterways and drainage projects. The English were busy transforming the place into London, with sooty facades and cobblestone streets.

Only the Lion remained from the old days. Drummond entered and was immediately assailed with memories so strong they nearly cut him off at the knees. The blades still waited in the rafters for the next riot. The same drunks at the same tables. The smell of beer and tobacco smoke.

And Ross Raeger. "Drummond!" his voice called out, and the two men embraced as though they were drowning men clinging to flotsam of the past. No need for secrecy or Sealed Knot passwords. Raeger seemed fatter and grayer, an old pirate retired to his tavern.

"Did ye bring the lass?" Raeger asked, and looked disappointed when Drummond told him no, Blandine remained at their trading outpost in the western wilderness.

They walked the town together as they had in the old days, not gathering intelligence about military defenses this time, but merely trying to grab on to the surviving shreds of New Amsterdam before they vanished for good. The town authorities were in the midst of filling in the canal, transforming it from a Dutch waterway into a proper English thoroughfare.

"Let me show you something," Raeger said. He guided Drummond along the old canal to where it branched off to the west. A thin finger of a ditch led toward the parade ground, now a bowling green.

"This was the Hendricksons' private canal," Raeger said. "It led over to the big one, the Heere Gracht."

"I remember," Drummond said.

"Look down there," Raeger said.

Where the little canal dead-ended behind the former Hendrickson grounds, a wooden door was set into the bulwark.

"Come along," Raeger said, leading Drummond to climb ten feet down into the ditch and approach the door.

He forced it open. The gaping mouth of a passageway, musty-smelling and dank. "Ye afraid of the dark?" Raeger asked.

"Not since I last slept at the Lion," Drummond said.

The passageway—a tunnel, really, faced with stone and big enough to roll a small cart through—ran to the south. The light spilling from the entrance faded, and they moved forward in pitch darkness.

Drummond knew where the tunnel led before they reached it. After thirty yards, the passage ended at another door. Raeger opened it, bringing in daylight along with an overpowering smell of burnt wood.

They stepped forward, and Drummond found himself in the understory of the old Hendrickson mansion. The dwelling-house had hidden its tunnel as one of its many secrets. A decade after the place burned, collapsed and fire-blackened timbers still lay in disarray, and a half foot of dirty rainwater pooled in the gutted subterranean chambers.

This was how the Devil was supposed to smell, Drummond thought, charred and rotten.

Raeger said, "Ye ever wonder how Martyn got out and about in his infernal witika gear, terrifying and murthering wee ones?"

"I did wonder," Drummond said.

"They made the tunnel in the old days," Raeger said. "For the Hendricksons to bring their trade goods in from the little canal."

Drummond looked around the site. He felt a cold distaste. "Nobody will build here," he said. "The place is cursed."

"Aye," said Raeger, "that it is."

Blandine and Edward never made it to *Cain-tuck-kee*. That mythic land floated in their imaginations, far off, fertile, where the grass, legend said, grew an uncanny shade of blue.

Instead, they founded a small trading post at the southern end of one of the odd, beautiful fingers of water in western New York, Honeoye Lake, close to the Genesee River and home country of the Seneca nation. Wilderness enough for Edward, trade enough for Blandine.

They had Jan with them there, and Anna and her children. The Bean grew up fat and happy, as did Blandine and Edward's own baby, Sarah. All they were was love.

Blandine swiftly fell in with the Seneca, continuing to import cloth from the old world, trading adroitly in New York's fur-rich interior, shipping the pelts back to her New Amsterdam customers and pocketing the profit. Far back in her *kas*, alongside the enameled rose her parents gave her, she kept an Emily Stavings miniature of Aet Visser, a brave bad man or a cowardly good one, she could never decide which.

For a home, Blandine and Edward built their own, not a squat clapboard-and-brick dwelling-house such as those on Manhattan, but a soaring, porch-enclosed, light-filled apparition that sat like a ship on the smoothly rolling horizon. The glass for its windows Edward poured himself.

They never saw Kitane. Rumor had him in Paris, the pet of a buxom French lady. Antony stayed in Manhattan and gained his own pulpit. He made the long trek to visit Honeoye Lake only once in a while, preaching his way to them through the growing string of hamlets and villages the Europeans established along the rivers of the southern tier.

Goffe, Whalley and Dixwell, the New Haven regicides, lived and prospered. Clarendon's assassins never came, primarily because Clarendon had other difficulties, most of them the creation of the Duke of Norfolk. Edward Hyde, first earl of Clarendon, the lord chancellor who stood in for the deceased father of the second Charles, guiding, teaching, protecting the young prince, exterminating the regicides, fell victim to court intrigue.

Drummond briefly thought of going to New Haven to do the job on Goffe, Whalley and Dixwell himself, just to get back his facility for killing, but had not the heart. With his daughter, Sarah, on his lap and Blandine talking peltry to a Seneca sachem on their front porch, that world seemed impossibly far away.

He enjoyed hearing from Antony of the decidedly cool reception given to Petrus Stuyvesant when the disgraced director general returned to Patria after the English takeover. In fact, the Dutch stateholders argued for putting the man before a punishment tribunal. For treason. Drummond thought he might have recommended a good man to act as counsel.

The witika continued to stalk the north woods, ranging up to Canada, out toward the Great Lakes, down into the American river valleys west of the mountains. Wherever the demon went, the witika sign appeared, like punctuation, like a challenge, like a warning.

AUTHOR'S NOTE

I have grounded this fictional narrative in verifiable facts and real situations. The orphanmaster as an official government function did exist in New Amsterdam, agents of the English king did search out the signatories of his father's death warrant, the North River did freeze over enough to admit sleigh traffic. The director general of the Dutch colony was indeed Latin-proud and possessed a peg leg set with silver. Details of geography and body politic, of colonial foodstuffs, the magic lantern and early optics are accurate as far as I could make them.

The novel centers around an apparition known as the witika, a flesh-eating demon that formed a crucial part of the psychic life of the Algonquin Indians. The name has many transliterated variants, including, most popularly, wendigo, but also witigo, witikow and windiga. Living amid native Americans, seventeenth-century Dutch and English colonists became intimately familiar with witika lore.

Perhaps the most frightening aspect of the phenomenon was "witika psychosis," which would grip the victim with the uncontrollable urge to consume human flesh. Since to most Algonquins, as much as to the European, man-eating was taboo, it was with unspeakable terror that sufferers felt themselves being invaded by the witika's cannibalistic impulses.

Some of the most useful research for this book comes from the monumental *Iconography of Manhattan Island*, by I. N. Phelps Stokes, which furnishes an intimate description of daily life in New Amsterdam during the seventeenth century. Such details as the botched hanging of an African giant, the discovery of missing human heads in a cow pasture and the exact layout of the settlement's streets appear there.

Chapter five's "two-legged cheese worm" quote is from a seventeenth-century pamphlet, *Tractaat van het Excellente Kryd Thee*, by Cornelis Bontekoe, excerpted in Simon Schama's excellent account of Dutch culture in the Golden Age, *The Embarrassment of Riches*. The sermon in chapter nineteen is modified from a text by the Puritan preacher Richard Baxter, "Directions Against Sinful Fear," in *The Practical Works of Richard*

Baxter. The dialogue exchange between the German "shiv-man" and the Polish sailor in chapter forty-seven is based on a passage in *Peter Stuyvesant: The Last Dutch Governor of New Amsterdam*, by John S. C. Abbott.

I'd like to acknowledge my debt to several people for their help and encouragement. Paul Slovak bowled me over with his immediate enthusiastic embrace of this project. Betsy Lerner acted as a superb sounding board, first editor and—most of all—friend. Betty and Steve Zimmerman provided support without which *The Orphanmaster* could not have been written. Maud Reavill offered her usual winning combination of intelligence, skepticism and ebullience. My husband, Gil Reavill, gave vital input throughout, including a nudge to get me started. "Write me a murder," Gil said, and I did.